I Can Read Book® is a trademark of HarperCollins Publishers.

The Berenstain Bears at the Aquarium

www.icanread.com
Library of Congress catalog card number: 2011930718
ISBN 978-0-06-207525-3 (trade bdg.)—ISBN 978-0-06-207524-6 (pbk.)

18    SCP    10  9  8  7  6  5  4  3  ❖    First Edition

# Dear Parent:
## Your child's love of reading starts here!

Every child learns to read in a different way and at his or her own speed. Some go back and forth between reading levels and read favorite books again and again. Others read through each level in order. You can help your young reader improve and become more confident by encouraging his or her own interests and abilities. From books your child reads with you to the first books he or she reads alone, there are I Can Read Books for every stage of reading:

### SHARED READING
Basic language, word repetition, and whimsical illustrations, ideal for sharing with your emergent reader

### BEGINNING READING
Short sentences, familiar words, and simple concepts for children eager to read on their own

### READING WITH HELP
Engaging stories, longer sentences, and language play for developing readers

### READING ALONE
Complex plots, challenging vocabulary, and high-interest topi( for the independent reader

### ADVANCED READING
Short paragraphs, chapters, and exciting themes for the perfect bridge to chapter books

**I Can Read Books** have introduced children to the joy of rea( since 1957. Featuring award-winning authors and illustrators an( fabulous cast of beloved characters, I Can Read Books set the standard for beginning readers.

A lifetime of discovery begins with the magical words "I Ca(

*Visit www.icanread.com for information
on enriching your child's reading experience.*

# I Can Read!

BEGINNING READING **1**

## The Berenstain Bears®

# at the AQUARIUM

Jan & Mike Berenstain

**HARPER**
*An Imprint of* HarperCollins*Publishers*

"Here we are at the aquarium,"

says Papa Bear.

"The what?" asks Sister.

"The ah-KWAIR-ee-um," says Mama.

"It is a zoo of the sea."

"There are many things to see,"

says Papa.

"I want to see the whale,"
says Brother.

"I want to see the dolphins,"
says Sister.

"What shall we see first?" asks Papa.

"The whale," says Brother.

"The dolphins," says Sister.

"First, let's see the fish," says Mama.

"This swordfish has a very long nose," says Papa.

"Pointy, too," says Brother.

"The flounder is very flat," says Mama.

"His eyes are on the same side,"

says Sister. "Ugh!"

"Here is a catfish," says Papa.

"It looks like a cat," says Brother.

"Here is a dogfish," says Mama.

"It does not look like a dog,"

says Sister.

"This way to the whale!" says Brother.

"This way to the dolphins!" says Sister.

In the next room they see an octopus.

"Which end is the front?" asks Mama.

"I'm not sure," says Papa.

They see jellyfish.

"Those long strings can sting you,"
says Papa.

"Not if we stay out of the tank,"
says Mama.

"Where is the whale?" asks Brother.

"And where are the dolphins?"
asks Sister.

"Look at those penguins swim!"
says Mama.

"Look at them dive!" says Papa.

"Why don't they fly?" asks Brother.

"Because they can't," says Papa.

"Why don't they walk?" asks Sister.

"Some of them do," says Brother.

15

"These are some big fish," says Papa.

"The sharks are very scary,"

says Brother.

"Look at their sharp teeth!"

"The sunfish is very funny," says Sister.

"Look at his big head!"

"The otters are so cute," says Mama.
"It is fun to watch them slide,"
says Papa.

"I wish I could see the whale,"
says Brother.

"I wish I could see the dolphins,"
says Sister.

The Bear family comes to the seal pool.

It is feeding time.

The seals make a lot of noise!

Their trainers give them fish to eat.

21

"This makes me so hungry," says Papa.

"Here is a place to eat," says Mama.
The Bears have lunch and watch
the seals.

After lunch, they spot a sign.

It says, WHALE AND DOLPHIN SHOW TODAY!

"Hooray! The whale, at last!"

says Brother.

"Hooray! The dolphins, at last!"

says Sister.

25

The show begins.

The dolphins jump and leap and spin.

The trainer tells them to do tricks.

The Bears clap and clap.

A whale leaps out of the water.

The trainer feeds him a fish.

The Bears clap and clap and clap.

What a show!

The trainer asks Brother and Sister

to help.

Sister tells a dolphin to leap.

Brother feeds a fish to the whale.

The whale and the dolphin

make a big splash.

The family gets all wet!

"SPLASH!" yells Honey.

They laugh and laugh and laugh.

# CONQUERING LYME DISEASE

Science Bridges the Great Divide

## Brian A. Fallon, MD, and Jennifer Sotsky, MD

with Carl Brenner, Carolyn Britton, MD,
Marina Makous, MD, Jenifer Nields, MD,
and Barbara Strobino, PhD

COLUMBIA UNIVERSITY PRESS
NEW YORK

The information in this book is not a substitute for medical evaluation or advice. If you are concerned that you might have Lyme disease or any other illness, please consult with a physician for a thorough evaluation and treatment plan.

Case histories in this book are either drawn from the published literature or represent fictionalized accounts drawn from our combined experiences with numerous patients.

All royalties from the sale of this book go to the Research Foundation for Mental Hygiene to support research at the Lyme and Tick-borne Disease Research Center.

Columbia University Press
*Publishers Since 1893*
New York    Chichester, West Sussex
cup.columbia.edu
Copyright © 2018 Brian Fallon
All rights reserved

Library of Congress Cataloging-in-Publication Data
Names: Fallon, Brian, M.D., author. | Sotsky, Jennifer, author.
Title: Conquering Lyme disease : science bridges the great divide / Brian A. Fallon and Jennifer Sotsky ; with Carl Brenner, Carolyn Britton, Marina Makous, and Jenifer Nields.
Description: New York : Columbia University Press, [2018] | Includes bibliographical references and index.
Identifiers: LCCN 2017031085 (print) | LCCN 2017031961 (ebook) | ISBN 9780231545181 | ISBN 9780231183840 (alk. paper)
Subjects: | MESH: Lyme Disease
Classification: LCC RC155.5 (ebook) | LCC RC155.5 (print) | NLM WC 406 | DDC 616.9/246—dc23
LC record available at https://lccn.loc.gov/2017031085

Columbia University Press books are printed on permanent and durable acid-free paper.
Printed in the United States of America

Cover design: Milenda Nan Ok Lee
Cover art: © Shutterstock

*To the patients with Lyme disease,*
*the doctors who treat them,*
*and the researchers seeking answers.*

William Blake, *Job's Tormentors*, 1793.

*Look deep into nature.*
*Then you will understand.*

—Albert Einstein

*Fall seven times and stand up eight.*

—Japanese Proverb

# CONTENTS

# ACKNOWLEDGMENTS

Many people should be thanked for their contributions to this book, only some of whom are included below.

First, we wish to thank the patients, the physicians, and the researchers, as each has played a key role in advancing our knowledge in the quest to conquer this illness.

Second, we thank the pioneer scientists and clinicians whose insights and encouragement helped us in key ways throughout the early years of our journey in clinical research on Lyme disease. These include Alan Barbour, Willy Burgdorfer, Joseph Burrascano, Patricia Coyle, Sam Donta, Paul Duray, Andrew Dwork, Christina Hoven, Kenneth Liegner, Ian Lipkin, Ben Luft, Ed Masters, James Miller, Mario Philipp, Gorazd Rosoklija, Steven Schutzer, Allen Steere, Reinhard Straubinger, and Richard Tilton. We have found essential supporters and collaborators among our Columbia University Medical Center and New York State Psychiatric Institute colleagues, including Harold Sackeim, Michael Liebowitz, Donald Klein, John Keilp, Eva Petkova, James Moeller, Kathy Corbera, Alla Landa, Armin Alaedini, Rafal Tokarz, Brian Scully, Jay Dobkin, Edward Dwyer, Angela Lignelli, Robert DelaPaz, Ronald Van Heertum, Gerald Fischbach, and Jeffrey Lieberman. We also thank the early patient advocates and community leaders, particularly Betty Gross, Karen and Tom Forschner, Pat Smith, Phyllis Mervine, Cathy Morrissey, Diane Blanchard, and Debbie Siciliano. We are grateful for the excellent historical accounts of Lyme disease, including those by Polly Murray, Jonathan Edlow, and Pamela Weintraub, as well as Alan Barbour's informative books on the fundamentals.

Third, we thank the Lyme Disease Association and the Global Lyme Alliance (GLA) who joined forces years ago to raise funds to establish the

Lyme and Tick-borne Diseases Research Center at the Columbia University Medical Center—the first research center in the United States at an academic medical center focused on the chronic aspects of Lyme and other tick-borne diseases. The center's focus has enabled us to investigate diagnostic, treatment, and brain imaging questions of pressing concern to patients; to build a biorepository that facilitates translational research and precision medicine by scientists at Columbia and internationally; and to educate future clinicians and researchers about Lyme and tick-borne diseases. (To learn more, go to: www.columbia-lyme.org.)

Fourth, we thank those who have contributed photos, answered questions, and the named and unnamed reviewers of various sections of this book for their valuable comments and suggestions. Some of these include Armin Alaedini, John Aucott, Stephen Barthold, Jorge Benach, Ed Breitswerdt, Charles Chiu, Tom Daniels, David Dorward, Kevin Esvelt, Elizabeth Maloney, Richard Marconi, Paul Mead, Rick Ostfeld, Kirby Stafford, and Sam Telford.

Fifth, we thank the National Institutes of Health New York State, the Research Foundation for Mental Hygiene, Columbia University Medical Center, and the private foundations and individuals who have supported our research over the years. In particular, we thank the Steven and Alexandra Cohen Foundation whose support facilitated the completion of this book. The National Research Fund for Tick-borne Diseases established an endowed medical student fellowship at our Columbia center that included co-author Dr. Jennifer Sotsky as a trainee. The Weis, Monsky, and Peck families and the Tick-borne Disease Alliance (now merged with GLA) supported a fellowship for family medicine doctors at our center that included co-author Dr. Marina Makous as a trainee.

Finally, we thank the people at Columbia University Press including Patrick Fitzgerald, Ryan Groendyk, and Milenda Lee in particular for collaborating in helping make possible what we hope is a highly informative, clinically helpful, and visually beautiful book.

We conclude by stating that the perspectives and content in this book represent the judgment and clinical experience of the authors. These are not the official viewpoints of a medical association or of a university or medical center.

# PREFACE

Picture the following:

- A ten-year-old schoolgirl complains of headaches and fogginess and keeps falling asleep in class. She has trouble recalling assignments. She arrives late to school because she routinely needs twelve to fourteen hours of sleep per night. Her teachers wonder what is going on at home.
- A twenty-two-year-old man notices palpitations and increasing shortness of breath. A few days later, he becomes weak, collapses, and is rushed to the emergency room, where a pacemaker is inserted to override his complete heart block.
- A thirty-year-old man, recently treated for the Lyme disease rash, develops persistent joint and muscle pains, headaches, marked irritability, and severe fatigue. He says, "I feel like a ninety-year-old." Doctors are not sure how to help him.
- A thirty-five-year-old woman gets a bull's eye rash following a tick bite, is treated within days with antibiotics, never feels sick, and wonders why her friends are so phobic of Lyme disease and of walking in the woods.
- A forty-five-year-old musician avoids going to concerts because the stage lights are far too bright and the sounds too painful; her brain seems to get scrambled even with normal-level sensory stimulation. Nine months earlier she developed joint pains and sharp radiating pains from her spine into her limbs. Dense fatigue now dominates her waking hours. She saw six doctors before Lyme disease was considered and diagnosed. She tested positive and now asks why did it take so long?

- A sixty-five-year-old professor, treated for Lyme arthritis three years earlier, reports that he is having trouble retrieving words as he speaks even though he has given fluent lectures for years; at times, he even uses the wrong words. He also reports recent numbness and tingling in his extremities. He wonders, am I getting dementia?

Each of these is a case of Lyme disease, representing just a small sample of the diverse presentations of this illness.

For those who do not have Lyme disease, it can be a fascinating illness. Fascinating because the illness is diverse in its presentation. Fascinating because the microbe causing it has evolved highly adaptive and brilliant ways of evading detection and destruction by the immune response. Fascinating because the societal and political response to Lyme disease has been so varied—at times helpful and productive, while at other times dismissive and divisive.

For those who do have Lyme disease, however, "fascinating" does not describe this illness. For many of those whose infection is caught early, Lyme disease is a mild to moderate illness that resolves with antibiotic treatment. For others, it is a painful, disturbing, and prolonged illness— disabling, frightening, confusing, isolating, and sometimes life-altering. Lyme disease can be a profoundly debilitating illness that has a major impact on an individual's life, with symptoms lasting from months to years.

How can one disease have so many presentations? Why do some patients relapse and then suffer with chronic symptoms? Why are the societal and medical responses to Lyme disease so filled with tension? How do the patients and physicians understand this illness? Is there any hope for the sicker patients? Why is there such a great chasm separating different medical communities?

This book addresses these questions. It provides an overview of Lyme disease and the most recent scientific advances. It describes the symptoms, diagnosis, treatments, and research. It presents a historical and scientific perspective on the controversies surrounding this illness. Most importantly, this book provides an update on how the extraordinary scientific advances of the past decade are helping to reshape our understanding of Lyme disease and accelerating the identification of new tools to diagnose and treat it.

We are writing for those affected by the illness and their families. We are also writing for the educated, interested nonmedical person and for the experienced medical professional because each can gain useful knowledge about Lyme disease and other tick-borne diseases from this book. The authors of this book are clinical researchers and front-line clinicians. Because we work closely with basic scientists and with the patient community, we provide a broad scope and unique perspective, bridging worlds that at times seem to be at war with one another. We hope that this book will inform readers and therefore enable them to better navigate the medical system to enhance the likelihood of improved outcomes.

We realize that some sections of this book are quite technical and more easily understood by a medically trained professional, while most other sections are more widely accessible to all readers. Writing a book for two audiences—the general public and the medical professional—may seem like a strange choice. We wrote in this fashion for two reasons. First, because of the vast amount of information on the Internet about Lyme disease and the many books about this illness already published by the popular press, a reader can easily be confused, terrified, or misled. Curious nonmedically trained people are trying to understand for themselves what is really going on in this field. Medical information previously only available to doctors from the shelves of a medical library is now obtained through a brief Internet search from home. By providing greater depth into some of the complexities of this illness, we aim to help nonmedically trained readers to gain a better understanding of the symptoms, diagnostic tests, treatment options, prevention strategies, reasons for persistent symptoms, and controversies. Second, we want to present the latest scientific research in sufficient detail to convince the open-minded reader or even the medical skeptic that transformative advances are now underway that will improve the health of our world for the better—and will allow us once again to walk in the woods without worry.

In this book, we present what is known, identify what is not known, and elucidate where the latest breakthroughs in science are leading us. We hope to clarify areas of confusion. Above all, this book aims to help patients and the health care providers who care for them as they seek to understand the complexities of this illness.

Patients may find certain sections of this book particularly accessible. Chapter 13, "Frequently Asked Questions," includes questions asked of us over the years by patients with specific queries of pressing clinical relevance. Chapter 12, "The Experience of the Patient with Chronic Symptoms," should resonate with patients and help clinicians get a better sense of what it might be like to have Lyme disease when the course is more complex. Chapter 11, "Suggestions to the Patient Seeking Evaluation or Treatment," offers pointers on optimizing the medical encounter. Chaper 10, "Lyme Disease Prevention and Transmission," provides numerous practical suggestions on how to reduce the risk of contracting Lyme disease.

Finally, to illustrate certain key points, we have inserted selected clinical case vignettes in different chapters of this book—of individuals with either "typical" or "atypical" Lyme disease or other common tick-borne diseases. The "typical" cases illustrate the usual course of illness, which in most individuals is one of rapid improvement after antibiotic treatment. The "atypical" cases, while far less common, are presented because they cause us to ponder and force us to stretch the limits of our understanding and even to challenge preexisting paradigms. Because these are unusual cases, we have drawn them from the published medical literature so that the reader can go to the original article to learn more.

This is an encouraging time in the history of Lyme disease—one characterized by extraordinary research and creative ideas. This novel research comes from research scientists in the United States and around the world. Many of the more recent studies are the products of collaborative efforts by scientists from many different institutions, reflecting both the diversity of skills needed to study a complex disease and the need for patient samples from diverse geographic areas to capture the variant strains of the Lyme disease spirochete and other tick-borne coinfections.

Most people—patients and physicians alike—are not aware of these advances. We present them in this book to instill hope and facilitate understanding.

Health care providers may not be aware of the diverse manifestations of Lyme disease, the limitations of existing diagnostic tests, the sophisticated survival strategies for immune evasion of the organism that causes Lyme disease (the bacterium *Borrelia burgdorferi*), and the complex challenges posed by patients with persistent symptoms. This is not a simple disease that can be easily dismissed. To help readers who wish to probe more deeply into specific areas, we provide references to journal articles throughout this book.

Vast progress has been made on the scientific front that will—in the not-too-distant future—have a hugely beneficial impact on public health. The expanding plague of Lyme disease and other tick-borne diseases is being confronted. This book purposely includes information that is "hot off the press"—describing scientific advances in diagnostics, treatment, and prevention—about advances made possible by the biotechnology revolution and by the generous support provided to researchers by private donors, private foundations, and governmental agencies such as the National Institutes of Health (NIH) and the Centers for Disease Control and Prevention (CDC).

Our goals in writing this book are to bring clarity to a murky field and to bring hope to both patients and their health care providers by demonstrating that breakthroughs are on the way.

## WHO ARE THE AUTHORS?

*Dr. Brian Fallon* is director of the Lyme and Tick-Borne Diseases Research Center at Columbia University Medical Center, a leading academic research center dedicated to multidisciplinary research on Lyme disease, focused primarily upon the chronic neurologic and neuropsychiatric aspects. He is a graduate of Harvard College, the Columbia University College of Physicians and Surgeons, and the Columbia University School of Public Health. Dr. Fallon is widely known for his expertise on post-treatment Lyme disease symptoms, particularly in regard to clarifying the impact of Lyme disease on the brain, the neuroimaging and cognitive changes that occur, and the neuropsychiatric and neurobehavioral problems that result. He has lectured internationally, conducted one of the four major NIH-funded placebo-controlled clinical treatment trials on post-treatment Lyme disease syndrome in the United States, and is the author of more than 120 articles and chapters. He has been invited to lecture on his research findings before members of the U.S. Congress, the Institutes of Medicine, and the Centers for Disease Control and Prevention, and he has presented overseas as well in Great Britain, Norway, Canada, and Germany. In addition to peer-reviewed scientific publications, Dr. Fallon's work on Lyme disease and other diseases has been featured in the media, including *The New Yorker*, *Time Magazine*, *New Scientist*, and National Public Radio. As a professor of clinical psychiatry at Columbia University Medical Center and director of the Center for Neuroinflammatory Disorders and Biobehavioral Medicine at the New York State Psychiatric Institute, Dr. Fallon is particularly interested in the interplay between infection, the immune system, and the brain—each interacting with the other to lead to the diversity of clinical manifestations that plague our patients.

*Dr. Jennifer Sotsky* is a physician in the residency training program in the Department of Psychiatry at Columbia University Medical Center. She received her BA in English from Dartmouth College, MS in Narrative Medicine from Columbia University, and MD from Columbia University's College of Physicians and Surgeons. Dr. Sotsky completed advanced training in Lyme and tick-borne diseases at the Lyme Disease Research Center at Columbia Medical Center as a medical student and continued her work there throughout her medical training.

*Carl Brenner* completed his college studies at Yale University and is a senior staff associate of research at the Lamont-Doherty Earth Observatory, a former member of the Research Advisory Board of the National Research Fund for Tick-Borne Diseases, and current director of the U.S. Science Support Program (USSSP) associated with the International Ocean Discovery Program. He has served on the Lyme Disease Advisory Panel to the National Institute of Allergy and Infectious Diseases and has presented testimony on Lyme disease to the U.S. Senate Committee on Labor and Human Resources and the New York State Assembly Standing Committee on Health.

*Dr. Carolyn B. Britton* is an associate professor of neurology at the Columbia University Medical Center. She received her medical degree from NYU School of Medicine, an MS in Virology at NYU, and residency and fellowship training in infectious disease and neurology at Columbia University Medical Center. Dr. Britton was one of the early pioneers delineating the neurologic manifestations of HIV infection, starting in 1981. Her interest expanded to Lyme disease in the late 1990s when in both research and clinical settings she evaluated and treated hundreds of patients with neurologic and neuropsychiatric manifestations of Lyme disease. Dr. Britton's work has included national leadership, both in state and national policy on battling the HIV epidemic and in her role as past president of the National Medical Association.

*Dr. Marina Makous* is a family medicine physician in private practice in Pennsylvania. A graduate of the Medical College of Pennsylvania and Drexel University College of Medicine (Philadelphia), she completed a two-year fellowship program in Lyme and tick-borne diseases at the Columbia University Medical Center and was subsequently appointed assistant clinical professor of family medicine in psychiatry at the Columbia University Medical Center. She has presented at regional and national conferences on Lyme disease. Dr. Makous's extensive background as a family medicine physician and her experience in diagnosing and treating people with tick-borne diseases help provide the primary care doctor's perspective for this book.

*Dr. Jenifer Nields* is an assistant clinical professor of psychiatry at Yale University School of Medicine and a graduate of Harvard College, the College of Physicians and Surgeons at Columbia University Medical Center, and the New Directions Program in Psychoanalytic Writing at the Washington Center for Psychoanalysis. Dr. Nields's early research on the neuropsychiatric aspects of Lyme disease highlighted its cognitive, sensory, and mood-altering features; this research was greeted with much enthusiasm by patients, as the clinical profile resonated so strongly with their clinical experience. Her published peer-reviewed journal articles, book chapters, and letters have led her to be recognized as one of the national experts on the neuropsychiatric aspects of Lyme disease. Dr. Nields currently supervises psychiatry residents at Yale University School of Medicine and treats patients in private practice in Connecticut.

*Dr. Barbara Strobino* previously served as Associate Director of Research at the Lyme and Tick-Borne Diseases Research Center at Columbia University Medical Center. She received an MPH from University of Pittsburgh and a PhD in epidemiology from Columbia University and has published numerous journal articles and book chapters on pregnancy risk factors and pediatrics. As principal or coinvestigator of several epidemiologic studies funded by NIH, the New York State Tick-Borne Disease Institute, and the March of Dimes, she investigated the relationship between miscarriages, stillbirth, preterm delivery, and congenital malformations and maternal Lyme disease.

## WHAT IS OUR PARTICULAR PERSPECTIVE AND PRIMARY CLINICAL FOCUS?

Since the early 1990s, we have focused our clinical and research skills on Lyme disease, particularly on the chronic aspects. Puzzled by the conflicts between patients and academic researchers, we have sought to apply careful clinical observation and the tools of research to test hypotheses regarding diagnosis and treatment. Many of these hypotheses emerged from the clinicians in the community who were struggling to find ways to help patients. These doctors witnessed what was happening to their patients in the long term and were trying empirical treatments to address the chronic symptoms. We wanted to test some of the clinical observations emerging from these clinicians to see if they held up under the scrutiny of the scientific method. Because of our unique position as clinical researchers associated with the Lyme and Tick-Borne Diseases Research Center at Columbia University Medical Center, we have had the privilege of designing studies and collaborating with outstanding research scientists at Columbia University and elsewhere to address some of the most pressing questions that plague our patients.

As physicians and scientists, we recognize that a growing number of patients have experienced ongoing or relapsing symptoms after having been treated for Lyme disease. We recognize that current diagnostic tests, while helpful, have limitations; foremost among these concerns is that the antibody-based tests that are the core of current Lyme disease testing do not provide definitive information regarding the presence or absence of *B. burgdorferi* infection. We also recognize that there are multiple complex mechanisms following *B. burgdorferi* infection that may cause patients to have persistent symptoms.

While we hope that most people who read this book will come away better informed and encouraged by the latest research, we also anticipate some individuals may feel that sections of this book are either too open to the patients' or community doctors' perspective or too focused on the academic researchers' perspective. Criticisms such as these are welcome because they suggest that we have struck a balance in this book.

The history of Lyme disease has been characterized by polarized positions on diagnosis and treatment, leading some patients, community doctors, and academic researchers to feel threatened by one another. To address these conflicts, we include a chapter on the "Lyme Wars" because this is part of the troubled history of Lyme disease. We strongly believe and hope, however, that the "Lyme Wars" are fading as novel results from recent science are serving to open up new lines of communication between the previously warring camps.

Conflict and uncertainty in science can be terribly discouraging for patients who need and want answers now, but conflict can also be enormously helpful in advancing science and focusing funding and talent on the most pressing questions. Because of the accelerated pace of scientific discovery over the past ten years and because patients and scientists have struck a new chord of collaboration, the most urgent questions are now being addressed.

# BASIC TERMINOLOGY

Because we are aware that most readers of this book will not have medical training, we have included a glossary at the end of this book. However, as an initial introduction to this topic, readers should understand the commonly used terms, listed below.

**Antibody** (also known as immunoglobulin) and **antigen:** A protein produced by the immune system to defend against microbes such as spirochetes, other bacteria, and viruses. The antibody binds to a protein (called an "antigen") on the microbe (for example, on the outer surface of the spirochete) to facilitate killing of the microbe. The smaller piece of this antigen that is the precise site for antibody binding is called an "**epitope**."

*Borrelia burgdorferi (B. burgdorferi)*: the bacterial microbe (a spirochete) that causes Lyme disease.

**Centers for Disease Control and Prevention (CDC)**: A U.S. government agency mandated to improve public health through health promotion, disease surveillance, and prevention.

**Cerebrospinal fluid**: The continuously produced watery fluid that flows in the ventricles and around the surface of the brain and spinal cord. A **lumbar puncture** ("spinal tap") is used to collect cerebrospinal fluid to detect signs of disease or infection.

**Chemokine**: A type of cytokine that guides white blood cells to sites of infection.

**Cytokine**: A hormone-like cell-signaling molecule that aids cell-to-cell communication and stimulates other cells to move toward sites of inflammation, infection, and trauma. Examples include interferon, interleukin, and tumor necrosis factor.

**Enzyme-linked immunosorbent assay (ELISA)**: A method of detecting and quantifying substances, such as antibodies in the blood or cerebrospinal fluid. Also referred to as enzyme immunoassay (EIA), this is often the first test for Lyme disease.

*Ixodes* **ticks**: Hard-bodied ticks that carry microbes (for example, viruses, bacteria, and protozoan parasites), some of which can be transmitted by the bite of a tick to humans to cause disease. These are considered "vectors" because they transmit infection.

**Lyme borreliosis**: Another term for Lyme disease, commonly used outside of the United States.

**Neuropathy**: Damage or malfunction of the nerves of the body. One common type affects the peripheral nervous system, causing symptoms such as tingling, intense pain, or weakness.

**Polymerase chain reaction (PCR)**: A test that detects genetic material (DNA or RNA) and is often considered a marker of current or recent infection or of remnant particles of infection.

**Serologic test**: A blood test that detects antibodies against microbes.

**Western blot**: A specific type of immunoblot that detects antibodies present in a serum sample. Often ordered as the second test after the ELISA for Lyme disease.

# CONQUERING
# LYME DISEASE

# 1

## WHAT IS LYME DISEASE?

### BASIC FACTS

Lyme disease (also known as Lyme borreliosis) is the most commonly reported vector-borne illness in the United States. The Centers for Disease Control and Prevention (CDC) estimates that more than 330,000 individuals are diagnosed with Lyme disease each year in the United States alone. Although the illness was named after a town in Connecticut, Lyme disease is not confined to the United States. In fact, more than eighty countries have reported cases, and the earliest reports come from Europe, not the United States.

The causative pathogen, *Borellia burgdorferi*, is a spirochete or spiral shaped bacterium that infects humans through the bite of the black-legged tick—sometimes referred to as a "deer tick." During the initial blood meal by the tick, the *B. burgdorferi* bacteria are injected into the skin. Among most patients, this then triggers an inflammatory response that manifests as an expanding red rash known as *erythema migrans*. This is the most common presenting sign of the disease and usually develops within two to thirty days after infection. It is typically a round or oval, solid red rash that grows in size over time; sometimes it resembles a bull's eye with a red perimeter and a paler central clearing. However, some patients never develop symptoms; the immune system clears the infection on its own and these individuals have no knowledge of having been infected with *B. burgdorferi*. Others don't see the rash or have only mild symptoms, so they don't seek medical attention; these patients may develop more serious manifestations weeks or a month later.

As the *B. burgdorferi* spirochete spreads locally within the skin tissue, it may enter the bloodstream—usually for just a brief period of time.

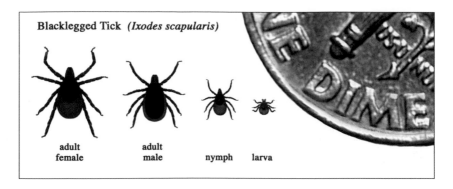

**FIGURE 1.1**

Relative sizes of black-legged ticks at different life stages. Adult ticks are the size of a sesame seed and nymphal ticks are the size of a poppy seed.

*Courtesy of the CDC.*

Once in the bloodstream, it gets distributed widely throughout the body. The spirochete seeds whichever organ or tissue it has reached (e.g., collagen tissue, joints, muscles, brain, peripheral nerves, heart), often causing inflammation in that tissue. The initial and ongoing immune response to this invading organism can lead to a wide range of symptoms, the most common being fever, joint pain or swelling, muscle pain, marked fatigue, headaches, stiff neck, nerve pain, irritability, cognitive problems, and, less often, cranial nerve palsy, meningitis, or cardiac inflammation or conduction block. The initial symptoms may be mild and may go noticed by the patient, or they may be quite severe, leading to emergency medical care. Among patients for whom the infection is initially unnoticed and untreated, the infection may resolve or remain quiescent for many months or even years, only later manifesting as an arthritic or neurologic illness.

Because of its initial presentation as a skin rash, its potential to involve many different organ systems, and its spirochetal etiology, Lyme disease has been compared to another disease caused by a spirochete, syphilis, which causes complex and chronic symptoms and in the twentieth century was called the "Great Imitator." Renowned physician Dr. William Osler said in the early twentieth century, "He who knows syphilis knows medicine," and today the same holds true for Lyme disease.

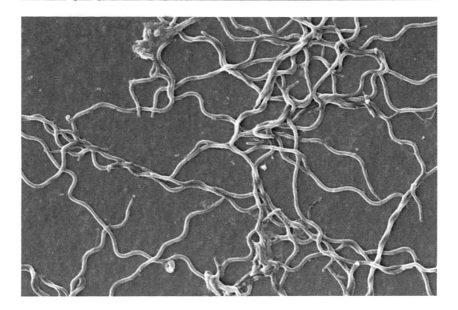

**FIGURE 1.2**

This digitally colorized scanning electron microscopic (SEM) image depicts a grouping of numerous *Borrelia burgdorferi* bacteria derived from a pure culture.

*Courtesy of the CDC/Claudia Molins.*

Because symptoms and signs of Lyme disease can be diverse and blood tests (as with other diseases) are not 100 percent reliable, diagnosis is based on a clinical history obtained from the patient and a thorough physical exam, supplemented by blood test results. This approach to testing is typical of the process physicians follow to make most diagnoses. First, the clinical presentation and risk factors are assessed and then the test is ordered. If the characteristic expanding rash is present, blood tests are not typically ordered, as at this early stage antibody-based tests are unlikely to be positive. Blood tests are not required to make a diagnosis of early Lyme disease when a patient presents with a characteristic rash after having been exposed to a Lyme endemic area. Clinicians who see this rash and know that the individual has been to a Lyme endemic area recently should immediately prescribe antibiotic treatment for presumed Lyme disease. Unfortunately, not all clinicians are aware that treatment should be started right away. Although initial blood tests for Lyme disease at the time of the rash are often negative (50 to 65 percent of the time), blood tests drawn several weeks later are more likely to be positive; at this later point, the blood tests have much better (but not perfect) sensitivity because the antibody response has had time to develop.

Many knowledgeable clinicians know to ask patients with suspected Lyme disease essential questions about tick bites, duration of tick attachment, expanding rashes, flu-like symptoms in the spring and summer, residence in or travel to Lyme endemic areas, and history of other tick-borne infections in themselves, close family members, or neighbors. Activities like golfing, gardening, hiking in the woods, and walking through leaves or tall grasses increase the likelihood of tick exposure. Forest workers and hunters are at high risk. In the United States, certain regions, including the Northeast, Mid-Atlantic States, upper Midwest, and Pacific coastal states, have a particularly heavy burden of *Borrelia*-infected ticks that lead to Lyme disease. Lyme disease, however, continues to spread geographically. The ticks that transmit the infection have now been identified in nearly 50 percent of the counties in the United States, spread across forty-three states (Eisen, Eisen, and Beard 2016). Because the geographic range of the disease is expanding and because people who don't reside in Lyme endemic areas may well vacation in areas where it is prevalent, all health care clinicians need to be aware of Lyme disease.

Outside of the United States, Lyme disease is generally referred to as borreliosis because it is recognized as being caused by multiple spirochetes of the *B. burgdorferi* genospecies complex. Lyme disease is the most commonly reported tick-borne infection in North America and Europe. Worldwide, Lyme disease has a particularly big impact on Europe and Asia. Its incidence is low in the United Kingdom, Japan, and Turkey, while it is quite high in Austria, Germany, the Netherlands, Belgium, Lithuania, Slovenia, and Estonia. In the northern and eastern regions of Europe (e.g., Croatia, Bulgaria, Slovakia, Scandinavia, Czech Republic, Baltic states), the ticks are most likely to carry *Borrelia afzellii*, which causes primarily a skin disease. In the Western countries (e.g., Switzerland, Austria, the United Kingdom), the ticks are more likely to carry *Borrelia garinii*, which causes primarily a neurologic disease. Lyme endemic areas have been identified as far west as Portugal and all the way east to Turkey and north to Russia (Mead 2015).

While similar across countries and continents, there are also important differences. In Europe, for example, there are three primary genospecies, while in the United States one genospecies causes most cases of Lyme disease. In Europe, there are more diverse skin manifestations, such as a chronic late-appearing rash called *erythema chronicum atrophicans* or an earlier blue-red rash or nodule called *Borrelia* lymphocytoma, which most often appears on the earlobe of children or nipple of adults. These different clinical manifestations reflect genetic differences in the species of the spirochete that causes Lyme disease. Not only are the initial and later-stage manifestations somewhat different among the United States and other countries, but these genetic differences also mean that diagnostic tests that work in one location may not work as well in another. Additionally, there are questions regarding whether the treatment response to antibiotics differs based on the infecting genospecies. For example, in Europe it has been reported that oral doxycycline is just as good as intravenous ceftriaxone for neurologic Lyme disease. Is this applicable to neurologic Lyme disease in the United States as well? We do not yet know, as these studies have not yet been done.

Consider the following case of a woman from the northeastern United States. While the initial course was typical, the subsequent symptoms led to important questions.

**CASE 1.** Lyme Disease with Rash and Disseminated Symptoms

A forty-year-old previously healthy woman living in a Lyme endemic area developed diffuse muscle aches, palpitations, and fatigue about four days after pulling weeds from her garden. Although she felt feverish, her temperature was normal. Two days later, her spouse noted an apple-sized rash on the back of her leg, followed a few days later by other round rashes elsewhere on her body. These rashes started small and grew larger, and they were not itchy. She also noted that normal light started to bother her—the television screen appeared abnormally bright and sunlight hurt her eyes such that she kept the window shades down during the day. Sounds in stores were uncomfortably loud. Chewing became difficult because of jaw pain. Headaches emerged. She felt dizzy at times and had trouble reading. About four weeks after the onset of symptoms, Lyme disease was diagnosed based on the rash and fully positive blood tests

*(Continued next page)*

*(Continued from previous page)*

for Lyme disease (enzyme-linked immunosorbent assay [ELISA] and Western blot—both IgM and IgG). After treatment with three weeks of doxycycline, the rashes, jaw pain, and headaches resolved, but her fatigue was still quite dense and she noticed cognitive problems emerging, such as problems with short-term memory and word-finding.

Comment: This woman did not recall a tick bite, but she had been gardening in a tick-infested area just days before development of the typical round red expanding rash of Lyme disease. The bacteria that cause Lyme disease, known as *B. burgdorferi*, were transmitted to her through the bite of a tick she hadn't seen; the spirochetes then spread through her skin and into her bloodstream, thereby reaching other parts of her body and causing rashes elsewhere. Had she seen the initial tick bite and removed it within the first twenty-four to thirty-six hours of attachment, she most likely would not have contracted Lyme disease. The early flu-like symptoms were followed by headaches, sensory sensitivity, profound fatigue, and, later, cognitive disturbances. She received the standard course of antibiotic therapy for early Lyme disease. In most cases, when Lyme disease is treated early, the symptoms resolve completely and quickly. In this case of an individual with multiple rashes indicating dissemination of the infection, this course of antibiotic treatment led to a resolution of some but not all of her symptoms.

The woman asked, "What should I do next?" Should her doctor recommend that she wait several months, as complete resolution of symptoms after antibiotic therapy can take time? Should her doctor recommend a lumbar puncture (spinal tap) to look for evidence of central nervous system infection given the new onset of memory and word-finding problems and then possibly treat with intravenous antibiotics to ensure better penetration of antibiotics into the central nervous system? Or should her doctor recommend returning in four weeks to see if the symptoms have improved? If not improved after four weeks, would a second round of oral antibiotics be considered? She asks, "How do I know if I still have the infection in my body? Is there a blood test that will answer this question? I don't like antibiotics, but if I need them I'll take them."

As this woman consults with other doctors, searches the Internet for answers, and listens to the advice of friends, she realizes that the tests are not as informative as she had hoped and that there are many different opinions about what she should do next. She becomes more confused. "Why do doctors not agree with one another? Whom should I trust? Which treatment path should I pursue?"

Lyme disease is often a short-lived illness that responds to early anti-biotic treatment without any long-term problems. However, in some individuals—especially if the infection is not treated until months later—the response to antibiotic treatment is incomplete and symptoms linger or return. Among these individuals, the delay in treatment may contribute to a more chronic and serious illness. These patients in particular want to know more about how to interpret the diagnostic tests, which treatment options are best for the chronic symptoms, and the reasons for persistent symptoms. These questions are obviously of paramount importance. This book presents much of what is now known in each of these areas. However, before going further, we would like to put all of this in context by taking the reader on a rapid tour of the history of Lyme disease.

## A BIRD'S EYE VIEW

At times it is helpful to simplify. From our perspective, the history of Lyme disease can be divided into three periods.

**Period 1. 1970–1990**    Discovery, openness, rich clinical descriptions

**Period 2. 1991–2007**    Epidemiologic surveillance, narrowed definitions, more specific tests, clarification of pathophysiology

**Period 3. 2008–Present**    Renewed openness and inquiry into multiple causes of persistent symptoms, discovery-based science and precision medicine tackle the illness

The timeline depicted in figure 1.3 presents some of the key highlights of these three periods. While we will be discussing all of these highlights and others in greater depth in the subsequent chapters, we present them here briefly for the advantage of the bird's eye view.

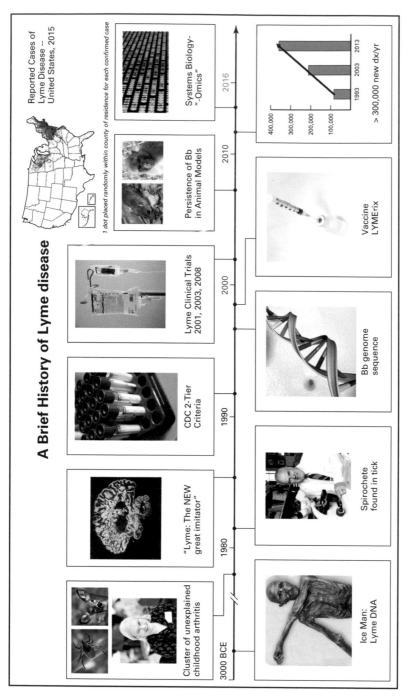

**FIGURE 1.3**

Counter clockwise from left: deer tick, courtesy of the CDC/James Gathany; deer, courtesy of Dr. Barbara Strobino; Polly Murray, courtesy of Dr. Kenneth Liegner; MRI scan Multiple Sclerosis, courtesy of Govind Bhagavatheeshwaran, Daniel Reich, NINDS, NIH; test tubes, courtesy of the CDC/Amanda Mills; IV bag, courtesy of NIH; incidence map, courtesy of the CDC; mouse, courtesy of The Connecticut Agricultural Experiment Station/Dr. Kirby Stafford; monkey, courtesy of Dr. Monica Embers; binary code, courtesy of Christiaan Colen/Creative commons; Lyme 1993–2003, courtesy of the CDC/ NCEZID and Nelson et al. 2015; vaccine, courtesy of NIH; double helix, courtesy of National Human Genome Research Institute, NIH; Willy Burgdorfer, courtesy of NIH; Ice Man, © Südtiroler Archäologiemuseum/EURAC/Marco Samadelli-Gregor Staschitz.

## Period 1. 1970–1990

Although first reported in Europe many decades earlier, the first publication in the United States describing the expanding red rash of Lyme disease was by a dermatologist from Wisconsin who recognized it as identical to a European rash known as *erythema chronicum migrans* (Scrimenti 1970). Similar rashes were seen in Groton, Connecticut (Mast and Burrows 1976a). The initial cases of what would soon become known as Lyme arthritis (Steere et al. 1977) were brought to the attention of Connecticut public health officials and clinical investigators at Yale University by two mothers who were very troubled by a strange epidemic in their New England town (Murray 1996). The cause of Lyme disease was uncertain until 1982, when a National Institutes of Health (NIH) researcher, Dr. Willy Burgdorfer, identified spiral-shaped *Borrelia* inside the guts of ticks sent to him from Long Island, New York (Burgdorfer et al. 1982).

After the initial reports of Lyme arthritis, the literature was filled with rich clinical descriptions of the multisystem manifestations of Lyme disease. One of the more striking clinical reports (Pachner 1988) went beyond the well-recognized symptom triad of neurologic Lyme disease—meningitis, cranial neuritis, and radiculitis—to describe some of the more atypical presentations of brain involvement: behavioral changes (e.g., compulsions, depression); memory difficulty; confusion and agitation (in a patient with subacute encephalitis); or a relapsing-remitting focal neurologic disease mimicking multiple sclerosis. The author of this paper, titled "*Borrelia burgdorferi* in the Nervous System: The New 'Great Imitator,'" suggested Lyme disease might replace syphilis for that distinction.

Among many advances made during these early years, the most important from a clinical perspective was the demonstration that antibiotic therapy was effective in treating Lyme disease, particularly when initiated early in the course of infection. Early antibiotic studies recommended penicillin and tetracycline (Steere et al. 1980). Subsequent studies demonstrated that amoxicillin and doxycycline were more effective for early Lyme disease and that intravenous ceftriaxone was more effective than penicillin for late Lyme disease (Dattwyler et al. 1988; Dattwyler et al. 1990). This initial period in the history of Lyme disease was one of ongoing discovery and clarification in which academics and community doctors saw a wide range of patients, sometimes collaborating to tackle this disease.

## Period 2. 1991–2007

Period 2 began with the initiation of national surveillance by the CDC, for which they delineated a set of objective case criteria for the surveillance diagnosis of Lyme disease. These surveillance criteria enhanced accuracy of national case reporting by focusing upon visible, verifiable, and objective clinical manifestations. A second action by the CDC that had a wide impact was to endorse a two-tiered approach for diagnostic testing of serum in the United States, as recommended by a meeting of diagnostic experts at a national conference (CDC 1995). This two-tiered algorithm (ELISA followed by a Western blot) for serologic diagnosis markedly reduced false positive test results, but it also had limitations—in particular, very poor sensitivity in early Lyme disease (35 to 50 percent) and insufficient sensitivity in neurologic Lyme disease (72 to 87 percent).

The CDC's set of objective clinical criteria were essential for epidemiologic surveillance. Problems arose, however, when clinicians inappropriately applied these surveillance clinical criteria as strict rules for diagnosis in the clinical setting, such that only individuals with the objective observable clinical manifestations could be diagnosed and treated for Lyme disease. An additional problem was that these CDC surveillance criteria became the benchmark set of criteria used by researchers when they were applying for grants from the government; the academic research community thus limited its focus to investigating those patients who met these narrow CDC surveillance criteria. Insurance companies began to deny payment for treatment of cases that didn't meet the CDC surveillance criteria. Frustration and anger erupted among patients, conflicts occurred among doctors with different perspectives on how to diagnose and treat this disease, and battles occurred with insurance companies, leading to the Lyme Wars, discussed in a later chapter in this book.

Four other highlights during this period had significant influence.

- The sequencing of the *Borrelia* genome led to a surge of research, including identification of many additional strains of *B. burgdorferi*, a better understanding of pathophysiology, the identification of new diagnostic tests, and the development of new vaccines (Fraser 1997). One fascinating application of this knowledge came when genetic material from the *Borrelia* spirochete was found in a 5,300-year-old ice mummy discovered in the northern Italian Alps, demonstrating that *B. burgdorferi* didn't first emerge in the twentieth century but was present over five thousand years ago (Callaway 2012).

- Investigators uncovered a variety of immune evasion strategies used by the *Borrelia* spirochete to enable it to escape host defense mechanisms and survive in the animal host. The *Borrelia* spirochete "hides" from immune surveillance by up- or down-regulating the proteins on its outer surface and by changing components or configuration of these outer surface proteins themselves (Norris 2006). The spirochetes also render the immune system less effective by binding inhibitory proteins from the animal host that diminish immune-mediated killing (Kraiczy et al. 2002).

- A Lyme disease vaccine ("LYMErix") came on the market in the United States in 1998. Initial excitement about a great public health advance was followed only a few years later by diminished interest and concerns about safety, such that the manufacturer of the vaccine removed it from the market after only four years.

- Four NIH-funded placebo-controlled clinical trials were conducted to determine whether repeated antibiotic therapy is helpful for patients with persistent symptoms (Krupp et al. 2003; Fallon et al. 2008; Klempner et al. 2001a). The results of these trials have led to different interpretations and much debate—an issue addressed in chapter 7.

## Period 3. 2008–Present

A major shift in understanding Lyme disease occurred in 2008 when a study was published demonstrating that the spirochete causing Lyme disease, *B. burgdorferi*, could persist in the mouse even after antibiotic treatment (Hodzic et al. 2008) This study was intriguing in that the *Borrelia* spirochete was identified not by standard mechanisms—such as blood testing—but by allowing a laboratory-raised uninfected tick to feed on the previously treated mouse and then testing the tick. This method (known as xenodiagnosis) demonstrated that the tick was able to attract and suck up persistent spirochetes when other efforts to find the spirochetes had failed.

This report was followed by another study that also demonstrated persistent infection despite antibiotics, but this time among animals much closer to humans—rhesus macaques (Embers et al. 2012). In this study, small numbers of intact spirochetes were recovered from the monkeys by xenodiagnoses, even though the monkeys had been previously treated with antibiotics known to be effective against the *Borrelia* infection. In addition, inflammation and positive immunofluorescence markers for *Borrelia* spirochetes were found in the cardiac tissue of three previously treated monkeys who had no other disease or infection to explain the cardiac inflammation. Further, *B. burgdorferi* DNA, RNA, and protein were detected in the tissues of the treated monkeys. These data from an animal quite close to humans confirmed that *Borrelia* spirochetes can persist despite antibiotic therapy and suggested that cardiac muscle inflammation may occur as a result.

These studies rocked the foundation of the long-standing conviction of many in the academic community who had argued for decades that repeated antibiotic treatment made no sense because the infection did not persist after antibiotics. These researchers then had to ask: Were these animal findings real? Was this research error?

The plethora of similar reports suggests this was not research error. The first major animal study to report persistent infection after antibiotic treatment had been published ten years earlier, using beagles as the animal model (Straubinger et al. 1997). These results were so unexpected that they were largely ignored by the academic community. A Finnish study of treated mice previously infected with *B. burgdorferi* detected persistent spirochetes after the mice were given an immunosuppressive agent (Yrjanainen et al. 2007). Another research group using the mouse model had visualized noninfectious persistent *Borrelia* spirochetes after treatment (Bockenstedt et al. 2002) and later identified spirochetal protein fragments that remained for months after antibiotic treatment (Bockenstedt et al. 2012). While concerns were raised by some scientists about research methodology that might have led to misleading results (Wormser and Schwartz 2009), many of these concerns were addressed by subsequent research by the same groups. What is clear is that researchers from different institutions using different animal models and different methods have come to the same conclusion that *Borrelia* spirochetes can persist after antibiotic therapy—but in nearly all studies the spirochetes were less robust and not able to grow in culture. The National Institutes of Health was so impressed by these animal studies that funding was provided for a similar study among humans; preliminary results from this human study (Marques et al. 2014) will be addressed in a later chapter.

While researchers were largely surprised by these animal model findings, many community clinicians felt vindicated. Many clinicians were aware of the beagle study from the mid-1990s as well as case reports from the medical literature suggesting persistent infection in humans despite treatment (Preac-Mursic et al. 1989; Nocton et al. 1994; Strle et al. 1996; Oksi et al. 1999), and their clinical experience with patients resonated with these animal model studies. While it remained to be demonstrated definitively in the animal model that these persistent spirochetes or protein fragments are causing disease, many clinicians felt relieved that finally the research community was beginning to take this possibility seriously.

The acceptance of persistent spirochetes in the animal model has subsequently led to a flurry of studies and new openness to some of the key questions patients have long asked researchers to address.

- Why do some patients have persistent symptoms? Do humans have persistent infection or a postinfectious process?
- Why do antibiotics eradicate most but not all spirochetes? Do we even need antibiotics to wipe out all of the remaining spirochetes that cause Lyme disease, or does a healthy immune system clear out the remaining infection?
- Why is it so rare to be able to culture the persisting spirochetes? If there are spirochetes that persist in the human and if their function is attenuated, are the persistent spirochetes even causing disease? Do the spirochetal remnants (protein fragments or genetic material) trigger symptoms through an ongoing inflammatory response and, if so, how long do these spirochetal remnants stay in the human body after the spirochete is gone? In other words, what do these persistent spirochetes signify? Are they causing disease or not?
- Can diagnostic tests be developed that detect active infection or confirm the eradication of infection?

Another highlight of this third period was the announcement in 2013 by the CDC that there are at least 300,000 cases of Lyme disease diagnosed each year in the United States—ten times greater than reported each year by physicians to the CDC. While some might consider this bad news in that it confirms an expanding epidemic, the large numbers of new cases brought national attention to Lyme disease and to the need for better diagnostics. This caught the attention of the private biomedical industry as well, which realized the financial opportunity provided by the development of better diagnostic tests.

Fortunately, the period from 2008 to the present has been accompanied by a burgeoning of new biotechnologies that allow researchers to obtain answers to questions within days or weeks that previously might have taken years. This revolution in biotechnology (which includes broader application of the omics approaches, next-generation sequencing, and a new gene-editing tool called CRISPR) has led to new research opportunities. The following are some examples of questions that have been explored in recent years and others that are now being investigated.

## PATHOPHYSIOLOGY

Among animals with persistent infection, is there evidence of local inflammation and of genetic transcription of inflammatory molecules at the site of the persistent spirochete? If local inflammation can be shown, could this explain chronic symptoms? Can it be shown in other animals as well, closer to the human?

## BIOMARKERS

Is there a biological fingerprint (e.g., proteins, metabolites, DNA/RNA, mitochondria) in the blood, spinal fluid, urine, or stool that differentiates humans with persistent symptoms from those who recover? If we can identify a fingerprint, then new "personalized" treatments can be devised that target the disease process.

## OTHER INFECTIONS

Are there other microbes that have not yet been discovered that exist inside ticks? Instead of guessing what might be there and searching one microbe at a time, can we use the latest technology to "uncover" or "discover" all the microbes that exist within ticks without knowing in advance what we are looking for?

## NEW DIAGNOSTICS

Can these "discovery-based" diagnostics be adapted for use in a health clinic that is far removed from a major medical center? For example, one recent project led to the development of a palm–sized device that can extract and analyze genetic material quickly from a drop of blood. Once extracted, the information is then conveyed by computer to a central database that then matches the genetic material in that sample with a massive cloud-based database to come up with a correct infectious diagnosis. Such a device could be used on a remote island off of Maine or in the remote health clinics of Asia. This is not a remote dream or science fiction. A hand-held device—a portable genome sequencer—was recently successfully tested for use in outer space by International Space Station scientists, enabling astronauts to rapidly identify potentially dangerous microbes (Karouia et al. 2017).

Can we move beyond the outdated diagnostic tests of the 1990s? Early assays were developed based on the proteins that were produced by the *B. burgdorferi* spirochete in the laboratory culture setting, not in the human. While it made sense at the time, now this approach is recognized as inadequate. Why? Because new proteins are actually produced by the spirochete after it infects the human that aren't produced in the laboratory culture setting. This means that the original antibody tests based on laboratory culture do not necessarily detect all of the antibodies against Lyme disease infection that are actually produced in the human. Next-generation diagnostic tests—based on the proteins that are actually produced at different stages of human infection—are being developed to improve the detection of infection at all stages of disease. Using only the exact location of the *B. burgdorferi* protein that the antibody actually binds (i.e., the epitope), these new diagnostic tests are leading to markedly enhanced precision. By including a wider array of outer surface proteins—those expressed later and those expressed earlier in the course of infection—these novel diagnostic tests can be made more sensitive for all stages of human infection.

## NEW TREATMENT STRATEGIES

If "persister spirochetes" are contributing to ongoing human disease, can we identify new antibiotic approaches that are effective at killing these persister spirochetes? Can new tissue-penetrating antibiotic approaches be identified that do not require intravenous administration?

If chronic symptoms are due to postinfectious immune dysregulation, can immune modulatory strategies be identified that will improve health outcomes?

If chronic symptoms are due to altered brain networks that govern pain, cognition, or fatigue, can these be targeted through brain stimulation or other neuromodulatory approaches?

## NEW PREVENTION STRATEGIES

Can we create a new vaccine that is safe and does not require frequent booster shots to maintain protection?

Can we genetically modify mice so that they create antibodies that kill the spirochetes inside them? Can we then safely release these genetically modified mice into the human population and allow these mice to propagate and pass on these genes from generation to generation?

The rationale is that if the *B. burgdorferi* spirochetes are killed inside these super mice, then the ticks will not be able to suck up the spirochetes during a blood meal. If the ticks do not get infected when they feed on mice, then the ticks cannot transmit the spirochete when they feed on humans and the incidence of human Lyme disease in the United States will be dramatically reduced.

When we are asked, "What's going on in the Lyme disease research world?," we can now state with confidence, "More than you could possibly imagine." Paradigm shifts have occurred. Massive progress is taking place. We have reason to expect major public health advances within the next several years.

# 2

# THE EARLY HISTORY AND EPIDEMIOLOGIC SURVEILLANCE

In the early twentieth century, long before reports appeared in the United States, the following cases appeared. In 1909, a red expanding rash at the site of a tick bite was described in a patient from Sweden (Afzelius 1921). Then there was a report from France of a patient who developed a similar rash (*erythema migrans* [EM]) after a tick bite, followed by radiating pains, arm paralysis, anxiety, and meningitis (Garin and Bujaudoux 1922). In 1930, a report from Sweden described a man who, three months after an EM rash, developed an encephalitis with disorientation, psychosis, and abnormal spinal fluid results (Hellerstrom 1930). Then in 1941, a neurologic syndrome was described in Germany that included meningitis, radicular pains, and peripheral nervous system involvement (Bannwarth 1941). These reports, now considered to be early descriptions of Lyme disease, demonstrate that Europeans have long known that Lyme disease is a multisystemic illness.

Although the EM rash was first described in the United States in 1970, Lyme disease didn't garner much attention until 1975 when two women—Polly Murray and Judith Mensch—grew increasingly concerned by an unusual clustering of arthritis among children in their small rural town of Old Lyme, Connecticut. Each woman contacted the Connecticut public health authorities to report this odd clustering because they recognized that there were too many reports of a rare childhood disease—juvenile rheumatoid arthritis—in their town. Concerned by these reports, the State Health Department contacted the Division of Rheumatology at Yale University to collaborate in exploring further. A young rheumatologist from Yale trained in clinical epidemiology, Dr. Allen Steere, led the investigation. These were exciting days for the investigators. They learned that the illness had a tight geographic clustering, as often several households on a block had a case; similarly, more cases might be found among households on one side of a river compared to the other side. The symptom profile was described as brief, intermittent attacks of asymmetric joint swelling and pain, primarily in the large joints. When asked about earlier clinical signs or symptoms, the investigators learned that about 25 percent of patients with arthritis recalled having had an unusual rash about four months prior to the development of arthritis (Steere et al. 1977).

After careful clinical interviews with the children and adults with new onset arthritis, Steere and his colleagues concluded that this was a new illness—Lyme arthritis—with geographic clustering and temporal variation (i.e., more common in the spring and summer) suggestive of a vector-borne illness, possibly from a tick. The infectious agent inside the vector, however, was unclear. Was it a virus, a parasite, a bacterium? Blood tests were conducted to determine whether this was a known infectious arthritis, but all blood tests were negative. It appeared that this was a new disease and, in the tradition of other infectious diseases (such as Legionnaires' disease, St. Louis Encephalitis, or Rocky Mountain Spotted Fever), it was named after the area in which it was discovered.

As noted earlier, the expanding red rash described by the Connecticut patients with Lyme arthritis had been described previously in the United States by a Wisconsin dermatologist (Scrimenti 1970). Next it was described by physicians working at the U.S. Naval Base in Connecticut (Mast and Burrows 1976). These latter clinicians—working in Groton, which is just eighteen miles from Old Lyme—had evaluated patients presenting with an unusual expanding red rash. They noted that this rash was quite similar to the descriptions of *erythema chronicum migrans* in Europe, which was thought to be infectious in origin; they were aware of European reports indicating that penicillin treatment shortened the course of illness (Hollstrom 1951, 1958).

It was not clear, however, whether *erythema migrans* in the United States had the same cause as the *erythema migrans* described in Europe. Because of this, in the early years of this illness, patients who presented with an EM rash were not routinely treated with antibiotics. To more carefully document the natural course of this illness, the Yale researchers initiated a six-year prospective naturalistic follow-up study of fifty-five patients to see how the illness evolved over time among patients who had not received antibiotics (Steere, Schoen, and Taylor 1987). Of the fifty-five untreated patients enrolled between 1976 and 1979, 20 percent had no subsequent manifestations of Lyme disease—that is, the illness resolved on its own. All of the others, however, did have subsequent problems: 20 percent had recurrent brief episodes of joint or musculoskeletal pain without objective joint abnormalities; 50 percent developed intermittent attacks of frank arthritis, usually in the large joints; and 10 percent developed a chronic erosive arthritis. Commonly involved joints included the knee, followed by the shoulder, ankle, elbow, and the temporomandibular, wrist, and hip joints.

Within a short period it became clear that this was a disease that affected not only the joints and skin but also the heart and the central and peripheral nervous system. In fact, the neurologic aspects of Lyme disease appeared quite similar to a disease in Europe described in the 1940s called Bannwarth's syndrome, characterized by the triad of meningitis, cranial nerve palsy, and an intensely painful sensory radiculitis. These early reports therefore established a clinical link between what was being discovered in the United States and what had long been observed in Europe.

The treatment of choice for Lyme disease was initially unclear. The Yale rheumatology group felt this was a rheumatologic disorder and should be treated with anti-inflammatory agents. One factor leading them away from the hypothesis that this disease was caused by a bacterial infection was that some patients fully recover after the characteristic rash even without antibiotics. When it began to become clearer that antibiotics did seem to be helpful, questions remained as to what the antibiotics were actually doing. Was early antibiotic therapy shortening the duration of the initial illness or serving to prevent later disease in other organs? Because of the uncertainty, a study was conducted to assess the outcome of four groups of patients with EM based on treatment (penicillin, tetracycline, erythromycin, or no antibiotic treatment) (Steere et al. 1980). The study demonstrated that those given penicillin or tetracycline resolved the EM and associated symptoms more quickly than those given no antibiotic treatment. The researchers found that these antibiotics did not diminish the likelihood of developing neurologic or cardiac complications. However, the study did suggest that penicillin may prevent or attenuate the course of Lyme arthritis. This study therefore supported the emerging hypothesis that a bacterial infection might be the cause of Lyme disease.

## WHAT WAS THE INFECTIOUS AGENT OF LYME DISEASE?

Early on, many researchers suspected that a virus was the cause of Lyme disease. However, no virus could be found. As it became clear that antibiotics that kill bacteria were helpful in Lyme disease, researchers began to focus on finding a bacterial agent. As had investigators in Europe in earlier years, they hypothesized that it might be a bacterium in the *Rickettsial* family. The actual agent, however, continued to elude investigators in the United States and Europe.

In 1981, Dr. Willy Burgdorfer at the NIH's Rocky Mountain Laboratories in Montana was dissecting ticks sent to him by a New York pathologist, Dr. Jorge Benach, that had been collected from eastern Long Island. Benach sent Burgdorfer forty-four black-legged hard-bodied ticks, *Ixodes scapularis*. After careful dissection of these tiny ticks, Burgdorfer found long, irregularly coiled spirochetes in the midgut of the ticks, among other microorganisms. This was a shock. While it was known that spirochetes

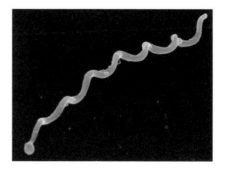

FIGURE 2.1

Electron micrograph of *Borrelia burgdorferi*.
*Courtesy of NIAID/David Dorward.*

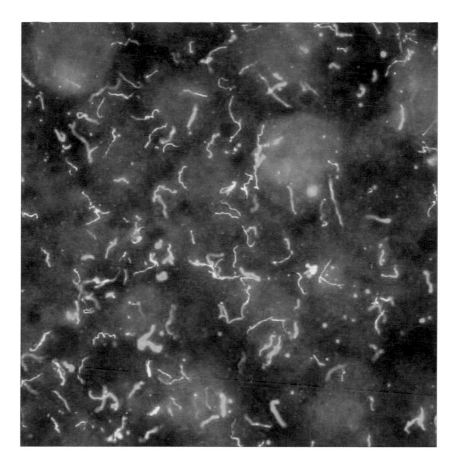

FIGURE 2.2

*B. burgdorferi* alters the proteins expressed on its outer surface. Here, immunofluorescent antibodies were used to identify spirochetes that express outer surface protein D (OspD in yellow and red). *B. burgdorferi* not expressing OspD are labeled in green.
*Courtesy of NIAID.*

could be found in soft-bodied ticks, spirochetes were not expected in hard-bodied ticks. Burgdorfer shared the exciting news with Benach. To test whether this finding in the tick had anything to do with the mysterious Lyme disease in humans, Benach sent Burgdorfer serum that had been collected from patients with Lyme disease on Long Island. Benach also sent serum from patients on Long Island who had been diagnosed with Babesiosis but who also reported having had an EM rash. Could these individuals have been infected with two microbes—the agent of Babesiosis and that of Lyme?

To assist with culturing the organism, Dr. Burgdorfer invited a colleague, Dr. Alan Barbour, also at the Rocky Mountain Laboratories, to join the scientific effort. Dr. Barbour—a physician and microbiologist with expertise on Relapsing Fever *Borrelia*, a related spirochete—developed the first culture medium (BSK) for this new spirochete isolated from the Long Island *Ixodes* ticks. When the spirochetes grew in culture known to be favorable for *Borrelia*, it became clear that these were spirochetes in the *Borrelia* genus. Once cultured, laboratory tests could be devised to detect these organisms. The first antibody test was an immunoflourescent assay derived from the spirochetes cultured from the ticks.

One important early animal study involved allowing infected ticks to feed on laboratory rabbits; these rabbits developed an EM rash and a positive Lyme antibody test, confirming a link between the spirochete and the dermatologic manifestation of Lyme disease. The human studies, however, were the essential next step. When the serum samples from a Long Island patient with a history of Lyme disease tested positive using the new antibody test, the hypothetical link between the newly discovered spirochete and human Lyme disease was confirmed for the first time.

The cause of Lyme disease was further strengthened when not only the blood but also the skin and spinal fluid from patients with Lyme disease tested positive using these new assays. The *Borrelia* spirochete found within the midgut of ticks was the cause of Lyme disease, the spirochete was named after its founder Willy Burgdorfer, and the strain was called B31 because it was the first isolate discovered by the three Bs—Burgdorfer, Barbour, and Benach. These findings were first published in the journal *Science* (Burgdorfer 1982) and the first isolates of these spirochetes from human patients were reported in the *New England Journal of Medicine* (Benach et al. 1983, Steere et al. 1983). Investigators throughout the world started testing their samples.

As Louis Pasteur said in the nineteenth century, "Chance favors only the prepared mind." Burgdorfer's mind had been primed. As a PhD student in Switzerland, Burgdorfer had studied the *Borrelia* spirochetes that caused Relapsing Fever in Africa. He knew what *Borrelia* spirochetes looked like.

He recalled a report by Hellerstrom from the late 1940s linking European *erythema chronicum migrans* with a prior tick bite and a possible spirochetal infection. Visualizing spirochetes in these ticks from eastern Long Island, he realized that he may have discovered the cause of not only Lyme disease in the United States but also the European *erythema chronicum migrans*. Shortly thereafter, he found these same spirochetes in *Ixodes ricinus* ticks, the vector linked to *erythema chronicum migrans* in Europe. With the new laboratory assays, the infectious cause in humans of two European skin diseases (*erythema chronicum migrans* and *acrodermatitis chronica atrophicans*) and the neurologic Bannwarth's syndrome was also confirmed as due to *B. burgdorferi*.

Over the subsequent years, numerous case reports, small series, and controlled studies demonstrated the effectiveness of a variety of antibiotics for Lyme disease (Wormser et al. 2006). Research studies conducted among patients with the EM rash indicate that about 75 to 80 percent of patients had excellent outcomes with three weeks of antibiotics. These studies led to the conclusion that treating Lyme disease with antibiotics at the time of the early EM rash is effective for many (but not all) individuals. Patients with disseminated Lyme disease, such as neurologic Lyme disease affecting the central nervous system or Lyme arthritis, however, might need a more potent therapy that could cross the blood–brain barrier or enter joint spaces more effectively—such as intravenous ceftriaxone (Dattwyler et al. 1987).

The logical flow of research in this historical account suggests that Lyme disease had been conquered decades ago. The clinical manifestations had been described, the infectious cause had been identified, diagnostic tests were developed, and effective treatments were demonstrated. This suggests that Lyme disease was all wrapped up by 1990. One more infectious disease had been put to rest. Or had it?

## THE SPREAD OF LYME DISEASE AND NATIONAL SURVEILLANCE

The public health authorities in the United States led by the Centers for Disease Control and Prevention (CDC) realized that Lyme disease was an emerging epidemic that needed to be studied more systematically from an epidemiologic perspective. In the early 1990s, the CDC delineated a set of objective clinical criteria for the diagnosis of Lyme disease that would be used by public health officials throughout the country to count the number of new cases of Lyme disease each year. Lyme disease became a "nationally reportable disease." Each physician was asked to report new cases of Lyme disease to the state public health officials. To ensure accurate identification of a "surveillance case" for the purpose of monitoring change in incidence of disease over time, the CDC's clinical surveillance criteria focused on those manifestations that are readily visible and objectively verifiable. Although it was recognized that the manifestations of Lyme disease are quite diverse and not thoroughly represented by the CDC "surveillance criteria," the monitoring criteria were narrowly defined on purpose to ensure with a high degree of certainty that all patients included had proven Lyme disease. These surveillance criteria were therefore mainly useful for the diagnosis of Lyme disease when an externally visible sign was present, such as the EM rash, arthritis, facial nerve palsy, or meningitis with abnormal spinal fluid markers.

What was learned? Since the early 1990s, when Lyme disease became nationally reportable, the incidence has dramatically increased and the geographic range of cases has spread (see figures 2.3a and 2.3b).

In 2013, the CDC issued a press release that made international news. It stated that new studies suggest that the number of Americans diagnosed with Lyme disease each year is approximately 300,000—not 30,000 as indicated by the annual case reports to the CDC. Because case reporting by physicians is known to underrepresent the true incidence of disease, the CDC had conducted three new studies to try to more accurately assess the actual case rate of Lyme disease. Their revised estimate suggested that the total number of people diagnosed with Lyme disease was actually ten times higher than the yearly reported number.

As Paul Mead, MD, MPH, and chief of epidemiology and surveillance for the CDC's Lyme disease program stated in that press release,

This new preliminary estimate confirms that Lyme disease is a tremendous public health problem in the United States, and clearly highlights the urgent need for prevention. (http://www.cdc.gov/media/releases/2013)

## Reported Cases of Lyme Disease -- United States, 2001

1 dot placed randomly within county of residence for each reported case

## Reported Cases of Lyme Disease -- United States, 2015

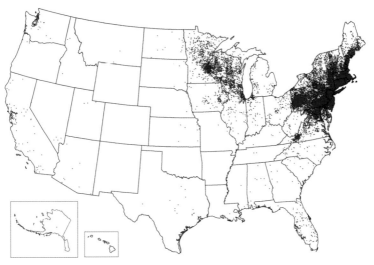

1 dot placed randomly within county of residence for each confirmed case

**FIGURE 2.3A AND 2.3B**

U.S. cases of Lyme disease in 2001 and 2015. One dot placed randomly within county of residence for each confirmed case.

*Courtesy of the CDC.*

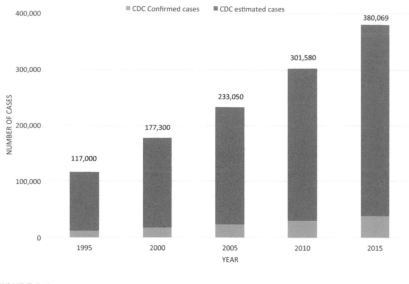

FIGURE 2.4

Confirmed and estimated cases of Lyme disease in the United States from 1995 to 2015.
*Courtesy of the CDC/NCEZID and Nelson et al. 2015.*

Figure 2.4 (using the estimate of ten times more cases than reported) high-lights the dramatic rise in reported and estimated cases of Lyme disease in the United States over a twenty-year period.

The geographic spread of Lyme disease is determined by whether the vectors that transmit the spirochete to humans (black-legged ticks known as *Ixodes scapularis* or *Ixodes pacificus*) are present in the geographic locale. Most commonly, Lyme disease cases in the United States are acquired in certain regions that are heavily populated by *Ixodes* ticks—the Northeast and Mid-Atlantic (from Maine to Virginia), the north central states (mainly Wisconsin and Minnesota), and the West Coast (particu-larly northern California). However, Lyme disease has been reported in all of the contiguous states as well as Alaska. The widely dispersed iden-tification of Lyme disease in the United States may be partly due to the fact that people from nonendemic areas travel to Lyme endemic areas and because cases reported to the CDC are attributed to the location of the report rather than the location of acquisition of the infection. Or it may be due to the spread of *Ixodes* ticks to new regions not yet recognized.

**FIGURE 2.5 AND 2.6**

The black-legged ticks, *Ixodes scapularus* and *Ixodes pacificus*, are known vectors for *Borrelia burgdorferi* bacteria.

*Courtesy of the CDC/James Gathany.*

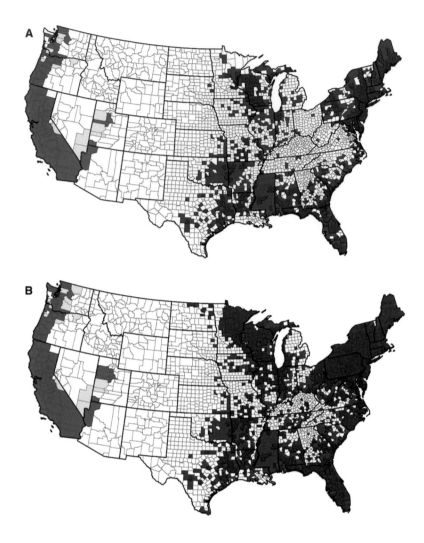

**FIGURE 2.7**

Distribution by county of the primary vectors of *B. burgdorferi*, the black-legged ticks, as summarized in 1998 (A) and in 2015 (B). Green and red refer to counties with an established population of *Ixodes* ticks, while yellow and blue refer to counties where *Ixodes pacificus* and *Ixodes scapularis*, respectively, have been reported.

*Eisen, Eisen, and Beard 2016.*

Between 1992 and 2015, the number of confirmed cases in the United States as a whole increased 300 percent. As examples of the continued rapid spread of Lyme disease in the United States, consider that certain states where there had previously been very little Lyme disease have seen marked increases in confirmed cases. Between 2005 and 2015, the number of confirmed cases increased 1,000 percent in Rhode Island; 900 percent in Vermont; 400 percent in Virginia, West Virginia, and Maine; 300 percent in Indiana; and 200 percent in Illinois and Florida.

The primary vector of the *B. burgdorferi* spirochete is now reported in 49.2 percent of the U.S. counties spread across forty-three states; this represents a 44.7 percent increase in the number of counties that have recorded tick presences since the survey in 1998 (Dennis et al. 1998; Eisen et al. 2016). As of 2015, Colorado, Idaho, Montana, New Mexico, and Wyoming did not have records of these ticks in their states. However, a small number of new cases of Lyme disease have been reported in each of these states based on CDC surveillance reports.

The spread of *Ixodes* ticks and of Lyme disease across the United States and in over eighty other countries is a public health crisis; some have called it a "public health failure." Despite decades of effort, this disease is not yet under control. Yet there is reason for hope. In the prevention chapter of this book, past, recent, and newer strategies for control of tick-borne diseases are described. While Lyme disease has not yet been conquered, new strategies offer promise of major breakthroughs.

# 3

## WHAT ARE THE SYMPTOMS AND SIGNS OF LYME DISEASE?

### EARLY LOCALIZED STAGE: DAYS TO WEEKS AFTER TICK BITE

Lyme disease is transmitted when an infected tick attaches to a human and injects *B. burgdorferi*, the spirochetal bacteria that cause Lyme disease, into the skin. It usually takes thirty-six hours of attachment for the tick to infect a human. If a tick is attached for a shorter period of time, the *Borrelia* spirochete can still be transmitted, but the likelihood of transmission is much lower. In 70 to 80 percent of cases, an *erythema migrans* (EM) rash will develop at the site of the bite, usually within three to thirty-two days (Steere and Sikand 2003). The rash typically starts as a red patch that is not painful but may be warm to the touch.

The name of the rash, "erythema," is from ancient Greek "to redden, to turn red." If untreated, the rash expands gradually over the next several weeks. As it grows, it may develop a central clearing or a "bull's eye" appearance. However, in most cases, the rash will be uniformly red. Alternatively, the rash may have a darker bluish-red center, a raised or blistery central region, or another atypical appearance. The shape of the rash varies from circular to oblong, oval, linear, or even triangular. Even though many patients and physicians would recognize a typical bull's eye rash as a marker of likely Lyme disease, only about 20 to 30 percent of Lyme rashes will have this classic bull's eye presentation. A diameter of two inches or more is seen in the majority of Lyme rashes.

A small bump or red rash occurring within several hours of a tick bite represents a hypersensitivity reaction rather than a Lyme rash. These

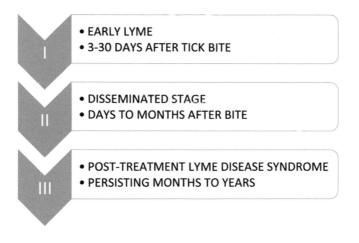

I
• EARLY LYME
• 3-30 DAYS AFTER TICK BITE

II
• DISSEMINATED STAGE
• DAYS TO MONTHS AFTER BITE

III
• POST-TREATMENT LYME DISEASE SYNDROME
• PERSISTING MONTHS TO YEARS

**FIGURE 3.1**

Some cases of early Lyme disease progress to disseminated disease with neurological, arthritic, or cardiac symptoms. Post-treatment Lyme disease syndrome occurs in 5 to 20 percent of cases.

hypersensitivity reactions are usually less than two inches in diameter, are sometimes raised in appearance, and typically begin to disappear within twenty-four to forty-eight hours. In contrast, an early primary Lyme rash usually increases in size over time and typically first appears days to weeks later.

Early symptoms of *B. burgdorferi* infection reflect the body's immunologic battle against the foreign bacteria. Because this initial immunologic response involves the release of small pro-inflammatory molecules called cytokines, many patients will experience moderate to severe systemic symptoms during this early phase of infection. These early systemic symptoms may include fatigue, headache, malaise, muscle and joint aches, swollen lymph nodes, and fever and chills. Because the classic Lyme rash may not occur or may not be seen in 20 to 30 percent of cases, the only sign of infection may be these flu-like symptoms. This symptom cluster of muscle and joint pain, fatigue, headache, and malaise is in fact the second most common presentation of Lyme disease, with the EM rash being the most common. Worth noting is that early symptoms of Lyme disease do *not* include upper

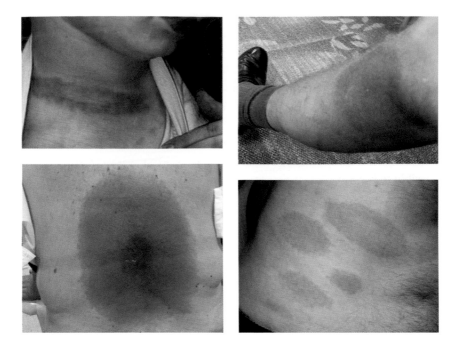

**FIGURE 3.2**

*Erythema migrans* rashes (clockwise from top left) **Figure 3.2a** Oval Lyme "bull's eye" rash with central clearing. **Figure 3.2b** Large, expanding Lyme rash. **Figure 3.2c** Multiple satellite EM rashes. **Figure 3.2d** Large, expanding Lyme rash with darker central area.

*Figure 3.2c courtesy of John Aucott, MD. Figure 3.2d courtesy of Carol Sotsky, MD.*

respiratory symptoms (e.g., cough, nasal congestion, runny nose) or significant diarrhea.

This high prevalence of symptoms without a rash, however, is not widely recognized as a manifestation of Lyme disease because only "objective" externally verifiable signs of disease are included in the CDC's epidemiologic surveillance criteria. These common symptoms can easily be ignored by doctors or even by the patients themselves, leading to an unrecognized and untreated illness. A *New England Journal of Medicine* article (Steere and Sikand 2003) reported this high prevalence of early symptoms without a rash:

Particularly when *erythema migrans* is not present early in the illness, patients may not go to a physician or Lyme disease may not be recognized until the more debilitating, harder-to-treat late manifestations of the infection become apparent. The challenge for patients and physicians is early recognition and treatment of the infection, particularly when patients present during the summer with non-specific systemic symptom.

Most doctors who work in areas where Lyme disease is common know that a flu-like illness during the spring or summer months suggests a possible tick-borne infection. Some doctors who work in areas in which Lyme disease is hyperendemic will treat patients who present with flu-like symptoms in the warmer months with antibiotics right away. They do not wait for blood test confirmation because they know that Lyme disease

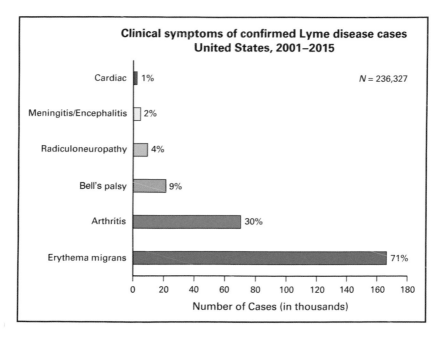

**FIGURE 3.3**

Clinical manifestations of confirmed Lyme disease cases.

*Courtesy of the CDC.*

tests can be falsely negative in the first few weeks of infection. Other risk factors suggesting that a flu-like illness might be Lyme disease include recent travel to a Lyme endemic area or spending time in the woods or other outdoor areas where ticks might be present. Flu-like symptoms in the absence of cough, runny nose, vomiting, or diarrhea should also raise suspicion for possible Lyme disease.

## EARLY DISSEMINATED STAGE: DAYS TO WEEKS AFTER TICK BITE

Dissemination of the *B. burgdorferi* spirochete beyond the initial localized area of the tick bite can occur quickly. When *B. burgdorferi* enters blood vessels or the lymphatic system, it has the potential to infect every tissue of the body. The trip through the bloodstream, however, is short, as the *B. burgdorferi* spirochete rapidly makes its way from the blood vessels back into the tissue where it typically resides; indeed, finding these bacteria in the blood is rarely possible after the initial infection. For example, the spirochete may exit the blood vessel and lodge in the skin, nerves, brain, heart, joints, or tendons. Wherever the *B. burgdorferi* spirochete lands, typically there is a local inflammatory response with cytokine production. When the *B. burgdorferi* spirochete disseminates to other skin regions, for example, it may cause "satellite" rashes that are far removed from the initial tick bite. These rashes may take on a different appearance, such as smaller red spots that may not resemble the original one.

### Joints and Muscles

Patients with Lyme disease often experience joint and muscle pain during the initial phase of skin infection. When *B. burgdorferi* disseminates beyond the skin to the joints, swelling and tenderness may occur, typically in the large joints and often migrating from one joint to another. Because the majority of patients don't develop joint inflammation until about six months after initial infection, arthritis is grouped into the "late disseminated stage" category. This, however, can be misleading because joint inflammation and swelling can occur as early as four days after initial infection. In other words, while different manifestations of Lyme disease are grouped for convenience into early and late disseminated stages based on the average time for onset, these stages are somewhat arbitrary in that there is often considerable variability as to when these signs and symptoms appear.

## Nervous System

When the *B. burgdorferi* spirochete targets the nervous system, conditions including meningitis, encephalitis, cranial neuritis, and radiculoneuritis may develop.

### MENINGITIS

Meningitis is an inflammation of the membranes covering the brain and spinal cord and is most often characterized by headaches that fluctuate in intensity from mild to severe. Additional symptoms may include neck stiffness, nausea, vomiting, light sensitivity, or fever. However, the symptoms of Lyme meningitis in the United States are often described as "smoldering" because they are generally less severe and their onset less abrupt than what is seen in other bacterial causes of meningitis; Lyme meningitis may mistakenly be considered viral meningitis. If a lumbar puncture (spinal tap) is performed on a patient with Lyme meningitis, the cerebrospinal fluid will by definition show an elevated number of lymphocytes (a type of white blood cell); the increased number of lymphocytes is often lower than seen in other bacterial infections. There may also be elevated protein and production of *B. burgdorferi*-specific antibodies. Some patients with no symptoms or only mild symptoms of neurologic Lyme disease will have signs of meningitis in their spinal fluid; in these cases, the meningitis will go undetected unless a lumbar puncture is conducted. Many patients with Lyme meningitis also have other symptoms or signs of Lyme disease.

### ENCEPHALITIS

Encephalitis is an inflammation of the brain tissue itself and is uncommon in Lyme disease. It can present as sleepiness, decreased level of consciousness, abnormal mood (mood swings, irritability, abnormal sudden tearfulness), confusion, cognitive changes, personality or behavior changes, hallucinations, or seizures. An electroencephalogram, a test of brain function, may show mild slowing. Magnetic resonance imaging (MRI) of the brain may show focal abnormalities suggesting inflammation, often affecting the white matter more than the gray matter. Functional brain imaging with positron emission tomography (PET) scans may show regions of increased metabolism or blood flow (Kalina et al. 2005). The spinal fluid may show oligoclonal bands and the synthesis of *B. burgdorferi*–specific antibodies.

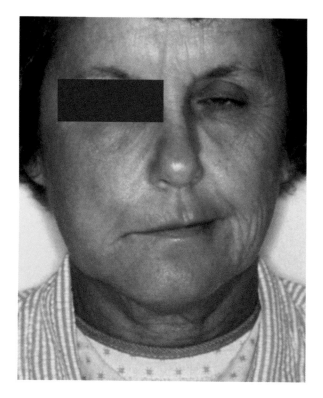

**FIGURE 3.4**

This patient presented with a right facial palsy and was subsequently diagnosed with Lyme disease.

*Courtesy of the CDC.*

## CRANIAL NEURITIS

Cranial neuritis, due to an inflammation of a cranial nerve, can cause a variety of sensory and motor problems:

- Facial nerve palsy (sometimes inaccurately referred to as Bell's Palsy) may be the first sign of Lyme disease and is the most commonly reported neurologic sign. The facial drooping indicates weakness or paralysis of the facial nerve. The weakness often comes on rapidly over one to two days, leading some patients to fear they are having a stroke. Typical symptoms include problems with lip movement, eye closure, and forehead wrinkling. Also common are pain behind the ear or an altered sense of taste. Involvement of the stapedial branch of the facial nerve may lead to hyperacusis (increased sound sensitivity). If a patient has weakness or paralysis of one side of the face and comes from a Lyme endemic area, Lyme disease should be strongly suspected. If both sides of the face are affected, Lyme disease is even more likely. Other factors that would increase the likelihood that a facial palsy is due to Lyme disease would include onset during tick season, fever, headache, and the absence of herpes lesions.
- Less commonly, other cranial nerves may be involved, sometimes in combination with one another. Patients may develop optic nerve inflammation causing changes in vision, abnormalities in facial sensation or facial pain, double vision, and/or hearing loss or tinnitus (ringing in the ears).

## PSEUDOTUMOR CEREBRI

Pseudotumor cerebri is characterized by an increase in intracranial pressure that if left untreated can lead to compression of the optic nerve and potential visual loss. Rarely, this condition is caused by infection with *B. burgdorferi*. A neurologic exam will reveal swelling of the optic disc (papilledema). Studies show diagnostic elevated cerebrospinal fluid pressure, sometimes with elevated white blood cells in the cerebrospinal fluid, a finding that is not otherwise associated with this condition. More often reported in children and young adults, the most common symptom is headache, followed by blurred vision or double vision. Very rarely, blindness may occur if the condition is not detected or treated early.

## RADICULONEURITIS

Radiculoneuritis (or radiculoneuropathy) refers to nerve dysfunction that stems from inflammation of the roots of the spinal nerve. Motor and/or sensory symptoms may occur. The sensory symptoms may include numbness or tingling on one or both sides of the body; there may be increased sensitivity to painful stimuli in the affected areas. Radicular pain may be experienced as sharp, stabbing, burning, or shooting pains that radiate down along the nerves into the limbs or across the trunk. A cluster of spinal nerves may be affected, such as in a brachial plexopathy that leads to numbness, tingling, pain, and weakness in various areas of the arm, hand, or shoulder.

## OTHER PRESENTATIONS OF LYME DISEASE–RELATED NEUROPATHIES

- Dysfunction of randomly distributed single or multiple nerves can occur (mononeuropathies or mononeuropathy multiplex). The symptoms, affecting one or more areas, may include numbness, tingling, loss of sensation, and/or trouble with movement.
- Rarely, patients may present with a syndrome typical of Guillain-Barré syndrome in which there is a rapidly progressive weakness and sensory changes, starting in the lower extremities and progressing to the upper body and arms (Kumar, Singh, and Rashid 2016; Celik et al. 2016). This is also called acute inflammatory demyelinating polyneuropathy (AIDP). When severe, certain muscles cannot be used at all and the person may become almost totally paralyzed. Respiratory muscles may be involved, resulting in need for ventilator support. This requires immediate medical attention.
- The C. Miller Fisher variant of AIDP also occurs, characterized by progressive dysfunction in multiple lower cranial nerves resulting in problems with speech and swallowing. A chronic inflammatory demyelinating polyneuropathy is also seen in the setting of Lyme disease. These neuropathic complications are mediated by immunologically driven attacks on nerves and require treatment with immune modulatory therapy such as intravenous immunoglobulin or steroids in addition to antibiotics.

## COMMENTS ABOUT ACUTE NEUROLOGIC LYME DISEASE

- The diagnosis of neurologic Lyme disease in the United States can be challenging in that some patients may have prominent symptoms of central neurologic Lyme disease without having abnormal spinal fluid test results when routine assays are employed (Coyle et al. 1995).
- Manifestations of neurologic Lyme disease may vary depending on the genetic profile of the Lyme disease spirochete. In Europe, where there are not one but three main types (genospecies) of *B. burgdorferi*, the manifestations are similar but also different in certain ways. For example:
  - Meningopolyneuritis is more common in Europe than in the United States, primarily caused by *B. garinii* rather than *B. burgdorferi*. With this neurologic manifestation, a painful radiculoneuropathy is present, accompanied by cerebrospinal fluid markers of meningitis but without a prominent headache; this is often followed by a cranial neuropathy or weakness of the extremities.
  - *B. afzelli* typically causes skin disease but can also lead to atypical neurologic presentations. In one study of ten patients in which *B. afzelli* was isolated from the cerebrospinal fluid, only one of the ten met the typical European criteria for neurologic Lyme disease. The other nine had symptoms such as headache, dizziness, and concentration and memory problems, while only two of the nine had increased white blood cells in the spinal fluid (Strle et al. 2006). This study demonstrates that neurologic Lyme disease may not always fit the typical profile and that factors such as the genospecies (or possibly strain) of the infecting *Borrelia* spirochete can alter the presentation.

**CASE 2.** Facial Nerve Palsy and Meningitis. The Case of Mr. E

Mr. E is a twenty-one-year-old man who developed a severe headache, followed two days later by a fever (38.3°C or 100.9°F) that recurred over the next four weeks. He then experienced muscle pains, poor appetite, progressive fatigue, and a marked sensitivity to loud sounds. About nine

*(Continued next page)*

(Continued from previous page)

days after the headache onset, he lost his ability to smile, to close his eyes tightly, and to wrinkle his forehead. His speech was mildly slurred and he drooled. The physician evaluating him learned that he was an outdoorsman and was recently exposed to a Lyme endemic area, but he did not recall a tick bite or a rash. The physical exam was normal except for the bilateral facial weakness, a stiff neck, and absent blink reflexes. The bilateral facial palsy led physicians to consider multiple causes, including Lyme disease, herpes-zoster infection, HIV infection, and sarcoidosis. A lumbar puncture revealed that the spinal fluid had elevated protein, normal glucose, and an increased number of white blood cells. Based on these clinical and laboratory findings, Mr. E was diagnosed as having a bilateral facial palsy and a lymphocytic meningitis.

This patient's blood tests for antibodies against *B. burgdorferi* over the course of the first month of illness showed an eight-fold increase in titer. Although the spinal fluid was not tested for *Borrelia*-specific antibodies, the diagnosis of neurologic Lyme disease was made based on the rise in titer in the serum and the classic clinical profile of neurologic Lyme disease combining meningitis and cranial neuritis. Because of the meningitis, he was treated with four weeks of intravenous ceftriaxone; the headaches, stiff neck, and fevers resolved quickly. The facial palsy and sound sensitivity resolved much more slowly over the subsequent six months.

Comment: Optimal testing for neuroborreliosis in this case would include Lyme enzyme-linked immunosorbent assay (ELISA) of the serum and spinal fluid antibody to calculate the "Lyme Index," which indicates whether *B. burgdorferi*–specific intracompartmental antibody production is occurring. A polymerase chain reaction (PCR) assay test for the DNA of *B. burgdorferi* is helpful if positive, but despite high specificity, this test is insensitive and is positive in only 25 to 38 percent of patients with confirmed neurologic Lyme disease in the United States. Culture assays for *B. burgdorferi* in the cerebrospinal fluid are also insensitive and not commonly available. Assays for the chemokine CXCL13, which attracts B-lymphocytes (more often used in Europe), would likely be positive in this patient. This biomarker is considered a sensitive, but not specific, indicator of neuroborreliosis. As in this case, when two or three of the primary manifestations of neurologic Lyme disease (meningitis, cranial neuropathy, radiculoneuropathy) are present in a patient exposed to a Lyme endemic area, the diagnosis of neurologic Lyme disease becomes highly likely.

(*Case modified and drawn partly from "Case 29–1984."*)

## Heart

Less commonly, *B. burgdorferi* infection may affect the heart, causing conduction abnormalities or muscular inflammation. This usually occurs within weeks to several months of the initial infection. When the heart's conduction system is involved, the transmission of electrical signals that control the heart rate and rhythm are disrupted. This is sometimes referred to as "heart block" or "atrioventricular conduction block." When the cardiac muscle tissue is infected and inflamed, there may be a decrease in the ability of the heart to pump with sufficient strength; this heart muscle inflammation is sometimes referred to as "myocarditis." When the sac-like membrane surrounding the heart is affected, this is called "pericarditis." In Europe a case was reported in which the spirochete *B. burgdorferi* was isolated from the cardiac muscle of a man with long-standing cardiomyopathy (Stanek et al. 1990).

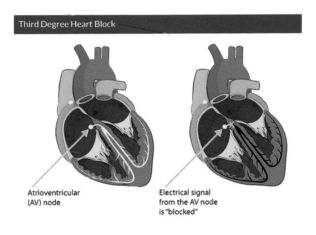

**FIGURE 3.5**

The heart on the left shows how an electrical signal flows from the atrioventricular node (AV node) to the chambers in the lower half of the heart (ventricles). The heart on the right shows a case of third-degree heart block. With the electrical signal from the AV node to the ventricle blocked, the ventricles beat at their own, slower rate.

*Courtesy of the CDC.*

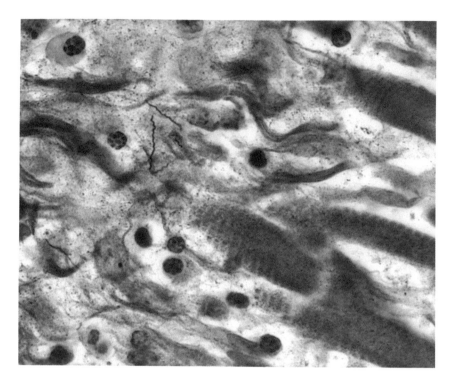

**FIGURE 3.6**

Photomicrograph of a heart tissue specimen (158X) reveals the presence of a number of *Borrelia burgdorferi* spirochetes. At this stage, after having infected the heart muscle, the disease is more specifically referred to as Lyme carditis.

*Courtesy of the CDC/Dr. Sherif Zaki; Anna Perea.*

Symptoms of cardiac Lyme disease may be mild or life-threatening. These can include lightheadedness, fainting, shortness of breath, heart palpitations, or chest pain. An individual with these symptoms should be evaluated by a doctor so the appropriate cause can be identified and treated. While palpitations and the sensation that the heart is pounding or racing can be benign and most often unrelated to Lyme disease, these symptoms should be evaluated by a clinician. A recent EM rash may not be recalled in many of the cases of cardiac Lyme disease. Because cardiac Lyme disease can be fatal, rapid recognition is essential because treatment with antibiotics is effective.

## CASE 3. Ms. B. Lyme Carditis

Ms. B, a thirty-three-year-old previously healthy woman living in the northeastern United States, presented to the emergency room with a fever of 101.4°F, light sensitivity, and headache. A lumbar puncture revealed that the cerebrospinal fluid had no abnormalities to suggest infection causing meningitis. Three weeks later, she returned to the ER because she had developed a dull, moderately intense chest discomfort, as well as episodes of shortness of breath and lightheadedness. Further history revealed that she was an avid hiker and had been in the mountains about one week prior to the initial ER visit. Her physical exam was unremarkable except for a round red rash five centimeters in diameter with central clearing on the back of her neck. Lyme disease was considered likely, but antibiotics were not started right away. Because her electrocardiogram demonstrated a first-degree atrioventricular conduction block, she was transferred to the cardiac unit for closer monitoring. Over the next four hours, the heart block worsened from first degree to second degree to complete heart block. A presumptive diagnosis of Lyme carditis was made and intravenous antibiotic (ceftriaxone) therapy was started. After three doses of ceftriaxone, the heart rhythm abnormality reversed from complete heart block to second-degree heart block to first-degree block. After twenty-one days of IV ceftriaxone, the heart rhythm had normalized. Serologic testing for Lyme disease revealed a positive ELISA and Western blot for both IgM and IgG antibodies.

Comment: It is likely that, prior to the first emergency room visit, Ms. B had an unseen tick bite while hiking. The EM rash may have been present at the initial ER visit but was missed by the clinicians as it occurred on the back of her neck. The EM rash can last several weeks if untreated, so it is not surprising that the rash was still present when she came to the ER three weeks later. As demonstrated by this case, progression from a low-grade conduction block to complete heart block can be rapid, so antibiotics should be started immediately. Although Lyme carditis is usually rapidly reversible with antibiotic therapy, a temporary pacemaker may be needed; only rarely, however, is a permanent pacemaker required.

*Adapted from Afari et al. 2016*

## Eyes

Lyme disease can manifest as a mild conjunctivitis, an inflammation of the transparent outer membrane of the eyeball, also known as "pink eye." As mentioned earlier, visual changes from Lyme disease may also manifest rarely as inflammation of the optic nerve, as compression of the optic nerve due to increased intracranial pressure, or as double vision due to weakness of the extraocular muscles.

**CASE 4.** Billy. An Eight-Year-Old Boy with Optic Neuritis

In the spring, shortly after visiting a Lyme endemic area, Billy complained of intermittent headaches and fatigue. Two months later, he told his parents that he was having trouble seeing the television screen. The only other symptoms were slowness in activities and an intermittent pain in his thigh. On examination, his visual acuity was markedly impaired—20/200 in one eye and 20/400 in the other. Both optic nerve discs were swollen. The retinas were elevated and both visual fields showed loss of central vision. A brain MRI scan was normal. The spinal tap showed a normal spinal fluid pressure and no abnormalities other than a mildly elevated protein; unfortunately, a spinal fluid test for Lyme antibodies was not done. Initial treatment with intravenous steroids led to improved vision (20/70 and 20/100). When Lyme disease was considered and the blood tests came back positive on both ELISA and Western blot (ten bands on IgG), the diagnosis of "bilateral optic neuritis secondary to Lyme disease" was made. Billy was then treated with one month of intravenous ceftriaxone; after treatment, his optic nerves and his vision almost fully normalized (20/20 and 20/30).

Comment: Lyme disease as a cause of optic neuritis is rare. It was considered in this case because, shortly before developing headaches and fatigue, Billy had visited a Lyme endemic area with his parents. Nymphal ticks known to transmit *B. Burgdorferi* actively seek blood meals by biting hosts (such as Billy) in the springtime. The deterioration of vision started about eight weeks later. This case is remarkable because there was no known history of tick bite, rash, facial palsy, meningitis, or arthritis, so consideration of Lyme disease might easily have been overlooked without the diligence of thorough and thoughtful clinicians.

*Adapted from Rothermel, Hedges, and Steere 2001.*

## Other Early Signs

Involvement of the liver is less common but may manifest as mild hepatitis (an inflammation of the liver tissue), which is usually accompanied by flu-like symptoms and loss of appetite.

# LATE DISSEMINATED STAGE:
# MONTHS TO YEARS AFTER TICK BITE

When the initial symptoms of Lyme disease are mild or if the presentation is atypical, the infection may go undetected. In some individuals, the immune system is so effective in killing the invading *B. burgdorferi* that the infection is eradicated without any antibiotic treatment; in this scenario, the symptoms resolve and the patient is well. Or if the immune system eradicates only some of the *Borrelia* spirochetes, the individual may feel reasonably well for months or years while the residual *B. burgdorferi* remain quiescent, settled in tissues without causing disease. However, if months or years later the residual *Borrelia* spirochetes become more active, the patient may then experience Lyme disease symptoms. This is called late disseminated disease.

At the late disseminated phase, the joints and nervous system tend to be most often affected. Common symptoms may include joint pain and swelling, fatigue, cognitive problems, sleep disturbance, irritability, or hypersensitivity to sensory stimuli.

## Joints

Approximately 60 percent of patients with untreated Lyme disease develop arthritis (i.e., joint swelling), which can be temporary or chronic (Steere, Schoen, and Taylor 1987). While the arthritis commonly emerges approximately six months after the initial infection, the range of onset is wide (four days to two years); because the emergence of arthritis may occur many months later, patients may not recall the initial tick bite, flu-like symptoms, or rash. The joint pain and swelling experienced in Lyme disease can be severe and often affect the large joints, particularly the knees. Swelling around the joint may also occur without pain. While monoarthritis is common, other joints may also be involved, such as the ankle, shoulder, elbow, wrist, or temporomandibular joint. Fever is usually absent. The pain and swelling may resolve completely on its own, may recur intermittently over time, or may be chronic and persistent.

Lyme arthritis can be distinguished from some other forms of arthritis because it only rarely causes a symmetric polyarthritis, is most often abrupt in onset rather than gradual, and is more often shorter in duration (weeks to months) rather than chronic (years).

For most patients with Lyme arthritis, joint pain and swelling will resolve after antibiotic treatment, which may require up to three separate courses of therapy. Approximately 10 percent of patients with Lyme arthritis will have ongoing symptoms despite antibiotics. Experts refer to this as "antibiotic-refractory arthritis" and consider it to be an inflammatory immune-perpetuated arthritis that is no longer due to active infection (Li 2011). Many of these patients benefit from other treatment modalities. Rare cases, however, have been reported suggesting persistent infection based on finding *Borrelial* DNA by PCR in the synovial membrane among patients with Lyme arthritis previously treated with antibiotics (Priem et al. 1998).

Certain strains of the Lyme disease spirochete that are found in the northeastern United States are highly inflammatory. Many factors contribute to the development of antibiotic-refractory Lyme arthritis, including characteristics of the infecting strain of *B. burgdorferi* (i.e., is it highly inflammatory?) and characteristics of the human host, such as the genetic profile (e.g., are certain HLA-DR alleles present?) and the immune response (e.g., has an autoimmune response been induced, as might be shown by endothelial cell growth factor antibodies?). Among patients with Lyme arthritis, the blood tests for Lyme disease (IgG and IgM antibodies) can stay positive for years. PCR testing of the joint fluid prior to antibiotic therapy may reveal positive results in more than half of the cases.

## Skin

In Europe, a slowly progressive purplish skin lesion called *acrodermatitis chronica atrophicans* is the most common late manifestation of Lyme disease occurring typically on the extensor surface of the extremities. This is

**CASE 5.** Lyme Arthritis. The Case of Ms. G.

Ms. G, a previously healthy forty-year-old woman living in western Pennsylvania, noticed pain in her right knee followed by swelling, making it difficult to walk. There was no history of trauma or fever. An x-ray and an ultrasonogram of the knee confirmed fluid in the joint. Due to the swelling, a tap was conducted to test for infection and to reduce the pressure from the fluid accumulation. She was told infection was ruled out, although a Lyme disease test was not conducted despite the fact that she lived in a Lyme endemic area. She was treated with a steroid to decrease inflammation, which relieved the pain for about one month, until the fluid reaccumulated and the swelling returned. The pain led to trouble walking. She also reported prominent fatigue and intermittent "brain fog," making it hard for her to keep track of conversations. Due to the knee swelling, the knee joint was tapped and drained once again and a corticosteroid was readministered. A PCR assay for *B. burgdorferi* on the synovial fluid was negative. A blood test for Lyme disease was then conducted, revealing a positive ELISA followed by a positive IgG Western blot for Lyme disease. She was diagnosed with Lyme arthritis and placed on oral doxycycline for three weeks, which she tolerated well. The swelling resolved and did not returned. Six months later, she noted mild pain in her elbows and knees, but she was functioning well. The brain fog resolved, though mild word-finding problems lingered on for an additional several months. The date of her initial infection was unclear because she did not recall ever having been bitten by a tick or developing a rash, or flu-like, neurologic, or cardiac symptoms.

Comment: In this case of a monoarthritis, blood tests for Lyme arthritis were not conducted until three months after initial presentation even though Ms. G came from a Lyme endemic area. Although nonsteroidal anti-inflammatory medications are useful to help reduce inflammation in Lyme arthritis, oral or intra-articular cortisone injections are not recommended before or during antibiotic therapy due to concerns of possible prolongation of joint inflammation and enhanced growth of spirochetes (Steere et al. 2016).

primarily associated with *B. afzelii* infection and can occur 6 months to 8 years after an initial EM rash.

## Nervous System

Some patients whose Lyme disease has been left untreated for months or years will develop neurological problems that are less common in the earlier phases of the disease. These complications include encephalopathy, a sensory polyneuropathy, and rarely quite severe presentations such as dementia, encephalomyelitis, and stroke-like presentations.

### ENCEPHALOPATHY

Cognitive problems may develop early in the course of Lyme disease or many months or years after the initial infection. If the disease is caught earlier in the course of infection and treated with antibiotics, the cognitive problems are usually mild in severity. More severe cognitive problems occurring later in the course of Lyme disease fall into the category of "encephalopathy"; these deficits typically affect one or more cognitive domains, such as memory, verbal fluency (name or word retrieval), and speed of thinking. Accompanying symptoms may include mild depressive symptoms, somnolence, headache, irritability, and hearing changes. Individuals with encephalopathy from Lyme disease may also have neuropathic symptoms (such as "numbness," "pins and needles," or "jabbing") or radiating/shooting pains in the extremities. Functional brain imaging using PET or single photon emission computerized tomography (SPECT) typically reveals regions of hypometabolism or hypoperfusion (Logigian et al. 1997; Fallon et al. 2009).

- In one report, eighteen patients with Lyme encephalopathy were treated with a four-week course of intravenous antibiotic (ceftriaxone) (Logigian et al. 1999). Of these eighteen, nearly all had been previously treated with antibiotics: four had received less than two weeks of intravenous ceftriaxone therapy previously and twelve had received ten to thirty days of prior oral antibiotic therapy. After treatment in this study with a four-week course of intravenous ceftriaxone, sixteen of the eighteen patients reported substantial gains in cognition twelve to twenty-four months later—with nine reporting they were "greatly improved" and seven reporting they were "back to normal."

- ◦ Notable is that improvement was reported by 61 percent at six months and by 89 percent at twelve to twenty-four months, indicating that improvement after treatment can take time.
- ◦ One patient was retreated with intravenous ceftriaxone at six months due to relapse of symptoms; after retreatment, his improvement in cognition was sustained to long-term follow up.
- ◦ Also notable is that improvement was reported by so many patients, despite the fact that the initial infection occurred many years earlier (average of six years) and even though the majority had had prior antibiotic therapy (although none had had two or more weeks of intravenous ceftriaxone therapy).
- ◦ Objective evidence of improvement in a subgroup was demonstrated by brain imaging scans. Seven of these patients had pretreatment SPECT scans that showed multifocal areas of decreased blood flow in the brain; after treatment, perfusion in the brain for this group of seven patients significantly improved.

## CHRONIC POLYNEUROPATHY

This is manifests most often as sensory changes, such as intermittent tingling or numbness of the extremities, beginning months to years after infection. The sensory symptoms may involve the arms, legs, or both on one or both sides of the body. Radicular pain may also occur. On physical examination, the doctor may note a reduction in vibration sensitivity in the lower extremities. Much less common would be weakness and decreased reflexes. Electrophysiologic testing typically shows that both the distal nerves and the nerve roots are affected and that the nerve conduction is slowed. This chronic polyneuropathy is considered uncommon.

## SEVERE RARE NEUROLOGIC PRESENTATIONS

- • Encephalomyelitis is a serious but rare condition that involves acute inflammation of both the brain (encephalitis) and spinal cord (myelitis). Symptoms of Lyme encephalomyelitis might include confusion and cognitive impairment; somnolence; severe psychiatric symptoms such as hallucinations, paranoia, mania; weakness in the extremities (paraparesis) with accompanying sensory loss; abnormal body movements; impaired coordination; and seizures. There may be autonomic nervous system involvement as well, causing symptoms such as disturbances in urination or defecation or impotence. Imaging scans (e.g., MRI) of patients with Lyme encephalomyelitis may show multiple areas of increased signal in the cerebral white matter, brain stem, and/or spinal cord. Encephalomyelitis related to an infection such as Lyme disease is typically a monophasic post- or para-infectious illness, not a relapsing remitting illness as in multiple sclerosis. There is some overlap, however. Rare cases of a progressive form of Lyme encephalomyelitis show a worsening over months or years that may in some cases be hard to differentiate from multiple sclerosis (Ackerman, Golmer, and Rehse-Küpper 1985).

- Although there are distinctive features to the increased signal seen on MRI among patients with multiple sclerosis, the brain MRI findings among patients with Lyme disease may at times be suggestive of a demyelinating disease (Hildenbrand et al. 2009). Typical of multiple sclerosis would be white matter hyperintensities that predominate in a periventricular location with "Dawson's fingers" and involve the corpus callosum. One test that can help distinguish multiple sclerosis from Lyme disease is a lumbar puncture, which commonly shows abnormal proteins called oligoclonal bands in multiple sclerosis that are less common or prominent in Lyme disease in the United States. In encephalomyelitis due to Lyme disease, typical abnormalities in the cerebrospinal fluid would include elevated white blood cell count, elevated protein, and the presence of antibodies specific for *B. burgdorferi*. In Europe, the chemokine CXCLXIII level has been reported to be much higher in neurologic Lyme disease than in other neuroinflammatory disorders, thus providing an additional test to help differentiate Lyme disease from multiple sclerosis (Van Burgel et al. 2011). See the next chapter for specifics on what tests should be ordered when a spinal tap is performed.

- Cerebral vasculitis and stroke are rare manifestations of neurologic Lyme disease that may manifest as an ischemic infarction or as an intracranial bleed (Topakian et al. 2008; Garkowski et al. 2017). The symptom profile may be quite diverse, ranging from sudden onset focal neurologic deficits (e.g., weakness on one side of the body) to slowly evolving cognitive impairment with confusion and speech difficulties. The brain MRI in some cases may be mistakenly interpreted as showing a malignant cancer (Oksi et al. 1996). In this report, the brain tissue from two of three cases was shown to harbor *B. burgdorferi* DNA at the site of the cerebral inflammation, suggesting that direct invasion by *B. burgdorferi* of the central nervous system may be the pathogenic mechanism for focal vasculitis and encephalitis in neurologic Lyme disease.

- Dementia due to Lyme disease, though rare, is reported, primarily in Europe. In one series of 1,594 patients with clinical signs of dementia, twenty (1.25 percent) had dementia with evidence of elevated production of *B. burgdorferi*–specific antibodies in the cerebrospinal fluid. After treatment with intravenous antibiotics, follow up over five years revealed that seven (0.44 percent) of these patients had either no further decline in their dementia or mildly improved; cerebrospinal fluid markers for other causes of dementia were not found in this group. The authors concluded that "pure Lyme dementia exists and has a good outcome after antibiotics" (Blanc 2014). It is important to note that a primary degenerative disease or dementia of other cause may be worsened by central nervous system Lyme disease, with reversal of the worsening after antibiotic treatment.

## Neuropsychiatric

Neuropsychiatric symptoms occur among patients with Lyme disease (Fallon et al. 1992; Fallon and Nields 1994; Kaplan and Jones-Woodward 1997; Keilp et al. 2006; Oczko-Grzesik et al. 2017). These primarily include disturbances of cognition and mood. When the cognitive deficits are severe, the patients would be considered to have an encephalopathy (as described earlier) or rarely a dementia. More commonly, the cognitive deficits are mild and may not be obvious to others but are disturbing to the patient. These neuropsychiatric symptoms can emerge either early or late in the course of infection, and they often manifest alongside the other arthritic and neurologic complications of Lyme disease. Neuropsychiatric symptoms, however, are reported much more often in neurologic Lyme disease than in Lyme arthritis (Oczko-Grzesik et al. 2017). Uncommonly, the neuropsychiatric symptoms may appear as the predominant initial manifestation with very few accompanying musculoskeletal signs or symptoms of Lyme disease, making it hard to distinguish Lyme disease from a standard psychiatric disorder (Hess et al. 1999). In some of these cases, a careful inquiry will reveal a history of Lyme disease or tick bite within the months or year prior to the onset of the neuropsychiatric symptoms (Pachner 1988). In other cases, the presenting psychiatric disorder may be followed weeks or months later by other more typical features of Lyme disease, such as encephalopathy, radicular pains, or migrating arthralgias.

Common neurocognitive problems include poor memory, slower speed of thinking, difficulty with retrieval of words, and impaired fine motor control. The slower mental processing speed contributes to the patient's experience of "brain fog." Adults, for example, may have trouble following the normal speed of conversations, and children might find it difficult to complete homework or to follow the teacher's comments during class.

Typically the impairment, when formally tested by a neuropsychologist, falls within the mild to moderate range of severity. The processing speed slowness is particularly noticeable when initiating a cognitive process; this slowness occurs independent of sensory, perceptual, or motor deficits (Pollina et al. 1999). Although patients with depression alone without Lyme disease can have problems with attention and slower speed of thinking, objective memory deficits are less severe in depression than in post-treatment Lyme disease. Several studies have demonstrated that the memory impairment among patients with post-treatment Lyme disease or Lyme encephalopathy cannot be explained away by a concurrent mood disorder (Barr et al. 1999; Keilp et al. 2006).

Common mood symptoms among patients with persistent symptoms after Lyme disease or chronic neurologic Lyme disease include irritability and depression (Barr et al. 1999; Fallon and Nields 1994; Logigian, Kaplan, and Steere 1990). Elevated rates of depression, however, are not found among adult patients at the earliest stage of Lyme disease (*erythema migrans*) who are treated with antibiotics and evaluated prospectively over six months (Aucott 2013). This may reflect the generally good outcome associated with early treatment; most patients will not have significant functional impairment or highly distressing symptoms at six months when treated early in the course of infection. Similar findings were reported among children who participated in an epidemiologic catchment area study of psychiatric disorders conducted in a Lyme endemic area of New York State (Fallon et al. 1994). In this study, among the fifteen children treated within one month of infection with Lyme disease, none reported long-term problems and none met criteria for major depression; the one child whose infection was not diagnosed until four months later had a more protracted, painful illness and she met criteria for major depression.

Elevated levels of depression may be found among individuals whose Lyme disease infection was not detected until long after the initial tick bite. These are often the patients who have more chronic symptoms despite antibiotic treatment (post-treatment Lyme disease syndrome). One well-designed cross-sectional study (Hassett et al. 2008) examined four patient groups who presented to a Lyme disease evaluation clinic with one of the following: a) well-defined past Lyme disease with persistent symptoms despite antibiotic treatment; b) medically unexplained symptoms attributed to past treated Lyme disease that persists after antibiotic treatment, but without good evidence of having had Lyme disease; c) recovered Lyme disease after treatment; and d) another non-Lyme medical illness. Notably, in this study, the group with excellent documentation of prior Lyme disease had a fourfold higher rate of major depressive disorder (45.2 percent) than the group who believed they had "chronic Lyme disease" but had poor documentation of prior infection (10.9 percent). In other words, just thinking one has chronic Lyme disease is not related to higher levels of depressive disorder; rather there appears to have been something specific about actually having had prior Lyme disease that may be related to depressive symptoms. Further study in this area is needed because the studies are few and the quality is limited.

Anxiety disorders are common (29 to 49 percent) among patients with well-documented disseminated Lyme disease and with post-treatment Lyme disease (Hassett 2008; Oczko-Grzesik 2017). While anxiety does occur among patients with a history of Lyme disease, our initial study did not demonstrate that it occurs at a higher rate than is seen among two rheumatologic disorders (Fallon and Nields 1994). The rate of panic attacks and generalized anxiety were comparable for patients with a history of treated Lyme disease compared to a disorder associated with pain (rheumatoid arthritis) and another associated with fatigue and immune activation (systemic lupus). An increased need for sleep and daytime fatigue are common among patients with late and post-treatment Lyme disease.

**FIGURE 3.7**

Sensory hyperarousal, "The Scream" by Edvard Munch.

Sensory hyperarousal may occur in the early disseminated or the later stages of infection (Batheja et al. 2013). Sensitivity to bright lights may lead patients to wear sunglasses indoors or to avoid going outside during the daylight. Sensitivity to loud sounds may lead patients to avoid crowds, restaurants, and movie theaters as unexpected loud sounds may be experienced as painful—as depicted in the The Scream, painted by Norwegian artist Edvard Munch and shown in figure 3.7.

Rarely patients with central nervous system manifestations of neuropsychiatric Lyme disease will develop paranoia, hallucinations, mania, and/or obsessive-compulsive symptoms (Pachner 1988; Hess et al. 1999; Pasareanu, Mygland, and Kristensen 2012). Lumbar puncture in these cases should be conducted (prior to antibiotic treatment) as it may reveal spinal fluid abnormalities consistent with central nervous system invasion by *B. burgdorferi*. In this circumstance, antibiotic treatment with intravenous ceftriaxone should be considered given its ability to cross the blood–brain barrier better than most oral antibiotics.

Neuropsychiatric symptoms may emerge for a variety of reasons.

- They may reflect active infection with *B. burgdorferi*, either in the central nervous system itself or elsewhere in the body, leading to the production of inflammatory mediators and consequent neuropsychiatric symptoms. Inflammation—whether due to active infection or past infection—has a strong association with several neuropsychiatric disorders (Bransfield 2012; Miller and Raison 2016; Fallon et al. 2010).
- These may reflect altered brain metabolism or perfusion, abnormal activation of neural pathways, or changes in neurotransmitter function in the brain as a result of current or past infection with *B. burgdorferi* (Fallon et al. 2009)
- Following the model of sudden-onset neuropsychiatric disorders after streptococcal infection (pediatric autoimmune neuropsychiatric disorders associated with Streptococcal infection [PANDAS]) (Swedo 2010), it is also possible that molecular mimicry is contributing to the onset of neuropsychiatric symptoms accompanying infection with *B. burgdorferi*. In this molecular mimicry model, antibodies that are generated against portions of the Lyme disease spirochete might be mistakenly targeting the host's own tissue, such as the nervous

system tissue or the heart, for example. With *B. burgdorferi*, this type of molecular mimicry has been demonstrated in the laboratory setting (Alaedini and Latov, 2005; Raveche et al. 2005) such that antibodies generated against the *Borrelia* spirochete do in fact also bind to human neural or heart tissue. This mechanism of causation for neuropsychiatric disorders in humans with Lyme disease is not yet proven.

- Although depressive symptoms and anxiety may emerge as a biologic response to central nervous system invasion or inflammation related to *B. burgdorferi* infection, depression and anxiety may also emerge as a secondary reaction to the stressors associated with this illness—for example, financial loss of income due to being unable to work or the expense of medical care; interpersonal tensions in the family because of being unable to keep up with role responsibilities at home; the physical impact of this illness itself leading to marked pain or profound fatigue; and the trauma of having one's symptoms constantly discounted. Depression and anxiety may also emerge due to fear and hopelessness, partly triggered by reading frightening stories about long-term outcomes on the Internet and partly due to the many uncertainties and controversies associated with Lyme disease. The stress of having been undiagnosed for a prolonged period while living with increasingly bizarre, painful, progressive, and unexplained symptoms can in itself lead to a cluster of anxiety symptoms akin to post-traumatic stress disorder. (For further elaboration on these topics, see chapters 5 and 12.)
- Neuropsychiatric symptoms may emerge due to a preexisting psychiatric disorder that is exacerbated and magnified by Lyme disease.

Psychiatric disorders are common in the general public; the vast majority of these disorders are, of course, not due to Lyme disease. As one would expect, psychiatric disorders may also be present among patients with Lyme disease as a concurrent but unrelated illness.

Factors that may lead a clinician to suspect that neuropsychiatric symptoms may be Lyme related would include history and clinical symptoms important for a Lyme disease diagnosis but also features that in general would lead one to search for another organic cause. These include:

- the presence of multisystemic symptoms (e.g., central and peripheral nervous system, joints, muscles, fatigue);
- symptoms that emerge after a flu-like illness or after exposure to *Ixodes* ticks;
- a new positive Lyme disease test, a marked increase in Lyme antibody titers, or abnormal spinal fluid;
- features of the psychiatric illness that are atypical:
  - prominent problems with memory and verbal fluency,
  - psychiatric symptoms developing de novo at an atypical age for the specific psychiatric disorder,
  - psychiatric symptoms occurring in an individual with no recent life stressor,
  - the individual having no prior personal or family history of psychiatric disorders,
  - the psychiatric disorder not resolving with medication or psychotherapeutic strategies that are usually highly effective.

Because psychiatric disorders can be disabling or life-threatening if left untreated, treatment of these disorders should not be delayed while trying to determine whether Lyme disease is the cause. In most cases, along with the care of the primary physician, mental health professionals can play a key role in the process of recovery.

Physicians evaluating patients with a history of Lyme disease should ask about suicidal ideation. Given the stressors associated with this illness and given its central nervous system effects, patients may become hopeless and begin to feel that life is not worth living. In our review of patients with persistent symptoms after being treated for Lyme disease, approximately one in six patients had suicidal thoughts, consistent with their severity of depressive symptoms (though not with the plan or desire to kill themselves). Concurrent moderate to severe depression markedly increases the rate of suicidal thoughts as well as the risk of a suicidal act. Patients with prominent depressive symptoms and/or suicidal thoughts should be under the care of a mental health provider.

Patients with a history of anxiety prior to Lyme disease may well become more anxious in the process of learning about Lyme disease. This may become a particular problem among those who have preexisting illness anxiety disorder because these individuals tend to imagine the worst possible outcome when faced with physical symptoms (a process called "catastrophizing") and to hyperfocus on information from the Internet or media that presents the most frightening consequences. The Internet chat rooms on Lyme disease are filled with so many stories of despair that an individual with preexisting anxiety will undoubtedly become more anxious after visiting one of these websites. Because some individuals may well have both Lyme disease and illness anxiety, optimal treatment would address both the underlying psychiatric disorder as well as Lyme disease, with the recommendation that web searches related to health be curtailed.

One particular case history, published in the early years of Lyme disease (Pachner 1988), caught the public's attention, raising questions about whether other atypical cases of Lyme disease were being missed. This case was dubbed the "Bicycle Boy."

**CASE 6.** The "Bicycle Boy." Lyme Arthritis followed by Compulsive Behaviors.

A twelve-year-old boy from the northeastern United States was psychiatrically hospitalized with the diagnosis of anorexia nervosa because of a thirty-pound weight loss associated with compulsive bicycling, depression, negligible eating, and uncommunicativeness. A medical history revealed that over the prior two years there had been four attacks of knee swelling, diagnosed eventually as Lyme arthritis and treated with one month of doxycycline. The psychiatric symptoms started shortly thereafter. Because anorexia in a twelve-year-old boy is unusual, the psychiatric inpatient team wondered: Could this boy's anorexia and compulsive behaviors be related to the prior Lyme disease? A neurology consultation led to confirmation of antibodies against *B. burgdorferi* in both the serum and cerebrospinal fluid. The boy was treated with two weeks of intravenous penicillin and within weeks he began to eat more, gain weight, and communicate. His compulsive bicycling and depression resolved. Within months he was able to return to school and had an excellent long-term outcome.

*(Continued next page)*

*(Continued from previous page)*

Comment: This represents a rare case. Because of the atypical presentation and the timing of onset shortly after the swollen joints, a connection with Lyme disease was considered and led to the successful outcome after antibiotic treatment, resolving the neuropsychiatric disorder. A reasonable neurologist might argue that because there were no white blood cells in the spinal fluid (pleocytosis) and because the concentration of antibodies in the spinal fluid was not greater than in the blood, we cannot be certain the *B. burgdorferi* spirochetes had actually entered his central nervous system. The neurologist treating this boy agreed with this concern, noting, however, that in certain cases of central neurologic Lyme disease in the United States, when the infection has been chronic, the spinal fluid may not show the typical markers of active infection.

## POST-TREATMENT LYME DISEASE SYNDROME

Approximately 5 to 20 percent of patients treated for Lyme disease have distressing or disabling symptoms that can last up to months or even years after treatment. This has been called post-treatment Lyme disease syndrome (PTLDS) by academics while many community doctors and patients prefer the term Chronic Lyme disease.

Common symptoms include:

- muscle and/or joint pains,
- memory or word retrieval problems,
- "brain fog" or a feeling of being mentally slowed down,
- severe fatigue, and
- sleep disturbance—usually an excessive need for sleep.

There are multiple possible causes of these symptoms. One way to think of this constellation of symptoms is that they represent an exaggerated "sickness response" (Dantzer et al. 2008). In other words, whenever one acquires an infection such as a virus or a bacterium, it is common to have extreme fatigue, pain in the muscles, increased need for sleep, and an overall feeling of being mentally and physically slowed down. This is the normal response of the body to infection and part of the healing process, forcing the individual to recuperate and rest. These symptoms are induced by the immune response to the infection; after five to ten days, the immune response in most people quiets down, recalibrates, and normalizes. However, among some individuals treated for Lyme disease, the sickness response takes much longer to resolve; indeed, this cluster of symptoms may last many months or even years.

A variety of hypotheses have emerged to explain why these symptoms persist:

- One possible explanation for the persistent symptoms of PTLDS is that a small number of *B. burgdorferi* bacteria or fragments of the bacteria persist in the body despite the prior antibiotic treatment, thus keeping the immune sickness response activated.
- Another possibility is that an ongoing post-infectious immune process was triggered by the prior *B. burgdorferi* infection and is now continuing unabated.
- A third possibility is that there are inappropriately activated brain circuits that lead to fatigue, sleep disturbance, cognitive problems, depression, or chronic pain—abnormalities in these circuits may have been triggered by the prior *B. burgdorferi* infection.

Emerging evidence from studies of other infectious diseases suggests that historical factors in an individual's life may increase the risk of having a prolonged sickness response. For example, an infection from years earlier may lead to a long-term impairment of the immune system's checks and balances, setting the stage for chronic illness (Fonseca et al. 2015). Or prior physical or mental trauma may be captured in central nervous system memory, leading to a prolonged activation of neural circuits governing pain, fatigue, or the immune response. This might be considered a "priming" of the brain; the prior injury or infection may prolong recovery from Lyme disease.

Additionally, it is possible that the individual with presumed PTLDS has another disorder or infection that occurred simultaneously or subsequent to the infection with *B. burgdorferi* that has not yet been diagnosed or treated. In other words, the individual did have Lyme disease, but the problem is now another disorder or infection and not the effects of Lyme disease. For example, because ticks may transmit more than *B. burgdorferi*, evaluating patients for these other tick-borne coinfections can be a very important part of the workup of the patient with PTLDS; this evaluation is guided by the clinical profile and atypical laboratory findings. Alternatively, the patient may have a disorder that is not tick-borne but shares some common signs and symptoms with Lyme disease. More about coinfections and these other disorders will be presented in later chapters.

There are multiple possible treatment approaches for PTLDS. With regard to whether additional antibiotic treatment is helpful for PTLDS, randomized placebo-controlled treatment studies, which are the gold standard for proof in medicine, have produced mixed results. Some studies show retreatment was beneficial, while other studies show no benefit. These research studies are discussed in detail in chapter 7. Physicians vary on how they interpret and act on the results of these studies. Some choose to retreat with antibiotics, while others recommend no further treatment. Treatment guidelines from national medical organizations, freely available online, also provide conflicting perspectives on treatment recommendations (e.g., the Infectious Diseases Society of America versus the International Lyme and Associated Diseases Society).

Patients who have persistent or recurring symptoms after antibiotic treatment for Lyme disease should return to their physician to discuss additional tests or treatment options. This is important to ensure that all other reasonable causes of persistent symptoms have been assessed and ruled out. If the physician is dismissive or not engaged, consideration should be given to seeking a second opinion from another health care provider. Some physicians enjoy evaluating and examining the challenging patient with a complex history; these doctors are like detectives who relish putting together the historical and laboratory clues that might lead to a new diagnosis. Other doctors prefer more straightforward cases in which a single narrow problem is the focus of attention, the disease has definitive laboratory tests, and decision making is less complex.

Certainly patients with a multitude of symptoms—as is a typical profile for patients with later stages of Lyme disease or those with PTLDS—need to find a doctor who is comfortable with complex cases. In other words, these patients should seek a physician who will listen attentively, spend time gathering the history, and carefully review the past and current test results.

Patients also need to remain open to the possibility that their current physical and/or cognitive symptoms are not due to Lyme disease. Other medical or psychiatric problems may emerge concurrently that have nothing to do with Lyme disease. This may seem obvious and unnecessary to state. However, when one is focused on Lyme disease and its many possible manifestations and when one has had the experience of being readily dismissed by doctors because of symptoms that were actually due to Lyme disease, it is easy to become defensive about even considering the possibility that there may be an additional problem or another explanation. Such defensiveness is dangerous for the patient because it could lead to a delay in obtaining treatment for other serious medical disorders.

Patients should also be aware that other problems may emerge as a result of Lyme disease that are no longer due to active infection; these include immune-mediated disorders (Arvikar et al. 2017) and changes in central nervous system circuitry or transmitters leading to pain, fatigue, and/or neuropsychiatric symptoms. Therefore both physicians and patients need to keep an open mind. Approaches to treatment that are essential in the early phases of Lyme disease (e.g., antibiotics) may no longer be as effective in helping to ameliorate longer-term symptoms.

# 4

## WHAT DO THE DIAGNOSTIC TESTS TELL US?

The diagnosis of Lyme disease is made based on a constellation of considerations, including the patient's history of exposure to *Ixodes* ticks, time spent in Lyme endemic areas, clinical symptoms and signs, findings on the physical exam, and results from laboratory tests. Patients who present with the characteristic *erythema migrans* (EM) rash do not require testing; indeed, antibody tests for Lyme disease in the early weeks of infection are often negative.

The ideal diagnostic test for Lyme disease would clarify with 100 percent certainty whether the individual has been infected with *B. burgdorferi* and whether—after treatment—the infection has resolved. Such a test would aid diagnosis and help in treatment planning. Given that many of the symptoms associated with Lyme disease are common to other diseases as well, this test should also have no false positives; in other words, patients who do not have Lyme disease would not test positive on the Lyme disease test. While these goals for a test are simple to understand, they are impossible to achieve in actual practice. Even the best tests for other infections do not have 100 percent sensitivity and specificity. The aim therefore is for diagnostic tests that come closer to these ambitious ideals. With Lyme disease testing, there is much room for improvement.

This chapter reviews many of the tests—those that are now standard as well as new tests that are under development or newly released. This chapter also reviews some of the additional tests that doctors might order; these tests do not inform the physician about the presence or absence of infection, but they do provide information about bodily processes that may be consistent with a diagnosis of Lyme disease. For example, tests of the brain or peripheral nerves may provide objective evidence of neurologic dysfunction that may be seen among patients with current or prior *B. burgdorferi* infection.

## BLOOD TESTS

The three types of blood tests most commonly used to check for Lyme disease are the indirect fluorescent antibody (IFA), the enzyme-linked immunosorbent assay (ELISA), and the Western blot. These blood tests do not detect the *B. burgdorferi* spirochete directly. They act indirectly instead. They detect antibodies present in the patient's blood formed in response to antigens of the *B. burgdorferi* spirochete. Because the immune system has a long memory, once an antibody response develops, it tends to last for years, even in the absence of infection.

Because these tests measure antibodies and because the antibody response to *B. burgdorferi* requires time to develop (one to three weeks), most patients with a solitary Lyme disease rash will test negative. An additional problem with these antibody-based tests is that they do not necessarily tell us whether the infection is currently present. A positive antibody test simply indicates that a *B. burgdorferi* infection occurred at some point in the past. This infection may have occurred recently or in the distant past, months or even years previously. The infection may be active now or it may have been killed off years ago by the immune system and is no longer present. Because these antibody-based tests are not sufficiently sensitive at all stages of disease, a person may have Lyme disease but test negative. Alternatively, a healthy person may have fully positive antibody tests but not recall ever having been sick with Lyme disease.

### The Two-Tiered Approach for Antibody Testing

In an effort to enhance diagnostic standards, in the mid-1990s the CDC adopted the criteria from a national review committee that recommended a two-tiered strategy for laboratory testing of Lyme disease. According to the two-tiered approach, the first step involves ordering an ELISA or IFA.

If the ELISA or IFA is negative, then no further testing is recommended. If the ELISA or IFA is equivocal or positive, then the next step is to order a Western blot. If the infection has been present for less than four weeks, then an equivocal or positive ELISA with a positive IgM and/or IgG Western blot is considered good evidence to confirm recent infection with *B. burgdorferi*. If the infection has been present longer than four weeks, then an equivocal or positive ELISA with a positive IgG Western blot is considered good evidence of prior or current infection with *B. burgdorferi*. According to the CDC guidelines, the IgM Western blot is not recommended for determining disease in persons with infection greater than four weeks in duration.

This two-tiered strategy is commonly used in the United States but is considered particularly problematic in Europe and other countries because there are several genospecies of *B. burgdorferi* in Europe that vary in their surface proteins and therefore may not be detected by the particular antigens chosen in the CDC's Western blot scoring criteria.

An additional problem with this two-tiered standard is that the individual tests—both the ELISA/IFA and the Western blot—have problems both in *sensitivity*, the ability of the test to correctly identify those with the disease, and in *specificity*, the ability of the test to rule out those who do not have the disease. For example, a patient may have Lyme disease but test negative on the initial ELISA or the follow-up Western blot. Or a patient may have a positive test on an ELISA and/or IgM Western blot but never have had Lyme disease. In general, the two-tiered approach errs on the side of enhancing specificity at the expense of sensitivity, especially in early Lyme disease.

Various research studies and reports have assessed the two-tiered strategy (Dressler et al. 1993; Bacon et al. 2003; Aguero-Rosenfeld et al. 2005; Branda et al. 2010; Wormser et al. 2013; Molins et al. 2016), revealing different estimates of the sensitivity and specificity of the two-tiered strategy. However, some general conclusions about the sensitivity of the two-tiered approach include:

- All studies agree that in early Lyme disease, the sensitivity of the two-tiered approach is poor—only 29 to 45 percent of patients will test positive using this two-tiered approach.

- In acute disseminated neurologic Lyme disease, the sensitivity of the two-tiered approach is much improved but still problematic—about 72 to 87 percent of patients will test positive.
- In Lyme arthritis, the sensitivity is excellent—97 to 100 percent of patients will test positive.

A central problem in the two-tiered method is that sensitivity varies depending both on how early in the course of infection one is tested and on the actual manifestation of Lyme disease. Equally problematic is that a patient may test positive using this two-tiered approach due to past exposure to Lyme disease but may not have a currently active *B. burgdorferi* infection. Another problem is that the IgM Western blot is recommended

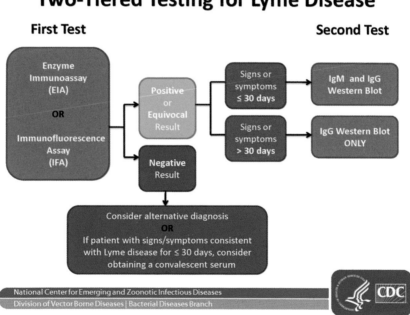

**FIGURE 4.1**

The two-tiered testing strategy recommended by the CDC.

*Courtesy of the CDC.*

for use only during the first four weeks after infection; unless the tick bite was seen, it is often difficult to know when infection actually occurred and data analyses from other researchers have recommended that six weeks would be a more useful interval (Branda et al. 2010). Finally, our research at Columbia among patients with chronic symptoms after previously treated Lyme disease indicates that about 10 percent of those who have an IgG Western blot positive serum (i.e., five or more CDC significant bands) will have a negative ELISA.

Physicians relying solely on the initial ELISA test could miss patients who have good evidence of prior infection by IgG Western blot. Indeed, the CDC surveillance criteria accept a single positive IgG Western blot as lab evidence of prior infection. The two-tiered criteria, while enhancing specificity, may actually be misleading if the physician stops after a negative ELISA, as the IgG Western blot may provide additional information that is quite useful even if the initial ELISA is negative.

The Western blot, however, has its own problems, one of which is that some of the bands that are labeled as meaningful also are known to have cross-reactive antigens. This means, for example, that a patient's serum might have multiple bands that are read as positive on Western blot that are actually not reflective of *B. burgdorferi* antibodies. This is because some of the *B. burgdorferi* proteins used in the Western blot contain regions (epitopes) that are similar to other proteins from other bacteria. In other words, test results may reveal positive bands for example on an IgG or IgM Western blot even though that person has never had Lyme disease. This is because the blood came from a person who was previously exposed to other non–Lyme disease bacteria that have similar protein profiles. This is discussed further under "cross-reactivity."

These tests and their interpretation can therefore be confusing to both patients and doctors alike. These first-generation assays—developed in the 1980s and 1990s—are clearly inadequate and outdated. The newer-generation antibody-based assays (described later) have markedly reduced the problem of cross-reactivity by selecting protein fragments (epitopes) that are unique to the *Borrelia* species and by eliminating other fragments that elicit this cross-reactivity with other bacterial species.

While many aspects of Lyme disease are open to discussion and disagreement in academic circles, the problem of testing is widely accepted as an area in need of novel ideas and solutions. The fact that in early Lyme disease the false negative rate is as high as 60 to 70 percent means that the testing is of little use at one of the most important phases of infection—early Lyme disease—when it is most responsive to treatment. Antibody-based tests will not be able to solve this problem because antibodies take time to develop. The additional problem is that antibody levels do not necessarily correlate with treatment success in eradicating the *B. burgdorferi* spirochete. Because of these problems, many scientists from around the world are focusing their energies on developing more sensitive and accurate Lyme disease tests.

The following sections are meant to provide reasonable guidelines regarding how best to understand and use tests for Lyme disease. Some of the problems—and potential solutions—are delineated. Some of the standard approaches as well as more novel approaches and developments are also presented.

## Indirect Fluorescent Antibody

This was the first Lyme antibody test and is less commonly used today. In this initial test, a dead *B. burgdorferi* spirochete is affixed to a glass slide, the patient's serum is applied to the slide, and any antibodies (IgM or IgG) from the patient's serum that bind to the spirochete on the slide are detected under a microscope after a fluorescent dye attached to a second antihuman antibody is applied. This test differs from the ELISA partly because it uses a fluorescent dye as opposed to an enzyme to signal spirochetal antigen detection. When observed under a microscope using ultraviolet light, serum antibodies bound to the spirochetes on the slide will light up a bright fluorescent color.

### PROS

- The IFA provides semiquantitative information by reporting the highest dilution at which fluorescent spirochetes are still visible.
- The IFA allows for visualization of the binding of the antibodies to the spirochetes.

## CONS

- The IFA requires a highly trained technician to interpret the results and is more subject to error than the ELISA or Western blot.
- The IFA is more labor intensive than the ELISA and thus more costly.

## Enzyme-Linked Immunosorbent Assay

This is an automated, widely used quantitative initial test for Lyme disease that most often uses a "whole-cell sonicate" (i.e., *B. burgdorferi* spirochetes grown in culture are broken apart by sound waves); typically, this is the first test performed. A single number (or in some cases dilution titer) is reported that shows the relative level of antibodies against *B. burgdorferi* in the patient's serum compared to the level usually found in the serum of individuals without Lyme disease. Some laboratories will not report the numerical value, instead reporting only whether the index or titer is positive, indeterminate, or negative. (The cutoff for a positive result requires that the patient's antibody levels be three standard deviations higher than the average level in the non-Lyme group.) In the two-tier testing strategy, an indeterminate or positive ELISA then would lead to a Western blot.

## PROS

- The ELISA is inexpensive.
- It is widely available, automated, and many samples can be run simultaneously.
- It is more quantitative than the IFA and Western blot.
- It produces a clear numeric value that reflects the magnitude of the antibody response (IgM and IgG) to the spirochetal proteins expressed under culture conditions.

## CONS

- *False positives and false negatives*: The whole cell sonicate ELISA sometimes produces false negative or false positive results. False negative rates on the ELISA have been reported as high as 67 percent in early Lyme disease and 21 percent in early neurologic Lyme disease. False positives also can occur, particularly in the context of certain diseases. One recent study (Schriefer 2015), for example, found that the ELISA had high false positive results among patients with syphilis (FP 85 percent), infectious mononucleosis (FP 53 percent), and multiple sclerosis (FP 18 percent); however, it performed well in this study with no false positives among patients with fibromyalgia and only 10 percent false positives among those with rheumatoid arthritis.

- Because many of the ELISA tests used today detect both IgM and IgG antibodies, there is a greater risk for false positive results because the IgM antibodies are known to be more "sticky" (and less specific) than the IgG antibodies. In other words, these antibodies may have been generated in response to another non-Lyme bacterial or viral infection but then bind to a Lyme disease spirochetal protein that is similar, thus leading to a false positive result. This phenomenon is known as "cross-reactivity."

- *Cross-reactivity*: ELISAs that are based on whole-cell sonicate *B. burgdorferi* have an inherent problem of cross-reactivity. This is because the whole-cell spirochete contains components that are common among other bacterial species—i.e., not unique to the organism and thus "non-specific." Some of the more nonspecific components of *B. burgdorferi* include the 21–23 kDa, 30 kDa, 41 kDa, 60 kDa, 66 kDa, and 73 kDa antigens that are known to have considerable cross-reactivity to other spirochetes (e.g., the oral treponemes common in the mouth may seed the blood in patients with periodontal disease), heat-shock proteins found on other microbes, and viruses (e.g, Epstein-Barr virus) or bacteria (e.g., *Helicobacter pylori*). False positives on the ELISA due to cross-reactivity may also occur among individuals with endocarditis or autoimmune disorders. Overall, the problem of cross-reactivity is recognized as a leading explanation for false positives on the ELISA (and Western blot).

- *Differences between the proteins expressed in culture and the proteins expressed in the actual infected human*: The traditional ELISA and Western blot assays are made most often with antigens obtained from *Borrelia* spirochetes grown in culture in a laboratory setting. However, what happens in culture is not the same as what happens in the human host. In culture some outer spirochetal surface proteins are expressed that are suppressed in the human host. Similarly, in the human host, some new surface proteins emerge that are not expressed in the culture setting. This means that a lab test that is developed based on what happens in culture may not be able to detect all of the outer surface proteins expressed in spirochetes in different stages of human *B. burgdorferi* infection. Some researchers speculate this may contribute to the variable sensitivity of the two-tiered assays in different stages of Lyme disease. Fortunately, newer assays with antigens expressed in the human (e.g., C6 and VlsE ELISAs) have been developed that begin to address this problem.

- *Inconsistency between blood and cerebrospinal fluid*: In our studies of Lyme disease, we have found occasional patient samples that test positive by Lyme ELISA in the cerebrospinal fluid but negative in the serum; this presents a problem when a physician relies solely on the ELISA in the serum to rule in or rule out neurologic Lyme disease.

  - In a study of eighteen patients with cognitive problems after Lyme disease, three of the eighteen patients tested negative in the serum but positive in the cerebrospinal fluid for *B. burgdorferi*–specific antibodies (Logigian, Kaplan, and Steere 1999). This suggests that as many as one in six patients with evidence of central nervous system invasion by *B. burgdorferi* would be at risk for misdiagnosis if clinicians relied solely on blood test studies.

## NEW DEVELOPMENTS

- *Recombinant or Synthetic Peptide ELISAs*. To reduce the number of false positives, more specific ELISAs (based on "recombinant" or "synthetic" proteins) have been developed that dramatically reduce the percentage of false positive results. One such test is the C6 Peptide ELISA. A similar test is the VlsE ELISA. Both provide tests for Lyme antibodies with improved sensitivity and specificity; each represents a much more specific test than the standard "whole-cell sonicate" ELISA.

  - In one large U.S. study (Branda et al. 2010), the C6 ELISA was shown to have a sensitivity of 56 percent in early Lyme disease compared to only 42 percent for the two-tiered approach. In that study both approaches had excellent specificity—98.4 percent for the C6 and 99.5 percent for the two-tiered method. In another large-sample-size study (Wormser et al. 2013) compared to two-tiered testing, the C6 ELISA as a stand-alone test had a sensitivity in early Lyme disease of 66.5 percent versus 35.2 percent; in early neurologic Lyme disease of 88.6 percent versus 77.3 percent; and in Lyme arthritis of 98.3 percent versus 95.6 percent. In this study, the specificity was only slightly less for the C6 assay at 98.9 percent versus 99.5 percent for the two-tiered method. While more sensitive than the standard ELISA, particularly in early Lyme disease, the C6 ELISA is still not sensitive enough to be considered an adequate test for early infection.

○ Some research studies on the C6 ELISA suggest that changes in the C6 ELISA value may reflect successful response to treatment. One study reported that six months or more after treatment there was a fourfold or greater decline in titer on the C6, corresponding with successful treatment in humans with culture-confirmed *erythema migrans* (Philipp et al. 2005). Other human studies, however, have not confirmed these findings. Additionally, in a primate animal study, C6 peptide ELISA antibody tests became negative over time in several rhesus macaques despite evidence of persistent *B. burgdorferi* infection (Embers et al. 2012).

• *Combining Multiple Synthetic Peptides.* To improve the sensitivity and specificity of the ELISA, other investigators are now creating ELISAs that combine multiple synthetic peptides, such as pepC10, OppA2, Decorin-binding protein A, and Decorin-binding protein B. The improved sensitivity is likely due to the use of multiple peptides that are expressed both at the very early localized phase and at the later stages of infection. The improved specificity may be due in part to the elimination of structures that are found in similar proteins expressed by other bacteria.

• *Point-of-Care tests.* More rapid and sensitive point-of-care ELISA tests are being developed that can provide results within minutes in the health care provider's office.

- *Adopting a two-tier ELISA.* To reduce problems associated with interpretation of the Western blot that can be technically complex and subjective, the Centers for Disease Control and Prevention may move to replace or complement their laboratory recommendation for diagnostic testing in clinical practice from the ELISA–Western blot combination of the two-tiered system with a two ELISA combination.
  - Recent analyses indicate that using a whole-cell sonicate ELISA as the first-tier test with the C6 ELISA as the second-tier test is either equivalent to or significantly better than any comparison algorithms that included immunoblots (Molins et al. 2016). This provides the advantages of simplicity and removes the subjective aspects of visually read immunoblots.

## Western Blot

The Western blot (a type of immunoblot) is also widely used as a test for Lyme disease antibodies, usually during the two-tiered testing as a follow-up test if the ELISA is equivocal or positive. While the ELISA is a quantitative test of the magnitude of the IgG/IgM antibody response, the Western blot provides qualitative data regarding which antibodies are actually present in the patient's serum that recognize proteins of *B. burgdorferi*. Interpretation of the Western blot is often conducted by a skilled laboratory expert who visually assesses the intensity of each "band." More recently, automated methods have been developed to measure each band's intensity and report whether it is present or absent based on a cutoff intensity. According to the CDC, a Western blot is considered positive if there is reactivity at two out of three bands of the IgM class (23, 39, or 41 kDa) *or* five out of ten bands of the IgG class (18, 23, 28, 30, 39, 41, 45, 58, 66, or 93 kDa). (The apparent molecular mass of OspC is dependent on the strain of *B. burgdorferi* being used and in the early Western blots was identified as 21 or 24 kDa, instead of the 23 kDa weight more commonly reported today.)

The Western blot IgM and IgG provide different information. Both IgM and IgG antibodies are produced during active infection, but the less specific IgM antibodies wane once the more specific IgG antibodies are generated. While it is generally known that the IgM antibody can be a

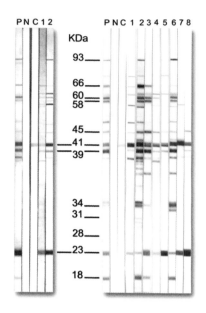

**FIGURE 4.2**

Western blot showing the location of significant bands that support the presence of *B. burgdorferi* antibodies.

*Courtesy of the CDC.*

marker of new or recent infection, it is not well known that the production of IgM antibodies does not necessarily stop, even after the infection has been treated and the organism eradicated. Both antibodies can stay elevated for long periods, although the IgG stays elevated for much longer. In the case of Lyme disease, IgM and even IgG do decline to undetectable levels in some patients, but in many patients they remain elevated (in comparison to baseline) for many years. This is likely a function of the duration of active infection, strain of organism, and genetic predisposition of the human. In almost everyone, these antibodies keep declining over the years at various rates after peaking at some point during or shortly after active infection. A persistent IgM antibody response therefore is of uncertain significance. The CDC and the IDSA state that the IgM Western blot result has meaning only during the first four weeks after infection. Subsequent to that interval, the IgG Western blot should be the focus of attention because by that time a healthy immune system in the human should be able to generate the more specific IgG response.

The IgG Western blot is considered highly specific when interpreted using the CDC criteria of five out of ten bands. In other words, if an IgG Western blot is positive, one can be almost certain that the person has had prior exposure to *B. burgdorferi*. This is obviously advantageous because knowledge of prior infection can help clarify why an individual might have persistent symptoms. On the other hand, a positive Western blot alone does not mean a person *has* active infection because the IgG antibody response can stay positive for many years, long after the infection has been eradicated.

## PROS

- The Western blot is widely available.
- It provides a fingerprint of the Lyme-specific antibody profile in the blood.
- A positive result (five out of ten bands) is highly specific for Lyme disease—in other words, a positive test is strong evidence that a patient had or has infection with the agent of Lyme disease.
  - A lab test that reveals four out of five IgG bands, while not positive by CDC standards, would be considered very highly suggestive of prior exposure to *B. burgdorferi*. In the setting of a carefully evaluated patient with good evidence of tick exposure and clinical features consistent with Lyme disease, such a test result would provide valuable supportive evidence of prior infection (although not confirmatory).
- The sensitivity of the IgG Western blot is considered to be excellent for Lyme arthritis. For acute neurologic Lyme disease, the sensitivity in various studies is less, falling between 72 and 87 percent (Dressler et al. 1993; Bacon et al. 2003).

## CONS

- Western blots are much more expensive than ELISAs.
- Unlike ELISAs, which are quantitative assays, the density of bands on a Western blot is usually visually interpreted by a technician, so there

is variability in results depending on the skills of the "reader." In other words, the test is more subjective. This problem is being addressed by new striped immunoblots that use a scanning densitometer (rather than a technician) to measure band intensity; this improves consistency and objectivity.

- There have been questions about the bands selected for inclusion in the list of Lyme-significant bands. For example, the CDC's list of significant bands excludes certain bands, such as the 31 kDa and 34 kDa, even though Lyme vaccines were developed or considered that target these specific proteins. If these markers are important enough to be the focus of vaccine development, clearly they should also be considered in Western blot interpretation. Why were these bands excluded?

  ○ Some speculate that the 31 kDa band was excluded in the mid-1990s because a vaccine was under development for the U.S. market that triggered the healthy patient's immune system to produce antibodies against the 31 kDa band. Vaccinated patients would therefore be more at risk of a misleading result on the Western blot if the 31 kDa band were included in the CDC list.

  ○ Another reason given for the exclusion of the 31 and 34 kDa bands is simpler. The CDC adopted the Dressler and colleagues criteria (1993) in which the ten most frequently observed IgG bands among patients with new-onset Lyme disease were chosen; although the 31 and 34 kDa bands were detectable among some patients with later stage disease (e.g., arthritis or neurologic Lyme), the frequency of antibody responses to these peptides did not make it to the top ten. In support of this conclusion, we examined the frequency of bands on IgG Western blots in a large sample of patients with chronic persistent symptoms after well-defined Lyme disease and found that the OspA and OspB antigens were the eleventh and twelfth most frequently elicited antibody responses.

  ○ Worth noting in regard to OspA and OspB antigens is that they are downregulated during tick feeding and not initially expressed in the human until later in the course of infection. Positive antibodies to OspA and OspB are therefore more relevant for the detection of later stage than earlier stage infection.

- As noted in the ELISA section earlier, cross-reactive antibodies originating from triggers unrelated to *B. burgdorferi* can occur. While it was originally thought that the Western blot would solve this limitation of the ELISA by selecting protein bands that were more specific to *B. burgdorferi*, it is now known that some of these proteins also have regions that are not specific and thus contribute to the problem of cross-reactivity. This is confusing to both patients and clinicians. The 21–23, 30, 41, 58, and 66 kDa antigens (included in the ten bands specified by the CDC) can each attract cross-reactive antibodies triggered by infections unrelated to *B. burgdorferi*. The common oral treponemes in the mouth, for example, can trigger the generation of antibodies that cross-react at the 41 kDa band (Magnarelli 1990) while the heat-shock proteins found on other microbes may lead to misleading reactivity on the 58 and 66 kDa bands (Hansen et al. 1988; Arnaboldi and Dattwyler 2015; Luft et al. 1991). Reactivity on a Western blot to other antigens previously thought to be "Lyme specific" may also reflect false positivity; these include the 31 kDa antigen (due to less specific protein migration to that 31 kDa location) and the 93 kDa antigen (Nowalk et al. 2006; Chandra et al. 2011). The problem of cross-reactivity common to these antibody-based tests is now being corrected by new tests that use peptide regions unique to the *B. burgdorferi* spirochete; the cross-reactive regions on the immunoblot bands that are common to other bacteria have been identified and eliminated from these new assays.
  - As an example of the problem of cross-reactivity, one study showed that 40 percent of healthy individuals with no history of Lyme disease had positive reactivity to the *Borrelia* flagellin (41 kDa) (Liang et al. 1999). In other words, reactivity to the 41 kDa band is common in the general public and should not be considered by itself as a sign of infection with *B. burgdorferi*.
- *Limitations of the IgM Western blot*: While a positive IgG Western blot is relatively easy to interpret, the considerable limitations of the IgM Western blot lead to problems.
  - *Unclear time course*: A positive IgM Western blot after the first one to two months can be confusing. It has been shown in Lyme disease that the IgM Western blot can stay positive for many

months, long after the infection has been treated and the patient has recovered.

- *Cross-reactivity*: The IgM Western blot is recognized as less specific than the IgG Western blot. That means that a positive Lyme IgM antibody test result may actually have been elicited by infection with a microbe other than *B. burgdorferi*. In other words, the Lyme IgM Western blot is more likely than the IgG Western blot to have problems with false positives as a result of cross-reactivity. This cross-reactivity creates quite a confusing situation for patients and doctors. Does an intermittently positive IgM Western blot reflect new *B. burgdorferi* infection, a failure to turn off a previously activated IgM response even after the infection is gone, or a false positive due to cross-reactivity with other common microbes in the human body? Patients may be told that they need more antibiotics because the IgM Western blot is positive—such a recommendation may be correct or it may be incorrect. The IgM Western blot is unfortunately not specific enough to allow us to make that determination.

- *CDC criteria versus "in-house" criteria*: To enhance the sensitivity of diagnostic tests, some Lyme specialty labs have devised an alternative ("in-house") set of criteria for determining whether a Western blot is positive; not surprisingly, when criteria are modified to enhance sensitivity, there is often also an increase in false positives. To assist clinicians, these labs report their interpretation of the Western blot results using the CDC criteria as well as the lab's in-house criteria.

  - *Limitations of in-house criteria*. The problem with interpretation of the IgM Western blot when using these in-house criteria was demonstrated in a study (Fallon et al. 2014) in which we reported that 37 percent of healthy individuals whose serum was tested at a Lyme specialty lab were found to have a positive IgM antibody response for Lyme disease, even though they did not feel sick and even though they had no knowledge of ever having had Lyme disease. Of course, while we cannot rule out that some of these healthy controls may have been previously bitten by a tick and gotten infected without a memorable illness, we consider it highly unlikely that this explanation would apply to most of these healthy individuals. This study demonstrated that these tests—when relied upon too strongly by clinicians—can be misleading, particularly when in-house criteria are used for the IgM Western blot.

## NEW DEVELOPMENTS

- *Switching from IgM to IgG may be impaired*: Recent research in mice indicates that *B. burgdorferi* infection damages the architecture of the lymph nodes in such a way as to diminish maturation from the production of IgM antibodies to IgG antibodies generated by long-lived plasma cells (Elsner et al. 2015). It is unclear whether this finding in mice has relevance to humans, as mice are the primary reservoir carriers of *B. burgdorferi* infection in nature. This is, however, an important area of current research as it could provide an additional explanation as to why people can get Lyme disease more than once, why in some patients IgM antibodies are more common than IgG antibodies, and why infection may persist in some hosts.
- *Use of recombinant or synthetic proteins on immunoblots*: To improve the accuracy of the Western blots, some laboratories are using recombinant or synthetic proteins rather than the protein mixture currently used to target the antibodies in the serum. These purified proteins ensure that the "positive" band is truly a Lyme-significant band as opposed to an antigenic marker that is not specific for *Borrelia* but has migrated to that location on the blot. The 31 kDa band, for example, is the site of one such migrating antigen that can lead to misleading conclusions. Some labs now provide Western blots that have a combination of antigens on the blot—one composed of synthetic antigens, recombinant antigens, and whole-cell sonicate antigens. These should improve the specificity of both the IgM and IgG Western blots.
- *Multiplex bead arrays*: Recent research has focused on identifying the best antigen combination or best cytokine/chemokine combination by screening a wide array of novel and established biomarkers to see which worked best to improve diagnosis and detect early infection.

○ Rather than relying solely on the ten antigens recommended on the CDC's IgG Western blot panel, one such approach screened multiple antigens to identify the ones most sensitive and specific (Lahey et al. 2015). In this study, the investigators screened sixty-two candidate antigens (including seven *B. burgdorferi* surface proteins and fifty-five synthetic peptides derived from *B. burgdorferi*–specific antigenic epitopes); of these, ten were selected for a multiplex bead array using Luminex technology. This detection strategy avoids the need for immunoblotting altogether by using specific peptides in a multiplex microsphere assay. The results from a sample of early Lyme disease cases demonstrated an improved sensitivity of 55 percent for detection rate of *B. burgdorferi* antibodies (using the multiplex array) compared to only 40 percent using the CDC two-tiered methodology; both approaches had excellent specificity (100 percent). The sensitivity of this multiplex assay however is similar to the sensitivity reported for the Lyme C6 ELISA assay in early Lyme disease. Both represent improvements for early detection compared to the two-tiered method, but one that falls short of the 90 percent or greater detection desired for an assay in early Lyme disease.

○ Another approach used a multiplex bead array to look not at antigens but at the immune signature associated with early Lyme disease (Soloski et al. 2014). In this study, fifty-eight immune mediators (cytokines and chemokines) and seven acute phase markers (e.g., C-reactive protein and serum amyloid) were measured. The analysis revealed an immune biosignature that differentiated the early patients with Lyme disease from the controls. Importantly, after antibiotic treatment of the EM rash, the levels of the three most highly expressed chemokines (CXCL9, CXCL10, and CCL19) returned to normal, suggesting that this immune signature may have a role as a diagnostic marker of early Lyme and/or a biomarker of treatment response. Could this research lead to the much-needed test for active infection? Possibly. Future studies need to examine how specific this immune signature is when compared to other inflammatory illnesses and whether this biosignature is also sensitive for active infection in later stages of acute Lyme disease.

## Culture

Culture is a test in which blood or tissue is placed in a special medium to see if *B. burgdorferi* will grow. Culture is the "gold standard" for diagnosis of any infection, but in the case of Lyme disease, culture is rarely used except in the research setting.

### PROS

- If the organism can be cultured, you know that the blood, spinal fluid, or tissue contains healthy *Borrelia* spirochetes. This is the definitive proof of active infection.
- In the research setting, *B. burgdorferi* spirochetes have been grown from approximately 50 percent of skin biopsy samples of patients presenting with the Lyme disease rash. This is helpful in clinical research because one can then be sure that the rash is indeed an EM rash. By conducting biopsies on all rashes on individuals after tick bite or exposure to a Lyme endemic area (regardless of whether it looked like a Lyme rash), this approach has demonstrated that the EM rash of Lyme disease may not always look like a Lyme rash (e.g., it could look like a spider bite).

### CONS

- Culturing *B. burgdorferi* is time consuming because the organism is slow growing.
- Not all *B. burgdorferi* will grow readily in standard culture.
- Test results may not come back for eight to sixteen weeks—far too long to be helpful to the doctor trying to decide what to do now for the patient currently in his or her office.
- Culture of *Borrelia* is not offered by the majority of commercial labs.
- Culture is less useful once the infection has disseminated outside the bloodstream and beyond the stage of the EM rash. Even at the EM stage, when the quantity of *Borrelia* spirochetes is greatest in the blood, only about 40 to 50 percent of patients will test positive using

the best culture techniques currently available (e.g., high-volume plasma culture).

- False positive results can occur even at the best labs due to inadvertent contamination of culture specimens.

## NEW DEVELOPMENTS

- *Modified Culture Medium.* There are increased efforts to improve the sensitivity of culture by modifying the culture medium. One lab in the United States has reported a remarkably improved sensitivity (greater than 90 percent after sixteen weeks) (Sapi et al. 2013). These results are extraordinary given prior studies that reported positive cultures using high volumes only 45 percent of the time after eight to twelve weeks (Wormser et al. 2001). The CDC has raised concerns about this new culture assay, particularly raising the question of implausibility and suspected contamination (Johnson, Pilgard, and Russell 2014; Nelson et al. 2014). For these reasons, the authors of this critique recommended additional validation studies of this new culture assay by an independent lab or academic medical center.

## Polymerase Chain Reaction

The polymerase chain reaction (PCR) detects genetic material of the *B. burgdorferi* spirochete itself. This is considered by many to be a direct test of active infection.

### PROS

- A positive PCR result is strongly suggestive of current or recent infection as the *Borrelia* genetic material does not linger in the body for long after the infection is gone.
- Because the PCR detects DNA, positive results can be seen immediately when infection first appears and does not require the delay of two or more weeks typical of antibody-based tests.
- PCR is a sensitive assay in skin biopsy samples from EM patients (approximately 64 percent) and in synovial fluid specimens (approximately 83 percent) from patients with Lyme arthritis.

## CONS

- PCR studies of blood from patients with early Lyme disease typically detect DNA of *B. burgdorferi* in only 18 to 26 percent of blood samples.
- PCR of the cerebrospinal fluid is insensitive in detecting active infection among patients with neurologic Lyme disease, with sensitivities as low as 38 percent in early neurologic Lyme and 25 percent in late neurologic Lyme disease.
- False negatives can occur when the genetic load in the blood specimen is just below the detection level of the assay.
- False negatives in the blood can also occur because spirochetes have already disseminated outside the bloodstream and have lodged in tissues; the test result is correct but the conclusion that the human is not infected with *Borrelia* spirochetes would be incorrect.

## NEW DEVELOPMENTS

- *Large volume sampling.* Recent studies have revealed an increased sensitivity by sampling larger blood volumes and by using different PCR techniques such as qPCR or nested PCR.
- *Discovery-based techniques.* One of the more promising research areas has been the introduction of "discovery" diagnostic methods to enhance microbe detection.

  Currently, doctors order a diagnostic assay such as a PCR based on a hypothesis that a specific organism, such as *B. burgdorferi*, may be present. This is a limited approach to microbial detection because it requires knowing in advance what microbe might be causing the infection.

  In research settings, we can now probe a sample of fluid and "discover" whatever microbes may be located within that sample. This is very helpful in biowarfare situations. In some hospital centers, it is now being used for patients who come in with "fevers of unknown origin." To be able to rapidly detect and label a foreign microbe is a major advance in medical science.
- This test is done through a variety of techniques, one of which is a combination of isothermal amplification followed by broad-range PCR and electrospray ionization mass spectrometry (PCR/ESI-MS).

This approach has been used to identify novel pathogens inside ticks as well as in blood samples of patients with recent Lyme disease (Eshoo et al. 2012, Marques et al. 2014). This technique has many advantages, including the ability to rapidly identify and genotype pathogens and to identify new genetic variants.

## Other Blood Tests

- In previous decades, various investigators have explored other laboratory methods for detecting Lyme disease, such as the immune complex dissociation assay and the borreliacidal assay. Most of these tests are no longer commercially available due to problems with sensitivity, specificity, or marketability.

## NEW DEVELOPMENTS

- *Lymphocyte or macrophage stimulation assays*: Much like the successful cell stimulation tests for tuberculosis, one of the newer approaches takes advantage of the immune cell's memory. When the infection with *B. burgdorferi* is current or recent, the patient's blood in the lab will show a much stronger release of a specific cytokine (immune mediator) when exposed to stimulation by *Borrelia* protein than when the infection has resolved. This is because the immune cells (for example, T-cells or macrophages) will have been "primed" by recent exposure to the *Borrelia* spirochete itself. These tests would be considered indirect markers of infection.
  - The application of this approach to early Lyme disease using monocytes or macrophages is partly based on the novel immunological discovery that the very early immune response is not just a shotgun response with no specificity but an immunologic attack that does retain some specificity for a period of time (Saeed et al. 2014).
  - Another report applied this approach to the stimulation of T-cells using peptide antigens derived from *B. burgdorferi* to stimulate the release of interferon-gamma (IFN-γ) (Callister et al. 2016). Among twenty-nine patients with early Lyme disease, 69 percent

tested positive; among these patients who initially tested positive on the T-cell stimulation assay, 80 percent were subsequently negative on this test when reevaluated two months post-treatment. This approach to testing bypasses the problems associated with the time delay for antibody generation and represents a significant departure from the antibody tests that remain positive for years, long after the infection is gone.

- o Most of these assays are still in the testing and validation phase and hence will not be discussed in further detail here. They do, however, provide the promise of a test that serves as a surrogate marker of active infection with the *Borrelia* spirochete at any stage of disease. As an alternative to serologic testing, this approach to diagnostic testing brings us closer to the clinically important goal: a test that is positive early in infection and one that becomes negative after the infection has resolved.

- *Next-generation "omics" and discovery-based science*: Rather than developing assays with a "best guess" of which proteins or markers are most important to use, discovery-based science starts with a blank slate. The method involves uncovering and identifying all of the molecules in a fluid (e.g., blood or spinal fluid) that distinguish individuals with Lyme disease from those who do not have Lyme disease. Or one could compare the blood or CSF components from patients with early Lyme disease to those components found in later stage Lyme disease. In this way, one is uncovering or discovering the markers that are there as opposed to searching for what one hypothesizes will be there. This breakthrough in science is made possible by recent advances in biotechnology. The components that are scrutinized might start at the most basic level or higher up the information chain; for example, studies probing a sample of human blood may seek to discover all the genetic material (DNA), genetic transcripts (mRNA), or the products of the gene transcriptions (proteins or other metabolic products). Metabalome-derived assays are an example of the application and power of this discovery approach.

  - o Recent work (Molins et al. 2015) has focused not just on the proteins and peptides but also on other features of the "metabolome" in the blood to distinguish early Lyme disease from healthy controls.

This approach examines the pattern of molecules produced in the patients' serum in response to *B. burgdorferi* infection. This research group identified a biosignature of early Lyme disease containing forty-four molecular features. The sensitivity of this assay was 88 percent in early Lyme disease with a specificity of 95 percent. These results are vastly superior to the current sensitivity of the two-tiered approach (ELISA and Western blot) while retaining high specificity. Given that many clinicians are most interested in highly sensitive tests so that they don't miss the opportunity to treat a case of Lyme disease early in the course of infection, this high degree of sensitivity represents a marked advance in the diagnosis of early Lyme disease. This assay combined mass spectrometry and liquid chromatography to identify metabolic patterns in the blood that differentiate early Lyme from other clinical or healthy states.

## URINE-BASED TESTS

### Nanotechnology and Urine-Based Assays

- An early version of urine-based tests that purported to detect *Borrelia* antigen was shown to be unreliable in one report (Klempner et al. 2001b).
- A more recent version has been reported using the extraordinary sensitivity of nanotube technology (Magni et al. 2015) to detect the OspA antigen, which is common to the *Borrelia* genospecies. OspA is a surprising choice because it is not thought to be expressed in early disease. However, another recent diagnostic study reported detection of OspA in the blood of three patients with acute Lyme disease (Cheung 2015). By directly detecting the spirochetal protein rather than the antibody response, these tests come closer to reaching the holy grail of clinically useful diagnostics—a test of active infection. If future studies are able to confirm that this is a reliable and sensitive marker of active infection at all stages of disease, many of the treatment decisions faced by clinicians would be made easier. While we cannot be certain the

persistent OspA antigen represents active infection, the detection of the protein does suggest that the *Borrelia* spirochete has been present in the recent past. The initial nanotechnology study reported excellent sensitivity and specificity. Because this is a relatively new assay and because OspA is an unexpected marker for early Lyme disease, this test requires independent validation for confirmation.

## SPINAL FLUID AND BRAIN TESTS

### Lumbar Puncture

Patients with symptoms suggestive of central nervous system involvement that may be due to Lyme disease should have a lumbar puncture, also known as a spinal tap. The cerebrospinal fluid (CSF) obtained in this test is sent for routine studies, including cell count as well as protein and glucose levels. In addition, the CSF is sent for studies of *B. burgdorferi*–specific antibodies and for *Borrelia* DNA by PCR. When spinal fluid is collected, it is equally important to collect serum from the patient so that the CSF-serum pair can be sent together to the lab for testing. This allows for a comparison of the relative levels of Lyme-specific antibodies in the CSF compared to the serum; with this information, the lab can then calculate the "intrathecal index." This index refers to the ratio of *B. burgdorferi* antibodies in the CSF compared to the serum. A positive index indicates that more antibodies are being produced in the CSF than in the blood, strongly suggesting that the *Borrelia* spirochete has invaded the central nervous system. Please note that the serum must be drawn *on the same day* as the lumbar puncture for this study to be effective. If the physician suspects the symptoms could also be caused by multiple sclerosis, he or she is likely to order more tests on the CSF, such as an assay for oligoclonal bands and an IgG index and synthesis rate.

#### PROS

- The spinal fluid is the closest fluid to the brain and thus provides information related to a variety of brain infections and diseases that may not be detectable from the blood alone. It is also relatively protected from the blood by the blood–brain barrier.

- A positive intrathecal index can confirm invasion of the central nervous system by *B. burgdorferi*.

## CONS

- In the setting of active Lyme disease in the central nervous system, a false negative result for *B. burgdorferi* antibodies in the CSF among U.S. patients may occur as often as 20 percent of the time (Coyle 1995). This false negative means that the *B. burgdorferi* antibodies are not always detected by routine tests and that the white blood cell count and protein level of the CSF may be normal even in the setting of neurologic Lyme disease; the 20 percent false negative was detected by "immune complex dissociation assays."
- Like the serum antibody tests, the intrathecal index may remain positive long after the initial infection has been treated and cleared as the antibody response can continue due to immunologic memory.

## NEW DEVELOPMENTS

- *Chemokine CXCL-13.* The chemokine CXCL13 was reported in early studies to be a highly sensitive (94 percent) and specific biomarker of early neurologic Lyme disease (Schmidt et al. 2011). This B-cell attractant, however, has also been found to be elevated in patients with neurosyphilis, B-cell lymphoma, and in patients with *N*-methyl-D-aspartate (NMDA)-receptor encephalitis. Therefore, while it may be a sensitive marker of active infection in Lyme neuroborreliosis, it is not 100 percent specific when compared to other diseases associated with CNS infection or B-cell mediated pathologies.
- *Recombinant Antigen Index.* A study (Wutte et al. 2014) demonstrated that the diagnosis of neurologic Lyme disease varies considerably depending on the test method used. Sensitivity of detection of neurologic Lyme disease was 24 percent higher when the intrathecal index used a recombinant antigen ELISA (OspC and VlsE) to identify *B. burgdorferi*–specific antibody production compared to when

another *B. burgdorferi*–specific antigen (flagellin) capture ELISA was used. When either the immunoblot alone or the CXCL13 assay were used to detect neurologic Lyme disease, the recombinant assay with OspC and VlsE continued to detect about 10 to 14 percent more cases. While this study is encouraging in demonstrating considerable improvement in diagnostic testing of the CSF, it also reminds us that a negative result using one testing method may be a false negative and that a clinician's decisions regarding treatment should not be based solely on the results of the CSF assay; further test improvements are needed to enhance the clinician's confidence regarding these tests.

- *CSF Proteome.* To determine whether the cerebrospinal fluid of patients with post-treatment neurologic Lyme disease contains a protein profile unique to patients with post-treatment Lyme disease when compared to patients with chronic fatigue syndrome and to healthy controls, a proteomic study (Schutzer et al. 2011) using samples from the Columbia Lyme encephalopathy clinical trial was conducted in collaboration with Pacific Northwest National Laboratories. The method enabled identification of all of the proteins contained in the spinal fluid from people in each of these three groups; this is known as the "proteome." The study demonstrated that post-treatment Lyme disease has 692 unique proteins in the cerebrospinal fluid and therefore can be differentiated from chronic fatigue syndrome, even though the clinical symptoms of each are quite similar. While not yet a diagnostic assay, studies such as these provide additional clues for diagnostic test development.

## Structural MRI

Magnetic resonance imaging (MRI) is a medical imaging technique that uses magnetic fields to show the anatomy of the brain without using radiation. MRI is able to detect abnormalities that may be seen in some patients with neurologic Lyme, such as white matter hyperintensities. White matter hyperintensities can occur as a result of Lyme disease, but can also occur for a wide variety of other reasons. It is important to note that these findings are not unique to Lyme disease. White matter hyperintensities tend to increase with age even in adults who do not have Lyme disease. Individuals with a history of stroke, multiple sclerosis, or smoking may also have large or numerous white matter hyperintensities. For these reasons, MRI is informative but it cannot be used to make a diagnosis of Lyme disease.

### PRO

- MRI does not use radiation and is noninvasive.

### CONS

- Lyme disease cannot be diagnosed on the basis of MRI findings, which are nonspecific.
- MRI cannot be used on patients with pacemakers or certain metallic implants.
- Some patients report feeling claustrophobic during the MRI scan, which takes approximately forty-five minutes. MRI scans are also somewhat noisy, making it hard for individuals with heightened sensitivity to sound (hyperacusis) to tolerate.

## Functional MRI

Functional MRI (fMRI) is an approach to magnetic resonance imaging that allows researchers to answer certain questions about brain function. It is not commonly used in the clinical setting in the assessment of patients. One example of its potential research use among patients with Lyme disease is to ask whether the brain function of patients with Lyme disease has been altered compared to those who are healthy. If we hypothesize, for example, that patients with post-treatment Lyme disease syndrome (PTLDS) might suffer from "central sensitization," we would expect that their central pain networks might be hyperactivated compared to healthy controls. In other words, a moderate level of pain would result in greater activation of the brain's pain networks in a patient with a history of Lyme disease than would occur in an individual without a history of Lyme disease. This "brain pain" can be studied using fMRI approaches; "brain pain" might help explain the chronic diffuse pain that many patients with PTLDS experience. At Columbia, we are conducting an fMRI study to address this question.

## Magnetic Resonance Spectroscopy

MR spectroscopy is not commonly used to assess patients with Lyme disease in routine clinical practice, but it is used in the research setting to teach us about the relative concentrations of different chemicals in the brain. For example, a study of brain chemistry among patients with fibromyalgia (Natelson et al. 2015) demonstrated using MR spectroscopy that the level of lactic acid in the cerebrospinal fluid was initially elevated but declined after successful pharmacologic treatment with a medication ("milnacipran"); this medication modulates important brain neurotransmitters involved in pain, fatigue, and depression. Whether patients with persistent fatigue or pain after Lyme disease also have elevated levels of lactic acid in the cerebrospinal fluid is a question that the Columbia Lyme Center is currently investigating using this noninvasive brain imaging approach.

## Single-Photon Emission Computerized Tomography Imaging

Unlike structural MRI, which provides a picture of the brain's anatomy, single-photon emission computerized tomography (SPECT) enables an examination of how the brain is actually functioning. In Lyme disease, the most common finding is "heterogeneous hypoperfusion" diffusely throughout the brain. This finding might lead one to conclude that there is a problem in the blood vessels because less blood is reaching various parts of the brain than normal. However, vascular narrowing or blockage is not the only reason for diminished blood flow. Decreased blood flow can also occur due to decreased demand by the brain tissue. In other words, if the brain tissue is not metabolically active or if it is impaired in its functioning, the demand for blood flow may be diminished. In fact, our studies at Columbia have documented that patients with Lyme disease have deficits in both metabolic demand and blood flow; the most striking finding, however, is that the brain tissue's reduced metabolism creates the appearance of insufficient cerebral blood flow (Fallon et al. 2009).

Approximately 50 percent of patients with persistent symptoms after Lyme disease may have multiple areas of hypoperfusion on SPECT imaging (Fallon et al. 1997). Unfortunately, this same pattern of heterogeneous hypoperfusion is also seen in Lupus, chronic cocaine users, and certain vasculitic inflammatory disorders. Although SPECT has limitations and the blood flow perfusion pattern does not provide a diagnosis, it may be a helpful tool to clarify whether or not the blood flow in the brain appears normal or abnormal in a patient with central nervous system symptoms.

In the research setting, repeated SPECT scans over time after treatment with intravenous ceftriaxone has been shown to result in improved perfusion among patients with Lyme encephalopathy (Logigian, Kaplan, and Steere 1999). In the clinical setting of an individual patient, however, it is not clear that monitoring changes in blood flow on SPECT imaging is helpful. We have seen patients whose clinical symptoms improved after treatment for Lyme disease but whose brain SPECT scan did not change; this led to considerable discouragement and in some cases despair. Our impression is therefore that improvement in blood flow on the brain SPECT scan may lag far behind the improvement in clinical symptoms. While helpful as a research tool, it is not yet clear that SPECT scans among individual patients with Lyme disease adds valuable information in the assessment of treatment response in the clinical setting.

## PROS

- It is relatively inexpensive compared to positron emission tomography (PET) scans and widely available.
- It can show brain function.
- It is particularly useful if a seizure is suspected as that area of the brain may reveal increased perfusion.
- It may be useful in the assessment of young adults: an abnormal brain SPECT demonstrating diffuse moderate to severe heterogeneous hypoperfusion in a young adult with Lyme disease would support brain involvement if the individual is not abusing drugs, has never had a brain injury, and does not suffer from another disease known to cause perfusion or metabolic brain problems, such as another autoimmune or infectious disease.

## CONS

- Lyme disease cannot be diagnosed on the basis of SPECT scans alone.
- SPECT scans may only be useful in patients with moderate to severe central nervous system disease, as healthy people may have mild to moderately decreased perfusion, especially associated with increased age.
- In many medical centers, the clinical reading of the brain SPECT is quite subjective—based on the clinical experience of the nuclear medicine physician and based on the assumption of normal flow in certain parts of the brain (such as the cerebellum or thalamus). In other words, unless the reading of the scan has been automated and compared to a large database of age- and gender-adjusted healthy controls, the subjective reading by an individual physician is vulnerable to considerable unreliability.
- Like PET imaging, SPECT imaging uses a small amount of a radioactive tracer; although the exposure is quite low and single or multiple scans are considered safe, repeated use over time would increase the risk of ionizing radiation toxicity and possibly place the individual at an increased risk for the development of cancer.

## Positron Emission Tomography Imaging

PET imaging also tells us about how the brain is functioning. The most common radioactive tracer is $^{18}$F-fluorodeoxygluclose ($^{18}$F-FDG) which assesses metabolism of brain cells. PET scan studies are common in research but also have a role in the clinical setting. The assumption behind all functional brain imaging, such as PET and SPECT, is that there is a close relationship among the brain's nerve activity, glucose metabolism, and blood flow. The advantage of PET compared to SPECT is that the images have enhanced resolution allowing for improved quantification of the metabolism and blood flow in different brain areas. When different radioligands are used, PET requires a highly trained multidisciplinary staff with expertise in physics, chemistry, computers, medicine, and technology. Certain radioligands are more stable over time (such as radioactively labeled glucose—FDG), and these are commonly used in most hospitals or outpatient clinics. In general, PET scans tend to be more expensive and less widely available than SPECT.

Before the scan, the patient is infused with a small amount of a radio-pharmaceutical, or "tracer," that allows one to measure the blood flow or metabolism on the scan. PET scans can be used to differentiate between the problem of inflammation or blockage in small blood vessels in the brain (as might be seen in inflammatory Lyme encephalopathy) versus a problem with the nerve itself. It is unclear at this point whether PET has any advantage over SPECT for evaluation of an individual patient with possible Lyme disease, but with further research PET scans may emerge as a helpful adjunctive clinical tool in Lyme diagnostics.

## PROS

- PET has enhanced resolution compared to SPECT scans.
- It is able to quantify both blood flow and brain metabolism, providing information that helps to tease out whether the brain problem is one of metabolism or blood flow.

## CONS

- It is expensive and less widely available than MRI scans.
- It cannot be used to diagnose Lyme disease because findings are nonspecific.
- It requires highly trained, multidisciplinary staff.

## Neuropsychological Testing

Neuropsychological testing assesses various aspects of brain function and is usually administered by a specially trained mental health professional or by a technician supervised by a neuropsychologist. Typically a comprehensive selection of tests is administered, including a measure of general intellectual functioning, verbal and visual memory and learning, attention/concentration, verbal fluency, processing speed, fine and gross motor functioning, and executive functioning. Testing may occur over one to two days

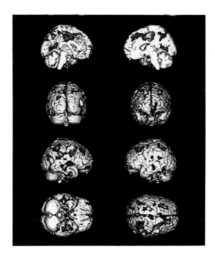

**FIGURE 4.3**

These are composite images representing areas of low blood flow in the brain of patients with memory impairment after Lyme disease (post-treatment Lyme encephalopathy). The low-flow regions are highlighted in yellow and red. To obtain these images, PET-$H_2O^{15}$ scans from thirty-seven patients with post-treatment Lyme disease syndrome were compared to the PET scans from eighteen age-, gender-, and education-matched healthy controls (Fallon et al. 2009).

and may span three to six hours or even longer. Shorter forty-five-minute to one-hour long computer-based neurocognitive batteries do exist; these are useful for screening but should not be considered a replacement for thorough neurocognitive assessment. Measures of depression, anxiety, and personality may also be administered because certain psychological states might affect cognitive performance. Lyme disease has been documented to cause impairments in memory, word finding, fine motor control, language conceptual ability, and motor functioning. The most consistently identified deficits in adults with Lyme disease have been problems with verbal memory, verbal fluency, and mental processing speed. Patients often refer to their cognitive limitations as "brain fog." Studies by various researches (Keilp et al. 2006; Kaplan and Jones-Woodward 1997; Elkins et al. 1999) support the conclusion that cognitive impairments are not secondary to a psychological response to chronic illness or due to a mood disorder.

## PROS

- Neuropsychological testing offers an objective measure of a patient's cognitive functioning at a specific point in time. Patients sometimes experience cognitive problems but perform well on objective testing. This may reflect a high level of intelligence on the part of the patient such that mild reductions in cognition function are not readily recognized as impairment. Alternatively, this may suggest that problems may have more to do with a distorted or negatively-biased perception of one's functioning than an actual deficit. This may be seen for example among patients with depression or anxiety. It is well known among neuropsychogists that patients' reports of cognitive difficulties, such as memory problems, do not necessarily correlate with objective data, so that without formal testing doctors may not be entirely sure that self-reported cognitive problems truly reflect a patient's cognitive capacity. Neuropsychological test results, when interpreted by an experienced neuropsychologist, may help to differentiate between neurological and psychiatric causes of cognitive problems.
- By providing a quantitative result, neuropsychological testing also allows for the monitoring of changes in response to treatment. This can be quite helpful as patients often ask, "Have I gotten any better over the last six months?"
- A better understanding of their own cognitive deficits may allow patients to better cope with them by advanced planning and special accommodations—for example, a patient with auditory attention problems might learn better from visually presented information.

## CONS

- Comprehensive neurocognitive testing can be costly. This is because the assessment requires not only hours to administer, but also hours after the testing to score the results, analyze the significance, and write the report. A neuropsychologist or psychiatrist may administer an abbreviated battery of tests as a screen to see if further testing is needed. Computer-assisted neurocognitive batteries are available online, but the cognitive domains that can be tested using this approach are not as comprehensive or informative as the in-person testing; this approach, however, is considerably less expensive.

- These tests are not able to diagnose Lyme disease specifically, although they are very effective at picking up brain dysfunction. These tests may be used as additional evidence in support of a suspected diagnosis of Lyme disease.

## OTHER TESTS

### Electromyography/Nerve Conduction Studies

Electromyography (EMG) and nerve conduction studies (NCS) assess the function of muscles and nerves, respectively. The EMG allows the neurologist to distinguish between muscle and nerve disease and to identify precisely the muscle involved. Nerve conduction studies inform the neurologist about the integrity of sensory and motor nerves. An electrical stimulation is applied to the skin overlying a peripheral nerve to enable a recording of the speed of conduction and the amplitude of the "downstream" action potential, or the electrical impulse traveling through a nerve. Nerve conduction studies assist in the diagnosis of nerve disorders, such as demyelinating neuropathy (slow conduction velocity), axonal neuropathy (reduced amplitude of compound muscle action potential), and nerve root compressions.

PRO

- EMG and NCS can detect muscle or nerve damage.

CON

- Lyme disease cannot be diagnosed on the basis of EMG or NCS alone.

### Skin Biopsy to Study Nerve Fibers

Lyme disease can cause a neuropathy, or nerve damage, that results in symptoms of burning, pain, tingling, or numbness, typically in the extremities. These sensory abnormalities may be due to damage to tiny pain and temperature nerve fibers in the skin (i.e., small nerve fibers). To detect small fiber damage, skin biopsies are performed. Many diseases may cause small fiber sensory neuropathy including diabetes, lupus sarcoidosis, Sjogren syndrome, celiac disease, hypothyroidism, and Lyme disease. The skin biopsy procedure is typically performed with a 3-mm disposable circular punch needle with a sterile technique using local anesthesia.

### PROS

- Skin biopsy can reliably detect sensory nerve damage.
- The procedure is minimally invasive.

### CON

- Lyme disease cannot be diagnosed on the basis of skin biopsy alone.

## Electrocardiogram or Echocardiogram

Electrocardiogram (ECG/EKG) and echocardiograms are widely performed to assess the structure and function of the heart. Though the abnormalities detected by these tests, such as partial or complete heart block or carditis, are not specific to Lyme disease alone, they are useful in detecting potential damage that may be caused by the infection.

### PROS

- ECG and echo are minimally invasive.
- They can detect abnormalities in the heart's rhythm and function that may be caused by Lyme disease.

### CON

- Lyme disease cannot be diagnosed on the basis of these tests alone.

## Autonomic Nervous System Testing

Because Lyme disease can affect the nervous system, tests that probe the autonomic nervous system can sometimes be quite helpful. *Heart rate variability* testing involves monitoring an ECG during cyclic deep breathing to assess the variability between beats. *Tilt table testing* involves measuring the heart rate and blood pressure response to a change in position from lying down to standing up (i.e., table tilts vertical). A systolic blood pressure drop of 20 to 30 mm Hg is considered abnormal and a diastolic drop of 10 mm Hg is considered significant. Disturbances of the ability to sweat—a marker of peripheral autonomic nervous system dysfunction—may be one of the earliest signs of a small fiber neuropathy. *Sweat gland function* can be assessed noninvasively. One such approach applies a low-voltage potential of varying current to the hands and feet; the electrochemical skin conductance is then measured to quantify the sweat gland functioning.

### PRO

- Autonomic testing is minimally invasive and inexpensive.

### CON

- Lyme disease cannot be diagnosed on the basis of these tests alone.

## SUMMARY

Most of the neurologic and imaging tools are ancillary tests used to document different effects of infection with *B. burgdorferi*. Only the *Borrelia*-specific lab tests—ELISA, immunoblot, IFA, PCR, or culture—can provide the biological evidence needed to confirm current or past infection with *B. burgdorferi* specifically. The antibody-based tests are being improved by using synthetic peptides that contain only the regions that are highly specific to *B. burgdorferi*. The emerging "biosignature" approaches that use inflammatory, proteomic, nucleic acid, cellular, or metabolomic biomarker profiles show promise, as do the T-cell stimulation assays. The ancillary tests that are not specific to Lyme disease may reinforce or refute the clinical suspicion of disseminated Lyme disease and may therefore help guide treatment. Because disseminated Lyme disease and PTLDS are complex multisystem diseases, the clinician may make use of many different tests, as if putting a puzzle together, to create a coherent composite picture to help guide diagnosis and treatment.

# 5

## THE GREAT DIVIDE AND
## THE LYME WARS

*"By whose authority do you do that? What are you doing,
stirring up trouble?"*[1]

—Polly Murray, *The Widening Circle* (1996)

From the earliest days of the Lyme story, there has been conflict. When two mothers from Connecticut—Polly Murray and Judith Mensch—independently observed that there appeared to be an unusual clustering of joint problems among children in their town, each was initially rebuffed by doctors and the response from public health officials was slow. But their persistence in conveying their observations to public health officials at the Connecticut State Health Department led to the discovery of Lyme arthritis (Steere et al. 1977).

Conflict reared its face again when doctors, using their best clinical judgment, came to strikingly different conclusions regarding treatment recommendations. The doctors at the health clinic at the Groton Naval Base in Connecticut recommended antibiotic therapy for their patients with *erythema migrans* (EM), based on the similarities with the European rash (Mast 1976b). The doctors from Yale, however, were rheumatologists whose attention was focused initially on the arthritic manifestations; they felt that this was a rheumatologic disease that required treatment with medications that reduced inflammation, such as aspirin. In addition, they had observed that some patients treated with penicillin for the rash went on to develop arthritis anyway. In these initial years, it did not seem to them that antibiotics were effective.

[1] A doctor's agitated reprimand in 1975 to Polly Murray, a concerned mother in Old Lyme Connecticut, who had called the State Health Department to report that there seemed to be an unusually high incidence of juvenile rheumatoid arthritis among children in her town.

Which theory was correct? Anti-inflammatories or antibiotics? These conflicting ideas were confusing to patients because some doctors were recommending antibiotic therapy to shorten the duration of disease, while others were recommending anti-inflammatory therapy because that was the appropriate treatment for arthritic illness. As alarm spread throughout Connecticut regarding the mysterious new illness, the local newspapers featured these scientific controversies.

Over the following years, as scientists followed their slow methodical pace of logical studies to test hypotheses about the cause, pathophysiology, and treatment of Lyme disease, the illness was spiraling out of control, spreading rapidly in the population. Some patients did not fully respond to the standard course of antibiotics, and others who had initially responded well to the antibiotic treatment relapsed. Was this a return of the original infection, or was this a new infection from a second tick bite? Were the original antibiotics studied for Lyme disease perhaps not effective enough? Realizing that too many patients were not doing well, researchers sought more effective antibiotic treatment for patients with Lyme disease. The early recommendations of treatment with penicillin or tetracycline switched to treatment with doxycycline, amoxicillin, or ceftriaxone when they were shown to be more effective (Luft et al. 1988).

The clinical manifestations of Lyme disease were also still under investigation. Some people were developing severe flu-like symptoms in the spring and summer after a tick bite, but no rash had been seen. Nor was there evidence of arthritis or facial palsy. Could these patients have Lyme disease?

Many of the typical cases of early Lyme disease responded well after a short course of doxycycline or amoxicillin. The atypical cases, however, often did not get recognized and thus many were not treated until months or years later. These patients responded less well to standard short-course treatment. The multi-systemic abundance of symptoms seemed more entrenched and more complex to treat. Some of these patients responded with sustained remission after treatment with intravenous ceftriaxone. Others, however, relapsed or didn't respond at all (Logigian et al. 1990).

In these early years, very little was known about how to treat these patients because no research studies on patients with atypical or chronic symptoms had yet been done. Clinicians were left with little guidance and many miserable patients. Some probed the medical literature for answers. Other clinicians contacted experts in academia and the CDC to find answers, collaborating with them by sharing blood samples from severely affected patients. However, these conversations were not always cordial or helpful. Sometimes when academic researchers and community physicians conversed with one another about these patients, sharp disagreements occurred about diagnosis and treatment. It was as if these clinicians worked and lived in parallel universes.

## WHAT IS THE GREAT DIVIDE?

It is the huge chasm that has existed for decades between the experience of academic researchers, hyper-focused on studying early Lyme disease, who saw nearly all patients recover with a short course of antibiotic therapy, and the experience of physicians working in Lyme endemic areas whose practices were inundated with patients suffering from relapsing or chronic symptoms after having gotten Lyme disease. The patients risked falling into the abyss, not sure whether to trust the esteemed expert physicians with considerable research experience on early Lyme disease but very little on its more chronic forms or the local community doctor working long hours to accommodate the increasingly long list of patients desperate to be seen because of relapsing symptoms after what they were told would be "curative" treatment.

This great divide created confusion, suspicion among those who held opposing views, and even condemnation. Patients mounted protests outside medical centers and scientific conferences, enraged that they were extremely sick yet were being ignored by the academic institutions.

When symptoms recurred after initial antibiotic treatment, patients were told by some academic Lyme experts: "Your remaining or relapsing symptoms can't possibly be due to Lyme. They must be psychological or fibromyalgia or chronic fatigue syndrome." The patients countered: "I was perfectly well before I got this tick bite. Why would I suddenly develop two illnesses? Isn't it more likely that these returning symptoms—which resolved when I got treated with antibiotics the first time—might once again respond to another course of antibiotic treatment? Isn't it possible that my current symptoms are related to my recent infection?"

Many academic experts—citing the literature—argued that an initial antibiotic course of two to three weeks was curative for nearly all cases and that persistent or relapsing symptoms were rare or completely unrelated to Lyme disease. Such confident statements about cure with short-term treatment to patients who initially responded to antibiotics but then relapsed was met with bewilderment, disbelief, fear, and at times anger. Patients were further troubled and enraged because many of their treating doctors in the community who saw a reasonable rationale for trying an additional course of antibiotic treatment or switching to different antibiotics were being investigated by state medical boards for practicing outside of the medical textbook standard. Such investigations threatened the patients with the loss of their doctor and threatened the doctor with medical sanction or the loss of the ongoing license to practice medicine.

To treat patients with chronic symptoms after acute Lyme disease with repeated or longer courses of antibiotics at this time in history was challenging to say the least because it taxed the limits of medical knowledge and it put one's career as a physician in jeopardy. Those doctors willing to consider retreating patients with an additional course of antibiotics needed courage and careful clinical judgment and risk assessment as their clinical practice ventured into yet unresearched clinical territory. Due to fear of being reported to the state medical boards for providing antibiotic courses longer than the accepted standard, doctors became wary of treating Lyme disease patients. Defending one's medical judgment before a State Medical Board was both emotionally intimidating and financially costly. Many doctors chose not to accept patients into their practice who carried the diagnosis of "chronic Lyme disease." Some doctors, however, not wanting to abandon their patients and aware of published reports in peer-reviewed journals indicating that there was culture and polymerase chain reaction (PCR) evidence that infection can persist in some patients despite antibiotic therapy, argued that science was lagging far behind the clinical need, that clinical trials would take years to conduct, and that they couldn't wait for the slow pace of science to catch up (Liegner 1993; Stricker 2007). After a careful discussion of risks and benefits and of the limits of medical knowledge with their patients, these doctors offered longer and repeated course of antibiotics—either individually or in combination with other antibiotics.

Other doctors—following the guidance of academic researchers and published medical articles—were persuaded that most patients with early Lyme disease recovered after the initial course of antibiotics, that demonstration by culture of persistent infection in the human had either never been demonstrated or was extremely rare, and that additional antibiotic therapy might lead to its own possibly more serious medical complications. These physicians would inform their patients with persistent or relapsing symptoms that additional antibiotic therapy was not advisable and suggest they try symptomatic therapies or seek care elsewhere.

Both sets of doctors, after reviewing their own clinical experience and the published evidence, concluded that their recommendations were in the best interest of their patients. However, these recommendations differed quite dramatically. One set of doctors stated that an antibiotic duration of two to three weeks was sufficient, while the other set recommended antibiotic courses that might extend to many months. One set relied strongly on the accuracy of the diagnostic tests, while the other set emphasized that false negative test results do occur. Patients were confused. Which doctor's guidance should be followed?

Fortunately, science has now created a bridge that brings together the opposing viewpoints.

- Previously chronic persistent subjective symptoms after Lyme disease were not studied because these were considered rare or inconsequential. Now this symptom complex is recognized as a potentially debilitating condition with widespread effects on the nervous, immune, and rheumatologic systems.
  - While the exact prevalence is debatable, various studies demonstrate that 5 percent to 20 percent of patients experience symptom persistence and functional impairment for six months or longer (Bechtold et al. 2017; Marques 2008).
  - Among patients with persistent symptoms seeking to participate in the U.S. clinical trials of post-treatment Lyme disease, the degree of physical functional impairment among patients was recorded as severe, comparable to patients with congestive heart failure (Klempner et al. 2001). The degree of fatigue was comparable to

that experienced by individuals with multiple sclerosis, and the degree of pain was comparable to that experienced by individuals after surgery (Fallon et al. 2008). While this does not mean that most patients with post-treatment Lyme disease syndrome experience such severe symptoms and functional deficits, these results do confirm that there is a range of symptoms and of functional impairment that in some cases can be quite severe.

- Previously the laboratory testing for Lyme disease was considered adequate. Now these tests are recognized as limited, outdated, and not sufficiently informative. Researchers around the world are competing with one another to develop assays that are more sensitive in early and late Lyme disease and that provide clarity on whether infection is still present.

- Previously the suggestion that infection with *B. burgdorferi* might persist after standard courses of antibiotic treatment was considered implausible. Now the persistence of nonculturable *B. burgdorferi* spirochetes or fragments despite treatment is recognized as a fact in numerous animal models of Lyme disease. Researchers are now trying to determine whether these persistent spirochetes induce local tissue inflammation; if they do, that might account for symptoms. A study (Hodzic et al. 2014) in mice demonstrated that the host tissue modulates its cytokine expression in response to the persistent spirochetes, but there was no evidence of local tissue inflammation. This research continues.

- Previously it was thought that standard antibiotics like doxycycline and amoxicillin eradicate all *Borrelia*. Now it is recognized in the laboratory setting that these antibiotics eradicate most of the spirochetes that cause Lyme disease but not all. Identifying better antimicrobials to eradicate the "persister *Borrelia*" is currently an intense focus of investigation, as is determining whether these new antimicrobial approaches, which are effective in the lab setting, will translate into better outcomes in the animal models.

Each of these paradigm-shifting changes in perspective represents a major leap in our understanding of Lyme disease.

## WHAT ARE THE LYME WARS?

The Lyme Wars refer to a painful battle that has involved patients, doctors, researchers, and insurance companies. This battle has been waged in doctor's offices, research conferences, journal articles, courtroom hearings, and even in Washington, DC, at Senate and congressional hearings.

Briefly, the conflict centers on the following points:

- What are the signs and symptoms needed to diagnose the disease?
- How accurate are the blood tests and how does one interpret them?
- Which antibiotic and what duration of treatment are optimal?
- Do some patients with persistent symptoms have persistent infection?

These are fundamental issues in Lyme disease, not simply theoretical questions. The answers to these questions have a profound impact on patient care.

- If physicians only diagnose Lyme disease if the CDC surveillance clinical criteria with "objective" signs are met, many patients with only "subjective" symptoms will go undiagnosed and untreated.
- If Lyme disease is only treated when the blood tests are fully positive, many patients with early Lyme disease and some patients with neurologic and other later forms of Lyme disease may go untreated.
- If two to three weeks of antibiotics are declared sufficient in the treatment guidelines published by leading specialist organizations (e.g., Infectious Diseases Society of America or American Academy of Neurology), many doctors will be unwilling to treat patients with relapsing symptoms and many insurance companies will choose to decline payment for retreatment.

In response to these issues about diagnosis and treatment, polarized positions emerged.

One might ask why the medical approach to the diagnosis of Lyme disease is so subjective. Why is it based so much on clinical judgment rather than on hard facts obtained from lab test results?

The shortest answer to this question is that the most common lab tests, while helpful, are inadequate because they are based on the antibody response. In the earliest stage of Lyme disease, the antibody test is often negative. In later stages of Lyme disease after antibiotic treatment, the antibody test may stay positive for years—thus not telling us whether the infection has been fully cleared. Because we do not yet have a diagnostic test that reliably tells whether infection with *B. burgdorferi* has been eradicated at all stages of disease, both patients and doctors are left in a conundrum. Without reliable biological markers to determine whether the persistent symptoms are due to persistent infection or a postinfectious process, doctors—as in many areas of medicine—are left with an uncertain science, forced to use their best judgment to guide clinical care based on the limited evidence currently available.

Another way to view the conflict is to consider how the science of medicine develops.

- Manifestations of disease, clinical course, and outcomes are based on the most common, normative, or typical profiles of patients with the disease.
- Lab test values are based on which lower and upper limits of normal can most reliably differentiate those who are healthy from those who are sick.

In other words, since the early 1990s, after the surveillance clinical criteria were delineated by the CDC, patients who had the major objective clinical manifestations and fully positive blood tests became the focus of research and the basis of diagnostic and treatment guidelines, while outliers were often ignored. This does not mean that the outliers do not have the disease; it does mean, however, that the outliers are met with uncertainty. The typical cases are accepted into research studies, while the atypical cases are sent to find help elsewhere. The typical Lyme disease cases are seen by the academic researchers, while the atypical ones are most often evaluated and treated by the community doctors. These two groups of doctors in general see different patients, hence their experience of the disease varies accordingly.

Most research studies have been done on patients who meet the CDC surveillance criteria—that is, those with the well-accepted objective manifestations of the disease. This was an important and wise decision because researchers needed to focus their work on those individuals who with absolute certainty had Lyme disease. If they included all comers into their studies, including those with atypical or possible Lyme disease, then the heterogeneity of the patient sample might dilute the actual biologic findings so much as to diminish the ability to find significant results. By including possible or atypical cases into clinical research, these more inclusive studies would undoubtedly include individuals who do not have Lyme disease.

Because the EM rash is the most common and earliest manifestation, most researchers have focused on this presentation. This facilitates research, as other manifestations such as arthritis, meningitis, or carditis are much less common. However, it has the disadvantage that the academic research community comes to base its understanding of this illness primarily on what happens to people after treatment of the rash. The majority of people with EM who are treated early do well without long-term sequelae. But how good are these antibiotics for patients who present with the flu-like symptoms without the rash or who present with other later symptoms?

A recent Cochrane review of treatment studies of neurologic Lyme disease (Cadavid et al. 2016), for example, concluded that "there is mostly low- to very low-quality clinical evidence from a limited number of mostly small heterogeneous trials" to assess the efficacy of antibiotics for neurologic Lyme disease in Europe. The authors further state that "there is a lack of evidence" on the efficacy of antibiotics for treatment of neurologic Lyme disease in the United States. This statement does not mean that the antibiotic treatment is not essential and helpful; it does mean, however, that treatment research on neurologic Lyme disease is of limited quality and firm conclusions can't be drawn about the relative efficacy of different antibiotic strategies.

One can therefore begin to understand how this narrowed scientific focus and the limited quality of treatment studies on later stages of Lyme disease helped fuel the Lyme Wars. Academic researchers, laden with data demonstrating that the long-term outcome after the EM rash is generally quite good, couldn't understand why Lyme disease had become perceived as such a devastating and debilitating epidemic. Clinicians in the community who were treating patients with these more chronic and sometimes quite severe sequelae could not understand why the academic community was treating this disease so lightly.

Some researchers and research-oriented clinicians have focused on the later stages of the disease—such as those with Lyme arthritis or those with persistent or relapsing symptoms despite antibiotic treatment. Later chapters in this book present some of the findings from these research groups.

## Narrow Spectrum for Lyme Diagnosis—CDC Surveillance Criteria

The objective, verifiable clinical criteria used to confirm cases for CDC surveillance, while essential for monitoring the course of disease over time for public health surveillance, have limitations when applied rigidly in the clinical setting where clinicians encounter patients who do not necessarily recall or have these "objective" markers.

- In a prospective study of individuals given placebo or a Lyme vaccine, about 18 percent of patients with new Lyme disease infections presented with a flu-like illness but did not have any "objective" signs such as the rash (Steere and Sikand 2003). These patients instead presented with marked fatigue, muscle pains, and headaches. Had these patients not been enrolled in a prospective study that required repeated serologic tests for Lyme disease to detect seroconversion (i.e., negative initial tests turning positive), these patients might easily have been diagnosed as having a viral illness. None of the clinical criteria required for a CDC surveillance case were present because none had developed "objective" externally visible signs of Lyme disease.

As noted in that *New England Journal of Medicine* report, "Particularly when *erythema migrans* is not present early in the illness, patients may not go to a physician or Lyme disease may not be recognized until the more debilitating, harder-to-treat late manifestations of the infection become apparent."

- In late-stage neurologic Lyme disease, one of the manifestations is a mild to moderate encephalopathy, which includes nonspecific symptoms of memory problems and fatigue. This manifestation of Lyme disease is also not included in the CDC surveillance case definition.

Physicians evaluating individuals presenting with either of these clinical syndromes—the sudden flu-like illness after tick exposure or the mild to moderate cognitive impairment in an individual without other known etiology—might not even include Lyme disease in the differential diagnosis if they rely exclusively on the CDC surveillance criteria as a set of comprehensive diagnostic criteria. Even if this patient is shown to have a positive blood test for Lyme disease, the physician may dismiss this finding either as a "false positive" or as insignificant and unrelated to that patient's current symptoms because the clinical manifestations fall outside of the CDC's objective clinical signs of a surveillance case.

What is the CDC's position on the use of their surveillance criteria for clinical care? The CDC recognizes that there are clinical manifestations of Lyme disease that fall outside of the narrow criteria used for the case definition. For over two decades, the CDC's website for the surveillance criteria has stated:

> This surveillance case definition was developed for national reporting of Lyme disease; it is not intended to be used in clinical diagnosis.

How many physicians in the community know this? How many medical reviewers for health insurance companies or managed care agencies acknowledge this when reviewing patient histories that do not meet the surveillance criteria?

At times the CDC has been inappropriately vilified for these narrow surveillance criteria. Why? Patient advocates are aware that these CDC surveillance criteria are being inappropriately used by some health insurance companies to deny coverage for Lyme disease treatment to patients. They also recognize that those without the more visible signs of Lyme disease may have gone undiagnosed by their health care provider. Inappropriate application of the narrow CDC surveillance criteria to diagnosis in the clinical setting or reimbursement in the insurance setting has fueled the Lyme Wars.

In 2008 the CDC modified their 1996 case definition by adding two new clinical categories. These would not be considered "confirmed" cases, but they would be counted for national surveillance.

### *"Suspected" Lyme disease* includes:

- a case of EM with no known exposure and no laboratory evidence of infection.
- a case with laboratory evidence of infection but no clinical history is available.

### *"Probable" Lyme disease* includes:

- any case of physician-diagnosed Lyme disease that has laboratory antibody evidence of infection using established criteria.

In summary, the narrow clinical criteria for surveillance that are important and necessary to objectively monitor disease incidence over time are not comprehensive enough to encompass all manifestations of this illness. Unfortunately, this surveillance case definition has caused confusion and controversy among physicians and patients regarding who should be diagnosed with and treated for Lyme disease.

Physicians who diagnose Lyme disease using a broader set of criteria without external clinical or laboratory verification risk exposing patients to unnecessary courses of antibiotic therapy and of misleading patients into a treatment path that does not address the actual problem; delay of correct diagnosis of another disease can be quite harmful. On the other hand, physicians who rely exclusively on these narrow CDC surveillance criteria for clinical diagnosis may fail to correctly diagnose some patients who present with less typical manifestations and do in fact have Lyme disease. In this situation antibiotic treatment may be delayed or absent altogether, resulting in unnecessary and possibly prolonged pain and disability. If detected and treated shortly after initial infection, Lyme disease in most individuals resolves with a short course of antibiotic treatment; however, delay in initiating antibiotic treatment is problematic. When treatment is initiated many months after infection, the symptoms that develop are generally less responsive to standard courses of treatment.

## Broader Symptom Spectrum for Lyme Diagnosis

With an awareness that the narrow CDC criteria are appropriate for national surveillance but not appropriate as the sole basis for clinical decision making in individual cases, some physicians use a broader, more inclusive set of clinical criteria for the diagnosis of Lyme disease. This group of doctors, after conducting a careful physical exam, collecting history of exposure to Lyme endemic areas, examining blood test results, and ruling out other possible causes of the patient's symptoms, may diagnose the patient as having "possible Lyme disease." In their judgment, the diagnosis is tentative but there is sufficient exposure history and clinical evidence to support the possibility of Lyme disease as the cause for the multiple symptoms of the patient. In this case, the physician explains that the diagnosis is not definitive and reviews the potential benefits and risks of treatment with the patient. These physicians recognize that Lyme disease can present in a variety of ways and will treat patients whose symptoms may not fit the narrower CDC surveillance guidelines.

While recognizing that there are significant risks associated with antibiotic treatment, particularly when administered intravenously, these physicians argue that the threat of serious physical, cognitive, and functional problems associated with long-term untreated Lyme disease infection outweighs the risks of antibiotic therapy. However, by taking this broader, more inclusive approach to diagnosis and treatment, it is likely that these physicians will treat some patients with antibiotics who do not have Lyme disease.

When a patient diagnosed with "possible Lyme disease" fails to improve after antibiotic treatment, the diagnosis should be reconsidered. An unwavering focus by the physician (or the patient) on Lyme disease as the diagnostic explanation for ongoing symptoms—even in the absence of improvement with antibiotics—can be harmful because other causes of the patient's ongoing symptoms may be ignored.

## Overdiagnosis versus Underdiagnosis

Is Lyme disease underdiagnosed or overdiagnosed? Both are occurring.

- When doctors fail to apply good clinical judgment in the interpretation of highly suggestive serologic tests (e.g., four bands on the IgG Western blot) in a patient with high probability of Lyme disease based on clinical history and exposure or when they fail to consider the possibility of new-onset Lyme disease in a patient from a Lyme endemic area who presents with prolonged flu-like symptoms during spring or early summer months without having noticed a tick bite or rash, it is likely that these doctors risk not treating someone who may well have Lyme disease.

- Conversely, when doctors fail to apply good clinical judgment in the interpretation of indeterminate serologic tests in the face of a patient from a Lyme endemic area with a set of symptoms not linked to Lyme disease (e.g., rhinitis) or with suggestive but extremely common symptoms with a broad differential diagnosis that have not been fully evaluated or treated (e.g., fatigue, depression, memory problems), this may be a situation of misdiagnosis of Lyme disease. Overdiagnosis might also be seen if a patient is given a diagnosis of Lyme disease but has had no known tick bites or EM rash and no known exposure to a region with *Ixodes* ticks, yet presents with typical Lyme disease symptoms that are also shared by other diseases (e.g., arthralgias, numbness/tingling, diffuse pain) or has weakly suggestive tests (e.g., a single positive IgM Western blot or enzyme-linked immunosorbent assay [ELISA]).

Misdiagnosis is a problem—whether it is overdiagnosis or underdiagnosis—because in each case the consequences can be serious. However, doctors often work in the setting of uncertainty and thus misdiagnoses will occur. In situations in which the diagnosis is tentative and a treatment course is initiated, physicians who follow their patients carefully and thoughtfully will reevaluate the initial diagnosis if the patient is not improving in the expected timeframe.

Referring to differences in diagnostic rigor when conducting epidemiologic surveillance versus the hands-on clinical situation in the individual doctor's office, a leading scientist from the Vector-Borne Disease branch of the CDC stated the following:

> A clinical diagnosis is made for the purpose of treating an individual patient and should consider the many details associated with that patient's illness. Surveillance case definitions are created for the purpose of standardization, not patient care; they exist so that health officials can reasonably compare the number and distribution of "cases" over space and time. Whereas physicians appropriately err on the side of overdiagnosis, thereby assuring they don't miss a case, surveillance case definitions appropriately err on the side of specificity, thereby assuring that they do not inadvertently capture illnesses due to other conditions. (Mead 2004)

## HOW HAVE PATIENTS RESPONDED TO THESE MEDICAL UNCERTAINTIES?

The introductory quote to this chapter documents one doctor's reaction to a mother trying to alert the health authorities of the State of Connecticut that a strange illness was afflicting the children in her town. Why was this doctor so hostile to his own patient? Perhaps this was an atypical reaction from an overworked physician frustrated at not being able to figure out what was wrong with his patient. Or perhaps this physician felt that this patient was uppity and not acting as a patient should. This is reminiscent of the parental dictum, "children are to be seen but not heard." Are patients not allowed to have a voice? Are patients meant to be collaborators in their own care or passive, dependent recipients of the wisdom transmitted by medically educated experts? In retrospect, all would agree that the two mothers who first reported the outbreak of Lyme disease—Polly Murray and Judith Mensch—deserve immense gratitude for their perceptiveness, persistence, and insistence on being heard.

As the disease spread and as more patients' lives were profoundly disrupted by this illness, patients wanted to know what was being done to help them. Faced with few answers and doctors who dismissed their concerns, patients became alarmed and angry and began to mobilize. They started support groups to educate and support one another. They wrote books and made documentary films. They started local, state, and national organizations. They organized national medical conferences for

While the patient community has not always been correct in their understanding of the complexities of the science and the approach of some individuals and groups has at times been stridently confrontational, causing increased distance between the "stakeholders," many of their efforts have borne fruit over the years. Coordinated patient and legislative efforts have reduced insurance coverage denials for Lyme disease treatment, have enhanced congressional attention and funding on the problem of Lyme disease, and have helped to shape the direction of research on the federal level.

## Patient and Nonprofit Foundation Funding of Research

"How can we educate our doctors about Lyme disease? They don't seem to want to listen to us. They seem annoyed when we bring in articles. They only listen to what they hear from the Lyme research experts in their hospital and professional organization.

"Why do doctors turn away from us? Some doctors dismiss us as 'antibiotic seekers'—acting as if our goal in life is to be on antibiotics! We don't care what helps us to get well. We just want to get well."

These were questions often asked and statements often made by Lyme disease patients.

In response, patients were told that health care providers are taught to base their clinical decisions on evidence derived from carefully conducted, well-controlled research studies published in top medical journals. Uncontrolled studies are hard to interpret. Studies published in less well-known journals are viewed with skepticism. If an article has passed peer review in a prominent medical journal, its results and conclusions are given considerable weight by the medical community.

The patients then asked, "Then why aren't the researchers conducting studies on the problem of persistent symptoms? What is stopping them?"

Patients were told that federal grants were quite hard to get; only about 6 to 10 percent of grants get funded by the NIH. Promising proposals that addressed "controversial" areas might be passed over for funding in favor of more traditional proposals. Patients probed further and learned that there might be bias in the NIH research committee reviewers. They learned that only researchers already funded by the NIH could serve on the grant review committees and that often both grant applicants and research reviewers were competing for the same pool of money. Many of these review committee members are either basic scientists with little or no clinical exposure to patients or experts on early Lyme disease who felt chronic persistent symptoms after Lyme disease were either too rare or too insignificant to commit NIH funds to study. Hence studies submitted for consideration for funding that focused on the problem of chronic symptoms might get scored poorly by these NIH review committee members. Even if two of the three primary reviewers on an NIH committee strongly favored the grant, the one dissenting voice would kill that grant proposal's chance of getting funded.

What did the patients do? They decided to act. "If the NIH won't fund them, then let's create our own funding mechanism to support top research scientists in their work. If medical research published in top journals is the way to answer questions and change medical paradigms, then let's fund researchers who are willing to take on this challenge." And that's what they did.

Over the past twenty years, a multitude of organizations have raised funds and supported medical research on Lyme disease. They have done this in two ways: by helping to establish Lyme centers at academic medical centers and by directly funding research studies.

Three research centers focused on Lyme disease have been established with their support, including centers at Columbia University Medical Center in New York, Johns Hopkins Medical Center in Maryland, and the Spaulding Rehabilitation Hospital, which is affiliated with Harvard Medical School in Massachusetts.

In the United States, these nonprofit patient organizations and private donors have committed over fifty million dollars to support Lyme and tick-borne diseases research. Research has been supported throughout the country by a variety of organizations, including the Lyme Disease Foundation, the Lyme Disease Association, Global Lyme Alliance, the National Research Fund for Tick-Borne Diseases, the Steven and Alexandra Cohen Foundation, the Bay Area Lyme Foundation, Stand4Lyme, and many others.

Initially some medical researchers were wary of accepting funds from these patient-organized Lyme associations. They feared that their reputations as unbiased independent researchers would be tarnished by accepting funds. They suspected that the funding organization might discourage them from publishing results that went against the organization's preconceived beliefs. Such fears proved unfounded.

Now researchers from throughout the United States and other countries compete with each other to receive grant support from these organizations. Why? The patient organizations wanted answers and the highest quality science. They urged publication without vetting or preapproval by the funding organization. In other words, "Let the results fall where they may."

This research has been published in prestigious peer-reviewed journals such as *Clinical Infectious Disease, Plos-One, Neurology, JAMA, Emerging Infectious Disease, Infection and Immunity, Journal of Clinical Microbiology, PNAS, Journal of Immunology,* and *Neurobiology of Disease.* The grant recipients include researchers at Harvard, Columbia, Johns Hopkins, Stanford, UC Davis, Rutgers, New York Medical College, Stonybrook, Brown, Mt. Sinai Medical Center, Virginia Commonwealth University, the University of Connecticut, UC San Francisco, the University of New Haven, Fox Chase Cancer Center, Northeastern University, and many others.

Funding support by these organizations has brought experts from other medical fields into the Lyme research arena, including experts in diagnostics, therapeutics, genomics, metabolomics, and proteomics. Precision medicine experts have set their sights on the problem of Lyme disease partly because of the availability of funding support by these generous donors and Lyme organizations.

In conclusion, patients have made a huge difference on many fronts in advancing research efforts to conquer this disease.

## HOW HAVE PHYSICIAN ASSOCIATIONS RESPONDED? ILADS VERSUS IDSA

The Infectious Diseases Society of America (IDSA) is a large organization of over nine thousand members founded in 1963 and composed primarily of physicians and scientists with specialty training in infectious disease.

In 2000, the IDSA published their first edition of guidelines for the diagnosis and treatment of Lyme and other tick-borne diseases in the society's journal, *Clinical Infectious Diseases* (Wormser et al. 2000). In 2006, the guidelines were revised (Wormser et al. 2006); an updated set of guidelines is expected in the near future. The IDSA's position statements on Lyme disease are followed closely by the CDC, funding agencies, and infectious disease societies in countries throughout the world. Other specialty organizations endorse the IDSA treatment guidelines, including the American Academy of Neurology and the American Academy of Pediatrics. The IDSA's treatment guidelines are available on the Internet.

The International Lyme and Associated Diseases Society (ILADS) is an international multidisciplinary medical society dedicated to promoting understanding of Lyme and other tick-borne disease through education. They published their first set of guidelines on the diagnosis and treatment of Lyme disease in 2004 and a second edition in 2014 in *Expert Review of Anti-Infective Therapy* (Cameron, Johnson, and Maloney 2014). A summary of their guidelines is available on the National Guidelines Clearinghouse website. ILADS hosts annual educational conferences in the United States and Europe.

These two organizations represent two different approaches to the diagnosis and treatment of Lyme disease. In the popular press, these two organizations have been referred to as leaders of the two camps in the Lyme Wars. Their positions can be briefly summarized as follows:

- The IDSA, the primary medical voice for the "conventional camp," recommends shorter-duration treatment of Lyme disease for ten to twenty-eight days and emphasizes the importance of objective criteria for diagnosis. The IDSA supports their recommendations by reference to published controlled studies. The IDSA recognizes that a minority of patients treated for Lyme disease go on to develop persistent relapsing symptoms (post-treatment Lyme disease syndrome); in 2006, they recommended against repeated or longer-term antibiotic therapy for these patients because they viewed the controlled trials as not providing sufficient evidence of benefit to justify the risk.
- The ILADS, the primary medical voice for the "alternative camp," recommends variable duration antibiotic treatment of Lyme disease based

on patient response and supports the use of more flexible guidelines to establish a clinical diagnosis. The ILADS also references published studies, but argues that there is insufficient high-quality published data for the later chronic stages of illness to formulate clear guidelines. Due to insufficient published evidence to justify not providing treatment and due to persistent suffering without other explanation, ILADS supports the use of repeated antibiotic therapies for patients with persistent symptoms. When there are few manifestations of disease, minimal quality of life impairments, and no evidence of disease progression, continued observation of the patient is recommended as an option.

The ILADS and IDSA guidelines and their contentious conflicts with each other have been well publicized and information for the interested reader on their positions is widely available in published journals, books, and on the Internet (Auwaerter et al. 2011; Lantos et al. 2010; Johnson and Stricker 2010, 2004; Weintraub 2013; Edlow 2004).

The battle between the two organizations or camps over the years has at times been quite hostile and disturbing, as each fears the other is putting the patients and public at risk. Leaders of these organizations at times take entrenched positions, refusing to budge, focusing on absolutes rather than acknowledging the areas of uncertainty, selectively pulling journal articles from the published literature that favor their position and not presenting those articles that suggest otherwise.

When members from either of the opposing camps present extreme views that represent only partial truths that serve to bolster their argument, the net result is to create distrust and confusion such that dialog is diminished and science is subverted. Patients who are not trained in the critical appraisal of scientific evidence can be easily misled.

In Lyme endemic communities, some physicians select a third approach to these treatment questions. Faced with a patient with persistent or relapsing symptoms with a good history of Lyme disease, these doctors might choose to provide a repeated course of antibiotics, switch to an antibiotic with a different mode of action, or extend treatment a few weeks longer than the IDSA guidelines but shorter than generally practiced by doctors affiliated with ILADS. These doctors—including infectious disease specialists who are members of the IDSA—would argue that

THE LYME WARS [1]
*The Lyme-disease infection rate is growing.*
*So is the battle over how to treat it.*

Still Lots of Unknowns [2] Associated with Lyme Disease

Drawing the lines in the Lyme disease battle [3]
Angry patients question treatment - or lack of it - yet with tests often inconclusive, some doctors think the condition is overdiagnosed. And the split is widening.

A big dispute behind a tiny tick bite: What to call [4] the lingering effects of Lyme disease?

Antibiotics Are Not [5] the Cure for 'Chronic' Lyme Symptoms

Is Chronic [6] Lyme Disease a Real Thing?

FIGURE 5.2

Media articles highlight Lyme controversies. (1. *The New Yorker,* July 1, 2013; 2. *New York Times,* August 11, 2013; 3. *Boston Globe,* June 2, 2013; 4. *Washington Post,* September 15, 2014; 5. *New York Times,* August 11, 2013; 6. *Healthline News,* September 15, 2014.)

guidelines are not meant to be the final word on clinical practice and that there may be certain patients whose course requires a more individualized treatment plan. This more personalized approach has not been well studied. The treatment chapter reviews what is known about the treatment of patients with persistent symptoms.

## Chronic Lyme Disease and Post-Treatment Lyme Disease Syndrome

Words matter. Although the term "chronic Lyme disease" was in common use in the 1990s in both academic and community settings to describe patients with persistent symptoms, the term itself has more recently become a bone of contention. Because the term seems to imply that Lyme disease may become a chronic infection, the IDSA avoids using this term. While members of both camps agree that patients with chronic symptoms after standard treatment for Lyme disease do exist, the prevalence of such patients and the cause of such symptoms is a matter of rancorous debate.

Various studies indicate that approximately 5 to 20 percent of patients who are treated for Lyme disease at the time of EM with the recommended two- to four-week course of antibiotics continue to have symptoms such as fatigue and joint or muscle pain, and functional impairment (Aucott, Crowder, and Kortee 2013; Marques 2008; Weitzner et al. 2015). Among patients with disseminated manifestations, such as neurologic Lyme disease, the percentage of patients with chronic symptoms is higher (Vrethem et al. 2002). These symptoms may be mild to moderate, may persist for months to years, and in a subgroup of cases are accompanied by functional disability.

- In one set of controlled studies of European neuroborreliosis assessed 2.5 years after treatment, moderate or more severe levels of fatigue occurred in 42 percent of patients and objective findings of neurologic deficit and/or neurocognitive impairment occurred in 36 percent of patients (Eikeland et al. 2011, 2012, 2013).
- A review of forty-four Lyme neuroborreliosis studies concluded that approximately 28 percent of patients experience residual symptoms, but impact on functioning was unclear (Dersch et al. 2016).
- In a long-term clinical outcome study of Lyme neuroborreliosis in childhood (Skogman et al. 2012), after a median of 5 years, 19 percent had "definite" mild objective neurologic sequelae, most often persistent facial nerve palsy and less often motor or sensory deficits. The functional and symptom outcomes were favorable however; compared to controls, the children with Lyme neuroborreliosis did not have significantly different school performance, activity levels, or subjective symptoms of headache, fatigue, or cognitive symptoms.

The exact cause of persistent symptoms such as fatigue and cognitive impairment is unknown. Some experts believe that the symptoms are due to residual damage from the original infection or a postinfectious process, such as the lingering effects of the previous infection on the tissues and immune system, while others believe that these symptoms reflect persistent residual infection with *B. burgdorferi*.

The term "post-treatment Lyme disease syndrome (PTLDS)" is preferred by many in the academic medical community because the pathophysiology is unknown (hence it is called a "syndrome"); as a syndrome, PTLDS encompasses the multiple reasons why patients may have persistent symptoms. The provisional criteria for PTLDS requires that the persistent symptoms develop within six months of diagnosis and treatment and that the narrower set of CDC surveillance criteria with objective markers are met at disease onset (e.g., the EM rash or arthritis) (Wormser et al. 2006). The designation of PTLDS should not be applied to an individual who has another concurrent or pre-Lyme disease medical or psychiatric condition that might better explain the ongoing symptoms.

The term "chronic Lyme disease" is more confusing than PTLDS as it is used differently by different groups.

- When patients use the term "chronic Lyme disease," they are often referring to the array of symptoms that emerged and persisted after Lyme disease regardless of the cause.
- When physicians use the term "chronic Lyme disease," they may be using the term in one of three ways based on their understanding of the cause of the symptoms.
  - *Unrelated to Lyme disease and due to another cause.* Physicians adhering to the IDSA terminology use this term to refer to those patients with symptoms of unknown cause who believe they have Lyme disease but who do not have good evidence of ever having had it. The patients identifying themselves as having "chronic Lyme disease" never had typical signs of clinical Lyme disease based on the CDC surveillance criteria and never had positive results on the two-tier Lyme disease assay; these patients therefore would not meet the more precise criteria for PTLDS. These patients are recognized as being sick and needing help, but the etiology of the sickness is not considered to be related to Lyme disease.
  - *Related to infectious or post-infectious causes from possible or definite past Lyme disease.* Health care providers not adhering to the IDSA terminology use the term chronic Lyme disease much the same as the patients do. The term would encompass those who have subjective symptoms common among patients with Lyme

disease but who may or may not have ever had positive blood tests or any of the objective clinical signs of prior Lyme disease. In this usage, chronic Lyme disease includes: a) symptomatic individuals with a past history of well-documented treated Lyme disease; or b) individuals with suggestive but not definitive evidence of prior infection ("possible or probable Lyme disease"). From this perspective, the term "chronic Lyme disease" is much broader than the term "post-treatment Lyme disease syndrome." It is more inclusive because it includes anyone with persistent symptoms after treatment who a physician thinks may have had Lyme disease, regardless of the strength of the serologic evidence or characteristic clinical signs; it is thus much less precise than PTLDS and will include some patients who may never have had Lyme disease. Among this group of health providers, there is acceptance that chronic symptoms may be due to either infectious or post-infectious processes.

○ *Related to persistent infection with B. burgdorferi.* On the other end of the spectrum, some physicians are persuaded that the vast majority of patients with chronic symptoms that persist after treatment for Lyme disease have chronic infection. While they recognize that immune processes are involved, they argue that the only rational cause for persistent symptoms is persistent infection with *B. burgdorferi.* Accordingly, among these physicians, the treatment of choice for persistent symptoms is antibiotics. The term "chronic Lyme disease" when used by these physicians carries the implicit assumption of chronic persistent infection.

While the term "chronic Lyme disease" is preferred by many patients in the community and by some of the community doctors who treat them, the lack of clarity regarding what defines chronic Lyme disease and the diversity of opinions on this issue create problems for diagnosis and treatment planning. For research purposes, when scientific questions are being addressed, it is critical to have well-defined patient groups. For this reason, the predominance of academic research on individuals with chronic symptoms has been focused on those who have post-treatment Lyme disease syndrome.

## Conflicts over How Strongly to Weigh Positive Blood Test Results

When the diagnostic net is cast so widely as to include patients who are quite unlikely to have Lyme disease, the clinician will have a much harder time trying to interpret blood test results. While it may not be obvious, serologic testing will yield more false positives when it is more broadly ordered among patients who are less likely to have Lyme disease. The fact that the interpretation of test results varies depending upon context is a concept that is extremely hard for the patient community and even some medical professionals to understand. The logical assumption is that the value of a blood test is the same regardless of who is tested or where that person comes from. If the latter weren't true, what good is the test?

The perfect test of the future would be 100 percent reliable all the time—no false positives and no false negatives. A test that has no false positives would have 100 percent specificity. A test that has no false negatives would have 100 percent sensitivity.

Perfection is not the case with Lyme disease tests, nor is it the case with most tests used by doctors to help guide clinical decisions. As a result, the "predictive value" of a test is heavily shaped by context. The predictive value of a positive test refers to the likelihood that an individual with a positive test result truly has the disease. Consider the following examples.

- The accuracy of the prostate-specific antigen assay as a screen for prostate cancer improves dramatically if the man being tested is over age sixty rather than between ages forty and sixty; this is because prostate cancer is so much more common in older men. Other parameters—in this case age—affect the probability that a positive test result is indeed indicative of prostate cancer. False positives might occur in a younger person because of prostate inflammation, for example, and not cancer cells.

- The same is true for Lyme disease. A positive test result for Lyme disease is more likely to be a true positive if the patient with new onset summer flu-like symptoms comes from a Lyme endemic area where perhaps 20 percent of the population has been exposed than if the patient comes from an area where Lyme disease is extremely rare and less than 0.5 percent of the population has ever been exposed.

- Similarly, a positive test for Lyme disease from someone in a Lyme endemic area is more likely to be a true positive if the patient being tested has a cluster of symptoms and signs quite characteristic of Lyme disease (e.g., multisystemic symptoms affecting the joints, muscles, and peripheral nerves) than if the person has only one such symptom.

Why would this be? This is a time when the frequency of disease in the population and a clinician's history taking, clinical exam, and medical judgment play a paramount role in increasing the likelihood that a test result will be a true positive. Consider the following two scenarios.

Assume that we have a test for Lyme disease that is excellent: it can detect a true case 99 percent of the time (i.e., sensitivity is 99 percent) and it incorrectly identifies a healthy person as having Lyme disease only 1 percent of the time (i.e., specificity is 99 percent).

*Scenario 1:* If the actual prevalence of Lyme disease in the population being tested is 50 percent, there is a 99 percent likelihood that a positive test is accurately identifying a person who has the disease.

*Scenario 2:* If the actual prevalence of Lyme disease in the population being tested is much lower (e.g., only 1 percent), there is only a 50 percent chance that the positive test is accurately identifying a person who has Lyme disease.

One might then conclude that a test that provides a 50/50 chance that a positive result is a true positive is a useless test. However, in this scenario in which the test had previously been shown to be 99 percent sensitive and 99 percent specific, that would be an erroneous conclusion. The test itself is clearly not useless; it is being misused. In other words, if a test is ordered on patients who are extremely unlikely to have Lyme disease based on symptoms and exposure history, this serologic test will yield hard to interpret results; the low prevalence rate of Lyme disease in these tested patients would lead to more false positives. On the other hand, if the serologic test is ordered based on a characteristic set of symptoms and exposure history suggesting the diagnosis, the prevalence of Lyme disease in the population being tested will be much higher than in the general population and thus a positive test result would more likely be a true positive. The clinician's clinical judgment and the base rate of infection in the community both matter because each contributes substantially to the predictive value of a test.

In the case of Lyme disease, as in all diseases, doctors typically don't order tests randomly just to see what might come up, and they don't order tests for Lyme disease on healthy people from the general population. Rather, they order tests on sick patients who are suspected of having Lyme disease based on their symptoms, history, and risk factors. This clinical process enhances the "pre-test probability" of having a disease. In other words, the clinician considers the following in the differential diagnosis: "In my best judgment as a clinician, given all that I know about this patient and about the geographic area to which this patient has been exposed, how likely is it that this patient actually has Lyme disease?"

Pre-test probability will be higher when the individual's clinical profile closely matches the typical clinical features of Lyme disease and when the individual's risk of recent exposure to *Ixodes* ticks is high. When these two criteria are met, the Lyme disease test will be much more likely to provide valuable information. Pre-test probability will be much lower if a patient has fewer signs or symptoms typical of Lyme disease and if the history of exposure to *Ixodes* ticks is minimal; in this clinical scenario of "low pre-test probability," the Lyme disease test will be more likely to give misleading results.

In other words, a positive Lyme test result in a patient whose exposure to *Ixodes* ticks is extremely low will more likely represent a false positive than a true positive. The likelihood that this positive test is a true positive, however, would dramatically increase if the patient had a recent *Ixodes* tick bite (or had recently returned from hiking in a Lyme endemic area) followed by the typical signs and symptoms of Lyme disease.

## Conflicts over How Strongly to Weigh Negative Test Results

Does a negative antibody test result indicate that a patient has not been infected with the spirochete that causes Lyme disease? In early Lyme disease, the answer is clearly no. The current antibody-based tests are insensitive at the earliest stages, with false negative results occurring 50 to 65 percent of the time. In contrast, in later stages of Lyme disease, a negative test is more likely to be an accurate true negative test. This is because in later stages of disease, the antibody-based tests have higher sensitivity.

But even at the later disseminated stages of illness, some patients may test negative on the serum antibody tests but have other evidence suggestive of active infection with *B. burgdorferi* (Holl-Wieden, Suerbaum, and Girschick 2007; Coyle et al. 1995). For example, in early neurologic Lyme disease, it has been estimated that 10 to 30 percent of patients test negative on the CDC-recommended two-tiered diagnostic assay (Dressler et al. 1993; Aguero-Rosenfeld et al. 2005; Marques 2015). This means that some patients with neurologic Lyme disease (e.g., meningitis or cranial nerve palsy) may not be given antibiotics because of an inadequately sensitive serologic assay for Lyme disease. That the diagnosis of neurologic Lyme disease may be missed based on a false negative blood test is highly problematic. For cases of meningitis, the clinician might understandably but incorrectly conclude that the patient has a viral meningitis that should not be treated with antibiotics. (Among these patients with early neurologic manifestations, many patients with initially negative tests will develop positive results if retested six weeks later.)

Proof of Lyme disease among these individuals who are negative on the two-tiered approach to testing may be hard to obtain, but occasionally one may get confirmation from other positive tests such as other antibody-based tests (C6 peptide ELISA or an IgG Western blot [even though the ELISA is negative]), a PCR assay for *Borrelia* DNA, or growth of the organism in culture. Experimental or newer tests (for example, tests of immune complexes or of *Borrelia* specific proteins) may also prove informative.

If the patient's serum is negative for antibodies against Lyme disease, examining the spinal fluid may also be helpful when there are central nervous system symptoms. In a study of eighteen patients with late neurologic Lyme disease (memory impairment—Lyme encephalopathy), on average six years after the initial Lyme disease infection (Logigian, Kaplan, and Steere 1999) three were negative for Lyme antibodies in the blood (both ELISA and Western blot) but their spinal fluid analysis showed evidence of past or current *B. burgdorferi* infection, as evidenced by antibody production or the presence of spirochetal DNA. In this sample of patients with late neurologic Lyme disease, 16.7 percent had negative blood tests. Had the

**CASE 7.** A Case of Seronegative Lyme Disease with Central Neurologic Invasion (Lawrence et al. 1995)

The following case report describes an unusual but well-documented case of an individual with seronegative Lyme disease.

A fifty-eight-year-old previously healthy woman developed a relapsing remitting central nervous system disorder with involvement of multiple peripheral and cranial nerves. Standard antibody-based tests of the serum were initially negative for Lyme disease, but cerebrospinal fluid tests on multiple occasions were positive. For example, the spinal fluid analysis revealed: a) PCR positive for *B. burgdorferi*–specific DNA at three different labs; b) positive for *B. burgdorferi* protein; and c) positive for complexed *B. burgdorferi* antibodies. As a result, this woman was diagnosed as having seronegative chronic relapsing neuroborreliosis.

Antibiotic treatment led to improvement or stabilization of her symptoms. After initiation of antibiotics, she often experienced a flare of symptoms characterized by fever, worsening motor deficits, and acute cognitive problems; this flare was thought to represent an inflammatory response to the killing of spirochetes (i.e., a Jarisch-Herxheimer reaction). Each relapse of symptoms led to a new course of antibiotics, therapeutic response, and a temporary arrest of neurologic deterioration.

Comment. One of the strengths of this unusual report is that positive PCR assays for *B. burgdorferi* DNA after antibiotic therapy were conducted independently at three well-respected research labs. In addition, after dissociation of the immune complexes, antibodies to *B. burgdorferi* antigens were demonstrated; cerebrospinal fluid *B. burgdorferi* antigen was also demonstrated in seven different spinal fluid taps over the course of five years. While this case is certainly not common, it highlights that seronegativity can occur and that the course of illness can be relapsing remitting. Clearly there are a variety of factors that may impact why most people get better after antibiotic treatment and some others do not. In this particular case, possibly unique attributes of this woman's immune response or of the microbe itself may have contributed to the chronic relapsing remitting course.

spinal tap not been done, a clinician might not have prescribed the intravenous antibiotic therapy. Although this study did not have a control comparison group, the one- to two-year follow up on the eighteen patients in this study after the initial one month of intravenous ceftriaxone treatment, revealed that sixteen of eighteen benefited substantially from retreatment: 50 percent were greatly improved and 39 percent were "back to normal."

While patients exposed to Lyme endemic areas can have Lyme disease but test negative on the antibody tests, the exact frequency of seronegative Lyme disease among untreated patients after the first month of infection is hard to determine. If a patient's serum tests negative for Lyme disease, considerable effort by the physician should be made to rule out other possible causes of the patient's symptoms. To assume the diagnosis of Lyme disease in the absence of confirmatory or strongly suggestive tests is risky, as it may delay detection of another as yet unrecognized cause of the patient's symptoms. When clinical suspicion is high that Lyme disease is the cause but serologic tests are indeterminate, clinicians at times do provide an empiric course of antibiotic therapy. If the patient's symptoms improve after antibiotic therapy, one can state that the patient appears to have an antibiotic-responsive illness that may or may not have been Lyme disease. Without specific confirmatory tests, however, definitive diagnoses cannot be made. This situation, however, is not uncommon in other areas of clinical medicine in which the cumulative evidence is convincing enough to recommend treatment even if the diagnosis is not absolutely certain.

Physicians following the IDSA guidelines tend to adhere closely to the actual test results using the CDC surveillance criteria for diagnosis, erring on the side of not exposing patients who do not have Lyme disease to unnecessary and potentially harmful antibiotic therapy. Physicians following the ILADS guidelines rely more on a clinical diagnosis, pointing to the problem of false negative test results and following their clinical hunch more closely, erring on the side of not failing to treat someone who might in fact have Lyme disease.

## Conflicts over the Possibility of Persistent Infection

Another major controversy that has fueled the Lyme Wars is whether infection with *B. burgdorferi* can persist despite antibiotic therapy. If the

*Borrelia* persist, then there is a biologic rationale for an additional course of antibiotic therapy if symptoms reemerge after initial treatment.

Animal models of Lyme disease confirm that infection can persist despite antibiotic therapy (Hodzic et al. 2008, 2014; Embers et al. 2012), although the remaining spirochetes do not grow in culture. In a study of rhesus macaques (Embers 2012), evidence of *B. burgdorferi* in cardiac and other tissues was found despite prior antibiotic therapy. In addition, inflammation was seen in the cardiac tissue of three previously treated, young, otherwise healthy monkeys; this raises the possibility that the inflammation may have been induced by persistent *B. burgdorferi* infection. Whether the persistent *Borrelia* in the animal models actually cause disease remains an open question that is currently under investigation.

Occasionally, reports have been published demonstrating *Borrelia* persistence in humans despite the standard course of antibiotic treatment for Lyme disease (Hunfeld 2005). For example, in two case series from Europe, Strle and colleagues (1993, 1996) examined patients treated with oral antibiotics for *Borrelia* culture-positive EM; in each report, two months after initiating treatment, *B. burgdorferi* spirochetes were isolated from normal appearing skin at the site of the previous EM rash—from five of twenty-eight treated patients in the first study and from two of one hundred treated patients in the second study.

In laboratory-based studies in which Lyme spirochetes are grown in culture, spirochetes are mainly in a spiral form during the growth phase, but they transform to other shapes (e.g., round bodies or microcolonies) in older, stationary phase cultures or when exposed to stressors such as antibiotics or heat. A recent set of in vitro studies (Feng et al. 2016; Sharma et al. 2015) demonstrated that the standard antibiotics used to combat Lyme disease in the human (e.g., amoxicillin, doxycycline) kill most *Borrelia* spirochetes but leave a small number of "persister" spirochetes unaffected. These have been called "drug-tolerant persister" spirochetes. Various research groups conducting studies in the lab have now identified different antibiotics or different approaches to antibiotic delivery that appear to be more effective than standard antibiotics in killing both the dormant variants as well as the actively multiplying ones. While it is known that what occurs in vitro in the laboratory setting may not be replicated or relevant to the human setting, these studies lend support to the hypothesis that there may be new approaches to help fight *Borrelia* infection that are more effective than the standard drugs.

Patients often become anxious when they learn that the *Borrelia* spirochetes may be able to persist despite antibiotics. What many patients may not understand is that antibiotic therapies are not meant to eradicate all of the target microbes in the human body. Rather, the goal of antibiotic therapy is to eradicate enough bacteria to shift the balance so that the immune system can then take over and either eradicate the remaining spirochetes or keep the microbial load in check. It is worth remembering that the human body harbors ten times more microbial cells than human cells. The goal in treatment is not to create a sterile human, but rather to reduce the burden of infection that causes disease such that the immune system can mop up the remaining spirochetes and resume its general surveillance, allowing for a healthy homeostasis between human and microbe.

Persistent infection in humans is challenging to document by blood testing given that *Borrelia* reside in tissue and are only transiently in the blood after initial infection. Some of the published case reports demonstrating persistent spirochetes have been criticized for using outdated methods or assays that are prone to false positives; they are further criticized for not confirming by immunohistochemistry or by genetic methods that the spirochetes visualized by microscopy were truly *B. burgdorferi* spirochetes. Concerns have also been raised that these results might be errors because the laboratory likely had contamination. Such criticisms certainly are reasonable and may well explain some of the positive case reports. However, some of the cases come from academic or government research centers in which the laboratory quality control is reputed to be excellent. Such was the situation in the case report (shown in case 7 earlier) published by Lawrence and colleagues (1995) because they used multiple laboratory methods and three different laboratories for the PCR studies, and in the case series from Slovenia where *Borrelia* was isolated from the skin (Strle 1993, 1996).

A fascinating study (Marques et al. 2014) recently examined the issue of persistent infection in humans using the same method—xenodiagnosis—that had been used in the earlier animal studies. In this study, laboratory-raised uninfected ticks were allowed to feed on humans with chronic symptoms after antibiotic treatment for Lyme disease to see if these ticks became infected with *B. burgdorferi* spirochetes. The preliminary results from this study indicated that although intact spirochetes could not be found in the feeding ticks, the ticks that fed on one of the study subjects did show DNA evidence of the *Borrelia* spirochete; this tick had fed on a person with chronic post-antibiotic symptoms who was serologically positive by C6 peptide ELISA. This finding supports the hypothesis that *B. burgdorferi* spirochetes (or at the very least *B. burgdorferi* DNA) can persist in the human host after antibiotic treatment.

Another notable case report of persistent infection after antibiotic therapy is described in box 5.2.

---

**CASE 8.** An Atypical Case of Culture Positivity for *B. burgdorferi* in the Cerebrospinal Fluid of a Previously Treated Woman (Liegner et al. 1997)

---

A thirty-nine-year-old woman from a Lyme endemic area presented with a two-year history of progressive spasticity and weakness of her arms and legs (quadraparesis), cranial nerve palsies, cognitive impairment, and persistent unexplained white blood cells (pleocytosis) in her spinal fluid. There was no history of tick attachment or of EM, and standard antibody tests for Lyme disease in the blood and cerebrospinal fluid were initially negative. Given the possibility that this might be a case of seronegative Lyme disease, she was treated with three weeks of intravenous antibiotic (cefotaxime) followed by four months of oral antibiotic (minocycline). Despite this prior antibiotic treatment, spinal fluid sent to the CDC for culture grew *B. burgdorferi* spirochetes. Subsequent testing of the blood revealed antibodies against *B. burgdorferi* in the serum. Her blood tested PCR positive for *B. burgdorferi* on two occasions, confirming the presence of genetic material of the spirochete that causes Lyme disease. Given the confirmation of infection in the central nervous system by culture, she was treated with longer courses of intravenous antibiotic therapy. This led to a partial improvement in symptoms and a resolution of the pleocytosis in the spinal fluid. Cognitive improvement during the intravenous therapy was documented by a battery of neurocognitive

*(Continued next page)*

*(Continued from previous page)*

tests. The patient's neurologic status, however, deteriorated when antibiotics were discontinued.

Comment: This case is rare in the international literature in that the *B. burgdorferi* was demonstrated by culture in the spinal fluid after intravenous and oral antibiotic therapy. The culture was conducted by scientists at the Division of Vector-Borne Diseases at the CDC. Further evidence of *B. burgdorferi* infection was provided by the positive PCR results of her blood. That intravenous antibiotic therapy had an objective impact in her central nervous system was supported by the normalization of the number of white blood cells in her spinal fluid. Given that *B. burgdorferi* is not known to develop antibiotic resistance, this may be a clinical case of an individual with antibiotic-tolerant *B. burgdorferi* causing a meningoencephalitis.

We present this case because documentation of persistent *B. burgdorferi* that has been shown to grow in culture after antibiotic therapy is rare. Could this patient have been reinfected? It is unlikely given that she was wheelchair bound and confined to the indoors. Could this be a case of a false positive culture due to inadvertent contamination at the CDC lab? This is unlikely given the CDC's high quality control standards. The subsequent positive PCR tests also lend support to the assumption of persistent infection.

This case demonstrates the value of collaborations among community clinicians who see very sick patients and academic and government scientists who have the expertise to conduct the microbiologic investigations. This case also raises scientific questions about treatment duration for individuals whose disease manifestations and course fall outside of the norm.

## Conflicts over Whether "Subjective" Symptoms Are Meaningful and Responsive to Treatment

The IDSA recommends that physicians focus on the verifiable objective signs required by the CDC surveillance criteria (e.g., rash, facial palsy, swollen joint) in assessing patients for Lyme disease to confirm a diagnosis.

Other manifestations of Lyme disease—fatigue or pain, for example—are considered "subjective" because they rely on the patient's self-report and cannot be externally validated. Some IDSA authors have noted that "subjective" symptoms are common in the general population and thus are being overvalued by clinicians who treat patients based on these symptoms. Because these subjective symptoms are part of everyday life, they should not be used as a basis upon which to make treatment decisions in Lyme disease.

These subjective symptoms, however, are often the most debilitating. Various studies have demonstrated that patients entering research studies for post-treatment Lyme disease symptoms are quite impaired by their "subjective symptoms." The Columbia study of patients with chronic cognitive impairment after Lyme disease found that the level of fatigue was comparable to those with multiple sclerosis, their pain was comparable to patients recovering from surgery, and their physical impairment was comparable to those with congestive heart failure (Fallon et al. 2008). These "subjective" symptoms are often of an intensity vastly greater than the minor fatigue and pain seen commonly in the general population.

Given the disability and distress associated with these subjective symptoms, patients might ask: "Why do researchers spend so much time studying patients with early Lyme disease when the rash is not disabling at all? It's the chronic symptoms of fatigue, pain, and brain fog that are wrecking my life!" The response of some in the scientific community might be: "These 'subjective' symptoms can't be studied. We should only focus on objective signs of disease."

Behavioral scientists have spent decades developing ways to assess and monitor subjective symptoms. This has led to well-validated self-report questionnaires that have been found to be quite sensitive in assessing symptom severity and in evaluating the effectiveness of treatments. They know how to study "subjective" symptoms in a reliable way. Indeed, studies of symptoms using validated behavioral measures coupled with modern biotechnologies (e.g., positron emission tomography imaging or functional magnetic resonance imaging) demonstrate that these "subjective" symptoms often have objective neurobiological or neuroimaging correlates that improve in parallel with symptom improvement (Logigian et al. 1997).

Treatment studies that have looked at responsiveness to initial antibiotic treatment in patients with early Lyme disease indicate that both objective and subjective symptoms improve (Kowalski et al. 2010). The conflict relates to whether subjective symptoms improve in a patient who does not have the objective clinical signs of active infection. In other words, will fatigue, headaches, and joint and muscle pain improve in patients who have positive blood tests for Lyme disease but who do not recall ever having had a typical sign of Lyme disease (such as the EM rash, migrating swollen joints, or facial nerve palsy)? In early Lyme disease, the answer is clearly yes; these symptoms can be a sign of acute infection and do respond well to antibiotic treatment (Steere and Sikand 2003). Given that one in six patients with early Lyme disease may not show these objective signs, the clinician working in a Lyme endemic area needs to keep Lyme disease in the differential diagnosis of acute "subjective" symptoms as well so that diagnosis and antibiotic treatment are not delayed. In later stage untreated Lyme disease, in which there may be prominent subjective symptoms without obvious external signs of disease, the answer to the treatment question is unknown as these studies have not yet been conducted; most clinicians and scientists, however, would agree that a course of antibiotic therapy would be warranted in these previously untreated seropositive patients. This position would be supported by the results of a controlled study of patients with chronic persistent fatigue after treated Lyme disease who were shown to be three times more likely to have a sustained reduction in fatigue if given one month of intravenous ceftriaxone compared to intravenous placebo (Krupp et al. 2003). The larger area of conflict regarding whether additional antibiotic therapy is effective for patients with subjective symptoms who have already received standard courses of antibiotic therapy is addressed further in chapter 7.

## Conflicts over How Strongly to Weigh Other Possible Causes of Persistent Symptoms

The two camps in the Lyme Wars also argue about how to weigh other possible causes of persistent symptoms. The IDSA camp highlights inaccurate diagnosis or postinfectious causes of persistent symptoms, such as an aberrantly regulated immune response triggered by the prior infection or remnant pieces of spirochetal material. The ILADS camp highlights persistent infection either by *B. burgdorferi* or by other microbes carried by the black-legged ticks as the likely cause for persistent symptoms in many patients. Both camps agree that persistent progression of symptoms after antibiotic treatment in which there has been minimal or no response to antibiotic treatment warrants a reevaluation of the original diagnosis.

Both camps agree that in certain areas up to one-third of black-legged ticks carry not only the agent of Lyme disease but also other microbial infections that cause human disease. Some have called these ticks "cess-pools of infection" given the diversity of microbes they may carry. Some research findings (but not all) suggest that being infected with *B. burgdorferi* as well as Babesia, for example, may worsen the course of illness (Krause et al. 1996).

While many other diseases can cause chronic multi-systemic symptoms (e.g., depression, thyroid abnormalities, sleep disorders, diabetes, cancer), when these symptoms emerge abruptly after a tick bite from a Lyme endemic area, infection with *B. burgdorferi* or other coinfections should be considered. Some of these coinfections cause elevated liver enzymes, low platelets, and low white or red blood cell counts; in this way, the laboratory profile alerts the clinician to consider other tick-borne infections because the profile is substantially different than what is typically seen with Lyme disease. The treatment selected for Lyme disease may not necessarily be effective in killing the unrecognized coinfection. A later chapter in this book addresses the diagnosis and treatment of many of the major tick-borne infections (and some of the less common ones as well).

## CONCLUDING COMMENTS REGARDING THE GREAT DIVIDE AND THE LYME WARS

In summary, the medical controversy surrounding Lyme disease is unfortunate but understandable. The controversy relates to the clinical and laboratory criteria used to diagnose the disease, the duration and type of antibiotic treatment for patients with persistent symptoms, the risk/benefit calculation when discussing the use of antibiotics with patients, the interpretation of test results, and the openness to considering other diagnoses and non-antibiotic treatments for patients with persistent symptoms. The controversy may also be fueled by the impact of other tick-borne coinfections (some not yet or only recently discovered) because these are not always considered in the differential diagnosis. That such controversy exists relates to the complexity of this illness and the very limited number of studies that have been done on those with later-stage disease. The controversy is also fueled by the inadequacies of laboratory testing. Until medical doctors have a test that definitively identifies the presence or absence of infection with *B. burgdorferi*, disagreements about the diagnosis and treatment of chronic symptoms triggered by Lyme disease will continue.

As science advances, new discoveries are made that help quell some of the controversies.

- A recent discovery helps to explain why some patients might have negative Lyme tests despite having symptoms that are Lyme-like that emerged after a tick bite and that resolve with the antibiotic treatment commonly used for Lyme disease. Some of these patients do suffer from a tick-borne illness, but it is not caused by the same spirochete that causes Lyme disease. A new tick-borne spirochete named *Borrelia miyamotoi* has been found in the same hard-bodied *Ixodes* ticks that transmit *B. burgdorferi*. This new spirochete causes a range of human symptoms very similar to Lyme disease but without the rash (Krause et al. 2015). The treatment for *B. miyamotoi* is the same as for Lyme disease, but the Western blot blood tests for Lyme disease will often be negative.

- As noted in the preceding diagnostic chapter, progress is being made on creating more sensitive diagnostic tests, including ones that are positive when the infection is present and negative when the infection has resolved. A test of active infection that is highly sensitive and does not have many false positives would represent a major breakthrough for patients and clinicians in clinical care. A test of active infection would help to quell the Lyme Wars by reducing the uncertainty and controversy about whether to treat patients with persistent symptoms with additional antibiotics.

Scientific progress is not possible without disciplined, open-minded research conducted by dedicated researchers. Many of the original pioneers in the Lyme disease research community continue to conduct pivotal studies that address key questions of concern to patients. New outstanding researchers from other medical fields have joined the effort. Most valuable is that dialog continues between patients, clinicians, and researchers so that the research scientists stay focused on the questions of pressing clinical importance.

How did this progress come about? Certainly the researchers conducting careful science were key, but this research wouldn't have been possible without funding support—and that has been provided by the U.S. government (NIH, DoD, CDC) as well as by private donors and foundations who realized that the only way to change the minds of doctors and achieve breakthroughs is through high-quality science.

This is a hopeful time in the world of Lyme disease. The biotechnology revolution has catapulted scientific advances, creating new bridges between previously polarized stakeholders and enabling researchers, clinicians, and patients to work together as they collaborate on conquering this disease.

# 6

# WHY WOULD SYMPTOMS PERSIST AFTER ANTIBIOTIC TREATMENT FOR LYME DISEASE?

Why do some patients experience persistent symptoms after having received the recommended antibiotic treatment for Lyme disease? The primary hypotheses to explain this problem include:

- Persistent infection with *B. burgdorferi*,
- Residual damage to tissue from the original infection,
- Persistent immune activation and inflammation, and
- *Borrelia*-triggered neural network dysregulation including central sensitization and neurotransmitter changes.

These hypotheses are discussed in greater detail in this chapter.

## PERSISTENT INFECTION HYPOTHESIS

While it has long been accepted in the medical community that *B. burgdorferi* can persist for months to years in a human who has not yet been treated with antibiotics, there has been significant debate over whether the infection could persist after initial antibiotic treatment of standard duration. A number of carefully conducted animal studies have now demonstrated convincingly that, even after antibiotic therapy, *B. burgdorferi* can persist in the animal host (Hodzic et al. 2008; Embers et al. 2012; Staubinger et al. 1997). The quantity of persistent *B. burgdorferi* is typically at lower levels than in a new infection. An animal study with mice has demonstrated that the *Borrelia* that persist are living, infectious, and

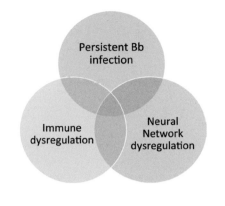

FIGURE 6.1

Treatment of post-treatment Lyme disease syndrome depends on the cause.

capable of stimulating an ongoing immune response (Hodzic et al. 2014). However, these persistent *Borrelia* are not able to be cultured in the standard culture medium for *Borrelia* spirochetes. While many of these studies have been conducted in mice, studies in dogs and rhesus macaques have also shown persistent *B. burgdorferi* spirochetes (Straubinger et al. 1997; Embers et al. 2012).

Culture is the gold standard for proving active infection with *B. burgdorferi*. Using the traditional culture medium (BSK), case reports in humans have been published confirming *B. burgdorferi* growth by culture after treatment—most of these are found in the early European literature on Lyme disease. There have been reports from Europe demonstrating culture of *Borrelia* from the skin of individuals with previously treated Lyme disease (Strle 1996). In the United States, as noted in chapter 5, a case report revealed positive growth of *B. burgdorferi* when the cerebrospinal fluid was cultured by the CDC from a patient who had received many months of prior antibiotic therapy for Lyme disease (Liegner et al. 1997). While rare, these cases prove that persistent infection in humans can occur.

Among those who agree that low levels of the bacteria can persist after initial treatment, there is additional debate over whether these low levels of spirochetes are causing clinically significant symptoms in patients and whether additional antibiotic treatment is helpful. For example, some studies in animals have shown that residual spirochetes do not cause the expected local inflammation when viewed microscopically, while more recent messenger RNA studies demonstrate that mice with residual spirochetes have altered tissue cytokine production, raising the hypotheses that these cytokines themselves, if produced in sufficient quantity, may be causing systemic symptoms (Hodzic et al. 2014).

How does the *Borrelia* spirochete persist despite the body's immune surveillance or despite antibiotic treatment? There are several possible explanations.

- Analysis of both human and experimental animal tissues indicate that *B. burgdorferi* spirochetes are found intercalated in extracellular collagen-rich matrixes (components of connective tissue); this location may be a unique niche for immune evasion. The central nervous system which is a relatively immune privileged site may also facilitate immune evasion.
- In vitro laboratory-based evidence demonstrates that *B. burgdorferi* may be able to survive inside human cells, including endothelial cells (lining blood vessels), astrocytes (in the brain), fibroblasts (in connective tissue), and macrophages (in the immune system). Intracellular sequestration, however, has not yet been demonstrated in vivo in the animal or human.
- *B. burgdorferi* is known to modify its outer surface protein expression depending on temperature, pH, and other factors. For example, the outer surface protein expression of the initial invading spirochete is different from the outer surface protein expression of the spirochete that has been in the host for more than four weeks. By up-regulating or down-regulating the expression of surface proteins that are usually recognized by the immune system, *B. burgdorferi* spirochetes can escape detection and killing by the immune system.
- *B. burgdorferi* has the ability to produce proteins that bind to and inactivate a key component of the immune system, called complement. The production of complement inactivators has the net effect of markedly decreasing the destructive capacity of the antibodies against the spirochete.

- Other laboratory-based in vitro experiments indicate that *Borrelia* can revert to round forms, which appear less susceptible to standard antibiotic therapy. Whether this also occurs during human infection remains unclear.
- Recent evidence conducted in vitro in the laboratory setting demonstrates convincingly that a subgroup of *Borrelia* spirochetes (called "drug-tolerant persisters") are not killed by the standard antibiotic therapy for Lyme disease. Research groups have identified different antibiotics or antibiotic combinations (Feng, Auwaerter, and Zhang 2015) or treatment regimens (Sharma et al. 2015) that are effective in the laboratory setting and now are being explored in animal studies. Until these novel agents or strategies identified by in vitro studies are tested in animal models to confirm improved efficacy over standard treatment, these antibiotic regimens are of uncertain clinical value.

By one or more of these mechanisms, *B. burgdorferi* may be able to persist inside the human body and it is possible that these persistent bacteria may be responsible for patients' ongoing symptoms.

In 2012, a leading authority on Lyme disease research in animals provided his perspective on Lyme disease to members of the U.S. Congress (Barthold 2012). Excerpts from his introductory comments are quoted here.

Lyme disease, caused by a number of closely related members of the *B. burgdorferi* sensu lato family (*B. burgdorferi* sensu stricto in the United States) that are transmitted by closely-related members of the *Ixodes persulcatus* family (*I. scapularis* and *I. pacificus* in the United States) is endemic in many parts of the world, with particularly high prevalence in the United States and Europe. Prevalence of human disease continues to rise, as does the geographic distribution of endemic areas. These events are enhanced by perturbation of the environment by humans, as well as global climate change, which favor habitation of the environment by *Ixodes spp.* vector ticks and suitable reservoir hosts. Interest in Lyme disease is rising globally, as Lyme disease is increasing in southern Canada, where infected ticks and reservoir hosts are extending their range from the United States, as well as an increase in prevalence throughout Europe and Asia.

During the course of my Lyme disease research career, I have become saddened by the negative discourse and division that exists among various factions of the Lyme disease community, including the lay community, the medical community, and the scientific community (the so called "Lyme Wars"). In particular, debate has intensified regarding efficacy and appropriate regimens for antibiotic treatment. Central to this debate is the Infectious Disease Society of America (IDSA) position that this is a simple bacterial infection that is amenable to simple antibiotic treatment, while also recognizing that something is happening in patients after treatment, known as Post Lyme Disease Syndrome (PLDS).

Lyme disease is exceedingly complex in humans, and this poses major challenges to accurate diagnosis and measuring outcome of treatment. It has been known for years that the acute signs of Lyme disease (*erythema migrans*, cardiac conduction abnormalities, arthritis, etc.) spontaneously regress without benefit of antibiotics, but their resolution is accelerated by treatment. There is overwhelming evidence in a variety of animal species as well as humans that *B. burgdorferi* persists without treatment, but the crucial question is does it survive following treatment, and if so, do surviving spirochetes cause "chronic" Lyme disease or PLDS? These questions cannot be answered by speculative and expensive human clinical trials motivated by firmly held dogmatism.

Something strange is happening with Lyme disease. *B. burgdorferi* persistently infects a myriad of fully immunocompetent hosts as the rule, not the norm of its basic biology. When such a situation occurs, antibiotics may fail, since it is generally accepted that antibiotics eliminate the majority of bacteria, and rely upon the host to "mop up" the rest. If the bacteria are able to evade host "mopping," then the logic of the scenario falters. It is not surprising, therefore, that experimental studies, using a broad spectrum of animal species (mice, dogs, monkeys) and a variety of antibiotics (doxycycline, amoxicillin, ceftriaxone, tigecycline) have all shown a failure to completely cure the animals of *B. burgdorferi* infection. What is surprising is that the surviving spirochetes can no longer be cultivated from tissues (culture is considered by some to be the gold standard for detecting viable *B. burgdorferi*), but their presence can be readily detected with a number of methods, including *B. burgdorferi*-specific DNA amplification (polymerase chain reaction [PCR]), xeno-diagnosis (feeding ticks upon the host and testing the ticks by PCR), detection of *B. burgdorferi*-specific RNA (indicating live spirochetes), and demonstration of intact spirochetes in tissues and xenodiagnostic ticks by labeling them with antibody against *B. burgdorferi*-specific targets. These surviving spirochetes are not simply "DNA debris" as some contend, but are rather persisting, but non-cultivable spirochetes. It remains to be determined if their persistence following treatment is medically significant. For example, humans are known to be persistently infected with a number of opportunistic pathogens, including viruses, bacteria, and fungi, which are held in abeyance by the immune response, without clinical symptoms. Their significance varies with individual human patients and their ability to keep them in check. Lyme disease is likely to be similar.

The key points from this statement are as follows:

- Lyme disease is not a simple disease because the agent of infection, *B. burgdorferi*, is highly complex.
- The basic biology of *B. burgdorferi* is that it can persist and survive immune attack, which can make it hard to eradicate.
- Antibiotics are expected to wipe out the majority of infection, but not all of it; a healthy immune system is meant to conduct the final sweep to eradicate the infection from the body. Because *B. burgdorferi* has evolved mechanisms by which it evades the immune system, it is not surprising that some spirochetes will persist.
- A preponderance of evidence now exists demonstrating persistent infection in the animal model despite antibiotic treatment, but these spirochetes can no longer be cultivated from the host's tissue. This suggests that the persistent *Borrelia* spirochetes are not as healthy as the initial infecting spirochete or that they are simply not actively replicating.
- The extent to which the residual noncultivable spirochetes cause clinically significant disease remains to be determined.

## RESIDUAL DAMAGE HYPOTHESIS

In general, Lyme disease is not associated with prominent tissue damage that persists after treatment. This is good news of course, but it is not necessarily true for all manifestations of Lyme disease. Patients with neuroborreliosis-induced vasculitis may experience long-term residual neurologic effects of a stroke. Patients with facial nerve palsy may have long-standing residual facial weakness.

## PERSISTENT IMMUNE ACTIVATION AND INFLAMMATION HYPOTHESIS

The immune response and inflammation may persist even after antibiotic treatment of the infection. This observation has led to the hypothesis that either a small amount of persistent infection or spirochetal residua continue to trigger the ongoing immune response or that this is a postinfectious process, triggered but not sustained by active infection.

This hypothesis is supported by several lines of evidence. For example, patients with Lyme arthritis who carry the HLA-DR4 gene are more vulnerable to developing a chronic immune-mediated antibiotic-resistant arthritis (Steere, Dwyer, and Winchester 1990). In addition, three auto-antibodies have been identified that are reasonably specific for antibiotic-refractory Lyme arthritis (antibodies against endothelial cell growth factor [ECGF], apolipoprotein B-100, and matrix metalloproteinase 10); supporting a role in pathogenesis, the levels of anti-ECGF auto-antibodies in one study were shown to correlate with obliterative microvascular lesions in synovial tissue (Londono et al. 2014).

Among patients with post-treatment Lyme disease syndrome (PTLDS), there is indirect evidence implicating "molecular mimicry" in pathogenesis, meaning that *B. burgdorferi* has outer surface proteins that mimic human cells so that the immune system accidentally attacks itself in addition to the invading bacteria (Jacek et al. 2013; Chandra et al. 2010). There is also evidence to suggest that remnants of the *Borrelia* spirochete in tissues may result in a persistent activation of the immune system, causing the production of inflammatory cytokines, such as interleukin-6 (IL-6) and tumor necrosis factor.

Evidence of post-treatment immune activation has emerged from several research groups:

- Several studies (Jacek et al. 2013; Chandra et al. 2010) document ongoing immune reactivity among patients with PTLDS.
  - Using samples from the Columbia University clinical trial, these researchers reported persistently elevated activity levels of the cytokine interferon-alpha in the serum of patients who were treated for Lyme disease but who continued to experience memory problems. This heightened immune response was proposed to have occurred due to prolonged exposure to *Borrelia* prior to treatment. The importance of this study was that it provided evidence in support of the hypothesis that patients with PTLDS have ongoing immune activation that may be contributing to some disabling PTLDS symptoms such as fatigue and malaise.
  - Using samples from the New England Medical Center clinical trial (Klempner et al. 2001) and the Columbia clinical trial (Fallon et al. 2008), these researchers demonstrated that patients with PTLDS have elevated levels of antineuronal antibodies—comparable in magnitude to what was seen in a comparison sample of those with an autoimmune disease, systemic lupus erythematosus. Of importance, individuals with recovered Lyme disease did not show elevated levels of these antineuronal antibody biomarkers.
- Using samples from a Slovenian clinical trial (Strle et al. 2014), serum from patients with early Lyme disease versus PTLDS was probed for the levels of twenty-three cytokines and chemokines before and after antibiotic treatment.
  - Of the forty-one patients with detectable IL-23 levels at initial presentation, twenty-five (61 percent) developed post-treatment symptoms, and all seven with high IL-23 levels had PTLDS symptoms.
  - Among those patients with post-treatment symptoms, antibody responses to the ECGF autoantigen were more common than in patients without post-treatment symptoms and ECGF antibody responses were correlated directly with IL-23 levels.
  - This study demonstrated that a particular immune response (high $T_H 1$) at initial presentation was correlated with more effective

immune-mediated spirochetal killing, whereas another immune response at initial presentation (high $T_H17$), often accompanied by autoantibodies, correlated with post-treatment Lyme symptoms. This study confirms that variable immune responses at the very start of infection may provide clues as to who will be vulnerable to developing PTLDS. Noteworthy is that the main function of IL-23 is to drive $T_H17$ cells, which are important in host defense against extracellular pathogens. It is also noteworthy that aberrant IL-23/$T_H17$ responses have been implicated in several autoimmune conditions, including rheumatoid arthritis, inflammatory bowel disease, lupus, and type 1 diabetes.

- Using samples from the Johns Hopkins biorepository of patients followed prospectively from the initial Lyme rash to the six-month follow-up after treatment, a study (Soloski et al. 2014) demonstrated that in some patient samples over six months there was an ongoing production of the inflammatory cytokine IL-6. The authors hypothesized that the persistent inflammatory process in a subset of individuals after treatment may be due to "residual antigen or infection in some treated Lyme disease patients," as has been observed in the animal model studies, but they note that to test this hypothesis in humans, a larger sample size and additional exploration are required.

## NEURAL NETWORK DYSREGULATION HYPOTHESIS

It is difficult to determine in a particular individual whether ongoing symptoms and immune activation are due to a small amount of persistent infection or to a postinfectious process. It is clear, however, that the brain is a central mediator of most bodily processes. Brain networks and the immune response may be triggered by active infection or remain aberrantly activated by past infection.

Why include the brain in this chapter? The brain can be viewed as the computer-processing center of the body. Neural activation networks can be viewed as the software that shapes how information is processed in the brain. Changes in brain hardware or software will have an impact on the patient's clinical presentation and the ability to resolve chronic illness. While it is easy to comprehend that problems with memory or mood are related to brain mechanisms, it is not as often recognized that inflammation and immune processes in the body are also shaped by input from the brain. This concept is of great importance for individuals with chronic illness because the problem may no longer be due to persistent infection but rather to the impact of the initial infection on the brain's activation patterns.

## Central Sensitization in the Brain and Pain

Central sensitization is a process that has been proposed to occur in chronic pain disorders, including fibromyalgia, chronic fatigue syndrome, migraine, and possibly PTLDS. These disorders share the symptoms of persistent pain and fatigue as well as sensory hyperarousal. Patients with central sensitization feel abnormally increased pain in response to a mildly uncomfortable stimulus, such as having blood drawn, and may even feel pain from a stimulus that is not painful to others at all, such as the sensation of clothing on the skin. It has been shown that patients with fibromyalgia have abnormally hyperactive brain pathways that control pain (Clauw 2014). Patients with central sensitization may also be intensely bothered by bright lights or loud sounds. It has been hypothesized that patients with central sensitization have a genetic predisposition to this condition that can be triggered by trauma or an infection. In the case of fibromyalgia, first-degree relatives of patients with this condition have an eightfold greater risk of developing it (Arnold et al. 2004). Central sensitivity may also result from an imbalance of neurotransmitters involved in the pain response including serotonin, norepinephrine, GABA, glutamate, and dopamine. Once central sensitization occurs, it may persist due to structural and functional changes in the brain. It is possible that chronic symptoms triggered by Lyme disease are caused, at least in part, by central sensitization, in which case treatments should focus on decreasing the hyperactivation of these pain pathways in the brain (Batheja et al. 2013).

It is reasonable to assume that some patients with chronic symptoms after initial treatment for Lyme disease suffer from persistent infection, whereas others suffer from a postinfectious ongoing immune process (autoimmune disease, infection-triggered immune activation) and others suffer from abnormally sensitized brain pathways (e.g., central sensitization), though more research needs to be done on each of these potential causes. Decisions about treatment have largely focused on antibiotic selection when acute infection is present, but emerging evidence suggests that patients with persistent symptoms after treatment may also benefit from immune modulatory strategies (Steere and Angelis 2006; Rupprecht et al. 2008) or from neurotransmitter modulatory strategies (Weissenbacher et al. 2005).

## The Immune-Body-Brain Link

The immune response has often been viewed inaccurately as an independent process that works by itself to defend the body against infections or other foreign substances. We know, for example, that the brain has an enormous influence on all bodily systems, such as the gastrointestinal tract and the cardiovascular and neuroendocrine systems. There is now considerable evidence that the immune system and the nervous system are functionally and anatomically connected.

This concept was demonstrated quite clearly by an experiment in the early 1990s in which the inflammatory cytokine (IL-1B) was injected into the abdomen of rodents (Watkins et al. 1995). Under normal circumstances, such an injection would cause a fever in the rodent. When one of the cranial nerves that innervates peripheral organs was cut (the vagus nerve), the fever did not occur. In other words, an intact nerve fiber connecting the brain to the abdomen was required to allow information from the abdomen about inflammation to be conveyed to the brain so that the fever response could occur. In a later rodent study, it was demonstrated that electrical stimulation of the vagus nerve decreases peripheral inflammation (Borovikova et al. 2000). Further evidence demonstrating the importance of the vagus nerve in controlling inflammation was provided by a study of humans with chronic refractory arthritis who received electrical stimulation of the vagus nerve (using a subcutaneous surgically implanted device); the results demonstrated an inhibition in the production of tumor necrosis factor (an inflammatory cytokine) and an improvement in clinical measures of pain and functioning (Koopman et al. 2016).

These studies therefore demonstrate that there are key neural pathways by which the brain modulates the inflammatory response. The immune system and the brain are intimately connected. This insight is critical as it suggests that abnormalities in brain function could also lead to abnormalities in immune response. This is relevant to Lyme disease in that infection with *B. burgdorferi* in some patients leads to altered brain metabolism and blood flow, as demonstrated by our group at Columbia (Fallon et al. 2009). Compared to well-matched controls, individuals with persistent cognitive impairment after Lyme disease (all of whom had received considerable prior antibiotic therapy) had multiple areas of decreased metabolism and blood flow, primarily in the temporal-parietal regions. Whether these regional brain alterations impact the immune response directly is not clear, but abnormalities in these brain regions are known to be associated with many of the cardinal symptoms experienced by patients with Lyme encephalopathy, including cognitive impairment and fatigue.

It remains an intriguing question whether normalization of brain function and metabolism would have a beneficial impact upon immune system function. Based on the vagal nerve stimulation studies that have demonstrated a reduction in the peripheral blood levels of several inflammatory cytokines (e.g., TNF-α, IL-1β, and IL-6), it is equally important to ask whether vagal nerve stimulation would reduce chronic Lyme arthritis or the diffuse musculoskeletal pain and fatigue associated with PTLDS.

## THE RELATIONSHIP BETWEEN IMMUNE ACTIVATION AND DEPRESSION

Recent studies in immunology have suggested a link between the long-term immune activation associated with many chronic illnesses and clinical depression. In response to infection, the innate immune system produces small signaling molecules called cytokines, some of which cause inflammation (examples of pro-inflammatory cytokines are TNF-α, IL-1α, IL-1β, and IL-6). These cytokines are thought to act on the brain to cause "sickness behavior" that includes loss of appetite, loss of interest in daily activities, sleeping problems, and irritability. When the infection lasts for months or years, so does the inflammation; the ongoing sickness behavior in certain vulnerable individuals may progress to clinical depression. Researchers now have good evidence to conclude that chronic inflammation increases the risk of major depressive episodes (Dantzer 2009; Hoyo-Becerra, Schlaak, and Hermann 2014).

- Studies of patients receiving cytokine therapy to treat chronic diseases such as for hepatitis C showed that these patients were at higher risk for developing major depressive episodes (Miller and Timmie 2009). Initially, these patients developed flu-like symptoms, fatigue, loss of appetite, chronic pain, and sleep disorders that were then followed by cognitive problems, depressed mood, anxiety, and irritability. Cytokines have also been shown to induce depression in animal studies.
- Additional research suggests that biomarkers of inflammation may help to guide treatment choice for depression. One study reported that depressed patients with signs of systemic inflammation such as elevations of C-reactive protein (CRP) were more likely to respond to a noradrenergic agent such as nortriptyline, whereas those with low CRP levels responded more favorably to serotonin reuptake inhibitors (Uher et al. 2014).
- A meta-analysis of twenty studies examined the impact of anticytokine drugs on depressive symptoms in chronic inflammatory diseases, including seven placebo-controlled randomized trials. The authors concluded that these immune modulators (most commonly agents that reduced tumor necrosis factor) resulted in significant improvement in depressive symptoms (Kappelmann et al. 2016). Of particular note is that improvement in depression was unrelated to improvement in physical symptoms. Modulation of inflammatory cytokines therefore may emerge as a novel approach to treatment of patients with depression, particularly when there is evidence of inflammation.

In addition to chronic illness, ageing and obesity are also thought to be associated with increased activity of the immune system and chronic inflammation. The interrelation of chronic illness, immune activation, and mood is an area of ongoing research.

## THE CONNECTION BETWEEN THE GUT MICROBIOME AND MOOD

The gut microbiome plays an important and as yet relatively unexplored role in the human. The likelihood that bacteria in the gut play a critical role in human health should not be surprising because the number of bacterial cells in the human body (i.e., predominantly in the gut) is ten times greater than the number of human cells; more dramatically, some state that the human body is simply a bag of microbes. The bacteria in the gut, while generally stable throughout life, can be altered by environmental factors such as infection, nutrition, antibiotics, and probiotic use.

One important area of future investigation is the impact of long-term antibiotic use on the rest of the body. Could the consequent imbalance in the intestinal flora be contributing to chronic symptoms such as fatigue, brain fog, and/or pain? Could immune-mediated diseases be triggered by these changes in the gut microbiome? These questions have not yet been studied in a systematic manner in regard to Lyme disease, though scientific interest is mounting.

Recent studies suggest that alterations in the gut microbiome may be key players in the pathophysiology of medical conditions as diverse as obesity and inflammatory bowel disease (Thomas et al. 2017). Rodent models have shown that bacteria in the gastrointestinal tract influence the development of autoimmunity. We also know that nutrition has an impact on the gut microbiome, which in turn can impact the innate and adaptive immune systems. This interaction is not always straightforward. For example, spore-forming bacteria have been found in animal models to support the development of autoimmune arthritis and encephalomyelitis (Block et al. 2016; Lee et al. 2011), but these same bacteria have been found to be protective against the development of type 1 diabetes (King and Sarvetnick 2011). This is a medical field at its earliest stages. The impact this research will have for patients experiencing persistent symptoms after Lyme disease remains to be determined.

Does the gut microbiome have anything to do with cognition or mood?

- Studies conducted in animals that have been depleted of their intestinal microbes demonstrate that the brain's neurotransmitter system (e.g., monoamines) then develops abnormally, resulting in memory and behavioral problems (Crumeyrolle-Arias et al. 2014).
- Germ-free mice have reduced fear responses. Remarkably, this can be reversed. If the intestinal bacteria are returned to the mice early in development, a normal fear response occurs once again (Cryan and Dinan 2012).
- The probiotic *Lactobacillus rhamnosus* causes major changes in the expression of the inhibitory neurotransmitter GABA (gamma-aminobutyric acid) receptors in the brain, resulting in an enhanced antianxiety response in animals (Bravo et al. 2011). Interestingly, this effect requires an intact vagus nerve. When the vagal connection between the gut and the brain is cut, the beneficial reduction of anxiety by the impact of *Lactobacillus* from the gut on the GABA receptors in the brain does not occur. This is one more animal study demonstrating that mood is modulated by the bacteria in the gut and that there is a direct interaction between the brain and the gut.
- A recent randomized double-blind placebo-controlled clinical trial of the probiotic *Bifidobacterium longum* among patients with irritable bowel syndrome revealed a modest reduction in depression, an improved quality of life, and reduced neural reactivity to negative emotional stimuli in limbic brain regions among the probiotic-treated patients compared to controls (Pinto-Sanchez et al. 2017).

These hypotheses about the role of the microbiome in chronic illness and its impact on brain activity are only just beginning to be tested. We present them here as examples of new directions in our efforts to understand the complexity of the human illness response and possible future relevance to Lyme disease.

## SOMATIZATION, ANXIETY, AND CHRONIC SYMPTOMS

Everybody has experienced somatization or anxiety at some point. Somatization is a process by which distressing physical symptoms arise due to psychological mechanisms. In its mild forms, individuals may experience "butterflies in the stomach" or a need to urinate when under stress. Somatization can become enhanced by excessive attention to one's bodily symptoms, by catastrophic beliefs about the potential significance of these symptoms, and by underlying mood or anxiety disorders.

- An example of attention and the power of suggestion leading to somatization would be if a patient is told that he or she may experience a flare of symptoms within the first few days of initiation of antibiotics, called a "Herxheimer reaction." This exacerbation of symptoms shortly after starting antibiotic therapy is thought to be due to a flare of the immune system in response to the killing of spirochetes. While this can indeed occur as an early consequence of antibiotic treatment, the anxious, hypervigilant patient may then hyperfocus so intensely on minor bodily symptoms that the sensation itself is experienced more intensely and the individual becomes increasingly distressed. At times, such hyperfocused attention on bodily symptoms and the resulting anxiety can lead to the shortness of breath, numbness and tingling, increased pain, or a systemic stress-related rash.
- Although Herxheimer reactions can be a valuable "tip" to the treating doctor that antibiotics are having an effect, the physician may be misled if the patient was previously warned to expect a Herxheimer reaction. We are not recommending that a patient not be warned because having such a reaction can be quite disconcerting to the patient. However, the clinician should be aware that how he or she discusses this potential reaction with the patient could influence the outcome. In other words, sometimes an exacerbation of symptoms is a Herxheimer reaction, while at other times it might be a sign of anxiety or somatization.
- Educating the patient about Lyme disease can be helpful in reducing anxiety. For example, here are several anxiety-reducing statements:

- The goal of antibiotic treatment is not to eradicate all *B. burgdorferi* bacteria in the body, but rather to give the immune system a head start by killing enough bacteria so that the immune system can then take over, mopping up any remaining spirochetes. Healthy immune systems are typically able to do this.

- In culture and in animal studies, *Borrelia* grow very slowly over the course of weeks and months. Patients who report feeling a resurgence of symptoms within a couple of weeks after ending an antibiotic course could be informed of *Borrelia*'s slow growth; because the growth is so slow and the remaining organisms (if present) would be quite few in number, it is unlikely that these symptoms are arising because of spirochetal activity. Rather, it may be that the antibiotics—in addition to their antimicrobial benefit—were also providing an anti-inflammatory effect. Not having this anti-inflammatory effect could lead to a rapid return of symptoms.

- Some symptoms may be due to the secondary effects of other primary symptoms of Lyme disease. For example, pain due to Lyme disease may lead to poor sleep. Poor sleep can lead to impaired attention, brain fog, irritability, and increased pain. In other words, the "foggy" brain and ongoing pain may be due to poor sleep rather than direct effects of active infection.

- Some physical symptoms may be due to anxiety itself. Patients are often relieved to learn that anxiety can manifest in quite diverse physical ways, such as chest pain, trouble breathing, numbness and tingling, and heart palpitations. These physical symptoms can arise out of the blue, when one is calm, or even while one is asleep. In fact, these symptoms among patients with primary anxiety (not Lyme disease but Panic Disorder) may be so severe as to lead symptomatic individuals to emergency rooms or to a host of medical specialists, such as cardiologists and neurologists. Fortunately, treatment of the anxiety leads to a remission in the physical symptoms.

# 7

# WHAT ARE THE TREATMENTS FOR LYME DISEASE?

This chapter addresses one of the greatest concerns for patients: How does one treat Lyme disease? It is not possible in this chapter to completely review the treatment of Lyme disease because to do so would require careful review of the many studies that have been conducted since Lyme disease was first discovered. That would take up too much space and time and has already been conducted by several expert review committees. Guidelines have been developed by the Infectious Disease Society of America (IDSA), the International Lyme and Associated Diseases Society (ILADS), and by other organizations such as the American Academy of Neurology. These guidelines—published in peer-reviewed journals—are available online and should be reviewed by clinicians. As noted in chapter 5, the IDSA guidelines and the ILADS guidelines differ considerably.

Controversies about treatment—particularly in regard to the treatment of post-treatment Lyme disease syndrome (PTLDS)—partly reflect the paucity of well-designed treatment studies that have been conducted and the inadequacy of current diagnostic tests to tell us whether active infection is still present. The IDSA guidelines (2006) convey that current treatment strategies are sufficient and successful in treating Lyme disease in the human host, while the ILADS guidelines (2014) state that current treatment strategies are sometimes insufficient and at times fail to eradicate the spirochete. The authors of the IDSA guidelines indicate that PTLDS is uncommon and not helped by repeated antibiotics; they argue that there is little evidence that infection persists in the human after antibiotic treatment and that the controlled clinical trials of PTLDS have been largely negative. The authors of the ILADS guidelines, on the other hand, state that PTLDS is not uncommon and that additional antibiotic treatment with either longer courses or different antibiotic combinations may be beneficial; they argue that persistent infection has been reported in humans in the peer-reviewed literature and that repeated antibiotic therapy has been shown to be helpful in some but not all of the clinical trials. Both the IDSA and ILADS physicians recognize that there are multiple possible causes of persistent symptoms among patients with PTLDS, including post-infectious causes, but the IDSA excludes persistent infection as a reasonable possibility given their review of the evidence, while the ILADS considers persistent infection a likely possibility. The main contention point in the treatment of PTLDS between these two guidelines is whether there is a role for repeated or longer courses of antibiotic therapy in certain individuals.

Readers should note that "guidelines" are meant to "guide" not "dictate." Because there are individual patients who may not experience a full remission after the standard treatment regimens, clinical treatment of the individual patient needs to be tailored, guided by both clinical guidelines and the particular genetics and clinical status of the patient.

Multiple factors may shape whether a person responds fully to initial treatment.

- Does the person have a compromised immune system such that immune-mediated killing of the invading spirochete is not sufficient to eradicate the organism?
- Was the level of antibiotic in the blood sufficient to kill the organism? Or did the individual's metabolism (or competing concurrent drugs) diminish the effectiveness of the antibiotic?
- Has the individual been infected not just by *B. burgdorferi* but also by other infections carried by the tick that together may compromise the immune response?
- If persister *B. burgdorferi* are present and if future research indicates that the recent in vitro findings are applicable to human disease, then could these *Borrelia* persisters be contributing to ongoing symptoms? What other antibiotics or antibiotic delivery strategies might be needed to kill not only actively dividing spirochetes but also the more quiescent persister ones?

- Has the individual developed a post-infectious disorder that now needs treatment with other approaches rather than antibiotics?
- Is there untreated depression or anxiety or a newly activated central pain sensitivity that may have been triggered by the prior infection but is no longer due to active infection?

Not all of these questions have been sufficiently studied, and clinicians do not yet have the tools needed to address these issues in a definitive way. Clinicians therefore must continue to use their "best judgment" in their care of patients, remaining committed to both the science and the art of medicine, which together allow for rational decisions to help shape individual treatment recommendations. The recommendations on the initial treatment of acute Lyme disease that follow are drawn from the IDSA guidelines (Wormser et al. 2006). It should be noted that these differ from the ILADS guidelines; for example, the ILADS report recommends at least twenty-one days of antibiotic therapy for the initial *erythema migrans* (EM) rash (Cameron et al. 2014).

## TREATMENT OF EARLY LYME DISEASE

Largely because the diagnosis is easy to confirm when the EM rash is present, the research community has in the past focused its efforts on studying the treatment of early Lyme disease. Treatment of EM or Lyme disease that presents with isolated facial nerve palsy (without other neurological symptoms suggestive of central nervous system involvement such as prominent headaches, neck rigidity, or abnormal spinal fluid) includes fourteen to twenty-one days of oral doxycycline, cefuroxime, or amoxicillin. However, not all cases result in cure. A small percentage of patients may develop later-stage disease or have persistent symptoms despite early antibiotic therapy.

## TREATMENT OF LATER-STAGE DISSEMINATED LYME DISEASE

Patients with Lyme arthritis who do not demonstrate signs of neurological or cardiac involvement can be treated initially with twenty-eight days of oral doxycycline, amoxicillin, or cefuroxime. If joint swelling and pain persist, additional antibiotic therapy is recommended with another course of either twenty-eight days of oral antibiotics or fourteen to twenty-eight days of intravenous (IV) ceftriaxone. For Lyme arthritis, it may take several months for the inflammation to resolve after treatment.

Acute neurologic Lyme disease (such as meningitis, radiculopathy, facial nerve palsy with likely central nervous system involvement) and *B. burgdorferi*–related heart disease in the United States is generally treated with fourteen to twenty-eight days of IV ceftriaxone. European studies suggest that treatment for fourteen days with oral doxycycline may have comparable efficacy to fourteen days of IV ceftriaxone for neurologic Lyme disease, but similar studies have not yet been done in the United States. For encephalomyelitis, twenty-eight days of IV ceftriaxone is recommended. As with treatment of EM rashes, not all patients recover fully after an initial course of antibiotic therapy.

A note of caution is needed regarding these antibiotic recommendations as many questions still remain.

- Is it good clinical practice to give both antibiotics and steroids to patients with acute facial palsy from *B. burgdorferi* infection? The rationale would be that the antibiotic would kill the infection and the steroids would decrease the inflammation and thereby possibly reduce long-term sequelae. However, a recent retrospective review of a clinical series reported that the facial palsy group receiving antibiotics and prednisone did worse on follow-up than the group receiving antibiotic alone (Jowett et al. 2017). Conclusions from this retrospective series are suggestive. Only a randomized controlled trial will answer this question definitively.

- A recent review of the literature on the treatment studies of neurologic Lyme disease concluded that the European studies were of limited quality and that no adequate quality studies of neurologic Lyme disease in the United States have been conducted (Cadavid et al. 2016). Does this mean that antibiotic treatment is not effective or recommended? Definitely not. This review, however, does indicate that the paucity of well-designed studies limits the conclusion that can be reached with regard to the relative efficacy of different antibiotic regimens for neurologic Lyme disease.

- The treatment of cardiac Lyme disease has not been studied adequately, but intravenous or oral antibiotic therapy is recommended. Because of the risk of life-threatening complications, hospitalization for continued monitoring and treatment is recommended for symptomatic patients, for those with second- or third-degree atrioventricular block, and for those with more severe first-degree block.

When *B. burgdorferi*–triggered symptoms return or persist despite the standard antibiotic recommendations, several options are considered by physicians to help the patient. This area in the treatment of Lyme disease is associated with considerable controversy. In the sections that follow, we address some of the scientific research on these issues.

## TREATMENT FAILURES AND *BORRELIA* PERSISTERS

Treatment relapse or poor response to initial antibiotic treatment for Lyme disease has been well documented. Do these individuals with persistent symptoms continue to have persistent infection? The most direct evidence would be provided by culture or RNA evidence of spirochetal presence. These methods however are rarely used outside of the research setting. Finding DNA of *B. burgdorferi* would also be strong supporting evidence of current or relatively recent infection, but even in early untreated acute infection the polymerase chain reaction (PCR) assays for DNA in the blood are not very sensitive. Pathological study of tissue is also rarely conducted and generally not available. Isolated case reports have been published that document persistent infection in humans despite prior antibiotic treatment; this has been demonstrated in both Europe and the United States, by both culture and/or PCR assays (Strle et al. 1993; Nocton et al. 1994; Strle et al. 1996; Oksi et al. 1999). While these reports are rare in the literature, their occurrence does provide proof of concept that persistent infection needs to be included as one possibility (among many) for persistent symptoms.

A central question that drives the current Lyme disease debates relates to how best to treat individuals with persistent symptoms. Many questions have been explored and new ones continue to be examined.

- Does retreatment with antibiotics offer any additional benefit if that patient has already been treated for Lyme disease with the IDSA-recommended course of antibiotics?
- Does a longer course of treatment confer greater benefit than a shorter course for those with later-stage Lyme disease?
- If one assumes that persister *Borrelia* exist in the human host (as they do in the animal model), are these persister spirochetes problematic or are they simply neutral microbes that reside in the host without causing disease? In other words, are the persister spirochetes causing an inflammatory response in the human host that is leading to symptoms or are they quiescent passive bystanders?
- Because of evidence from in vitro studies that the round forms of *Borrelia* or persister *Borrelia* require a different antibiotic for eradication (Feng et al. 2015, Sharma et al. 2015), is it similarly important for effective treatment of human Lyme disease to provide these different antibiotics as well, particularly in the case of relapsing illness? Does what we are now learning about persister spirochetes in the laboratory setting have any relevance for disease in humans?

## New Developments Regarding Persister Spirochetes

### ANTIPERSISTER ANTIBIOTICS

A laboratory-based in vitro study (Feng et al. 2014) screened a library of 1,524 drugs approved by the Food and Drug Administration (FDA) to see which were most effective against actively replicating and persister *Borrelia*. Ideally, a drug would excel against both the stationary phase and the active growth phase of the bacteria. What they learned was quite interesting. The standard antibiotics for Lyme disease (doxycycline and amoxicillin), while showing good activity against growing bacteria, had low activity against stationary phase *Borrelia* persisters. FDA-approved drugs that did have good activity against both actively growing and stationary spirochetes included carbomycin, cephalosporins (cefoperazone and cefotiam), and sulfamethoxazole. Two agents that were less potent against replicating *Borrelia* but demonstrated excellent antipersister activity included daptomycin and clofazimine. Studies are now underway to assess whether these in vitro efficacy findings can be replicated in the animal model.

## ROUND FORMS

What is the significance of different *Borrelia* morphologies for antibiotic success in eradicating the persister spirochetes? In vitro studies demonstrate that when *B. burgdorferi* are actively growing, they are primarily in the elongated spirochetal form. When *Borrelia* are not actively growing in vitro, they are more often in coccoid or round-body forms, referred to by some incorrectly as "cysts." Standard antibiotics for Lyme disease can impact both the morphology and the outer surface protein expression. In vitro studies, for example, have demonstrated that amoxicillin, which inhibits the synthesis of the bacterial cell wall, induces transformation of *Borrelia* from the elongated spiral form into the round-body form (Feng, Auwaerter, and Zhang 2015).

## BIOFILMS

It has been described that some *Borrelia* form aggregates or colonies that are embedded in biofilms in the laboratory setting (Sapi et al. 2012). *Borrelia* biofilms, as with other microbes, would be expected to enhance the ability of the microbe to survive in hostile environments and to contain both growing organisms and non-growing persister microbes. Biofilm structures not only create problems for antibiotic penetration but they make it easier for bacteria to evade immune detection. Further work is underway to determine whether this finding in the laboratory setting has relevance in the animal or human setting.

## PULSE DOSING TO ERADICATE *BORRELIA* PERSISTERS

Other research groups have also tested large numbers of compounds to see which were most effective in the laboratory setting in killing *B. burgdorferi* persisters (Sharma et al. 2015). One initially promising result of this investigation was that the agent that most readily led to eradication of the persister Lyme spirochetes in vitro was a well-known drug for Lyme disease—ceftriaxone. Ceftriaxone is commonly given intravenously to patients with refractory Lyme arthritis or to those with neurologic Lyme disease, usually for twenty-eight days. The novel finding in this study was that ceftriaxone led to eradication of *B. burgdorferi* only when it was given in a pulse fashion. In other words, the initial single pulse of ceftriaxone killed a substantial percentage of spirochetes quite quickly. By letting the spirochetes grow for an interval "ceftriaxone free," an additional proportion of spirochetes came out of dormancy and were thus vulnerable to being killed with the next brief round of ceftriaxone. After just three pulse courses of ceftriaxone in the laboratory setting, the *Borrelia* spirochetes were eradicated. Unfortunately, efforts to replicate this finding by another research group did not support the anti-persister efficacy of pulse dosing of ceftriaxone (Feng et al. 2016).

## ESSENTIAL OILS TO TREAT BORRELIA INFECTIONS

Essential oils have emerged as potentially valuable new antimicrobial agents with bacteriostatic and/or bacteriocidal activity against multi-drug resistant Gram-negative bacteria (Sakkas 2016). Recently researchers have begun to investigate whether essential oils may be effective in the eradication of *Borrelia* persisters (Feng et al. 2017). These in vitro studies are preliminary and should not be confused as evidence that essential oils should be taken by patients for Lyme disease. Indeed, essential oils need to be tested in the animal model first to assess whether they are effective. Then, these can be evaluated for safety and possible efficacy in humans.

## NOTES ON IN VITRO STUDIES AND THE ROLE OF THE IMMUNE RESPONSE

We highlight a cautionary note for the reader. There is a big difference between what happens "in vitro" in the laboratory setting and what happens in the animal or human when infected. Antimicrobials in the laboratory setting may be rendered ineffective when tested in the in vivo animal model. In other words, one cannot assume that an antibiotic that has been shown to be effective in the laboratory setting will also be effective or safe when given to humans. That is why animal studies (prior to human studies) have been so helpful as the requisite next set of studies after the laboratory in vitro study.

Many patients assume that the goal of antibiotic treatment is to wipe out all remaining Lyme spirochetes. While this is an understandable desire, it is most often not necessary because the human's immune system should be able to fight off the infection once it gets to a low enough level in the body. The role of antibiotics is therefore to lower the load of spirochetes, leaving the rest of the "cleanup" to the host immune response. However, certain questions remain.

- Is the human immune response always capable of wiping out the remaining *Borrelia* spirochetes?
- Given that the microbe *B. burgdorferi* has evolved over time to persistently infect an immunocompetent host (such as a mouse) and given that it has developed sophisticated immune evasion strategies to allow it to persist, is it really possible for the human immune system to fully "mop up" the spirochetes that may remain after antibiotic killing?
- Given that we know from animal research that the persister spirochetes are less robust (i.e., they often cannot be cultured), is it even necessary to completely wipe out the remaining residual spirochetes?

These are questions that challenge researchers. These are also the questions that challenge clinicians as they struggle to make treatment decisions for a particular patient. These questions can only be answered by carefully controlled animal studies and clinical trials in humans.

## RISKS AND BENEFITS OF ANTIBIOTICS

While this chapter primarily addresses the benefits of antibiotics in the treatment of active Lyme disease, it is important to recognize that antibiotic treatment—while generally well tolerated—carries risks as well. A physician typically discusses these risks with the patient at the time of prescribing the medication. All antibiotics carry a risk of allergic reactions and changes in the gastrointestinal flora (which in some cases can lead to a dangerous colitis, for example with *Clostridrium difficile*).

A few examples of other risks follow.

- Doxycycline can commonly lead to increased sensitivity of the skin to sunlight, moderately severe gastric symptoms (nausea, vomiting, diarrhea), vaginal yeast infections, decreased effectiveness of birth control pills, and rarely more serious problems (e.g., liver damage, esophageal irritation).

- Minocycline can cause an immune-mediated lupus-like reaction with symptoms such as arthralgias, lymphadenopathy, rash, and fever.
- Azithromycin and clarithromycin may lead to mild gastric distress (diarrhea, nausea, abdominal pain), headaches and dizziness, and rarely tinnitus, reversible hearing loss, liver damage, and fatal cardiac arrhythmias.
- Ceftriaxone can lead to gall bladder disease and rarely hemolytic anemia and pancreatitis. The use of indwelling intravenous catheters to provide antibiotics can increase the risk of life-threatening *Staphylococcus* infections and thrombus formation (leading to the risk of pulmonary emboli).
- The fluoroquinolone antibiotics (e.g., ciprofloxacin and levofloxacin) can cause gastric distress, mild headache and dizziness, and—of most concern—carry an increased risk of disabling and potentially serious side effects involving the tendons (tendonitis and tendon rupture), muscles, joints, nerves, and central nervous system.

Many antibiotics interact with other medications, sometimes in dangerous ways. For example, the acne drug isotretinoin when combined with tetracycline (or doxycycline) can lead to increased intracranial pressure with the potential for vision loss. Clarithromycin or azithromycin when combined with the antidepressant citalopram or escitalopram may rarely cause a prolongation of cardiac conduction and a potentially serious irregular heart rhythm.

The other risk of antibiotics that is of considerable public health concern relates to propagation of drug-resistant microbes that no longer respond to available antibiotics. This is a problem stemming from both the use of antibiotics to fight disease in humans and the widespread use of antibiotics in agriculture as pesticides or as growth promotants for food animals. The list of risks from antibiotics is extensive (and readily available on the Internet), but the point is that antibiotics should only be used when they are needed; careful risk/benefit discussions should occur between the physician and patient.

## TREATMENT OF POST-TREATMENT LYME DISEASE SYNDROME

Placebo-controlled randomized clinical trials are the gold standard for helping to determine whether a specific treatment is effective. Most treatment strategies currently given to patients with persistent symptoms have not been subjected to this rigorous scientific test. That is not surprising because these clinical trials are expensive. Before committing to the expense of a clinical trial in humans, scientists usually conduct a trial of the medication in animal models. This is especially important if the antibiotic regimen has not yet been shown to be safe in human studies. Although in vitro laboratory studies are the initial step in demonstrating that an antibiotic can "kill" or "slow the growth" of bacteria, what happens in the lab setting (as previously noted) is not the same as what happens in a living creature.

This was demonstrated, for example, with a novel antibiotic called tigecycline that offered considerable promise because it had a novel mechanism of action. In vitro studies demonstrated that this new first-in-class antibiotic tigecycline was far more effective in eradicating multiple strains of *B. burgdorferi* compared to the gold standard antibiotic ceftriaxone. The hope, therefore, was that tigecycline would be the next great treatment for human Lyme disease, permanently eliminating the spirochete and thus the problem of relapse and potential for antibiotic tolerance. The theory sounded great as to why it would work, but the mouse model study demonstrated that tigecycline did not have greater efficacy than standard antibiotic therapy; rather, persistence of *B. burgdorferi* with both antibiotic approaches was demonstrated (Barthold et al. 2010). Although animal studies do not always replicate how a drug would work in the human host, they do provide critically valuable guides.

### Controlled Trials of Repeated Antibiotic Treatment for PTLDS

As of 2018, there have been four NIH-funded controlled studies of repeated antibiotics for patients with PTLDS in the United States. Because these studies have helped shape treatment guidelines for patients with chronic symptoms and because there are subtleties to these studies that require review before conclusions can be drawn, we will provide detail of the study design, results, and conclusions. A more thorough review of our critique of these trials is available online (Fallon et al. 2012).

Each of the four studies recruited patients with a history of well-documented Lyme disease and a history of persistent symptoms despite prior antibiotic therapy. For ease of reference, these patients will be labeled as having PTLDS. It should be noted that each of these studies recruited patients who had already had considerable prior treatment; patients who have had persistent symptoms despite large amounts of prior antibiotics might be less likely to respond to retreatment with antibiotics than those who only had a single course of the standard IDSA-recommended therapy. By including patients who had already failed multiple courses of prior antibiotics (including IV ceftriaxone), some would argue that these trials were biased toward failure. This is not meant to be a criticism of the study design because physicians sometimes do offer repeated courses of antibiotics to those who have had prior antibiotic therapy, so testing this practice in a controlled setting is helpful. However, for the design of future research studies, it is worth remembering that the likelihood of a successful outcome in a repeated antibiotic trial would be enhanced by excluding patients who had already demonstrated a failure to respond to multiple prior courses of antibiotics. Given that none of the U.S. controlled trials had such an exclusion, successful outcome in any one of these trials would therefore be quite remarkable.

## STUDIES 1 AND 2—FUNCTIONAL STATUS

### Design

Studies 1 and 2 (Klempner et al. 2001) recruited PTLDS patients who reported persistent symptoms of pain or cognitive problems that caused impairment in functioning that began within six months of infection. The pain profiles included chronic musculoskeletal pain, radicular pain, and/or peripheral nervous system sensory symptoms (e.g., numbness, tingling, burning). Although the treatment regimen and assessments for the two clinical studies were identical, the two studies differed on the serologic status of individuals at the time of enrollment; one study recruited those who were currently seropositive (IgG Western blot positive) and the other study recruited those who were seronegative (IgG Western blot negative). For the first three months, the patients were randomly assigned to receive either one month of intravenous ceftriaxone (2 gm/day) followed by two months of oral doxycycline (100 mg twice daily) or one month of IV placebo injections followed by two months of oral placebo pills twice daily. Between months four and six, all patients remained off antibiotics. The primary outcome measure that defined success was improvement in the physical and mental function domains as assessed by self-report using a functional status measure (the Short Form 36). The end point for primary outcome analysis was six months.

## Results

Seventy-eight seropositive and fifty-one seronegative patients were included in the data analysis. A midtrial data analysis revealed no difference between the drug and placebo groups; the study was therefore stopped early because it was deemed unlikely that enrollment of additional patients would substantially change the study outcome. Ultimately, no difference was found on the self-reported functional disability measure between those treated with the antibiotics and those given the placebo. The authors also noted that the treatment itself can cause significant risk—one patient experienced pulmonary embolism (a life-threatening blood clot in the lung). The study concluded that this regimen of antibiotic treatment (three months of antibiotic therapy—one month of IV ceftriaxone and two months of oral doxycycline) was ineffective and potentially harmful for patients with persistent symptoms.

## Comments

The investigators of these two studies decided to enhance the power of the data analysis by combining both seropositive and seronegative patients into one larger pool of patients, thus creating a relatively large sample size of 129 subjects. Because this study has the largest sample size among the U.S. studies, its results have been weighed more strongly than the two subsequent smaller sample size studies. A weakness of this study—and one that makes it hard to know whether this was truly a negative study—is that the final data analysis did not control for differences in severity on the functional status measure at the start of the study. Although patients reported functional impairment, a severity threshold was not used to ensure people were impaired at study entry; although as a whole, the group did have impairment in physical functioning, the range of impairment was wide within this enrolled sample, indicating that some of the patients would not have been meaningfully functionally impaired at the start of the study on the primary outcome measure used to assess efficacy (SF-36). In other words, because the sample contained a mixed group of patients—those who had mild or little impairment and those who had substantial impairment—the final results of the study are hard to interpret. If a person is not significantly impaired at the time of study entry on the primary outcome measure, one would not expect any treatment to result in meaningful change. Typically studies would address this problem by controlling for differences in baseline severity at the time of the data analysis. That was not done when the data in this study were analyzed.

## STUDY 3—FATIGUE

### Design

Study 3 (Krupp et al. 2003) recruited patients with persistent fatigue after treatment for well-documented Lyme disease. During the first month, patients received daily intravenous treatment with either ceftriaxone (2 gm/day) or placebo. During the post-IV period from months two to six, patients were antibiotic free. To be accepted into the study, patients had to report at least moderate levels of fatigue, as determined by a threshold cutoff score on the Fatigue Severity Scale. Fatigue severity was the primary clinical outcome measured in this study. Additional primary study outcome evaluations included cognitive processing speed and the presence of a spirochetal protein (OspA antigen) in the patient's cerebrospinal fluid. Unlike the fatigue outcome for which all patients at the time of enrollment had at least moderately severe fatigue, the patients as a group at the start of this study were not significantly cognitively impaired and only nine of the fifty-five patients had the cerebrospinal fluid protein marker. The primary end point of the study to assess efficacy was six months.

Results

Fifty-five subjects enrolled. Those who were randomized to receive ceftriaxone were three times more likely to be judged as responders on the fatigue measure than those randomly assigned to placebo (69 percent responders with ceftriaxone versus 23 percent responders with placebo, p<0.01). This p-value indicates that there is less than 1 percent likelihood that these results occurred by chance. These results demonstrated that IV ceftriaxone was effective in improving the debilitating fatigue experienced by patients with PTLDS. This does not mean that the fatigue was lessened in all patients, nor does it mean that all of the "responder" patients returned to a normal level of energy by the end of the study. The results do indicate, however, that ceftriaxone clearly led to more patients feeling less fatigued than did intravenous placebo. Equally remarkable was that the authors found that those most likely to benefit were those who had a positive blood test for *B. burgdorferi* antibodies at the time of study entry. Patients who were IgG Western blot positive at study entry were six times more likely to benefit from IV ceftriaxone compared to IV placebo (80 percent responders to IV ceftriaxone versus 13 percent responders to IV placebo, p<0.01). In other words, this study not only showed that IV ceftriaxone led to a sustained reduction in fatigue but it also showed that a subgroup of those with chronic persistent symptoms who had a specific biomarker (i.e., those who still test positive on the IgG Western blot) have a very high chance of improving with repeated antibiotic treatment.

Some patients in this study had adverse effects related either to the antibiotics themselves or to the peripherally inserted central catheter (PICC) used to deliver them, including three cases of sepsis and one case of anaphylaxis. These are dangerous side effects. Sepsis refers to an infection in the bloodstream that can be mild to severe in its consequences; it usually requires inpatient hospitalization because it can lead to blood clots, decreased blood flow to vital organs, organ damage, and/or death. Anaphylaxis refers to a serious life-threatening allergic reaction that requires immediate treatment.

Although thrice as many patients given IV ceftriaxone for one month showed a meaningful improvement in fatigue, compared to those given the placebo, the study authors recommended against a month-long course of IV antibiotics for patients with persistent fatigue after prior treatment for Lyme disease. While the rationale for the final recommendation against offering repeated antibiotic therapy to patients with post-Lyme fatigue is not entirely clear because the treatment itself was shown to be effective for fatigue, considerations included the lack of improvement in other measures (such as cognition) and the risk of serious adverse events. The lack of improvement in cognition is not surprising, however, as patients had only mild cognitive impairment at study entry. Similarly, the lack of an active treatment effect on the OspA protein is impossible to interpret as only nine patients had that protein marker at the start of the study.

## Comments

Because at least moderate fatigue was required for entry into this study and it was assessed using a validated measure, the enrolled sample was ideal for hypothesis testing because the individuals were relatively homogeneous on the primary measure of interest—fatigue. Among the four studies, this was the one study with the most favorable results. Sustained reduction in fatigue was observed at six months three times more often among those who received IV ceftriaxone than among those who received IV placebo. IV ceftriaxone was therefore shown to be effective as a treatment for persistent fatigue among patients with PTLDS. Clearly, given the risks associated with IV ceftriaxone therapy, the identification of a safer therapeutic would be beneficial. Given the profound negative impact of living with debilitating persistent fatigue, however, the potential benefit of IV ceftriaxone should not be disregarded. It would be reasonable for physicians to carefully discuss the risk to benefit ratio with patients to create a personalized, optimized treatment plan.

## STUDY 4—COGNITIVE IMPAIRMENT

### Design

Study 4 (Fallon et al. 2008) recruited patients with persistent Lyme encephalopathy to examine whether a repeated course of IV antibiotic therapy would be beneficial for patients with cognitive impairment and a prior history of having been treated with IV antibiotics for well documented Lyme disease. In this study, all patients had to meet criteria for memory impairment, as well as have a positive IgG Western blot for Lyme disease at the time of enrollment. Unlike earlier studies that relied on self-report measures to assess primary outcome, the primary outcome in this study was an objective measure of cognition (neuropsychological tests). The primary domain of interest was memory.

Patients completed self-report questionnaires, such as a measure of physical and mental functioning (SF-36), which was also used in the Klempner and colleagues study (2001), and the Fatigue Severity Scale, which was also used in the Krupp and colleagues study (2003). The primary end point for efficacy was three months. Durability of response was assessed at six months. Patients were randomly assigned to ten weeks of either IV ceftriaxone or IV placebo. A longer duration of IV treatment (ten weeks) was chosen than is typically given (three to four weeks) because all patients in this study had already failed to experience sustained benefit from a prior standard shorter course of IV antibiotic treatment. Because this was a study evaluating cognition and it is well known that people do better when the same tests are repeatedly administered over a short period of time, this study included the assessment of healthy volunteers to control for the "repeated practice effect." The study therefore had three groups—patients given IV ceftriaxone, patients given IV placebo, and untreated healthy volunteers (who had no prior history of Lyme disease and tested negative on serologic tests for Lyme disease).

## Results

Thirty-seven patients with Lyme encephalopathy (twenty-three randomized to IV ceftriaxone and fourteen randomized to IV placebo) and eighteen healthy controls enrolled. The primary finding was that there was a significant difference in the pattern of cognitive change across the twenty-four weeks for all three groups (p = .04). There was overall greater cognitive improvement in the drug-treated group apparent at three months compared to placebo, which fell just above the border of statistical significance (p = .053). On the primary domain of interest (memory), however, there was no significant difference between groups at either week twelve or week twenty-four. While patients receiving placebo (as well as healthy volunteers) showed a gradual improvement in cognition over time, the patients given IV ceftriaxone showed a greater improvement in cognition compared to placebo at the primary end point of three months. The IV antibiotic–treated patients, however, lost their cognitive gains during the antibiotic-free interval, as measured at six months. On the secondary measures of fatigue, pain, and physical functioning, patients who were more impaired at baseline showed a greater improvement at week twelve when given IV ceftriaxone than when given IV placebo. This improvement was sustained to week twenty-four in the pain and physical functioning domains.

Similar to the other studies mentioned previously, this study confirmed concerns about the adverse effects of IV antibiotic treatment. Approximately 20 percent of enrolled patients had adverse effects that resulted in either hospitalization or withdrawal of study medication. Side effects included allergic reactions, biliary pain from ceftriaxone-induced gallbladder stones and sludge, blood clots forming on the PICC line, and systemic infection with *Staphylococcus* bacteria.

Because the improvement in cognition at three months was not sustained to six months and because IV treatment was associated with significant risks, including blood clots and sepsis, the conclusion was that treatment with ten weeks of IV antibiotics is not recommended for sustained improvement in cognition among patients with PTLDS.

Comments

The Lyme encephalopathy study results must be taken in context. First, the enrolled patients were among the most "treatment refractory" because all had previously been treated with oral and intravenous antibiotic therapy. Indeed, these patients had had on average seven months of prior oral antibiotics and two months of prior IV antibiotics. Second, because the sample size was so small (thirty-seven patients), even an effective treatment would be unlikely to be shown to be helpful. In other words, a small sample size raises the bar high for demonstrating efficacy because only the most robustly effective treatment could ever prove to be effective. Given these two detrimental factors for a study, the fact that there was greater improvement in cognition for the ceftriaxone group compared to placebo at twelve weeks that fell just above the margin of statistical significance is remarkable. Also notable was that repeated IV antibiotic therapy resulted in sustained improvement over six months in the secondary outcome measures of pain and physical impairment among the more impaired subgroups when baseline severity was included in the statistical analysis of the entire sample. However, these self-report measures were not the primary outcome domains chosen before the study; proof of efficacy requires an independent study to assess these measures as a primary outcome before definitive conclusions can be drawn.

One question of interest is why cognitive gains were lost during the antibiotic-free interval to week twenty-four but other physical symptom domains seemed to have sustained improvement among the more impaired (pain and physical functioning). One explanation is that perhaps the mechanism for improvement differed. If one is treating a central nervous system infection, one would expect long-term sustained improvement. It is unlikely that the relapse in cognition was due to resurgence of persister *Borrelia* because in that case one would also have expected a loss of the improvement in pain and physical functioning. Perhaps the benefit in cognition was not due to the antimicrobial effect of ceftriaxone but rather to the glutamate modulating effect of ceftriaxone on the central nervous system, which might require continued pharmacotherapy for sustained clinical response. Conversely, the benefit in other more physical domains may have reflected a true antimicrobial effect and that may be why improvement in these areas was sustained. These are speculations— that is, hypotheses that emerge from these data analyses that may serve to guide future investigations.

Some research scientists argue that persistent infection is not likely given that there was no evidence by PCR or culture that infection was present. While this would be a logical argument for many blood-borne infections, we would not consider this to be a logical argument for *B. burgdorferi* infection, which resides in the blood only transiently at the earliest stage of infection. It is widely recognized that the PCR assay and culture are extremely insensitive in detecting infection in the blood if one is testing individuals with active infection *after the initial stage* of the EM rash. Even in cases of acute neurologic Lyme disease, it is extremely difficult to document by culture or PCR that the organism is present. In the case of Lyme disease, therefore, one needs to remain careful about one's assertions. While we cannot claim that infection persists without demonstration of the infection, we also cannot claim that it is absent because the infection cannot be detected by direct techniques such as PCR and culture.

## WHAT CAN WE CONCLUDE FROM THESE NIH-FUNDED ANTIBIOTIC RETREATMENT STUDIES FOR PATIENTS WITH CHRONIC SYMPTOMS AFTER TREATMENT FOR LYME DISEASE?

Comparing studies can be informative. The reviewers for the Fallon study prior to publication asked that the Lyme encephalopathy data be reanalyzed using the same enrollment criteria, fatigue measure, and "responder" definitions as in the Krupp study. When this was done, the results were striking. As shown in figure 7.1, nearly identical treatment

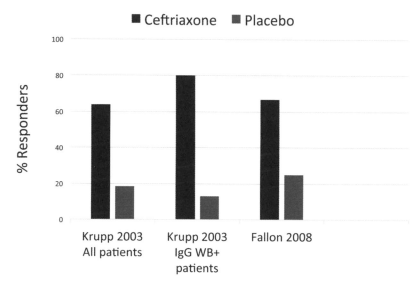

**FIGURE 7.1**

Percentage of patients who had sustained improvement in fatigue over six months. Data from two controlled clinical trials of repeated IV antibiotic therapy among patients with post-treatment Lyme disease syndrome.

improvement was noted in both studies on the fatigue measure at six months. That an independent second study (Fallon et al. 2008) found nearly identical results reinforces the conclusion that the original findings in the Krupp study are valid and reproducible—indeed, repeated antibiotic therapy with IV ceftriaxone does lead to sustained improvement in fatigue more often than IV placebo.

Among the two-thirds of responders to the IV antibiotic, was the reduction in fatigue clinically meaningful? The best way to answer this question is to look at the "effect size," which quantifies the size of the difference between the drug and placebo groups. In the Krupp study (2003), the improvement in fatigue was estimated to be moderate to large (Fallon et al. 2012); this is an effect that makes a meaningful difference in patients' lives and is greater than that found for many drugs that have received FDA approval (e.g., antidepressants).

In summary, the Klempner and colleagues studies (2001) were negative, while the Krupp and colleagues study (2003) showed sustained improvement on the primary measure of fatigue following IV ceftriaxone. The Fallon and colleagues study (2008) showed a moderate improvement in cognition in the ceftriaxone group at three months, but improvement in the primary outcome of cognition was not sustained. In the Fallon study, secondary planned and requested analyses suggested that individuals with more severe secondary symptoms (pain, fatigue, physical functioning) showed sustained improvement over six months if randomized to IV ceftriaxone.

As with many findings in scientific research, there are those in the academic community who disagree with the conclusions presented here. We encourage the reader—if interested—to read the different perspectives on these clinical trials by reviewing the following articles: Fallon et al. 2012; Delong et al. 2012; Klempner et al. 2013.

What take-aways can be drawn from these complex studies?

- IV ceftriaxone treatment results are mixed: some studies show clinical improvement in response to repeated antibiotic therapy, while others do not.
- IV antibiotics are associated with serious risks.

- While repeated antibiotic therapy can be helpful for post-treatment Lyme fatigue in some patients, it is clear that safer delivery methods are needed. It is also clear that these antibiotic treatment approaches, while leading to improved energy among many patients (about 60 percent) with persistent fatigue after getting Lyme disease, are not helpful to all. Novel treatment approaches are needed, as are diagnostic assays and biomarker predictors to help guide treatment selection.

## WHAT TREATMENT STUDIES FROM OTHER COUNTRIES HAVE ADDRESSED POST-TREATMENT LYME DISEASE?

The PLEASE study (Persistent Lyme Empiric Antibiotic Study Europe), a recent trial from the Netherlands (Berende et al. 2016) of 280 patients with persistent symptoms attributed to Lyme disease, asked an interesting question: Among patients who have all been given two weeks of intravenous ceftriaxone therapy, is it beneficial to extend that treatment by giving an additional twelve weeks of oral antibiotic therapy?

### Design

Patients with persistent symptoms attributed to Lyme disease were eligible if their symptoms were either a) temporally related to an EM rash or an otherwise proven case of symptomatic Lyme disease or b) accompanied by an immunoblot assay demonstrating *B. burgdorferi* IgG or IgM antibodies, regardless of prior enzyme-linked immunosorbent assay IgG/IgM results.

All patients received two grams of ceftriaxone administered intravenously for two weeks followed by random assignment to twelve weeks of masked treatment with one of the following oral regimens: a) doxycycline (100 mg twice daily); b) clarithromycin (Biaxin 500 mg twice daily) and hydroxychloroquine (Plaquenil 200 mg twice daily); or c) placebo (two different placebo capsules twice daily).

Improvement in physical functioning was assessed by the composite score of the Short Form 36. Assessments were conducted fourteen, twenty-six, forty, and fifty-two weeks after the start of therapy.

## Results

The study failed to show a benefit of *extended* antibiotic therapy because there was no difference among patient groups after intravenous antibiotic therapy on improvement in physical functioning; those who got placebo performed just as well as those who got doxycycline or the combination of clarithromycin and hydroxychloroquine.

All groups improved over time; this is notable because all of the patients received two weeks of intravenous ceftriaxone prior to being randomized to extended antibiotic therapy or placebo.

Using the specific antibiotic type and duration given in this study, the authors concluded that in patients with persistent symptoms attributed to Lyme disease, longer-term antibiotic treatment did not confer additional beneficial effects on health-related quality of life beyond those obtained with shorter-term treatment.

## Comments

While the study results did not support the benefit of longer-term therapy, the results did suggest that a two-week course of intravenous antibiotic therapy (given to people most of whom have already received prior antibiotic therapy) may be effective in improving physical functioning. Although this study suggests that *repeated* antibiotic therapy may be useful, it does not prove it. Why? Because there was no placebo control group when the IV ceftriaxone was first given, it is possible that patients may have improved with the passage of time alone or that positive expectations about a treatment effect led to improved outcome. In other words, without a placebo control, it remains impossible to know whether IV ceftriaxone was a positive instrument of change. While there are many strengths to this study (e.g., large sample size, sophisticated data analysis, inclusion of baseline functional severity as a covariate, a study design that replicates community-based practice), there are design limitations that limit our ability to draw useful clinical conclusions from this study. These limitations include:

- Because only 96 of 280 participants (34 percent) had objective evidence of Lyme disease such as the characteristic EM rash, the majority of the study population had nonspecific symptoms that were attributed to Lyme disease solely on the basis of positive IgM or IgG (or both) immunoblot assays for *B. burgdorferi*. Therefore the results of this clinical trial may not be generalizable to patients with persistent symptoms who have had well-documented previously treated Lyme disease. This study does what it says—it shows that extended treatment using these particular antibiotics are not helpful among a heterogeneous sample of patients, some of whom may not have had Lyme disease in the past.

- 9 percent of the study sample had only an IgM immunoblot as the positive lab test for enrollment—as previously discussed in the lab test section, the IgM immunoblot has a greater risk of false positive results due to cross-reactivity and there is debate as to whether the IgM immunoblot is informative after the initial stage of infection. (This limitation was partially mitigated in subsequent analysis by the study's authors [Kullberg et al. 2016] in which they report that when this latter IgM positive group was excluded from the analysis, the results of the study did not change.)

- Prior treatment for Lyme disease was not a requirement for study entry; indeed, in this study, 11 percent of the patients had not been treated for Lyme disease previously. Although 89 percent of the patients might be considered to have post-treatment Lyme disease, these 11 percent would not. It would have been helpful in the data analysis to remove this 11 percent to determine whether the improvement with IV ceftriaxone continued to be seen and to analyze the extended treatment results with a sample who truly might be considered to have post-treatment Lyme disease. Results from these secondary analyses, however, were not provided or perhaps were not done.

## OTHER THERAPEUTIC STRATEGIES

### Intravenous Immunoglobulins

Intravenous immunoglobulins (IVIG) contain the pooled IgG antibodies from the plasma of approximately a thousand blood donors. Immunoglobulin products were administered initially by intramuscular injection but now are given intravenously. IVIG is considered a relatively safe and effective, although expensive, treatment for neuropathies associated with autoimmune diseases. IVIG administration is known to decrease circulating inflammatory molecules and thereby decrease the body's inflammatory response. It can play a significant role in immunomodulation and suppressing autoimmune diseases.

Neurologists are beginning to investigate how to treat what appears to be a postinfectious *B. burgdorferi*–triggered small fiber peripheral neuropathy, a condition in which nerve damage causes tingling, burning, or stabbing sensation in the limbs. Based on the hypothesis and emerging evidence that *B. burgdorferi*–triggered peripheral neuropathy may be due in part to an autoimmune process, similar to the process that causes nerve damage in inflammatory demyelinating polyneuropathies, some physicians hypothesize that IVIG treatment may be beneficial. In small fiber neuropathy, patients may have severe symptoms with normal electromyography and minimal findings on exam. Pathology is limited to loss of small fibers as detected by epidermal biopsy; the large nerve fibers are not affected. Although there are anecdotal reports of the effectiveness of IVIG for small fiber neuropathy, there are no randomized controlled trials that allow conclusions to be drawn about the true effectiveness of IVIG.

A case report described an individual with polyneuropathy triggered by *Borrelial* infection that did not respond adequately to antibiotic therapy but did respond to treatment with intravenous immunoglobulins (Rupprecht et al. 2008). In a new research presentation at an American Academy of Neurology annual meeting (Katz and Berkley 2009), results were presented on the use of IVIG among a series of patients with neuropathic symptoms, a history of Lyme disease, and OspA reactivity in the serum demonstrated on Western blot. After six months of treatment with IVIG, these patients had objective improvement in small fiber nerve density as demonstrated by skin biopsy before and after treatment as well as subjective improvement in clinical symptoms. While not a controlled study, this open label clinical series provided preliminary evidence in support of IVIG as a potentially effective treatment for patients with post-antibiotic *B. burgdorferi*–triggered immune mediated neuropathy.

The most common side effects of IVIG treatment include headache, flushing, chills, muscle pains, palpitations, wheezing, nausea, and back pain. If these side effects occur during an infusion, these can often be diminished by slowing or discontinuing the infusion. In patients who have experienced these symptoms in the past, some physicians recommend premedication with antihistamines and intravenous hydrocortisone before the start of the infusion as this may help reduce adverse effects.

Serious adverse effects, although rare, may include blood clots (especially among patients with preexisting vascular disease), kidney failure (among patients with renal insufficiency), anaphylaxis (especially among patients with IgA deficiency), or septic meningitis (especially among patients with migraine). Physicians should carefully discuss the risks and benefits of IVIG treatment with their patients. At this point, given the lack of systematic or controlled studies, IVIG for small fiber neuropathies triggered by Lyme disease remains an experimental treatment. The IDSA currently recommends against this treatment due to its potential risks and its unproven effectiveness for Lyme disease. However, for large fiber neuropathies (e.g., autoimmune demyelinating polyneuropathy or chronic inflammatory demyelinating polyneuropathy), IVIG is recognized as an effective treatment.

## Nonsteroidal Anti-Inflammatory Drugs, Methotrexate, and Hydroxychloroquine

A small number of patients with Lyme arthritis who have already received extensive antibiotic therapy still have significant swelling and pain in their joints. For patients with persistent arthritis after sixty days of antibiotics who no longer have a positive PCR for *B. burgdorferi* in the synovial fluid, nonsteroidal anti-inflammatory (NSAID) drugs such as aspirin or ibuprofen may be helpful in reducing pain and inflammation. Although NSAIDs can be purchased over the counter, a physician should still be consulted about whether a patient would benefit from taking them because there are risks associated with their long-term use, including gastric ulcers and kidney damage.

If patients have tried antibiotics and NSAIDs and still have significant joint swelling and pain, disease-modifying anti-rheumatic drugs (DMARDs) such as methotrexate or hydroxychloroquine may be recommended (Steere et al. 2016). Methotrexate is a chemotherapy agent as well as an immune system suppressant used in a variety of autoimmune diseases including psoriasis, rheumatoid arthritis, and Crohn's disease. Hydroxychloroquine is a prescription oral antimalarial medication that is helpful in treating autoimmune disorders as well as persistent Lyme arthritis.

## Synovectomy Surgery

If antibiotics, NSAIDs, and DMARDs have all been attempted but severe antibiotic-refractory Lyme arthritis has persisted for over twelve months, arthroscopic synovectomy surgery may be considered. During this operation, the membrane lining the affected joint, often a knee joint, is removed in order to reduce pain, swelling, and inflammation (Steere et al. 2016). This procedure can usually be performed in the outpatient setting.

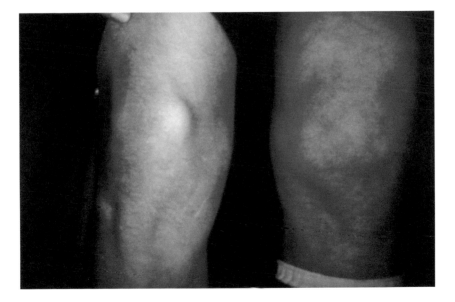

**FIGURE 7.2**

Approximately 60 percent of patients with untreated *B. burgdorferi* infection may develop Lyme arthritis.

*Courtesy of the CDC.*

## Neuropsychiatric Pharmacologic Treatment

Consultation with a psychiatrist and/or neurologist can be very helpful for patients who suffer from continued symptoms both to address the psychological impact of a chronic illness and to obtain relief from the psychiatric and neurologic symptoms that may have been triggered by *B. burgdorferi* infection. There have been well-documented cases of *B. burgdorferi* infection leading to the development of psychosis, depression, anxiety, obsessive compulsive symptoms, and other serious psychiatric problems and resolution of these psychiatric symptoms after antibiotic therapy (Pachner 1988; Fallon and Nields 1994; Hess et al. 1999; Banerjee, Liu, and Minhas 2013). Although the acute psychiatric effects of Lyme disease may resolve with antibiotic treatment, the more chronic psychiatric symptoms that persist after initial Lyme disease treatment may not respond to additional antibiotics but rather require a more traditional neuropsychiatric treatment. Unfortunately, treatment studies addressing the neuropsychiatric sequelae of Lyme disease have lagged far behind other areas of progress in Lyme disease. While there have been placebo-controlled studies examining whether cognition improves after repeated antibiotic therapy (Krupp et al. 2003; Klempner et al. 2001; Fallon et al. 2008), there have been almost no studies assessing efficacy of nonantibiotic therapies for neuropsychiatric symptoms that persist after antibiotics.

In the acute phase of a central nervous system infection (e.g., Lyme encephalitis), the initial presentation may well be neuropsychiatric—confusion, disorientation, memory loss, agitation, paranoia, mood swings, psychosis, severe startle, and sensory hyperacuities. Neuropsychiatric symptoms related to acute central neurologic Lyme disease will resolve most readily with antibiotics that cross the blood-brain barrier, such as IV ceftriaxone. (European studies suggest oral doxycycline is comparable in efficacy to IV ceftriaxone for acute neurologic Lyme disease. However, because similar studies have not yet been conducted in the United States, oral doxycycline cannot yet be considered an acceptable alternative to IV ceftriaxone in the United States.)

When the acute infection has been treated but the neuropsychiatric symptoms persist, other symptom-based treatment approaches are essential. Some of these approaches have long-lasting curative effects in resolving the symptoms of PTLDS. Reduction of the neuropsychiatric sequelae also has the advantage of reducing the long-term negative impact of the disease on the patient, the family, and the patient's ability to function in daily life.

The medications in the discussion that follows may be helpful for many of the symptoms associated with PTLDS. We emphasize, however, that none of these agents have been carefully studied among patients with PTLDS. In addition, because the recommendations may extend beyond the list of FDA-approved indications, discussion of risks and benefits should occur with the treating clinician. Many of our suggestions are based on the assumption that agents demonstrated to be effective in other disorders and syndromes with similar symptom profiles may also be helpful for patients whose symptoms persist despite antibiotic therapy. Controlled studies of non-antibiotic approaches for the treatment of PTLDS are needed to demonstrate efficacy, tolerability, and long-term sustained benefit. Antidepressant and antianxiety medication have a role in the treatment of PTLDS. Selective serotonin reuptake inhibitors (SSRIs) such as sertraline, fluoxetine, paroxetine, fluvoxamine, citalopram, and escitalopram may be helpful for patients with depressed mood, irritability, or anxiety.

Similarly, serotonin-norepinephrine reuptake inhibitors (SNRIs) can help improve depressed mood and anxiety. Because of their dual neurotransmitter actions, these medications also have pain-reducing properties.

Certain medications in this class (e.g., duloxetine and milnacipran) are FDA-approved for the treatment of pain disorders as well. As a class, therefore, SNRIs are often used by neurologists, rheumatologists, and primary care physicians to treat chronic neuropathic pain, fibromyalgia, mood disorders, and menopausal symptoms.

Typical SNRIs in the United States include venlafaxine, desvenlafaxine, duloxetine, milnacipran, and levomilnacipran. Because SNRIs are helpful in the treatment of both chronic pain (neurologic and muscular) and depression, their use is likely to have a particular benefit for patients with PTLDS who often suffer with both pain and depressed mood. Among the SNRIs, levomilnacipran is among the most noradrenergically active; this suggests it may also be more potent in relieving pain syndromes as well as in reducing depression among those with signs of active inflammation.

One medication that may be particularly helpful for patients with PTLDS is bupropion, given that it is generally well-tolerated and it has positive effects on mood, energy, and attention.

Certain antiseizure medications, such as gabapentin, valproate, and carbamazepine, have mood-stabilizing properties and may also be helpful in controlling chronic pain, migraines, peripheral neuropathy, and/or sensory hypersensitivities.

- Patients with an increased sensitivity to sound may benefit from gabapentin or carbamazepine treatment (Nields, Fallon, and Jastreboff 1999). In addition to sound sensitivity, carbamazepine can also be particularly helpful in reducing skin sensory hypersensitivity and headaches.
- A pilot study of gabapentin (dose 500 to 1,200 mg/day) given to ten patients for chronic neuropathic pain after Lyme disease (Weissenbacher, Ring, and Hoffman 2005) revealed improvement among nine of ten patients in "crawling" and "burning" pain sensations and in the neck and radiating lumbar pain, as well as improvement among five of ten patients in mood, general feeling of health, and quality of sleep.

Low-dose naltrexone may also be helpful in reducing pain among patients with PTLDS given studies of its use for chronic pain associated with inflammatory processes. Small placebo controlled studies among patients with fibromyalgia demonstrate benefit in pain reduction with low dose naltrexone (4.5 mg daily) greater than that seen with placebo (Younger, Parkitny, and McLain 2014).

Treatment of sleep disturbances should be a priority in the care of the patient with chronic symptoms, as the sequelae of poor sleep include daytime fatigue, impaired cognition, and musculoskeletal pain. Given that the latter symptoms are most common among patients with PTLDS symptoms, a careful sleep assessment is needed. The clinician should always start with an assessment of sleep hygiene, as simple behavioral changes can enhance sleep onset and duration. Cognitive behavioral therapy and relaxation techniques for insomnia can also be quite effective.

There are a variety of approved medications for insomnia that include benzodiazepines, non-benzodiazepine sedatives, melatonin agonists, doxepin, and suvorexant. Given the wide-range of medication options, selection can be guided by the type of insomnia. For patients with sleep onset insomnia, a short-acting medication with duration of less than eight hours may be preferable as it may also reduce the risk of residual somnolence on awakening; these would include agents such as zolpidem, zaleplon, lorazepam, and ramelteon. For patients who have a hard time maintaining sleep, longer-acting medications such as extended-release zolpidem, temazepam, eszopiclone, suvorexant, and low dose-doxepin can be helpful, but these would also increase the risk of somnolence on awakening. Suvorexant, which acts through antagonism of the orexin receptors, is not recommend for patients already on medications that inhibit the liver enzyme CYP3A, such as ketoconazole or clarithromycin.

Benzodiazepine receptor agonists (e.g., clonazepam, lorazepam, temazepam, or alprazolam) enhance sleep onset and duration and also have muscle relaxant and anxiolytic properties. However, benzodiazepines can have significant adverse effects, including cognitive impairment and motor incoordination. Benzodiazepines have also been associated with an increased risk of falls leading to hip fracture in the elderly, an increased risk of motor vehicle accidents, and respiratory depression in patients with severely impaired pulmonary function.

Other medications to consider for insomnia include:

- Low doses of amitriptyline, cyclobenzaprine, trazodone, mirtazapine, or quetiapine can be effective in improving sleep onset and duration. Amitriptyline, cyclobenzaprine, and doxepin would also be helpful in reducing musculoskeletal and neuropathic pain syndromes. Sedating antihistamines such as diphenhydramine also can improve sleep onset and duration.
- Gabapentin has been reported to lead to improved sleep quality and would be particularly appropriate for the sleep-disordered individual

with neuropathic pain or restless leg syndrome (Weissenbacher, Ring, and Hoffman 2005).

• Over-the-counter melatonin can also decrease subjective sleep latency.

Patients with marked distractibility and inattention may benefit from medicines used to treat attention deficit disorder, such as the stimulant medications methylphenidate, lisdexamfetamine, and dextroamphetamine; these medications however should be avoided among individuals with addiction histories. Alternatively non-stimulant medications may be helpful, such as bupropion, modafinil, or atomoxetine. Other medications that help enhance attention (e.g., clonidine and guanfacine) may be considered, but their side effect profile may be less favorable for patients with PTLDS symptoms. Typically starting with bupropion is a preferred option because, if effective, it alleviates the risk of adverse effects associated with stimulant drugs.

For patients who suffer from overwhelming fatigue, agents shown in double-blind placebo-controlled studies to be helpful in reducing fatigue among patients with multiple sclerosis may also be helpful for patents with PTLDS; these include modafinil and amantadine.

Patients should be made aware of potential drug interactions between these medications and antimicrobial agents. For example, ketoconazole and erythromycin increase the blood levels of benzodiazepines, such as clonazepam and alprazolam, possibly leading to increased fatigue and cognitive impairment. Fluvoxamine, citalopram, and azithryomycin can each delay cardiac conduction, causing a prolonged QT interval and leading to arrhythmias; combinations of these medications can be dangerous. While most psychiatric medications are well tolerated with few significant interactions, knowledge of drug interactions is essential given that patients with PTLDS are often on multiple medications.

While psychiatric medications can be very helpful, they may also cause a range of mild to serious side effects, such as sexual dysfunction, weight gain, and birth defects if used during pregnancy (especially for certain antiseizure medications). Central nervous system stimulants can lead to agitation in some patients and rarely paranoia. Modafanil may rarely cause severe skin reactions or systemic hypersensitivity. Therefore a careful evaluation by a physician and detailed discussion of the risks and benefits of each medication is necessary prior to starting any treatment. Patients taking these medications should continue to be monitored regularly by a physician for improvement and for any side effects.

## Psychotherapy

Chronic symptoms can cause an enormous amount of stress in a person's life and may even trigger or exacerbate a psychiatric illness, such as major depression or an anxiety disorder. Working with a mental health professional can be very helpful in coping with symptoms or in treating any psychiatric illness that may have arisen. There are many different types of psychotherapy.

### COGNITIVE BEHAVIORAL THERAPY

Cognitive behavioral therapy (CBT) focuses on identifying and changing unhelpful thoughts, beliefs, and behaviors. More emphasis is placed on current problems and solutions to those problems than on a patient's past. The patient needs to be an active participant, do homework assignments, and collaborate with the therapist. This is a highly effective, time-limited treatment for depression and anxiety. There are excellent self-help books that explicate CBT approaches to depression, anxiety, insomnia, and other problems.

### PSYCHODYNAMIC THERAPY

Psychodynamic therapy helps the patient gain more awareness of his or her own troubling unconscious thoughts, coping style, and defense mechanisms. By doing so, many patients are able to change their response to life events and find a new perspective on themselves and a new understanding of others, resulting in improved quality of life. Psychoanalysis is a more intensive form of psychodynamic therapy that often requires therapy two to four times a week; this therapy is typically reserved for individuals with personality disorders or for healthier people who seek a deeper understanding of their own psychological structure.

## INTERPERSONAL THERAPY

Interpersonal therapy (IPT) focuses on identifying how a patient communicates with others and how certain distressing emotions may be triggered. This often entails exploring a patient's past and current relationships with others and typically lasts twelve to sixteen weeks. IPT has been shown to be helpful in a variety of psychiatric disorders and is well tolerated, particularly by those who find psychodynamic therapy too vague and cognitive behavioral therapy too formulaic and bound to homework assignments.

## DIALECTICAL BEHAVIOR THERAPY

Dialectical behavior therapy (DBT) draws from sources as diverse as CBT and Buddhist meditation to treat patients with mood and personality disorders among other psychiatric conditions. DBT is very structured and similar to CBT in that the patient is an active participant in therapy and is often required to complete homework assignments. DBT focuses on mindfulness and skills training for emotion regulation and distress tolerance. Typically a DBT program includes individual and group therapy with a focus on specific exercises to enhance the consolidation of newly learned coping skills.

## TRAUMA- AND GRIEF-FOCUSED THERAPIES

Traumatic events include severe life stressors, such as loss of job, death of a loved one, break up of a relationship, witnessing or experience violence, or sudden severe illness. The multiple stressors associated with Lyme disease and the related losses for some individuals can be extreme. While some individuals have a natural capacity to reach out to others to talk about their trauma or loss, other individuals are prone to keep their emotional pain private or even to repress it to such an extent that one is not aware that the emotional pain exists. In these latter individuals, unexpressed emotional pain may come out as bodily pain, new onset somatic symptoms, "nonepileptic" seizures, or loss of neurologic function. Henry Maudsley, a British physician from the nineteenth century, said, "The sorrow that has no vent in tears makes other organs weep." When individuals with unexpressed grief come into a therapy that encourages the expression of emotions related to loss, progress can be substantial. Obviously psychotherapy cannot eliminate the residual effects of Lyme disease, but therapy may lead to a variety of positive changes. These include renewed energy, better sleep, less anxiety, improved neurologic function, fewer somatic symptoms, abatement of "nonepileptic" seizures, and an enhanced outlook on present and future.

Mental health professionals often use a combination of these psychological therapies, augmented as needed with pharmacotherapy, to help the individual patient with the challenging task of living with a waxing-waning or chronic illness.

## Cognitive Remediation

Consultation with a neuropsychologist with expertise in cognitive remediation may also be helpful. Cognitive remediation refers to the retraining of the brain to accomplish tasks that were previously done automatically. Cognitive strengths are used to compensate for current weaknesses. Such approaches have been developed for patients with persistent cognitive deficits after brain injury, for example. Similar strategies may be helpful for patients with persistent cognitive problems after Lyme disease. The best place to find an experienced remediation therapist is at a center for brain injury rehabilitation.

## Neurofeedback

Neurofeedback is a technique in which the clinician uses electroencephalogram (EEG) patterns or functional magnetic resonance imaging (fMRI) to view the patient's brain activity while teaching self-regulation skills to the patient. Neurofeedback is commonly used in the management of chronic pain, as well as memory, mood, and attention problems. There is a particular interest in the use of neurofeedback for disorders of chronic pain because the brain plays a crucial role in the experience of pain. Brain imaging studies of patients with chronic pain show structural and functional abnormalities compared to healthy controls (May 2008).

EEG neurofeedback is an older method that is noninvasive and relatively inexpensive, but it has limitations, chief of which is that it is not able to target specific areas of the brain. Real-time fMRI neurofeedback is also noninvasive, but it has the advantage of allowing the clinician to better localize specific brain areas that are being stimulated. This intervention, however, is quite expensive, requires highly trained individuals for administration, processing, and interpretation, and is presently used primarily as a research tool. Studies with real-time fMRI neurofeedback suggest that this treatment may help patients with mood regulation and pain control.

The goal of neurofeedback therapy is to train patients to be able to manage their symptoms by retraining their nervous system. There have been no studies to date on neurofeedback as treatment for Lyme disease specifically, but some scientists hypothesize that it could be effective based on its preliminary success with other chronic pain conditions and attention disorders, such as fibromyalgia, migraines, and attention deficit hyperactivity disorder (Jensen et al. 2008; Chapin, Bagarinao, and Mackey 2012).

## Exercise

Because patients with PTLDS often experience dramatic fatigue (much akin to patients with chronic fatigue syndrome) and spend significant amounts of time in bed, their muscles can lose strength and tone over time in a process called deconditioning. This can lead to a downward spiral in physical well-being in which patients become extremely fatigued after exercise and so avoid it in the future. Avoidance of exercise leads to further deconditioning, accompanied by greater loss of strength and endurance. To counter this cycle, planning a very gradual but progressive daily exercise regimen with a health professional can assist in a patient's gradual return to health. Among patients with widespread musculoskeletal pain, numerous studies have demonstrated that mild-to-moderate intensity aerobic and weight-bearing exercise can help to reduce pain, depression, fatigue, and improve overall health-related quality of life (Busch 2007).

## Nutrition

The effect of diet on Lyme disease has not been studied, but nutrition has been shown to affect the progression of many common chronic diseases.

**FIGURE 7.3**

Mackerel at market.

*Courtesy of Vincent van Zeijst.*

For example, the "Mediterranean diet," which is rich in omega-3 fatty acids found in certain fish (herring, mackerel, salmon, and several others), olive oil, fruits, vegetables, and nuts as well as rich in whole grains and low in saturated fats, trans-fats, and refined grains has been demonstrated to reduce the incidence of heart disease (Estruch et al. 2013). On the other hand, diets high in refined sugars, trans-fats, etc., and low in fruits, vegetables, and whole grains have been implicated in the development of heart disease (Mozaffarian et al. 2006; Yang et al. 2014). Although there have been no specific studies addressing the impact of diet on Lyme disease symptoms, adhering to a healthy diet may be beneficial to a patient's overall health and warrants a discussion with a physician and nutritionist.

There has also been an increased interest in the potentially beneficial effects of other diets—such as a gluten-free diet. While a gluten-free diet is essential for those who have celiac disease, there is increasing interest in the possibility that a gluten-free diet may help those with "non-celiac gluten sensitivity." Controlled research suggests that these individuals experience less pain, fewer gastrointestinal symptoms, and better mood when on a gluten-free diet (Biesiekierski et al. 2011). Recent research (Uhde 2016) suggests that patients with non-celiac gluten sensitivity suffer from a weakened intestinal barrier, which leads to a systemic immune activation after they eat foods that contain the gluten protein (e.g., wheat, rye, or barley). Typical symptoms include bloating, abdominal pain, and diarrhea, but other symptoms also occur including fatigue, headache, anxiety, and problems with memory and thinking.

## Yoga and Meditation

The stress of a chronic disease affects the nervous, endocrine, and immune systems, impacting the body, brain, and mind. A review published in the *Yale Journal of Biology and Medicine* concluded that yoga and meditation have the power to reduce physical symptoms of chronic disease by way of suppressing the hypothalamic-pituitary-adrenal (HPA) axis and the sympathetic nervous system (Purdy 2013). Activation of the HPA axis and sympathetic nervous system results in higher levels of cortisol and catecholamines, which are stress response molecules that in turn cause heightened anxiety and other deleterious symptoms. In addition to decreasing the stress response, some studies have also suggested that yoga can boost the immune system by increasing levels of IgA antibodies and "natural killer" immune cells, while decreasing markers of inflammation, such as pro-inflammatory cytokines and C-reactive protein. Furthermore, preliminary neuroimaging research demonstrates that mindfulness meditation can induce "neuroplastic changes" in several areas of the brain, including the anterior cingulate cortex, insula, temporo-parietal junction, and fronto-limbic network (Marchand 2014). These changes are associated with the reduction of stress-related symptoms. While there are no published studies yet that address the impact of yoga and meditation on Lyme disease, yoga and meditation are typically very safe and may contribute to patients' feelings of overall health and wellness.

## Probiotics

Antibiotics alter the microbiome and may lead to diarrhea. Probiotics are live microorganisms that are thought to balance the gastrointestinal microflora. Generally, lactobacilli, bifidobacteria, and lactococci are regarded as safe. Moderate quality evidence from twenty-three randomized controlled trials suggests that probiotics are both safe and effective for preventing *Clostridium difficile*-associated diarrhea (Goldenberg et al. 2013). Probiotics have shown promising results in mouse models and some human trials in decreasing symptoms of inflammatory bowel disease (Saez-Lara et al. 2015). Some concern about the safety of probiotics has been raised among those with central venous catheters, those who are immune-compromised, those with cardiac valve disease, and those with short bowel syndrome (Doron and Snydman 2015).

## Herbs and Supplements

Herbs and supplements including vitamins, plants, and spices have long been used for a variety of illnesses by practitioners of complementary and alternative medicine. Various alternative therapies have been suggested that could theoretically target different steps of infection with Lyme disease, for example, inhibition of tick binding to the skin by lemon eucalyptus extract and inhibition of pro-inflammatory cytokine production by capsaicin, boswellia, probiotics, or Cat's Claw, among others (Ali 2017). Some herbs have shown preliminary effectiveness in treating infectious diseases in animal-based scientific studies. For example, the oral administration of crude ethonolic leaf extract of *Artemisia vulgaris* was shown to have antiparasitic effect against malaria in a mouse model (Bamunuarachchi et al. 2013). Rhodiola rosea is a botanical adaptogen that has been shown in controlled research to reduce fatigue under stressful conditions and to improve endurance (Darbinyan et al. 2000). However, based on our review of the published literature, there have been no specific controlled studies showing the effectiveness of any herb or supplement for Lyme disease in humans; such studies are needed to determine efficacy and safety. Due to the paucity of controlled research in this area, physicians may be reluctant to recommend herbs or supplements despite the fact that some individuals may feel that they experienced significant symptomatic improvement after taking a supplement. At this time, herbs and supplements are of unclear benefit for Lyme disease, so it is recommended that any patient who wishes to begin treatment with an herb or supplement discuss its safety and potential for drug interactions with a physician.

## Oxygen Therapy

Some patients have reported improvements in symptoms after using hyperbaric oxygen (HBO) or ozone/hydrogen peroxide infusions. HBO is typically administered in a hyperbaric oxygen chamber. One controlled study assessed the effect of HBO therapy on strains of *B. burgdorferi* in vitro and in infected mice (Pavia 2003). Although *B. burgdorferi* is not an anaerobic microbe, it does prefer to grow in an environment with low oxygen tension. This study found that treatment with hyperbaric oxygen reduced the number of *B. burgdorferi* in culture and the number of mice with *Borrelia* cultured from their bladders; *Borrelia* spirochetes grew out in only 20 percent of the bladder cultures of the HBO treated mice whereas live *Borrelia* were recovered from 90 percent of the mice bladder extracts not given HBO. No studies have assessed the effectiveness of this therapy in humans, and there are risks associated with this therapy, such as middle ear damage.

Ozone or hydrogen peroxide intravenous infusions or rectal/vaginal insufflations have been used by some patients, but there is no known scientific evidence demonstrating their effectiveness, and there are significant risks associated with these methods, including infection.

## Energy, Heat, and Radiation

Chronotherapy, using a light box, has been shown in scientific studies to be effective in treating seasonally related depressive symptoms (Lam et al. 2006). The light box is relatively inexpensive, has few risks, and may be helpful for symptoms, although it has never been studied specifically in Lyme disease. Malariotherapy has been raised for consideration as a possible treatment for Lyme disease (Heimlich 1990); the rationale for this approach is that prior to the discovery of penicillin in the 1940s, malariotherapy was the primary therapy used to help fight another spirochetal disease, syphilis. The mechanism of action is unclear, but may relate to the inflammatory mediators triggered by malaria infection and/or the elevation of core body temperature. Malariotherapy is not recommended, however, for Lyme disease given the many antibiotic options for Lyme disease, the unknown efficacy of this approach, and the dangers associated with acquiring malaria. Some patients have reported success with use of lasers or electromagnetic radio signals (administered by an electromagnetic device called the Rife machine) that are purported to destroy bacteria; with Lyme disease, to our knowledge, these approaches have not been examined in scientific studies. These therapies can be very costly (often thousands of dollars) and have not been proven to be effective.

## Transcranial Magnetic Stimulation and Transcranial Direct Current Stimulation

Transcranial magnetic stimulation (TMS) is an FDA-approved treatment for depression for which numerous studies has shown efficacy (Brunoni et al. 2016). Administered in the outpatient setting, TMS works through a series of magnetic impulses applied to the cerebral cortex in order to modulate neuronal activity. While not yet studied for the neuropsychiatric symptoms associated with post-treatment Lyme disease, this approach has an appeal for those patients with mood disorders who either are not willing to try pharmacologic approaches or have not responded well to medication treatment. These noninvasive brain stimulation techniques have also been reported to reduce neuropathic pain in other disorders by modulating maladaptive neuroplasticity (Naro et al. 2016). An alternative noninvasive approach to brain stimulation—transcranial direct current stimulation (tDCS)—has been reported to relieve central pain in fibromyalgia patients and to reduce fatigue in patients with multiple sclerosis (Ferrucci 2014). One advantage of this technique is that portable devices allow for in-home treatments. Given potential benefits in reducing fatigue, pain, and depression, the efficacy of this treatment should be studied among patients with persistent symptoms despite antibiotic therapy for Lyme disease.

## Vagus Nerve Stimulation

Vagus nerve stimulation (VNS) using an electronic device implanted under the skin in the chest is an FDA-approved treatment for depression and for intractable epilepsy. An uncontrolled trial reported that vagus nerve stimulation was also helpful in reducing the chronic musculoskeletal pain associated with severe fibromyalgia (Lange et al. 2011). A more recent trial among patients with rheumatoid arthritis demonstrated that vagus nerve stimulation led to a reduction in pain and improvement in functioning as well as a decline in the production of the inflammatory cytokine, tumor necrosis factor (Koopman et al. 2016). There is also increased interest in determining whether external vagus nerve stimulators (i.e., noninvasive VNS) can be effective as well, with reports suggesting a potential benefit in reducing migraines (Puledda 2016). The FDA in 2017 approved a hand-held noninvasive vagus nerve stimulator for the treatment of pain associated with episodic cluster headache. This has not yet been studied for PTLDS, but studies should be done given the benefits in reducing pain, improving mood, and decreasing inflammatory cytokine production.

## Placebo and Nocebo

What is known about placebos and nocebos in other medical conditions? Simply stated, patient expectations in regards to treatment benefit and prior experiences have a strong effect on the success or failure of any treatment intervention.

The placebo effect refers to the improvement that occurs after patients are given an inert substance (i.e., something that has no biologically active ingredients) or a procedure without known biological effects. The improvement can be substantial. This usually occurs because the patient expects that the medication will lead to improvement. In the context of Lyme disease or any other infection, placebos will not eradicate the infection, but they can affect central brain processing of pain, mood, cognition, motor functioning, and energy.

Just as with antibiotic therapy, individuals with PTLDS who get better with placebo may show substantial improvements in pain, cognition, and energy levels. How could this happen? While the placebo response is typically not sustained for more than one to two months, it is important to recognize that the placebo effect can lead to physiologic changes in the body.

In a brain-imaging study of patients with Parkinson's disease (de la Fuente-Fernandez et al. 2001), placebo was shown to increase dopamine levels in the brain, helping Parkinson's patients to move more easily. This only occurred, however, among those patients who believed there was a 75 percent chance or greater that they would be getting actual L-dopa. In other words, a high anticipation of benefit led to enhanced dopamine in the brain in response to a placebo pill.

The nocebo effect refers to the deterioration that occurs when patients are given an inert substance, or when they are told a negative reaction might occur from a certain intervention or procedure. This is thought to be due to a combination of heightened expectations of harmful effects as well as from prior experiences (i.e., behavioral conditioning). This would be similar to the rat that learns to associate an electric shock with a bell. When the bell is rung, the rat cringes in fear, even though no more shocks are given.

As an example of the nocebo effect, consider the following randomized controlled study of individuals with back pain (Pfingstein et al. 2001). Fifty patients with chronic low back pain were randomly assigned to the experimental or the control condition. Prior to a simple leg flexion task, the experimental group was told that the movement might result in pain while the control group was told there would be no increase in pain. As one might expect, those patients who were pre-warned that pain might occur also reported increased pain intensity and fear during the test and their avoidance behavior during the test correlated with their fears. Negative expectations and fear associated with pain contributes to chronic pain ("chronification") and leads to disability due to pain avoidance behaviors. This is an important area of investigation in all chronic illnesses, particularly those associated with chronic pain or fatigue.

The message then for health care providers is to make use of the placebo effect by instilling positive expectations for improvement and to reduce nocebo effects by listening carefully to the patient and addressing negative or frightening beliefs about the ineffectiveness or harmful effects of treatments for the disease. Given that patients acquire considerable medical information on-line and some of it can be quite convincing and disturbing, physicians should explore patients' beliefs and fears and advise patients to be wary of Internet sites that present harrowing and hopeless stories. (See chapter 11 for tips on navigating the Internet).

# 8

---

# OTHER TICK-BORNE INFECTIONS

In addition to the *Borrelia* spirochete that causes Lyme disease, ticks may carry many other microbes—including other bacteria, viruses, and parasites. Infection by one of these other tick-borne microbes may lead to a spectrum of human illness, ranging from a mild illness that resolves on its own without treatment to a more severe illness, in some cases leading to death. The type of microbe in ticks varies depending on geographic location and on the species of tick. Some of these coinfecting microbes are relatively common in ticks from Lyme endemic areas, while others are rarely or never found in ticks from these areas. Some of these microbes can be transmitted within fifteen minutes after tick attachment (e.g., Powassan virus), while others may take twenty-four hours or longer (e.g., Babesia microti).

Awareness that ticks may transmit other microbes that cause human disease has obvious clinical relevance. First, a patient may have had a tick bite and subsequent flu-like symptoms but test negative for Lyme disease. Why would this occur? One possibility is that the test for early Lyme disease is insensitive and thus this represents a false negative. Another possibility is that although this patient was bitten by a tick and did get sick, this patient does not have Lyme disease. In other words, the negative Lyme disease test was accurate but the tick transmitted another microbe that also causes a flu-like illness (e.g., Anaplasma or *Borrelia miyamotoi*) that requires a different test for detection. Another reason that knowledge about coinfections is important is because patients may experience a more severe illness if they have been coinfected by more than one tick-borne microbe. This hypothesis was supported by a large study demonstrating that individuals who were coinfected with the microbes causing Lyme disease and Babesiosis had a more prolonged illness and experienced more severe symptoms (fatigue, headache, sweats, nausea, emotional lability, splenomegaly) than those with Lyme disease alone (Krause et al. 1996); this is an area of ongoing research, as another study did not find coinfection complicated the course of Lyme disease (Wang et al. 2000).

Is coinfection common? In certain regions of the country, yes. In a study of 192 residents from the northeastern United States confirmed to be infected with at least one of three common tick-borne infections (agents of Lyme disease, Babesiosis, or Anaplasmosis), 39 percent carried at least two of these infections at the same time (Krause 2002). Similarly, 30 percent of *Ixodes* ticks collected from Lyme endemic areas in the northeastern United States were shown to carry more than one human disease–causing microbe (Tokarz et al. 2010); the risk is therefore high of acquiring more than one microbe when bitten by an *Ixodes* tick.

Because the symptoms of coinfections may overlap with Lyme disease or may be nonspecific, the diagnosis and treatment of another tick-borne infection may be delayed. However, the clinician may be alerted to consider another tick-borne disease by the presence of other clinical or laboratory features such as recurring fever or a declining white blood cell count, decrease in platelets, or anemia. Faced with a patient who has negative tests for Lyme disease but has Lyme disease–like symptoms or a recent tick bite, the health care clinician from a Lyme endemic area must ask the following question: Could this patient have acquired another tick-borne infection?

In this chapter we present a brief overview of other tick-borne infections. This is not a comprehensive list. We start with the major tick-borne microbes that health care professionals should consider when evaluating symptoms in a patient with new onset Lyme disease—Anaplasma, Babesia, and *Borrelia miyamotoi*. We then present other tick-borne microbial infections that are less common or not transmitted by *Ixodes* ticks, one that is primarily transmitted by other nontick vectors (but possibly also by ticks), and two clinical syndromes not due to a tick-transmitted infection but triggered by the tick bite.

Each section is organized by a brief overview, signs and symptoms, diagnosis, and treatment. This is not meant as a clinical manual of tick-borne diseases but as a clinical introduction to this important area. As in all sections of this book, treatment decisions for an individual patient should be guided by physicians knowledgeable in these diseases.

## COMMON TICK-BORNE INFECTIOUS DISEASES

### Anaplasmosis

#### OVERVIEW

An important coinfection of Lyme disease is human granulocytic anaplasmosis (HGA) caused by *Anaplasma phagocytophilum*, a small, intracellular bacterium that invades neutrophils (the most abundant type of white blood cell in humans) (Dumler et al. 2001; Bakken and Dumler 2008). *A. phagocytophilum* organisms form bacterial microcolonies, called morulae, within these cells and disturb their function in human hosts. Most of the damage appears to be related to host inflammatory processes because there is little evidence of a correlation between the number of organisms and host disease severity.

#### SIGNS AND SYMPTOMS

The clinical course of HGA is very wide, ranging from asymptomatic infection to fatal disease. (The first case of human Anaplasmosis was described in 1990, when a Wisconsin patient developed a severe febrile illness following a tick bite and died two weeks later.) When initial symptoms appear, usually five to ten days after the tick bite, they are largely nonspecific: fever, chills, headache, and muscle aches. Nausea, cough, and arthralgias also occur. Rash is uncommon but has been reported. Nervous system involvement can occur, most often in the form of peripheral neuropathies (e.g., causing numbness and tingling). In patients with compromised immune systems, death can result from opportunistic infections, but the overall mortality from HGA is very low, less than 1 percent.

## DIAGNOSIS

Standard blood tests may reveal a low number of white blood cells, low number of platelets, and elevated liver enzymes. However, these abnormalities frequently resolve by the second week of symptoms, so their absence at this stage does not preclude Anaplasma infection. In general, empiric antibiotic treatment should be considered for patients in endemic areas who present with an acute febrile illness suggestive of HGA.

Very early in illness (during the first week) infection by Anaplasma may be detected by polymerase chain reaction (PCR); a negative result, however, does not rule out current infection. Also helpful in early infection is to ask the laboratory technicians to examine a blood smear to look for microscopic evidence of microcolonies of Anaplasma in the white blood cells; these can be detected, however, only in about 20 percent of cases of early disease.

Serologic testing is useful to confirm the diagnosis of Anaplasmosis after the first 7–10 days of infection. The most commonly used method is an indirect immunofluorescence assay (IFA) of IgM and IgG anti–A. *phagocytophilum* antibodies. Seroconversion (a negative test becomes positive several weeks later) is perhaps the most sensitive laboratory evidence of *A. phagocytophilum* infection, but is not always obtained in a timely enough manner to provide useful input on clinical (i.e., treatment) decisions. If samples are taken at initial presentation and then two to four weeks later, a fourfold increase in IgG titer on the follow-up test is considered strong evidence of HGA. Patients with HGA most often have titers of 1:640 or greater (Horowitz et al. 2013).

## TREATMENT

Although laboratory testing is important for the confirmation of the diagnosis of Anaplasmosis, antibiotic therapy should be initiated immediately in a patient with a suggestive clinical presentation, as a delay in treatment may result in severe illness and even death. Doxycycline is recommended for Anaplasmosis in patients of all ages, including children under 8 years. The usual treatment duration is ten to fourteen days given the possibility of coinfection with B. burgdorferi. Response to treatment is usually rapid;

A thirty-year-old woman living in Florida reported feeling increasingly tired with diffuse body aches over a two-week period. She felt febrile and recorded a temperature of 103°F (39.4°C). Accompanying symptoms included intermittent nausea, mild headache, and stiff neck. When asked by her physician, Ms. C denied having had an upper respiratory illness, vomiting, diarrhea, unprotected sex, exposure to farm animals, or symptoms of a urinary tract infection. Because this fever occurred during the summer and was associated with a headache, infection by a microbe acquired outdoors (e.g., mosquito- or tick-borne microbe) was considered more likely than infections occurring during the winter months that are common in temperate zones (e.g., influenza, adenoviruses, and rhinoviruses).

Ms. C asked the physician to test for Lyme disease because two of her family members had had Lyme disease. At first, the physician considered this to be an extremely unlikely cause of Ms. C's symptoms because Lyme disease—although reported in Florida—is not common and usually does not present with such a high fever. The physician inquired further and learned that Ms. C had visited her parents who live in northern California about two weeks prior to the onset of symptoms. Ms. C denied a history of tick bites, rashes, joint swelling, shooting or stabbing pains, facial palsy, meningitis, or numbness/tingling. However, she did acknowledge that while visiting her parents she had spent a lot of time with her mother helping weed the garden. This physician did some quick research and learned the western black-legged tick that is prevalent on the Pacific Coast carries the agents of Lyme disease and Anaplasmosis; although Anaplasmosis is uncommon in California, the physician ordered antibody tests. The routine laboratory tests came back first, revealing a low white blood cell count, low platelets, and elevated liver function test. Given these results, the physician felt that it was certainly possible that Anaplasmosis (or possibly Ehrlichiosis) was the explanation for this woman's symptoms. Although blood tests were drawn to check for antibodies against the agents of these tick-borne diseases, the physician did not want to wait until these test results came back to start treatment as Anaplasmosis and Ehrlichiosis could be quite serious illnesses; she immediately started Ms. C on doxycycline. The tests for Lyme disease and Ehrlichiosis came back negative, but the initial Anaplasma IgM and IgG antibody tests from the lab one week later were positive. The diagnosis was confirmed. Ms. C's fever and headaches remitted and the abnormal routine blood test results returned to normal. The fatigue diminished and Ms. C returned to her normal state of good health over the course of the following six weeks.

if the patient remains febrile for more than two days after the initiation of antibiotic therapy, the diagnosis should be revisited (Biggs et al. 2016).

## Babesiosis

### OVERVIEW

*Babesia microti* is a malaria-like protozoan that parasitizes and destroys human red blood cells. This infection is transmitted by the bite of *Ixodes scapularis*, the same tick species that transmits Lyme disease. Similar to Lyme disease, Babesiosis affects primarily southern New England and the northern Midwest with a peak incidence during the warmer months. In some areas of the United States, *B. microti* infection is almost as common as Lyme disease; on Nantucket Island off of Massachusetts, for example, this common illness is called "Nantucket Fever." A related tick-borne microbe, *Babesia duncani* (WA1), is primarily found in the Pacific coastal states. *Babesia divergens* is the primary cause of Babesiosis in Europe, but cases have also been reported in the United States. Rarely, Babesia can be transmitted via a blood transfusion or from mother to child. In most states, the blood supply is not currently screened for Babesia microbes, even though Babesiosis is a frequently reported transfusion-related parasitic infection in the United States, found in 3 to 8 percent of blood donations. This is of growing concern because some infected adults may have few symptoms and so would have no awareness when considering a blood donation that the donated blood might harm or even kill a sick individual with a weakened immune system.

The time from Babesia infection to onset of symptoms after a tick bite is typically one to four weeks but can be as long as three months; after transfusion of infected blood, the symptoms may not emerge until six months later. The actual frequency of Babesia infection is unclear because Babesiosis is mild and self-limiting in most cases. Coinfection of *B. microti* with other tick-borne infections may lead to more severe manifestations.

### SIGNS AND SYMPTOMS

Signs and symptoms of Babesiosis typically start with malaise and fatigue, followed by a fever as high as 105.6°F (40.9°C) and often accompanied by chills and sweats. Additional symptoms may include headaches, nausea, vomiting, joint pains, abdominal pain, muscle pains, and depression. The spleen and liver may be enlarged. Individuals with Babesiosis often have quite profound fatigue. A sizeable proportion of infected individuals, however, do not become ill and are asymptomatic, including up to 50 percent of children and 25 percent of previously health adults; for these individuals, the infection is often self-limiting. But for others, particularly the elderly, those without a spleen, those with functional asplenia (e.g., from lymphoma or sickle cell disease), those with an underlying illness that suppresses the immune system (e.g., HIV or cancer) or among those receiving immune modulatory treatment (e.g., with rituximab), *Babesia* infection can have a severe or even fatal course.

## DIAGNOSIS

Diagnosis usually begins with nonspecific lab tests that may show hemolytic anemia, blood in the urine, low platelets, and elevated liver enzymes. Microscopic examination of a blood smear can confirm the presence of Babesia; however, less than 1 percent of red blood cells may be infected during early illness so multiple blood smears may be required for diagnosis. The thin blood smear may reveal the ring forms of Babesia inside the red blood cells or rarely the pathognomonic cross-like pattern ("Maltese cross") indicated by an arrow in figure 8.1. Given low rates of red blood cell infection in acute illness, PCR assays are now often used because they are highly sensitive and specific. IFA of IgM and IgG antibodies is sometimes used to confirm diagnosis, but this test cannot differentiate past and current infection. During acute infection with Babesia, the IgG titers typically exceed 1:1024 and drop to 1:64 or less within six to twelve months after treatment. Specific antibody tests are needed to detect *B. duncani* (WA1) or *B. divergens*. Current serologic tests for *B. duncani* are more prone to cross-reactivity and consequent false positives than tests for *B. microti*. Because patients with Lyme disease may also be coinfected with Babesiosis, persistent fatigue with sweats after receiving treatment for Lyme disease should prompt tests for Babesiosis.

**FIGURE 8.1**

A Babesia species
in human red blood
cells stained with 10%
Giemsa, 100X magni-
fication. The typical
morphological forms
of Babesia are visible:
tetrad, or dividing
form, top center; ame-
boid, center; and ring
forms, bottom center.

*Courtesy Anne Kjemtrup.*

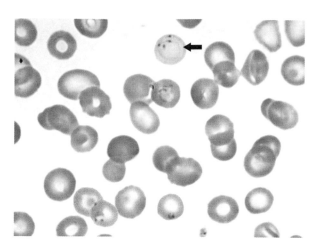

## TREATMENT

Treatment for mild to moderate symptomatic Babesiosis usually involves
combination therapy with oral atovaquone and azithromycin for seven to
ten days. The combination of clindamycin and quinine is also effective but
have a higher rate of side effects. Severe Babesiosis often requires hospital
admission, close monitoring, and possibly longer courses of antibiotic
therapy. The risk of not treating an individual with mild Babesiosis is that
the infection may not be cleared and severe disease may develop months
or even years later or that the infection may be inadvertently transmitted
to an immunocompromised patient by transfusion after a blood donation
(Cunha, Mickail, and Laguerre 2012; Vannier, Gewurz, and Krause 2008;
Vannier and Krause 2012; Wormser et al. 2006).

## *Borrelia miyamotoi* Disease

### OVERVIEW

*Borrelia miyamotoi* (BMD) is a newly recognized spirochete that is genetically related to the organism that causes relapsing fever. It was discovered
in Japan in 1995 and the first human cases were identified in Russia in

Mr. D, a fifty-five-year-old previously healthy New Yorker living in a Manhattan high rise, developed achiness and increasing fatigue; after two weeks, he mounted a fever of 103°F, with accompanying chills, headache, stiff neck, joint pain, nausea, and night sweats. He noticed that his urine was darker than usual. His physician took a careful history and learned that he had vacationed on the eastern end of Long Island about two weeks before the onset of symptoms. Mr. D did not recall a tick bite or unusual rashes, but he had been jogging through leaf-covered paths in the woods. The physician suspected that this man might have acquired a tick-borne infection because the black-legged ticks on eastern Long Island are plentiful in the leaf litter and are known to have high rates of coinfection with both *Babesia microti* and *B. burgdorferi*. The high fever led him to wonder about Anaplasmosis and Babesiosis, but he also wanted to test for Lyme disease. The lab tests revealed that this man had an anemia caused by destruction of red blood cells (hemolytic anemia); this is what caused his urine to appear darker. Mr. D was not on medicines that might cause a hemolytic anemia nor did he have an inherited disease that could predispose to hemolysis. Because neither Anaplasma nor *B. burdorferi* infection cause a hemolytic anemia, the physician narrowed his diagnostic suspicion to infection with *Babesia microti*; even though Babesiosis is more common among individuals who are immunocompromised, this physician knew that adults over age fifty also are at higher risk. The physician ordered a blood smear, but the technician could not find any Babesia-like organisms in the red blood cells. Not willing to give up his strong clinical suspicion, the physician then ordered a real-time PCR; the presence of Babesia DNA was confirmed. This man was diagnosed with Babesiosis and treated with azithromycin and atovaquone for ten days. The fever subsided, the clinical symptoms resolved, and his blood count returned to normal. Mr. D felt well again. IgG antibody tests against *Babesia microti* were initially elevated at 1:1024; titers dropped to 1:64 after one year, consistent with a past infection.

Comment: This is a typical case of Babesia infection. Notable, however, is that antibody tests for Lyme disease and Anaplasma had also been conducted. The Anaplasma test was negative, but the Lyme disease tests revealed a low positive on the enzyme-linked immunosorbent assay (ELISA) and four CDC significant bands on the IgG Western blot. Given that this man was clinically asymptomatic after treatment for Babesiosis, the physician concluded that Mr. D did not need treatment for Lyme disease. He interpreted the "almost positive" two-tier Lyme antibody tests as likely indicating an unrecognized but resolved infection in the distant past because this man had a long history of exposure to areas endemic for Lyme disease.

2011 and then in North America in 2013; human cases have now also been identified in The Netherlands and Japan. The organism is transmitted to humans by the bite of the same *Ixodes* tick species that is responsible for transmitting Lyme disease, Babesiosis, and Anaplasmosis. Recent studies show that approximately 1 to 15 percent of *Ixodes scapularis* ticks in Lyme endemic regions also carry *B. miyamotoi*. Surveys of the serum from people living in Lyme endemic areas of the United States indicate that as many as 10 percent may have been exposed to *B. miyamotoi*. Unlike the agent of Lyme disease, *B. miyamotoi* has been experimentally transmitted by tick larvae; in contrast, Lyme disease transmission only occurs with the later stages of tick development (nymph or adults). Given that these youngest ticks are barely detectable due to their small size, personal protection measures are essential in early and late summer months when the larval ticks are most active.

## SIGNS AND SYMPTOMS

Signs and symptoms of *B. miyamotoi* disease (BMD) are similar to those found in Lyme disease including fever, shaking chills, headache, fatigue, muscle and joint pains, and very rarely—among immune compromised patients—meningoencephalitis (severe headache, seizures, altered consciousness). In contrast to Lyme disease, BMD is not typically associated with a rash. About 25 percent of patients will present with such a severe illness that they are hospitalized.

## DIAGNOSIS

Diagnosis is difficult because patients usually exhibit nonspecific flu-like symptoms and the full clinical spectrum of this newly identified disease is not yet known. Conventional lab tests may show low white blood cell count, elevated liver function tests, low platelets, and protein in the urine. Because of the fever and the laboratory findings (low white blood cells and platelets), Anaplasmosis is another tick-borne infection in the differential diagnosis to consider. Certain commercial labs now offer *B. miyamotoi*–specific serologic tests as well as PCR assays. Early in infection only about 16 percent will test positive on the serologic antibody-based tests for

*B. miyamotoi*, but over 75 percent will test positive about six weeks later. BMD should be considered in any patient with a Lyme-like illness who tests negative for Lyme disease.

Misdiagnosis as Lyme disease is possible if one relies solely on a single whole-cell sonicate ELISA for Lyme disease because patients with *B. miyamotoi* infection may test positive on the whole-cell sonicate Lyme ELISA test but only rarely on the Lyme Western blot. This is a valuable clinical point to emphasize because a patient presenting with a "summer flu," no rash, and a positive whole-cell sonicate ELISA but negative Lyme Western blot may actually have *B. miyamotoi* infection rather than Lyme disease.

## TREATMENT

Treatment includes doxycycline for uncomplicated infections, but ceftriaxone or penicillin G may be more appropriate for severe cases, such as those that include meningoencephalitis. Early studies suggest that full recovery is expected if infection is treated early with doxycycline (Telford et al. 2015; Branda and Rosenberg 2013; Krause et al. 2015).

## OTHER TICK-BORNE INFECTIOUS DISEASES

### Ehrlichiosis

#### OVERVIEW

Similar to Anaplasmosis, discussed earlier, Ehrlichiosis is an infection involving microbes that invade and parasitize human immune cells. (In fact, the earliest described cases of human Anaplasmosis were initially thought to be caused by bacteria from the Ehrlichia genus.) However, the two species of Ehrlichia that appear to be responsible for most human infections, *E. chaffeensis* and *E. ewingii*, are transmitted to humans not by *Ixodes* ticks but rather by the lone star tick, *Amblyomma americanum*.

*E. chaffeensis* targets monocytes, a type of white blood cell, and is therefore referred to as the agent of human monocytic ehrlichiosis (HME).

**FIGURE 8.2**

Lone star tick with characteristic marking.

*Courtesy of the CDC/James Gathany.*

In contrast, *E. ewingii* preferentially invades neutrophil granulocytes. In this regard, it resembles the Anaplasma pathogen (*A. phagocytophilum*), the agent of human granulocytic anaplasmosis (HGA), although it is genetically and serologically much closer to *E. chaffeensis*. To avoid confusion with HGA, most researchers prefer to call this disease entity "human ewingii ehrlichiosis."

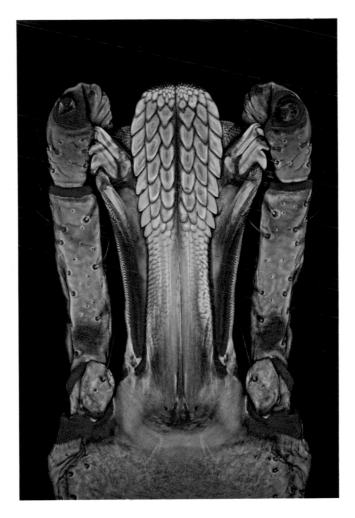

**FIGURE 8.3**

A digitally enhanced colored image of the mouth parts of a lone star tick. The center of the mouth (yellow) is covered with many tiny barbs. These barbs keep the tick securely lodged inside the host while feeding.

*Courtesy of Igor Siwanowicz, Janelia Farm Research Campus, Howard Hughes Medical Institute, Ashburn, Virginia.*

## SIGNS AND SYMPTOMS

Although *E. chaffeensis* and *E. ewingii* invade different host cells, they seem to produce a similar clinical course in humans. Most patients develop symptoms one to two weeks after the tick bite, and over 70 percent will have fever, chills, severe headache, and myalgias. Less common symptoms include nausea and vomiting, as well as confusion. A rash can also occur. As with many other tick-borne diseases, the symptoms are largely non-specific, thus confounding diagnosis.

Although most cases of HME are uncomplicated, it is a potentially serious illness. Hospitalization rates in symptomatic patients are estimated to be 40 to 50 percent, and fatalities run in the 2 to 3 percent range. At greatest risk are patients with underlying immunosuppression, such as organ transplant recipients or HIV or cancer patients.

## DIAGNOSIS

Common findings on conventional blood tests include a low white blood cell count, low platelets, and elevated serum liver function tests. From the standpoint of timeliness, the most useful diagnostic test for Ehrlichiosis is probably PCR. Sensitivity has been reported to range between 60 and 85 percent for *E. chaffeensis*; the sensitivity for *E. ewingii* infections is not known, but PCR is the only definitive diagnostic test for *E. ewingii*, which has proven to be extremely difficult to culture (Killmaster and Levin 2016). Culture of *E. chaffeensis* is possible from either blood or cerebrospinal fluid, but usually takes at least two weeks. Thus this method is useful only for retrospective confirmation of the diagnosis. Similarly, changes in antibody titers detected by IFA from acute infection to the convalescent phase can buttress the diagnosis of Ehrlichiosis, but this testing method is not useful during acute illness, when treatment decisions need to be formulated. Also, IgG antibodies can remain high for years after the infection, and false positive results have been associated with many other conditions, including several tick-borne diseases (Lyme disease, Rocky Mountain Spotted Fever, and Q fever).

## TREATMENT

Empiric evidence indicates that tetracyclines are highly effective against both *E. chaffeensis* and *E. ewingii*. The recommended therapy is doxycycline with a typical minimum duration of five to seven days. In severe cases, intravenous therapy is used or antibiotic treatment is extended. Consensus exists that in all cases, treatment should be continued in all patients for at least three to five days after the fever subsides and until clinical improvement is noted (Biggs et al. 2016).

# Rocky Mountain Spotted Fever

## OVERVIEW

Rocky Mountain Spotted Fever (RMSF) is caused by *Rickettsia rickettsii* bacteria and is transmitted to humans by two primary tick vectors, the American dog tick (*Dermacentor variabilis*) and the Rocky Mountain wood tick (*Dermacentor andersoni*). The American dog tick is widely distributed in all states east of the Rocky Mountains and in certain areas along the Pacific Coast. Despite its name, RMSF is actually most common in the south Atlantic and south central parts of the United States. The CDC reports between 300 and 1,200 cases per year, with a seasonal peak in the late spring and summer months. The disease is most common in children under fifteen years old, particularly those ages five to nine.

## SIGNS AND SYMPTOMS

Symptoms usually appear five to ten days after infection and include fever, severe headache, myalgia, nausea, and yellowing of the skin or eyes. In a patient with central nervous system involvement, confusion, seizures, dizziness, and coma may develop. Late in the disease course, approximately half of patients will develop the disease's hallmark rash, which classically involves small red spots starting on the hands and feet and extending inward toward the trunk over time. RMSF can affect the respiratory system, gastrointestinal system, kidneys, and heart, leading to a variety of serious or

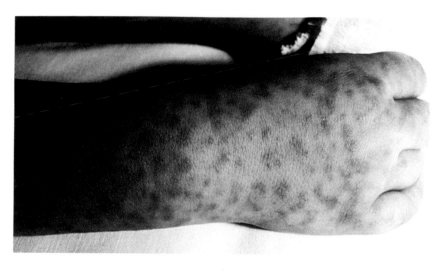

**FIGURE 8.4**

An early stage rash in a patient with Rocky Mountain Spotted Fever.
*Courtesy of the CDC.*

even fatal complications. Prior to the antibiotic era, RMSF had a mortality rate of up to 30 percent and, even today, about 5 to 10 percent of patients who acquire the infection will die from it. Most of these fatalities occur in the very young and very old and are due to delayed diagnosis and treatment.

## DIAGNOSIS

Diagnosis often must be made on the basis of the history and physical exam because available lab tests are neither rapid nor sensitive enough, and prompt treatment of RMSF is critical to a positive outcome. This can be challenging because many patients will not recall the tick bite. Conventional blood tests might show hyponatremia (low blood sodium concentration), thrombocytopenia (low platelets), white blood cell abnormalities, and elevated liver enzymes. Serological assays are used mostly to confirm the diagnosis after treatment has been initiated. Indirect IFA of both IgM and IgG antibodies are most commonly employed, but ELISA and dot immunoassays are also available. Complement fixation is less sensitive and less frequently used. Immunostaining of biopsied skin rashes can also be performed and is very rapid; results are available in a few hours. PCR assays for *R. rickettsii* DNA are considered perhaps the most timely and specific test for RMSF overall but are still not widely available.

## TREATMENT

Treatment with antibiotics should be rapidly initiated if RMSF is suspected. Doxycycline is the recommended treatment for suspected RMSF in patients of all ages. Both the CDC and the American Academy of Pediatrics recommend the use of doxycycline to treat suspected RMSF in children (include those under 8 years), as with the standard dose and duration there is no evidence that doxycycline causes staining of permanent teeth. Antibiotics should be continued for at least three days after the fever subsides and until there is evidence of clinical improvement. A typical course of treatment is 5 to 7 days. Severe cases may require intravenous administration or longer treatment duration. (CDC "Rocky Mountain Spotted Fever"; Chen and Sexton 2008; Cunha 2013).

## *Borrelia mayonii*

### OVERVIEW

Scientists detected *Borrelia mayonii*—a new *Borrelia* genospecies—when lab tests from six patients sent from Minnesota, North Dakota, and Wisconsin showed a unique pattern not found among patients infected with *B. burgdorferi* (Pritt et al. 2016). When twenty-five thousand blood samples were screened from other Lyme endemic areas such as the northeastern United States and the mid-Atlantic states, no new cases of *B. mayonii* were identified. *B. mayonii* has been found in *Ixodes* ticks in Wisconsin and is therefore thought to be transmitted by these ticks in the neighboring upper Midwestern states as well.

### SIGNS AND SYMPTOMS

Because so few cases of *B. mayonii* have been reported, the full spectrum of this illness is not yet known. The cases thus far demonstrated fever, headaches, rash, and neck and muscle pain in the early stages of infection and arthritis weeks after exposure; in this profile, the clinical symptoms were similar to Lyme disease. This small series suggested that *B. mayonii* differed from *B. burgdorferi* infection by leading to more gastrointestinal symptoms (nausea and vomiting), higher fevers, and diffuse flat rashes (rather than the characteristic Lyme disease *erythema migrans* rash with central clearing).

## DIAGNOSIS

Because *B. mayonii* bacteria are found in a higher concentration in the blood than is typical for Lyme disease, a blood smear may be helpful in diagnosis. Half of the six patients tested positive on the ELISA and Western blot tests for Lyme disease. A PCR assay, however, was able to identify *B. mayonii* in all cases.

## TREATMENT

Treatment of *B. mayonii* is similar to that for Lyme disease. All six patients responded well to treatment with the standard antibiotics used for Lyme disease. Early studies suggest this spirochete only rarely affects humans and so is unlikely to have much bearing on the majority of cases of blood test–negative Lyme disease.

## Colorado Tick Fever

### OVERVIEW

Colorado tick fever is a febrile illness caused by an RNA virus belonging to the genus *Coltivirus* (short for Colorado tick virus). The disease is transmitted to humans exclusively by the Rocky Mountain wood tick, *Dermacentor andersoni*, which acquires the virus from infected small- and medium-sized mammals, such as chipmunks, squirrels, mice, rats, and porcupines. It is most often found in the Rocky Mountains as well as in the Canadian provinces of Alberta and British Columbia, with the majority of cases occurring at four thousand to ten thousand feet above sea level. The illness is typically acquired between late March and October with most cases occurring in the late spring and early summer. This disease is rare in the United States with fewer than ten cases per year.

## SIGNS AND SYMPTOMS

Symptoms usually begin abruptly, three to five days after infection, and include fever, headache, chills, photophobia (light sensitivity), muscle aches, malaise, nausea, vomiting, diarrhea, abdominal pain, and rash (only in 5 to 15 percent of patients). About half of patients report a single recurrence of fever after initial resolution; this is called a "saddleback fever." Neurologic complications such as meningitis and encephalitis are uncommon but can occur, particularly in children. In rare cases, Colorado tick fever can cause pneumonitis, myocarditis, hepatitis, coma, or death. Although children are more prone to severe acute disease, their symptoms typically resolve in days to weeks, whereas approximately 70 percent of patients thirty years or older have lingering symptoms, such as fatigue and malaise, for weeks to months.

## DIAGNOSIS

Diagnosis can be difficult because other than the "saddleback fever" pattern, signs and symptoms of Colorado tick fever are nonspecific. Some patients may have leukopenia (low white blood cell count), low platelets, and/or abnormal liver function tests. In cases of central nervous system involvement, studies of cerebrospinal fluid obtained in a spinal tap may show a lymphocytic pleocytosis, elevated protein, and/or mildly decreased glucose concentration, but these findings are also nonspecific. Serologic diagnosis can be made by indirect immunofluorescence, enzyme immunoassay, and Western blot. PCR tests are also available for the virus and can be useful in cases with active infection. However, it is likely that many cases of Colorado tick fever are attributed to other viral infections and never correctly diagnosed.

## TREATMENT

Treatment consists primarily of supportive care, as there are no specific therapies available and most cases resolve uneventfully without treatment in any case. Infection with the Colorado tick fever virus almost always confers lifelong immunity (Romero and Simonsen 2008).

## Heartland Virus

### OVERVIEW

This virus, discovered in 2009, is a newly identified disease-causing tick-borne phlebovirus (named Heartland virus, *Bunyaviridae*). It is transmitted by the bite of the lone star tick (*Amblyomma americanum*). Case reports of human disease have come from Missouri, Tennessee, and Oklahoma. Recent field research, however, indicates that Heartland virus is quite common in animals (approximately 60 percent of raccoons and deer tested in Missouri have been exposed to Heartland virus) and geographically dispersed, with seropositive deer or raccoons found in thirteen states in the United States ranging from Texas to Florida to Maine and across the Midwest.

### SIGNS AND SYMPTOMS

Because human cases are rare, the case description is based on a total of nine cases. These were male patients older than fifty years who had fever, fatigue, and some had headaches, muscle aches, diarrhea, and poor appetite. Blood tests indicated leukopenia and thrombocytopenia; two individuals died.

### DIAGNOSIS

Patients with a history of exposure to lone star ticks who present with fever, leukopenia, and thrombocytopenia who do not respond to doxycycline and who test negative for other known tick-borne infections should be considered for possible Heartland virus infection. Antibody tests can be used to assess infection and RT-PCR can be done to detect the virus' genetic material (ssRNA) in the blood.

### TREATMENT

As with other viruses, the treatment is supportive because there is no known specific therapy for Heartland virus.

## Powassan Virus

### OVERVIEW

Powassan virus is a flavivrus that has been found in 1 to 2 percent of the *Ixodes scapularis* ticks in the northeastern United States. The virus can be transmitted by ticks from deer, groundhogs, and woodchucks. Transmission of the virus can occur very quickly, within minutes of the original tick attachment, which highlights the importance of rapid removal of ticks to decrease chances of transmission of other infections as well as *B. burgdorferi*. There have been only seventy-five cases of Powassan virus encephalitis reported in the United States in a recent ten-year interval. While this likely represents an underestimate of the actual number of cases, Powassan virus is clearly an infrequent cause of human disease.

### SIGNS AND SYMPTOMS

Signs and symptoms include fever, headaches, vomiting, confusion, lack of coordination, muscle weakness, speech and memory problems, and seizures. The severity of disease after infection ranges widely, from none to death. When it infects the central nervous system, it can cause meningitis or encephalitis with seizures. Approximately half of symptomatic individuals who survive infection with Powassan virus experience lasting neurological symptoms such as muscle wasting, chronic headaches, and memory problems. Approximately 10 percent of cases with serious neurologic disease are fatal.

### DIAGNOSIS

Diagnosis involves testing the blood and/or cerebrospinal fluid for antibodies.

### TREATMENT

Treatment consists of supportive measures, such as respiratory support and intravenous fluids, as there is no known specific therapy for Powassan virus (Romero and Simonsen 2008).

## CASE 11. Powassan Virus Disease in an Infant

Sam, a previously healthy five-month-old infant from the northeastern United States, was bitten by a tick that was removed by his parents within three hours of initial attachment. Several days later he developed a fever and vomiting, followed by facial twitching that progressed to seizures. He was hospitalized for seizure management and diagnostic evaluation. His spinal fluid showed an elevated number of white blood cells. His brain magnetic resonance imaging (MRI) scan showed a pattern of restricted diffusion that was suggestive of cellular edema consistent with encephalitis. Testing for various non-arthropod–transmitted causes of encephalitis was negative, as were bacterial and respiratory viral cultures. Because of the history of a tick bite prior to the onset of symptoms, the cerebrospinal fluid obtained four days after illness onset was sent to the CDC and tested for Powassan virus (POWV), which revealed a positive IgM specific antibody for POWV.

Because there is no specific treatment for POWV infection, the management was symptomatic. The infant's seizures were controlled with anticonvulsant therapy and he was discharged after one week. One month after symptom onset, however, he was no longer able to sit up unaided—a reversal of prior developmental gains. By four months after symptom onset, he had made considerable progress and was crawling, walking with a walker, and babbling normally. By this time he no longer needed physical therapy and he was taken off of the anti-convulsant medication. A second MRI performed four months after the first revealed gliosis and encephalomalacia in the thalami and basal ganglia bilaterally, with volume loss and evidence of early mineralization in the left basal ganglia.

Comment: Despite the high prevalence and expanding range of *Ixodes* ticks in the United States, POWV disease is rare. Because POWV infection is found in about 1 to 2 percent of *Ixodes* ticks in certain regions of the United States and because transmission can occur within fifteen minutes of a tick bite, one would expect more than the seven to eight cases that are reported in the United States annually. This suggests that there may be a high number of asymptomatic or unrecognized mild human infections. Most cases come from the Great Lakes region and the northeastern United States.

Even though Sam's parents were diligent and removed the tick quickly, transmission of the POWV had already occurred. This rare case highlights the importance of testing for POWV when evaluating a patient with encephalitis from an *Ixodes* tick-endemic region. This case also highlights the importance of prevention strategies to avoid tick bites (covered in chapter 10).

*(Adapted from Tutolo et al. 2017)*

## Q Fever

### OVERVIEW

Q fever is caused by infection with the intracellular bacterium *Coxiella burnetii* primarily through inhalation or ingestion of particles from contaminated soil or animal waste, but it can be transmitted by ticks as well. *C. burnetii* is commonly found in livestock on farms; as a result, infection in humans is strongly associated with exposure to farm animals including cows, sheep, and goats. Usually, humans acquire the pathogen by inhaling air contaminated with digestive waste products, birth fluids, and/or placental remains of farm livestock. *C. burnetii* is highly infectious and is also resistant to heat, drying, and many disinfectants. Because of this, it is considered a significant threat for biowarfare.

**FIGURE 8.5**

*Coxiella burnetii* bacteria can be transmitted from goats, sheep, and cattle to humans through inhalation of animal waste products.

*Courtesy of Barbara Strobino.*

## SIGNS AND SYMPTOMS

Signs and symptoms are nonspecific but may include high fever, headache, sore throat, malaise, nausea, diarrhea, chest pain, nonproductive cough, pneumonia, and hepatitis. About 1 percent of patients with Q fever develop neurological manifestations such as meningitis, encephalitis, myelitis, and/ or peripheral neuropathy. Although the vast majority of patients with acute Q fever recover even without treatment, a chronic form of the disease can develop anywhere from one to twenty years after initial exposure. These patients with chronic Q fever may need months of antibiotic treatment. The most serious manifestation of chronic Q fever is endocarditis

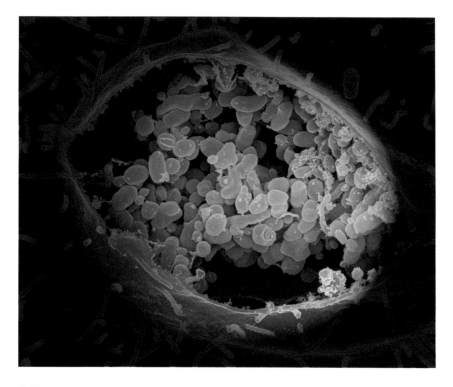

**FIGURE 8.6**

A fractured cell exposing the contents of a vacuole where *Coxiella burnetii* bacteria, the cause of Q fever, are growing.

*Courtesy of NIAID.*

(infection of the heart valves), usually found in patients with preexisting valvular disease. Infected patients with prior kidney disease or cancer are more likely to develop chronic Q fever, as are organ transplant recipients. The mortality rate for chronic Q fever is high, approaching 65 percent.

## DIAGNOSIS

Diagnosis is based on a combination of clinical history and blood tests. The most frequently used and dependable serologic method for Q fever diagnosis is indirect IFA testing. ELISA, complement fixation analyses, and immunohistochemical staining tests are also available. PCR tests exist, but are generally used only in research. Culture is possible but rarely performed due to the risk of laboratory-transmitted cases. Chest X-ray may show an atypical pneumonia pattern, but this same pattern can be found in many other diseases as well.

## TREATMENT

Many cases of acute Q fever recover without antibiotic treatment. Treatment of acute infection with doxycycline will shorten the course of the illness, ideally initiated within three days of illness onset. A post-Q fever syndrome occurs in about 20 percent of patients, characterized by recurring fatigue, severe headaches, night sweats, muscle and joint pain, mood changes, photophobia, and trouble sleeping. Chronic Q fever is significantly more difficult to treat, may involve treatment for several months with a combination of agents, and should be guided by an infectious disease physician (Anderson et al. 2013; Tissot-Dupont and Raoult 2008).

## Relapsing Fever

### OVERVIEW

Relapsing fever is an illness caused by at least fifteen spirochete species belonging to the genus *Borrelia* and can be transmitted to humans by either lice or soft-bodied ticks. Louse-borne relapsing fever (LBRF) is caused by *Borrelia recurrentis* and is transmitted from human to human by the body louse. LBRF tends to occur in epidemic waves, usually in times of human crisis such as war, poverty, and/or overcrowding. It is primarily a disease of the developing world, with foci in East Africa, South America, and parts of China.

Tick-borne relapsing fever (TBRF) is caused by more than a dozen species of *Borrelia* and is transmitted by soft-bodied ticks from the genus *Ornithodoros*. *Ornithodoros* ticks feed for short periods, usually at night, and their bites are painless; thus most humans are infected while asleep and

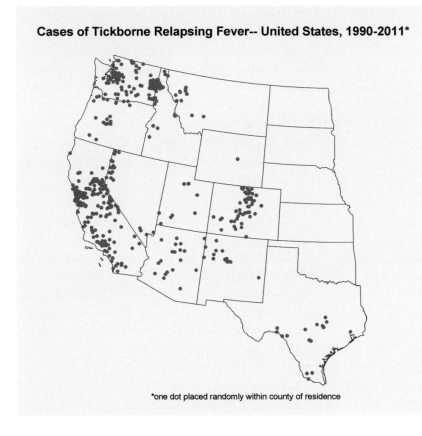

**Cases of Tickborne Relapsing Fever-- United States, 1990-2011***

*one dot placed randomly within county of residence

**FIGURE 8.7**

Geographic distribution of cases of tick-borne relapsing fever.

*Courtesy of the CDC.*

have no recollection of being bitten. TBRF is endemic primarily in Africa, Central Asia, the Mediterranean, and Central and South America, but cases occur in the western United States including California, Colorado, Washington, Idaho, and Oregon as well as southern British Columbia. Most cases occur in the summer months. This is an uncommon disease in the United States with only 483 cases reported from 1990 to 2011.

## SIGNS AND SYMPTOMS

Signs and symptoms usually appear around one week after infection. Symptom onset is abrupt and consists of episodic febrile "crises" that entail high fever up to 106°F with rapid breathing and fast heart rate, followed by drop in body temperature and profuse sweating. This cycle can repeat up to ten times, separated by only a few days. Patients also have headache, myalgias, arthralgias, nausea, vomiting, loss of appetite, conjunctivitis, and dry cough. Less common complications include liver and spleen enlargement, meningitis, seizures, facial palsy (muscle weakness), myocarditis (inflammation of the heart muscle), and pregnancy complications or loss. In general, relapsing fever is a more severe, acute disease than Borrelia Miyamotoi Disease or Lyme disease.

## DIAGNOSIS

Diagnosis should be considered in any patient who has recurrent fevers and has spent time in an endemic area. Conventional blood tests may show increased white blood cell count, low platelets, mildly increased bilirubin, elevated erythrocyte sedimentation rate or "sed rate," and increase in prothrombin time (PT) and partial thromboplastin time (PTT) coagulation tests. However, none of these are diagnostic. Serologic tests (direct and indirect IFA) for relapsing fever can be performed, but they are not useful for timely diagnosis. Cross-reaction with antibodies to Lyme disease and syphilis have also been reported. PCR tests exist but are not widely available. The gold standard for relapsing fever diagnosis is the visualization of spirochetes in smears of peripheral blood or cerebrospinal fluid with dark field microscopy. The number of circulating spirochetes tends to decrease with each febrile episode, making the disease more difficult to diagnose

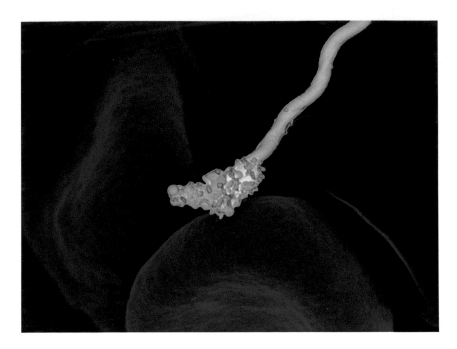

**FIGURE 8.8**

Scanning electron micrograph of *Borrelia hermsii*, the causative agent of relapsing fever, interacting with red blood cells.

*Courtesy of NIAID.*

later in its course. Without treatment, the mortality rate can approach 70 percent for LBRF and 5 to 10 percent for TBRF. Treated properly, the death rate is reduced to around 1 percent, but TBRF patients, particularly those who were diagnosed late, often report ongoing symptoms.

## TREATMENT

Treatment for LBRF usually involves a single dose of antibiotic, usually doxycycline or erythromycin, along with an antipyretic, such as aspirin, ibuprofen, or acetaminophen. TBRF treatment utilizes the same antibiotics for a longer duration, typically one week. IV penicillin is recommended in cases of central nervous system involvement. A potentially serious complication of treatment is the Jarisch-Herxheimer (J-H) reaction. As discussed

**TABLE 8.1 Clinical characteristics of other tick-borne diseases**

| DISEASE | VECTOR(S) | INCUBATION PERIOD | COMMON INITIAL SIGNS AND SYMPTOMS | CUTANEOUS SIGNS | COMMON LABORATORY FINDINGS | ESTIMATED CASE FATALITY RATE |
|---|---|---|---|---|---|---|
| *Rocky Mountain Spotted Fever* | - American dog tick<br>- Brown dog tick<br>- Rocky mountain wood tick | Three to twelve days | Fever, headache, chills malaise, myalgia, nausea, vomiting, abdominal pain, photophobia, anorexia | Maculopapular rash approximately two to four days after fever onset in most, might become petechial and involve palms and soles | Thrombocytopenia, slightly increased hepatic transaminase levels, normal or slightly increased white blood cell count with increased immature neutrophils, hyponatremia | 5 to 10% |
| *Ehrlichia chaffeensis ehrlichiosis (human monocytic ehrlichiosis)* | Lone star tick | Five to fourteen days | Fever, headache, malaise, myalgia, nausea, diarrhea, vomiting | Rash in approximately 30% of adults and 60% of children, variable rash pattern that might involve palms and soles, appears a median of five days after illness onset | Leukopenia, thrombocytopenia, increased hepatic transaminase levels, hyponatremia, anemia | 3% |
| Human anaplasmosis (human granulocytic anaplasmosis) | - Black-legged tick<br>- Western black-legged tick | Five to fourteen days | Fever, headache, malaise, myalgia, chills | Rash rare, in <10% | Thrombocytopenia, leukopenia, mild anemia, increased hepatic transaminase levels, increased numbers of immature neutrophils | <1% |
| Babesia | - Black-legged tick | One to nine or more weeks | Fever, chills, sweats, malaise, fatigue, myalgia, arthralgia, headache, anorexia, nausea, dark urine | None | Decreased hematocrit, thrombocytopenia, elevated serum creatinine and blood urea nitrogen (BUN) values, mildly elevated hepatic transaminase values, identification of intraerythrocytic Babesia parasites | 2 to 5% |

*Sources:* Biggs et al. 2016; Meldrum et al. 1992; MMWR 2011.

earlier for Lyme disease, the J-H reaction is caused by the massive release of small inflammatory molecules when the spirochetes begin to die off. Among relapsing fever patients, the reaction usually begins two to four hours after antibiotic administration and is similar to the crisis stage of the fever cycle. Typical presentations are fever, increased respiration and heart rate, excessive sweating, chills, and sudden changes in blood pressure. Fatalities from the J-H reaction can occur. Several agents have been reported to be of partial benefit in reducing J-H reaction severity (e.g., anti-TNF antibodies and opioid antagonist meptazinol), but with supportive care and fluids alone most patients reach full recovery in a few hours."

## Southern Tick Associated Rash Illness

### OVERVIEW

Since the late 1980s, physicians in the south central and southeast United States have observed Lyme disease–like rashes on patients with a recent history of tick bite. However, the tick associated with these lesions is *Amblyomma americanum*, the lone star tick, rather than the *Ixodes* tick species known to transmit Lyme disease. In addition, patients with these rashes seldom test positive for Lyme disease, suggesting that the cause of the rash is not *B. burgdorferi*. The resulting clinical entity has been differentiated from Lyme disease and is called southern tick-associated rash illness (STARI) or occasionally Masters disease in honor of Edwin Masters, the Missouri family physician who first reported these cases to his state's Department of Health.

Despite vigorous efforts, the causative agent of STARI has never been cultured and is not currently known. Early speculation focused on a recently discovered spirochete, *Borrelia lonestari*, but a microbiological study of skin biopsies from the rashes of thirty STARI patients failed to confirm this hypothesis (Wormser et al. 2005). Thus the etiology of STARI remains elusive.

### SIGNS AND SYMPTOMS

Symptoms of STARI include a circular or elliptical red rash that appears within seven days of a tick bite along with fever, headache, stiff neck, and mild muscle or joint pain. The full clinical picture of STARI is not well understood, but post-rash sequelae of STARI are thought to be significantly milder than those of Lyme disease. Some physicians have reported post-rash neurologic and cardiac manifestations in rare cases, but these are not universally accepted findings. Long-term follow-up studies of STARI patients have never been performed. Because lone star ticks are also vectors of Q fever and Ehrlichiosis, it is possible for STARI patients to be coinfected with these other entities.

## DIAGNOSIS

Diagnosis of STARI is based primarily on the existence of the typical rash; in the absence of a known etiological agent, it is not possible to develop serologic tests for the disease. Compared to the Lyme disease rash, STARI lesions are generally smaller, less variable in shape, and have more central clearing—ironically, making them more likely to resemble the iconic "bull's eye" rash of Lyme disease than Lyme rashes themselves. Secondary (multiple) lesions tend to be less common in STARI than in Lyme.

## TREATMENT

Treatment involves antibiotics, such as doxycycline or amoxicillin, for two to three weeks and sometimes longer in patients with more severe symptoms such as fever. Despite the lack of a known causative agent for STARI, most physicians and health agencies recommend treating STARI similarly to early Lyme disease. Most cases of STARI recover fully with timely antibiotic treatment (CDC "Southern Tick-Associated Rash Illness"; Masters, Grigery, and Masters 2008).

# Tick-Borne Encephalitis

## OVERVIEW

Tick-borne encephalitis (TBE) is caused by an RNA virus known simply as "tick-borne encephalitis virus" (TBEV), which belongs to the genus *Flavivirus*. It is transmitted to humans by the bite of infected arthropods, primarily mosquitoes and ticks, usually within minutes of the bite.

The range of tick-borne encephalitis spans from Western Europe to East Asia, although Eastern Europe and Russia are thought to have the highest number of cases. Because the *Ixodes ricinus* tick is both the vector for TBEV and for Lyme disease in Europe, coinfection can occur. Recently, a novel, closely related virus has emerged in North American *Ixodes scapularis* ticks known as "deer tick virus," which is serologically indistinguishable from Powassan virus, another *Flavivirus*, but represents a distinct lineage.

## SIGNS AND SYMPTOMS

Signs and symptoms usually appear about one week after the tick bite, but on rare occasions can be delayed by as much as a month. Manifestations in the first phase are nonspecific, with the primary symptoms being fever, headache, fatigue, and malaise, which last for about five days. Then many patients are symptom-free for about one week before the second stage begins. In this stage, manifestations are more serious and include meningitis (severe headache), encephalitis (seizures, altered consciousness), myelitis (tremors, motor problems, paralysis), and cranial neuritis (vision or hearing problems, facial paralysis, trouble swallowing). The overall death rate for TBE is about 1 percent, but studies have shown up to one-third of patients will experience incomplete recovery, often having lasting neuropsychiatric symptoms. A recent study revealed that approximately two-thirds of children who had the disease were experiencing ongoing symptoms, particularly cognitive problems, headaches, fatigue, and irritability (Fowler et al. 2013).

## DIAGNOSIS

Diagnosis can be made with ELISA, which can detect IgM and IgG antibodies to TBEV. Cross-reactivity with antibodies to other *Flaviviruses* can occur. Cerebrospinal fluid can also be analyzed for antibodies to TBEV, which are almost always present by the tenth day of illness. If TBE is suspected early on, the virus can be detected in serum by PCR before the development of antibodies. Lumbar puncture of TBE patients usually shows a moderate pleocytosis (white blood cells in the spinal fluid) and increased albumin. Brain MRI reveals abnormalities in 15 to 20 percent of patients, most commonly in the thalamus, cerebellum, and brainstem. electroencephalogram is abnormal in 75 percent of all patients. However, all of these findings are nonspecific and the diagnosis of TBE cannot be based solely on them.

## TREATMENT

Treatment is geared toward symptom amelioration because there is no specific treatment for TBE. One German study found that about 12 percent of patients required intensive care and 5 percent needed assisted ventilation. No data exist to support the use of corticosteroids in TBE (Ebel et al. 1999; Ebel 2010; Fowler et al. 2013; Lindquist and Vapalahti 2008).

## Tularemia

### OVERVIEW

Tularemia is a rare but serious infection caused by the small, rod-shaped, nonmotile bacterium *Francisella tularensis*. The disease occurs throughout North America and Eurasia, but in the United States it is most prevalent in the western and south central parts of the country. The main animal hosts of *F. tularensis* are small mammals such as mice, voles, squirrels, rabbits, and hares. In humans, infection is usually caused by bites from *Dermacentor* or *Amblyomma* ticks in the summer or from contact with rabbit carcasses in the winter, but other modes of transmission occur, including contact with contaminated water, air, or soil. Tularemia is divided into six forms: ulceroglandular, oculoglandular, glandular, oropharyngeal, typhoidal, and pneumonic.

Ulceroglandular is the most common form by far, comprising around three-fourths of all cases of tularemia. In ulceroglandular tularemia, the organism is acquired through the skin via the bite of a tick, deer fly, or mosquito. Typhoidal tularemia (or septicemic tularemia) accounts for 10 to 15 percent of cases and is the most serious form, often resulting in pneumonia. It is probably acquired by ingestion, although the precise mode of transmission is not completely clear. Pneumonic tularemia is acquired by inhalation and is quite uncommon. Oculoglandular tularemia is also rare and occurs when *F. tularensis* is introduced into the eye via a splash of infected blood or perhaps when the eyes are rubbed after handling an infected animal carcass. Oropharyngeal tularemia is similarly uncommon and is caused by ingesting undercooked meat from an infected animal, usually a rabbit. Glandular tularemia is also rare, and is clinically similar to the ulceroglandular form, except without the development of a skin ulcer. It is acquired through the skin and may not require a scratch or abrasion.

## SIGNS AND SYMPTOMS

Signs and symptoms usually develop within three or four days of inoculation, though in some cases it can take up to ten days for the disease to manifest. In all forms of tularemia patients may experience fever, enlarged/painful liver and spleen, a generalized red rash that may develop into pustules, and rarely meningitis.

In ulceroglandular and glandular tularemia, patients may also have a skin ulcer at the infection site (ulceroglandular form), chills, swollen glands, headache, and extreme fatigue.

Typhoidal tularemia is characterized by exhaustion, weight loss, and pneumonia. In oropharyngeal tularemia, sore throat, nausea, vomiting, diarrhea, abdominal pain, and intestinal ulcerations are common. Oculoglandular tularemia is characterized by redness and pain in the eyes (conjunctivitis), often accompanied by discharge and swollen glands. Pnuemonic tularemia causes dry cough, shortness of breath, and chest pain.

One-third of untreated patients will die, usually from pneumonia, meningitis, or peritonitis, but with appropriate and timely treatment, the mortality rate for tularemia is relatively low, around 1 to 2 percent.

## DIAGNOSIS

Diagnosis is based on the signs and symptoms described earlier, ideally combined with a history of recent arthropod bite or possible environmental exposure to *F. tularensis*, such as on a farm. The index of suspicion increases strongly with the presence of the characteristic ulcer at the infection site. About half of all patients will exhibit nonspecific

**FIGURE 8.9**

An engorged female lone star tick. A number of round, amber-colored eggs are showing from beneath the head region. An engorged female of this species can lay approximately 2,000 to 2,500 eggs.

*Courtesy of the CDC/James Gathany photo; Dr. Amanda Loftis, Dr. William Nicholson, Dr. Will
Reeves, Dr. Chris Paddock content.*

abnormalities in liver function and some may have elevated creatine
kinase levels as a result of muscle breakdown, but these results are not
specific to tularemia. Direct examination of biopsy specimens or secretions by fluorescent antibody, gram, or histochemical stains is often
helpful in diagnosis. *F. tularensis* can also be demonstrated microscopically with fluorescent-labeled antibodies. PCR tests can also be utilized.
*F. tularensis* can be grown in culture, although laboratory personnel are
advised to take strong precautions before attempting to do so because
workers can themselves become infected. Ideally, patient samples should
come from sputum or pharyngeal washings because the organism is not
present in large numbers in blood.

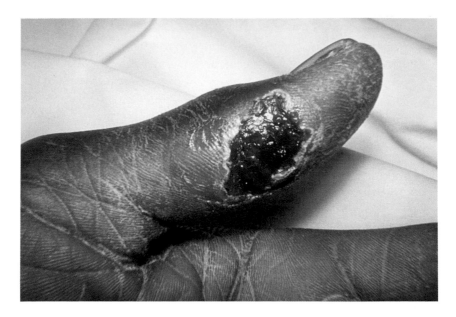

**FIGURE 8.10**

A skin ulcer caused by *Francisella tularensis*.
*Courtesy of the CDC.*

## TREATMENT

Treatment includes antibiotics such as streptomycin, gentamicin, or doxy-cycline. Treatment duration is typically two to three weeks. (Maurelus 2011; Mayo Clinic 2012; Nigrovic and Wingerter 2008).

## OTHER VECTOR-TRANSMITTED INFECTIONS (POSSIBLY BY TICKS)

### Bartonellosis

### OVERVIEW

*Bartonella* is included in this chapter because of the considerable concern in the patient community about this infection. *Bartonella* is known to be transmitted by a vector, primarily fleas, as well as by animal bites, scratches, or by needle sticks. Whether *Bartonella* can be transmitted to humans by ticks is an area of investigation. Laboratory studies demonstrate that *Ixodes* ticks can be competent vectors of *Bartonella henselae* (Cotté et al. 2008). *Ixodes ricinus* ticks have also been shown to be capable of acquiring *Bartonella birtiesii* infection from an infected mouse and transmitting this infection to an uninfected mouse (Reis et al. 2011). However, the ability of *Ixodes* ticks to actually transmit *B. henselae* to humans has not been specifically demonstrated.

*Bartonella* is a Gram-negative alphaproteobacteria composed of at least fifteen different species that cause a Bartonellosis in humans. This bacterium has been shown in vitro to invade red blood cells, macrophages, and endothelial cells. Among individuals with healthy immune systems, these bacteria may not cause disease. The full clinical spectrum of all *Bartonella* infections is still not completely understood. Cats are the main reservoir for *B. henselae*, with approximately twenty thousand reported cases of human *B. henselae* disease (called "cat scratch disease") per year in the United States.

## SIGNS AND SYMPTOMS

Signs and symptoms of Bartonellosis depend on the *Bartonella* species causing infection. Signs and symptoms of *B. henselae* infection appear about a week or so after exposure and include a small red bump at the transmission site (usually develops into a pustule), swelling of regional lymph nodes, and fever. Rarely patients may develop eye disorders or infection of the liver, spleen, or bones. Some may develop neurological involvement including encephalopathy (confusion, seizures), myelitis (sensory and motor problems in the limbs), and cranial neuritis or retinitis (trouble speaking, hearing, or seeing). Healthy patients generally experience an acute illness that resolves on its own. However, recent case reports, particularly from one research group that uses a special blood culture technique followed by PCR and DNA sequencing, suggest that various species of *Bartonella* (*henselae, vinsonii, koehlerae*) may lead to a chronic intravascular infection in some healthy patients lasting months to years and possibly causing a range of neuropsychiatric symptoms, including hallucinations, seizures, memory loss, fatigue, insomnia, and ataxia (Balakrishnan et al. 2016). Immunocompromised patients, such as those with HIV, can develop more serious manifestations such as endocarditis and bacillary angiomatosis (tumor-like masses caused by the abnormal overgrowth of blood vessels).

## DIAGNOSIS

Diagnosis requires laboratory confirmation of infection because clinical signs and symptoms may be nonspecific. Serological tests for *Bartonella* infections include IFA for both IgM and IgG antibodies. False negative serological results can occur, especially in immunocompromised patients; in one study, positive titers were found in only 30 percent of patients in whom *Bartonella* infection was confirmed by PCR and DNA sequencing. However, false positive reactions may also occur due to cross-reactivity by antibodies to *Coxiella burnetti*, chlamydia, and certain *rickettsial* infections. Western blot antibody tests appear to have greater specificity. The DNA of various *Bartonella* species can be amplified by PCR in blood, spinal fluid, and tissue; PCR may be the most reliable and useful test for *Bartonella* infection. In cases in which serology is negative or equivocal, fine needle aspiration or biopsy of an involved lymph node can be sent for histopathology, PCR, and culture. Culture of *Bartonella* organisms is possible from blood or cerebrospinal fluid, particularly using enriched medium, but the bacteria are generally slow growing in the laboratory. Culture using standard medium is insensitive. It is important to recognize that animal studies reveal that *Bartonella* infection is not always pathogenic. Indeed, a high percentage of healthy individuals may test positive serologically but not recall a prior infection consistent with a Bartonellosis.

## TREATMENT

Uncomplicated disease caused by *B. henselae* infection usually resolves even without antibiotic treatment. Studies are sparse and there is insufficient evidence to support the conclusion that antibiotics (e.g., tetracycline, macrolides, or aminoglycosides) shorten the duration of the disease. However, for complicated *Bartonella* infections, such as when it infects the central nervous system, management by a specialist is recommended and there is general agreement that antibiotic treatment is warranted. The optimal length of therapy for central nervous system infection has yet to be determined, but most guidelines suggest that treatment should last for at

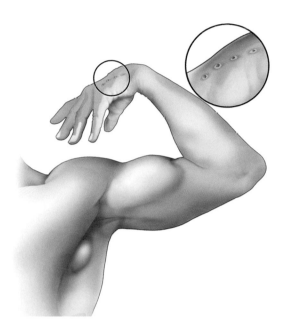

**FIGURE 8.11**

An enlarged lymph node in the armpit of a person with cat scratch disease and wounds from a cat scratch on the hand.

*Courtesy of the CDC.*

least four to six weeks. No data exist to support the use of corticosteroids in central nervous system *Bartonella* infections (Adelson et al. 2004; Eskow and Rao 2001; Reis et al. 2011; Rolain et al. 2004, Breitschwerdt 2014).

## OTHER DISORDERS CAUSED BY TICKS BUT NOT INDUCING HUMAN INFECTION

### Tick Paralysis

#### OVERVIEW

Tick paralysis results from exposure to a neurotoxin released by tick salivary glands during a bite. Worldwide, over forty tick species have been associated with tick paralysis, but in North America the most common culprits are the

American dog tick (*Dermacentor variabilis*) and the Rocky Mountain wood tick (*Dermacentor andersoni*), although it has also been linked to *Amblyomma* and *Ixodes* ticks as well. Tick paralysis, occurring most often during the summer months, is most commonly found in the Pacific Northwest, Rocky Mountain states, and southeastern part of the United States.

## SIGNS AND SYMPTOMS

Signs and symptoms typically appear within two to six days of tick attachment and include ataxia (poor coordination) followed by paralysis that starts in the feet and legs and moves upward, often accompanied by numbness and tingling in the face or limbs. Reflexes in affected areas are reduced or absent. Fever is rare, and flu-like symptoms, which only sometimes occur before the paralysis, are limited to malaise and fatigue. Tick paralysis is most commonly seen in children under sixteen. If the tick is not found and removed from the patient, the paralysis can ascend to the trunk and affect respiratory muscles, causing difficulty breathing, which can be life-threatening.

## DIAGNOSIS

Diagnosis of tick paralysis involves a thorough physical examination of any patient with a history suspicious for this condition. Specifically, any case involving sudden-onset ataxia and ascending paralysis, especially in a patient who lives in a tick endemic area and who fits the demographic profile described earlier, should be considered suspicious for tick paralysis. Such patients should be searched immediately for ticks, particularly in body areas where the tick might not be immediately apparent, such as the scalp, hairline, ear canals, or pubic region. Tick paralysis is often confused with Guillain-Barré syndrome, a clinically similar, but much more common condition. Diagnostic testing cannot distinguish between these two diseases and therefore a thorough history and physical is the key to diagnosis.

## TREATMENT

Treatment involves simply removing the tick, after which patients usually recover quickly. Improvement is commonly noted within hours, and further treatment is not required (Edlow and Mcgillicuddy 2008; Vedana-rayanan, Sorey, and Subramony 2004).

## Alpha-Gal Meat Allergy

### OVERVIEW

A syndrome of delayed anaphylaxis to red meat was first described in 2009 with thousands of cases reported across the southern and eastern United States, as well as in Europe and Australia. The reaction can be rapidly progressive and fatal. It is associated with an IgE antibody response to an oligosaccharide epitope, galactose-alpha-1,3-galactose (alpha-gal), which is found in red meat, such as beef and pork. The allergic reaction is not associated with rhinitis or asthma and is delayed, with symptoms emerging about three to six hours after eating mammalian meat (but not chicken, turkey, or fish). There is considerable evidence suggesting that lone star tick bites are a significant cause of the IgE antibody response to meat, with anaphylaxis occurring more often among those reporting a tick bite in the prior four weeks (Commins and Platts-Mills 2013).

# 9

## WHAT OTHER NONINFECTIOUS DISEASES CAUSE LYME-LIKE SYMPTOMS?

Because Lyme disease has such a wide range of possible symptoms, many non-tick-borne diseases may be misdiagnosed as Lyme disease or, conversely, a patient with Lyme disease may be misdiagnosed with another medical or psychiatric disorder, thereby delaying an opportunity for early treatment and rapid recovery. Just as it is important not to miss a case of Lyme disease because of the many less common manifestations, it is equally important not to misdiagnose someone as having Lyme disease when in fact another disease is the cause. Indeed, the cluster of symptoms so typical of patients with post-treatment Lyme disease syndrome (PTLDS) is often found in other diseases as well. Patients who have persistent fatigue or other concerning symptoms after treatment for Lyme disease should undergo a thorough medical evaluation because another undetected medical cause may be the etiology of the ongoing symptoms. Assuming that a patient's ongoing non-antibiotic responsive symptoms are due to PTLDS may delay diagnosis of and treatment for another treatable illness. The list of diseases discussed in this chapter is incomplete, but it may help remind clinicians and patients to consider some of the other possible causes of clinical symptoms that are common among patents with PTLDS.

### CELIAC DISEASE

Celiac disease is an autoimmune disorder in which patients have an abnormal immune response to gluten, a type of protein in wheat, barley, and rye. Gluten is found in many of the foods we consume and is even present in certain medicines, vitamins, or lip balms. When a patient with celiac disease eats gluten, the ensuing immune response damages the small intestine, resulting in malabsorption of nutrients. Symptoms of celiac disease include diarrhea, vomiting, abdominal bloating, constipation, weight loss, and fatigue. Many patients and even clinicians do not realize that there are symptoms of celiac disease that occur outside of the gastrointestinal tract; these may include headache (tension type or migraines), neuropathies (numbness, tingling, pain), ataxia (poor coordination), anemia, arthralgias, arthritis, depression, and irritability (a common symptom in children). Sometimes patients with celiac disease develop an itchy rash called *dermatitis herpetiformis* that is similar in appearance to blisters and often appears on the arms, knees, and buttocks. However, some people may not experience any symptoms at all. Celiac disease is genetic, so it runs in families, and patients with celiac disease may be at increased risk for other autoimmune diseases. Sometimes, but not always, the disease begins after a stressor to the body such as a viral illness, pregnancy, or even severe emotional distress. Diagnosis of celiac disease involves blood tests for specific antibodies (EMA, TTG, DGP) and/or biopsy of the small bowel or the skin, if the patient has skin lesions. Treatment is a gluten-free diet, which typically alleviates the gastrointestinal symptoms but may not be as effective for other symptoms, such as headaches. Individuals with confirmed celiac disease are cautioned to be careful of cross-contamination, which can occur by eating at a restaurant that stores or cooks foods with gluten in the same place as food that is supposed to be gluten-free.

## CHRONIC FATIGUE SYNDROME

Chronic fatigue syndrome (CFS) is also known as myalgic encephalomyelitis or systemic exertion intolerance disease. In this condition, chronic fatigue often develops suddenly following an infection, such as an upper respiratory infection or mononucleosis; however, it is not always preceded by an infectious illness. This fatigue is severe and debilitating, worsens with exercise, and lasts for at least six consecutive months. In order for CFS to be diagnosed, fatigue must not be due to ongoing exertion or other medical conditions associated with fatigue. Other CFS symptoms include sore throat, memory and concentration problems, generalized pain, headaches, insomnia, lack of refreshing sleep, and feeling unwell for more than twenty-four hours after physical activity. CFS commonly presents in young and middle-aged adults, and it is significantly more common in women. This condition often interferes with the patient's ability to engage in daily activities and work. The cause of CFS is currently unknown. Many patients with CFS have experienced frustration when told that their symptoms are "all in their head," similar to patients with chronic symptoms after Lyme disease. Two studies recently offered new perspectives on CFS. A metabolomics study (Naviaux et al. 2016) suggests that CFS may be a hypometabolic response to environmental stress that traces to mitochondria dysfunction. A microbiome study of CFS (Nagy-Szakal et al. 2017) suggests that CFS may result from a breakdown in the bidirectional communication between the brain and the gut mediated by bacteria, their metabolites, and the molecules they influence. Although there are no specific diagnostic tests for CFS or treatments that work for all patients, there are several studies reporting benefit among some patients from graded exercise therapy (Larun et al. 2016). Patients who believe they have CFS should be evaluated by a physician because CFS shares symptoms with other serious, treatable diseases including infections, autoimmune diseases, malignancies, psychiatric illnesses, and others.

## CHRONIC HEAVY METAL POISONING

Chronic heavy metal poisoning refers to exposure to usually small amounts of heavy metals over a long period of time, typically months or years. Exposure often occurs at work but can also occur in the home or sometimes outdoors. Common metals involved in chronic poisoning include lead, mercury, arsenic, cadmium, and manganese. Diagnosis of heavy metal poisoning involves identifying individuals who are at risk through a detailed medical history and physical exam; this is then followed by lab tests, such as blood and urine tests. If elevated levels of heavy metals are detected, treatment involves both removing the patient from the exposure and, most often, chelation therapy (McGuigan 2012).

## Lead

Chronic lead poisoning involves symptoms such as high blood pressure, peripheral neuropathy, reproductive problems in women, anemia, kidney failure, and encephalopathic symptoms such as memory problems, changes in mood, sleep problems, fatigue, and irritability. Occupations that may put adults at risk for lead poisoning include smelting, manufacturing of batteries, construction, mining, automobile repair, gas, and sanitary service. Nonoccupational sources of exposure for adults include shooting firearms, remodeling or renovation activities, ceramics, and contaminated food.

## Mercury

Organic mercurials are the type of mercury with which fish can be contaminated. Consumption of fish is the source of exposure for nearly all methyl mercury poisoning in the general population. The highest mercury concentrations are found in king mackerel, shark, swordfish, and tilefish

**FIGURE 9.1**

A fur hat factory worker in a Connecticut plant is "blocking" a hat. This man is not wearing protective equipment. Working with newly processed fur, which had been fixed with mercury nitrate, workers could be exposed to airborne mercury, thereby suffering the detrimental neurologic consequences from its inhalation.

*Courtesy of NIOSH/United States Government Work.*

from the Gulf of Mexico. Fish with medium concentrations of mercury include fresh tuna steak, canned white or albacore tuna, grouper, orange roughy, saltwater trout, bluefish, lobster, halibut, haddock, snapper, and crab. Methyl mercury in larger amounts has potentially toxic effects on the central nervous system of a fetus, so pregnant women should consult their physicians about what is safe to eat. Fish from local lakes and ponds may be more polluted than commercial fish sources. Initial symptoms of methyl mercury poisoning are fatigue and tingling in the extremities followed by difficulty with hand movements and visual disturbances. There is a gradual onset of motor problems, visual problems, and difficulty speaking, sometimes over a period of years.

## Arsenic

The trivalent form of arsenic is responsible for the majority of human arsenic toxicity. Sources of exposure include seafood, groundwater (often from water wells), mining, pesticides, pigments, wood preservatives, glass or metal manufacturing, electronics, and folk remedies. Poisoning develops after weeks to months of ingestion or inhalation. Typical initial symptoms are metallic taste in the mouth, loss of appetite, weight loss, malaise, and weakness. Skin lesions and brittle nails are also common early findings. Chronic cough, type 2 diabetes, and reproductive abnormalities in women have also been linked to arsenic exposure. Later-stage findings are alopecia (hair loss) and neurologic problems such as headache, peripheral neuropathy, muscle weakness, and coordination problems. Arsenic exposure has also been linked to various forms of cancer and cardiovascular disease.

## Cadmium

Sources of cadmium include industrial chemicals, fertilizer, fuel, nickel-cadmium batteries, and pigment in coloring the red bags used for infectious hospital waste (which release cadmium into the environment when they are incinerated). Most people, however, are exposed to cadmium through their diet. Smoking is a risk factor that increases a person's likelihood of cadmium poisoning. Chronic cadmium poisoning can result in kidney failure, osteoporosis, bone fractures, male infertility, slowing of visual-motor function, and peripheral neuropathy. Treatment of cadmium poisoning is symptomatic and supportive because there is no specific chelating agent that helps eliminate cadmium from the body (McGuigan 2012).

## Manganese

Exposure to manganese can occur through steel production, animal feed, batteries, fertilizers, fireworks, fungicides, matches, and potassium perman ganate. People who work in the welding, mining, and foundry industries are particularly at risk. Manganese is also an essential nutrient for the body so it is often a component of intravenous (IV) nutrition preparations. Therefore long-term use of IV nutrition therapy can result in manganese toxicity. People with manganese toxicity may exhibit unusual behaviors including aggression, irritability, nervousness, and destructive tendencies as well as spasmodic crying, laughing, singing, or dancing. Patients may also develop a syndrome similar to Parkinson's disease with tremors of the extremities, a shuffling walk, a mask-like face, and slowed or stiff body movements.

## Chelation for Heavy Metals

Heavy metal toxicity can lead to a wide array of adverse consequences (e.g., fatigue, headaches, nausea, gastrointestinal distress, and mild to severe neurologic, cognitive, and psychiatric symptoms). Some of these symptoms overlap with the symptoms of PTLDS, leading some clinicians to screen patients for heavy metals. While many heavy metals (e.g., zinc, copper, iron, manganese) are needed in small amounts for normal cellular processes, higher levels can lead to toxicity. Lead, mercury, and arsenic have no known biologic function and their presence in tissue is often associated with human toxicity. A history of exposure to heavy metals (e.g., occupational exposure or excessive fish consumption) and clinical symptoms would prompt a clinician to test the blood and urine for elevated levels of certain heavy metals. When elevated levels are found, detoxification is recommended with appropriate chelating agents. Some alternative medicine practitioners recommend, in addition to chelation, the removal of all mercury-containing amalgam dental fillings and root canals. However, the American College of Medical Toxicology recommends against this practice given the lack of evidence that mercury-containing amalgram fill-ings leads to illness and given that removal of such amalgams subjects the individuals to absorption of greater doses of mercury than if left in place (ABIM, 2014). While it is wise to pursue evaluation for and treatment of heavy metal toxicity if a patient has an exposure history and symptoms consistent with this diagnosis, it is not recommended that patients pursue chelation therapy if there is no well-substantiated biologic and clinical evidence of heavy metal toxicity.

Questions arise about the role of "challenge" testing. Some medical practitioners advocate a "provocation" with chemical chelators such as dimercaptosuccinic acid (DMSA) and ethylene diamine tetraacetic acid (EDTA) prior to urine testing. Patients should be aware that heavy metal testing of urine samples can be misleading if the urine samples are col-lected after a provocation or chelation challenge. This conclusion is based on the observation that the normative levels used to assess toxic levels of heavy metals are based on healthy individuals who had not under-gone the chelation challenge or provoked testing. Since chelation extracts metals from tissue, it is not surprising that the urine may show elevated levels even in healthy individuals after chelation. When assessing acute exposure to heavy metals, a nonchelator-challenged collection of urine or blood should be obtained as a baseline assessment. In 2009, the American College of Medical Toxicology stated that provoked testing "has not been scientifically validated, has no demonstrated benefit, and may be harmful when applied in the assessment and treatment of patients in whom there is concern for metal poisoning" (Charlton and Wallace 2010).

## CHRONIC INFLAMMATORY DEMYELINATING POLYNEUROPATHY

Chronic inflammatory demyelinating polyneuropathy (CIDP) is the most common treatable chronic neuropathy with a prevalence of one to nine cases per 100,000 population in worldwide studies (Mathey et al. 2015). There are several ways in which CIDP can present in terms of clini-cal symptoms and type of distribution on the body. Symptoms can be sensory (tingling, burning, stabbing, or numbness in the limbs) or motor (weakness in the limbs). Symptoms can be symmetrical (affecting both sides of the body) or asymmetrical (affecting one side predominantly). The most common type, affecting 53 to 67 percent of individuals with CIDP, includes both proximal and distal sensory and motor symptoms. Most of these cases have an onset that develops over a period of at least eight weeks (Van den Bergh et al. 2010), but there can be a sudden onset of symptoms. Additionally, the clinical course can be relapsing remitting or one of steady progression (Hughes et al. 2006). Physical findings on exam may reveal absent or diminished reflexes, loss of position sense or vibration, and/or weakness of the thighs or upper arms.

Although the precise cause of CIDP is not known, it is considered to be an autoimmune disease because there is evidence of an impaired immune response and of inflammation around the peripheral nerves and segmental demyelination. Electromyography (EMG) is abnormal in large fiber neuropathies (CIDP and autoimmune demyelinating polyneuropathy), showing slowing and sometimes conduction block. Treatments that affect the immune system (corticosteroids, plasma exchange, and intravenous immunoglobulin) have been found to be effective in some cases (Hughes et al. 2006). Diagnosis of CIDP is based on clinical symptoms as well as electrodiagnostic testing, supplemented by nerve biopsy and laboratory studies.

Although large fiber neuropathy can occur due to Lyme disease, the more common presentation among patients with PTLDS appears to be a small fiber neuropathy detected by epidermal biopsy. Among these patients the EMG is often normal as pathology is limited to the small nerve fibers. There are anecdotal reports and a small case series suggesting benefit of intravenous immunoglobins (IVIG) for small fiber neuropathy associated with PTLDS, but conclusions about efficacy and safety must await placebo-controlled randomized clinical trials and these have not yet been conducted (Katz and Berkley 2009).

## FIBROMYALGIA

The primary symptom of fibromyalgia is chronic, widespread musculoskeletal pain for at least three consecutive months. Other symptoms include fatigue, sleep disturbances, stiffness, physical or sexual dysfunction, brain fog, and anxiety and mood disturbances. Fibromyalgia may occur with a coexisting rheumatologic disorder. In general, there are no abnormal laboratory or imaging findings. Similar to chronic fatigue syndrome, the cause of fibromyalgia is currently unknown. Recent work has led to the conceptualization of fibromyalgia as a "centralized pain state" that can be triggered by a variety of stressors, including infections, early life stressors, and physical trauma (Clauw 2014). Treatments strategies may include pharmacotherapy or non-pharmacologic treatments.

Because it is viewed as a pain-processing problem in the brain, fibromyalgia is treated by medications that focus on modulating the brain's pain pathways including agents with dual actions on the neurotransmitters serotonin and norepinephrine. These medications include amitriptyline, cyclobenzaprine, milnacipran, duloxetine, venlafaxine, pregabalin, gabapentin, and low-dose naltrexone. Of importance is that opioids such as oxycodone and morphine do not work for patients with centralized pain; indeed, new evidence suggests opioids may worsen centralized pain in a process called opioid induced hyperalgesia (Lee et al. 2011).

Treatments for fibromyalgia should be individualized to the particular patient and may include a combination of an exercise program, psychotherapy, pharmacotherapy, and patient education regarding the disease. While it may be hard for patients to understand how psychotherapy could help reduce pain, it is worth noting that anger, sadness, and interpersonal rejection increase the experience of pain (van Middendorp et al. 2010; Landa, Peterson, and Fallon 2012); psychotherapy that enhances emotional regulation and reduces emotional distress may therefore be effective in reducing chronic pain.

Patients with widespread musculoskeletal pain should consider an online treatment program that is available at www.fibroguide.med.umich.edu. Clinicians should of course remember that it is important to treat co-occurring depression and anxiety that commonly accompany this disease and, similar to CFS, to conduct a thorough history and physical exam to evaluate for other potentially serious, treatable causes of chronic musculoskeletal pain.

## LUPUS

Lupus is a chronic inflammatory autoimmune disease that can affect the skin, joints, kidneys, lungs, and nervous system, causing a wide variety of symptoms. Often patients will have periods of remission with acute or chronic relapses. Young women are most frequently affected by this disease. Patients may experience chronic fatigue, fever with no known cause, and weight loss. Other symptoms include joint pain and swelling, rash (such as a "butterfly rash" across the nose and cheeks after sun exposure), hair loss, brain fog, and Raynaud's phenomenon, in which cold air induces a change in the color of the skin on fingers and toes. Lupus is a very diverse disease and has a variable prognosis. There is no one test used to diagnose the disease, and it may take months or even years to make the diagnosis. Treatment depends on the individual patient's symptoms but often includes recommendations regarding sun protection, diet and nutrition, smoking cessation, and avoidance of certain medications known to precipitate relapses. Treatment may or may not include immunosuppressants, such as steroids.

## MAJOR DEPRESSIVE DISORDER

Major depressive disorder is a common and disabling illness. Symptoms include depressed mood, irritability, fatigue, insomnia, decreased appetite, poor concentration, and problems with short-term memory. These symptoms overlap with those of many other illnesses, including Lyme disease. Major depression may be triggered by a medical illness, such as infection, endocrine abnormalities, or inflammatory disorders. If there is an underlying medical illness, the physical illness needs to be treated to achieve an optimal response to mental health interventions. Patients may feel that depression is a sign of "weak character," not understanding that depression itself is biologically mediated. Some people who are not educated about mental illness might dismiss mood problems as "not real," "in your head," or "purely subjective." However, major depression (as is also true for many anxiety disorders) is associated with "objective" brain changes. Brain imaging studies may show a global decrease in blood flow or a more regional pattern of decreased blood flow in the frontal and temporal lobes. Interventional treatment that electrically stimulates a certain area of the brain can lead to a rapid reduction in depression in 40 percent of patients with treatment refractory depression (Mayberg, Riva-Posse, and Crowell 2016). Neuropathologic studies may show abnormal neurotransmitter receptor density or function or even reduced brain volume in certain areas, such as the hippocampus. Failure to treat depression and anxiety can lead to a failure of neurogenesis in the brain, so that new healthy neural connections in the brain are not established and the brain may diminish in size. It is therefore widely recognized in the medical community that major depression is a very real biological illness. The good news is that it can be successfully treated with medication and/or therapy. Treatments include cognitive behavioral therapy, psychodynamic therapy, and pharmacotherapy—most often selective serotonin reuptake inhibitors (SSRIs) and serotonin and norepinephrine reuptake inhibitors (SNRIs).

## MALIGNANCY (CANCER)

An article in the *Journal of the American Medical Association* described cases of patients who were misdiagnosed as having PTLDS but actually had different malignancies (cancers) including pituitary adenoma and Hodgkin's lymphoma (Nelson, Elmendorf, and Mead 2015). In the first case, a man in his thirties presented to his physician with a twelve-year history of joint pain and memory loss as well as several years of tingling in his hands. After being diagnosed with Lyme disease despite a negative Lyme serology and treated with tetracycline, the patient's symptoms continued to worsen. He also developed syncope (fainting) and vision problems. He was eventually found to have a large pituitary gland tumor. The tumor was able to be partially removed but the patient had lasting symptoms. The second case entailed a man in his late thirties who presented with a four-year history of fatigue, abdominal pain, and diarrhea. The patient was diagnosed with Lyme disease and treated with several courses of antibiotics. When his symptoms did not improve, he was reevaluated by a gastroenterologist and an oncologist and found to have advanced lymphoma. The patient died two years later of complications from lymphoma. These cases are important in demonstrating that PTLDS symptoms can overlap with those of other serious treatable illnesses, including several forms of cancer. Furthermore, even in cases of confirmed Lyme disease, continuing severe symptoms after antibiotic treatment should lead to a further medical workup to seek other causes.

## MULTIPLE SCLEROSIS

Multiple sclerosis (MS) is an inflammatory disease of the optic nerves, spinal cord, and brain that can have diverse presentations ranging from mild to severe. The course can be relapsing remitting with long periods of remission or one of progressive decline. The primary pathology of untreated MS is that of demyelination followed by axonal degeneration. It affects women twice as often as men. The signs and symptoms of MS can vary widely, depending on the degree and extent of nerve damage. It often presents in young adults with symptoms of visual changes, loss of balance, numbness, impaired speech, weakness, urinary incontinence, tremors, fatigue, and depression. While there is no cure, there are many new treatments for MS that can serve to shorten the course of MS attacks, modify the progression of the disease, and reduce disability.

A variety of diseases can mimic MS, including a rare form of Lyme disease known as encephalomyelitis, which can lead to demyelinating-like lesions in the central nervous system; in this situation, treatment with intravenous antibiotics can help reverse the Lyme-induced inflammatory illness. Lyme disease may also affect the optic nerve, causing local inflammation; in this situation, MS would also be considered. For both diseases (neurologic Lyme and MS), brain magnetic resonance imaging  and examination of the cerebrospinal fluid are critical for diagnosis. To assess for Lyme disease, the cerebrospinal fluid should be tested for *B. burgdorferi*–specific antibodies, comparing the quantity present in the cerebrospinal fluid to the quantity in the serum to assess whether there is preferential production of *B. burgdorferi*–specific antibodies in the central nervous system. In rare cases, a patient may have both MS and Lyme disease; it would be important to treat both conditions—the Lyme disease with antibiotics and the MS with immune modulating agents. In the situation of an individual with known Lyme disease and MS-like symptoms, treatment with intravenous antibiotics may be reasonable to assess treatment response even in the absence of *B. burgdorferi*–specific production because an elevated Lyme index is not always present in neurologic Lyme disease in the United States. It is essential to emphasize that there are excellent disease-modifying treatments for MS; while Lyme-induced MS-like symptoms should not be missed, it is also critical that true MS be treated appropriately to reduce and prevent further disability.

## PANIC DISORDER

Patients with panic disorder have repeated episodes or attacks of intense fear accompanied by sweating, trembling, tingling, palpitations, lightheadedness, chest pain, and/or feelings of unreality. Two startling facts about this anxiety disorder is that the symptoms are predominantly physical and that the panic attacks may occur completely out of the blue—when one is calm, at rest, or even during sleep. Patients with panic disorder can present to an emergency room fearing a heart attack or might consult a neurologist because of dizziness, numbness, and tingling. Patients may feel like they are dying or "going crazy" during a panic attack. These episodes usually peak in intensity within ten or fifteen minutes. While the first episode may come out of the blue, patients often begin to worry about these attacks and avoid certain activities that they believe might bring them on, such as taking public transportation or going to a crowded place alone. Patients who are suspected to have panic disorder should have a thorough medical workup to ensure that there is not another medical cause for their symptoms. Panic disorder can be successfully treated with cognitive behavioral therapy or pharmacotherapy including SSRIs and SNRIs. In the very short term, benzodiazepines can be helpful at alleviating the acute symptoms of a panic attack, but SSRIs and SNRIs are the medications of choice for the longer term.

## PEDIATRIC AUTOIMMUNE NEUROPSYCHIATRIC DISORDERS ASSOCIATED WITH STREPTOCOCCUS

A small number of children (this disorder can only be diagnosed in children) develop new or worsened neurological or psychiatric symptoms that arise quite suddenly and intensely after infection with Group A Beta hemolytic streptococcus (GABHS). These symptoms can include motor or vocal tics similar to those seen in Tourette's syndrome and obsessions and/or compulsions, often along with moodiness and irritability. This disorder is called Pediatric Autoimmune Neuropsychiatric Disorders Associated with Streptococcus (PANDAS). Although the origin of this disorder is not completely understood, it is believed that it might be due to an autoimmune reaction to streptococcal infection. In this reaction, antibodies that formed in response to the GABHS infection begin attacking the patient's own tissues. Treatments include cognitive behavioral therapy and SSRI medication as well as plasmapheresis and IVIG for severe cases. Controlled studies to date of IVIG therapy have been few and small in size; larger studies are needed. There have been case reports of new-onset pediatric neuropsychiatric disorders after other infections, such as after *mycoplasma pneumoniae* or after *B. burgdorferi* infection. These infection-related case reports and other environmental triggers have led to the delineation of a new broader diagnostic syndrome called PANS (pediatric acute-onset neuropsychiatric syndrome). Whether patients with PANS also show a favorable response to IVIG and/or plasmapheresis in controlled studies remains to be determined.

## POSTURAL ORTHOSTATIC TACHYCARDIA SYNDROME

Postural orthostatic tachycardia syndrome (POTS) involves a dysregulation of the autonomic nervous system that can be triggered by or accompanied by Lyme disease. Symptoms include tachycardia (rapid heart rate), exercise intolerance, sleep disturbance, lightheadedness, extreme fatigue, headache, and mental clouding. Patients with POTS have a heart rate increase of greater than or equal to thirty beats per minute with prolonged standing (approximately ten minutes). With this heart rate increase, patients begin to feel lightheaded and some actually faint. This condition often affects a patient's ability to work or go to school. Diagnosis is made based on a clinical history and a tilt table test. There is no single preferred long-term treatment, but there are several effective alternatives for alleviating symptoms in the short term. These include adding more salt to the diet to increase blood volume, staying adequately hydrated throughout the day, and drinking two glasses of water before standing up after prolonged sitting. Low doses of the medications fludrocortisone and midodrine can also be helpful in some cases. Other individuals are helped by beta blocker medications or exercise programs (Kanjwal et al. 2011).

## SLEEP DISORDERS

Not uncommonly, patients with acute Lyme disease or PTLDS find that they need to sleep much longer and often do not feel rested on awakening. Or they may feel as if they are dragging their body and their mind through the steps of daily life, constantly fighting a background of dense fatigue. These symptoms may be due to ongoing Lyme disease or to its postinfectious sequelae. It is also possible, however, that the patient may have an underlying sleep disorder that has not been detected or properly treated. Hypersomnia disorders include Klein Levin syndrome and narcolepsy. Klein Levin syndrome is rare, typically reported in teenagers, and is characterized by periods of intense long-duration sleep such that the individual sleeps for days or weeks with only a very short period of awakening during a twenty-four-hour interval; accompanying symptoms may include hyperphagia and hypersexuality. Narcolepsy is a more common sleep disorder characterized by excessive daytime sleepiness, with or without cataplexy; cataplexy refers to sudden attacks of loss of muscle tone that may be triggered by strong emotions. Sleep apnea—best diagnosed with a sleep study—refers to the condition in which a person's brain and body fail to get sufficient oxygen at night during sleep due to either obstructed airways or central brain mechanisms; as a result, the individual feels exhausted during the day. Individuals with obstructive sleep apnea may snore loudly or make choking noises as they try to breathe at night. Restless leg syndrome refers to the overwhelming urge to move one's legs, thus impairing sleep at night and leading to exhaustion during the day; this more often develops in women and after the age of forty-five.

Impaired sleep—regardless of the cause—will lead to poor concentration, poor memory, irritability, and in many individuals depression. Fragmented sleep has also been shown to mediate the relationship between clinical pain, brain circuits, and central sensitization (Burton et al. 2016). Proper diagnosis is essential because there are effective treatments for a wide range of sleep disturbances.

## SOMATIC SYMPTOM DISORDER

Somatic symptom disorder (SSD) is characterized by distressing symptoms, such as headaches, musculoskeletal pain, and stomach aches, that persist for at least six months. There may or may not be an identifiable medical cause for the symptoms, but the key to this diagnosis is that the symptoms are accompanied by excessive emotional, cognitive, or behavior responses. While unexplained somatic symptoms are common (90 percent of individuals report at least one unexplained symptom over a two-week period), SSD is only diagnosed if the reaction to the symptoms is considered excessive and so distressing that patients are unable to function normally. Typically, family, interpersonal relationships, and/or work are significantly affected. The determination of what is "excessive" is challenging and in some cases prone to judgment errors by the clinician. If a person does have an undetected medical disorder, it is reasonable to be distressed because the person may be getting worse but no cause has yet been identified. However, in the typical scenario, the individual with SSD has often been to dozens of doctors and received a vast amount of testing for an exhaustive differential diagnoses—all to no avail. The patient with SSD who is open-minded and has good insight eventually comes to agree that there is an emotional component that exacerbates the somatic symptoms. The manifestations might include excessive thoughts, feelings, and behaviors in relation to the somatic symptom. The individual might have obsessive thoughts that the symptom means something terrible is going to happen, or the individual might engage in repeated health-seeking behaviors even though many past visits to different doctors had led to being told there is nothing medically wrong.

Before receiving a diagnosis of SSD, a patient should have a thorough medical workup to rule out any possible medical cause of the symptoms that need treatment. In Lyme endemic areas, the workup should include tests for Lyme disease and if clinically indicated various coinfections. SSD can occur on its own or at the same time as a medical illness. One can certainly have other disorders with prominent somatic symptoms, such as fibromyalgia or PTLDS, and not be diagnosed with SSD. In this scenario, the medically ill patient may be symptomatic but does not have an excessive response to the somatic symptoms. Clinicians who work with patients who have SSD emphasize to the patient that their experience of symptoms is real; these clinicians may then clarify that the psychophysiology of heightened somatic sensation and concerns include a combination of factors, including neurotransmitter and neural network alterations in the brain that govern affective and somatic sensations as well as cognitive distortions partly fueled by catastrophic thinking. Treatments can be quite effective and include cognitive behavioral therapy and a class of medications called selective serotonin-norepinephrine reuptake inhibitors (SNRIs), which are particularly helpful in reducing widespread pain, neuropathic pain, depression, and anxiety.

## VITAMIN B12 DEFICIENCY

Vitamin B12 (cobalamin) deficiency can present with a range of neurologic and neuropsychiatric signs and symptoms including confusion, depression, sensory loss, ataxia (trouble walking), and tingling or weakness in the limbs that can mimic Lyme disease. In addition, patients can have optic atrophy (visual loss), loss of taste, impaired sense of position and vibration, and abnormal reflexes. Because vitamin B12 is typically found in foods of animal origin, vegans and vegetarians are particularly prone to developing this vitamin deficiency. Absorption of cobalamin requires the presence of intrinsic factor; patients who lack intrinsic factor due to autoimmune atrophic gastritis can develop severe vitamin B12 deficiency, known as "pernicious anemia." Vitamin B12 is critical for the myelination of the central nervous system and the preservation of its function. Absence of B12 can lead to demyelination of areas of the spinal cord as well as demyelination of the white matter in the brain, eventually leading to irreversible loss of function. Classic findings on routine labs in patients with B12 deficiency include anemia (low hemoglobin and hematocrit), macrocytosis (abnormally large red blood cells), leukopenia (low white blood cell count), thrombocytopenia (low platelets), and elevated liver function tests. However, many patients do not present with the classic laboratory findings. In a study of 141 patients with neuropsychiatric abnormalities due to vitamin B12 deficiency, forty (28 percent) had no anemia or macrocytosis (Lindenbaum et al. 1988). Although measuring the serum vitamin B12 level is helpful, one can have normal serum vitamin B12 levels but still have a B12 deficiency. Serum methylmalonic acid and total homocysteine are also very useful because they are elevated in the majority (more than 98 percent) of patients with clinical B12 deficiency (Stabler 2013). However, these two tests should be obtained before any treatment is given because they typically lower rapidly with B12 supplementation.

Treatment of severe vitamin B12 deficiency initially includes intramuscular injections several times per week, then weekly until clear improvement is shown, followed by monthly injections. Daily high-dose oral treatment may have similar effectiveness. With treatment, blood tests normally improve within two months and neurologic signs and symptoms improve within six months. Diagnosing a patient with vitamin B12 deficiency can be challenging given that it may not always present with typical findings of anemia and low-serum B12 but is extremely important considering that its disabling effects can be fully reversible with timely treatment.

# 10

## LYME DISEASE PREVENTION AND TRANSMISSION

The best prevention against Lyme and other tick-borne diseases involves reducing exposure to ticks. This can be done in a variety of ways using both personal and environmental protection methods. This chapter describes ways to reduce the risk of tick bites, as well as fascinating new strategies to prevent Lyme disease that are now under development.

## THE TICKS

### Life Cycle of the Tick

Before embarking on specific recommendations and descriptions of new research, it is worth reviewing the three stage of the life cycle of the *Ixodes* tick: larva, nymph, and adult. See figure 10.1.

In each of the three stages of its life, the tick has to have a blood meal before transforming (molting) into the next stage. The smallest and youngest ticks—larva—feed primarily on small mammals, usually for about four days. If the small mammals are carriers (that is, reservoir hosts) and infected with *B. burgdorferi*, the ticks will likely suck up some spirochetes in the process of feeding on the blood of the animal. These small mammals include the white-footed mice (the primary reservoir of *B. burgdorferi*) as well as chipmunks, voles, shrews, squirrels, raccoons, skunks, and opossums. The ticks may also feed on other carriers (reservoir hosts) of *B. burgdorferi* such as the American robin or other ground-foraging birds. After feeding, the newly infected larval ticks then molt

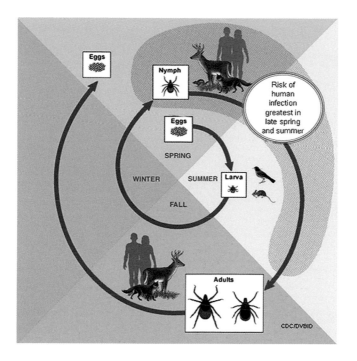

**FIGURE 10.1**

The life cycle of black-legged ticks through the four seasons.

*Courtesy of the CDC.*

into the nymphal stage—about the size of a poppy seed. The infected nymph then seeks another small mammal for a blood meal; if a human is nearby, the nymph may opt to bite the human instead. The feeding infected nymph thereby transmits whatever microbes might be inside its gut, such as *Borrelia* spirochetes, to mice, birds, squirrels, or humans. After this blood meal, the nymph molts into the adult stage. In the adult stage of the tick life cycle, this larger tick (sesame seed size) feeds predominantly on large animals such as deer (or humans). The deer are not reservoirs of *B. burgdorferi*. However, even though they are not carriers of the *Borrelia* spirochete, deer are important for the life cycle of the tick because they are a source for a blood meal for the adult ticks and ticks mate with one another on them.

## COMMON TICKS

- ***Ixodes* ticks**, commonly known as "deer ticks," are hard-bodied ticks, specifically identified in the United States as *Ixodes scapularis* and *Ixodes pacificus*. They can transmit microbes, including the agents of Lyme disease, Babesiosis, and Anaplasmosis. Younger *Ixodes* nymphal ticks are active in the spring and summer months. They are easily missed because they are light colored and as small as a freckle.

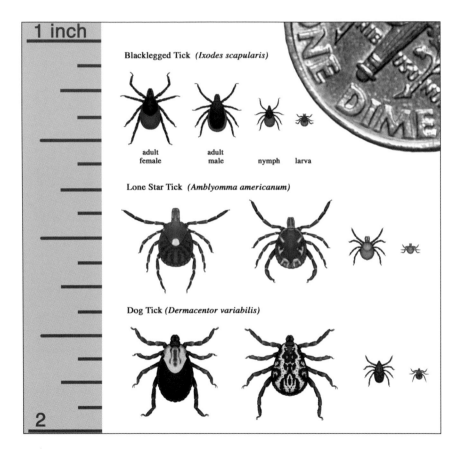

**FIGURE 10.2**

Relative size of black-legged, lone star, and dog ticks at different life stages.

*Courtesy of the CDC.*

**FIGURE 10.3**

Female *Ixodes* deer tick laying eggs.

*Courtesy of Griffin Dill, University of Maine Cooperative Extension.*

The adult ticks are more readily visible because they are larger and darker in color and are active in the autumn months in the northeastern United States. When bloated after a prolonged blood meal, they may grow to the size of a raisin.

- **Dog ticks or wood ticks**, *Dermacentor variabilis*, are much larger than *Ixodes* ticks and do not carry the spirochete causing Lyme disease. However, they can transmit microbes that cause other human diseases, such as Rocky Mountain Spotted Fever or tularemia.
- **Lone star ticks**, *Amblyomma americanum*, can also carry microbes that cause disease in humans, such as ehrlichiosis, southern tick-associated rash illness, and tularemia. The lone star tick is also thought to transmit the newly discovered Heartland virus. The lone star tick is more aggressive and moves faster than the *Ixodes* tick and has been expanding its geographic range from the known heavy density areas in southeastern and Atlantic states to previously less dense areas such

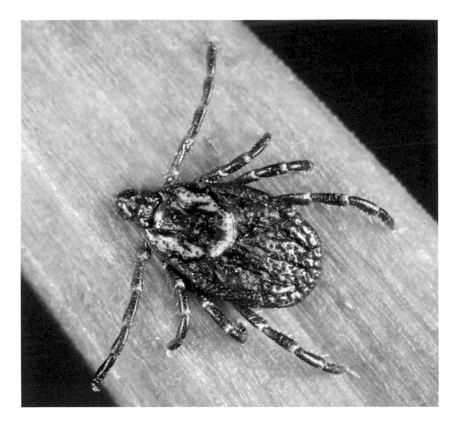

**FIGURE 10.4**

Female American dog tick.

*Courtesy of the CDC/DVBID/James Gathany.*

as the northeast and midwest United States. As noted in chapter 8, there have been clinical reports indicating that a lone star tick bite can induce a delayed allergic reaction to meats in humans, known as an alpha-gal allergy (Wolver et al. 2013).

## Additional facts about *Ixodes* ticks

- Dogs and cats, if bitten by an *Ixodes* tick, might get infected with *B. burgdorferi*, but these animals are not good carriers of *B. burgdorferi*.

An uninfected tick is unlikely to acquire the *B. burgdorferi* microbe by biting a dog or cat.

- In the United States there are now over thirty million deer, whereas in the early 1900s in the United States it is estimated that there were only about 500,000 deer. Because there are fewer natural predators of deer (e.g., coyotes, wolves, mountain lions) and more restrictions on hunting, the deer population has exploded. This is a favorable scenario for the adult tick.

- When our society was agrarian and hunting and farming with wide open fields were the norm, the life cycle of the tick was interrupted because there were fewer small and large mammals on which they could feed. Given the return of the land to forest and the increase in deer and small mammals, the late twentieth and early twenty-first century has seen a marked increase in the density and distribution of ticks and consequently of tick-borne diseases.

- Climate makes a difference for ticks. The *Ixodes* ticks do not do well under dry, arid, or hot conditions because they risk becoming dehydrated.

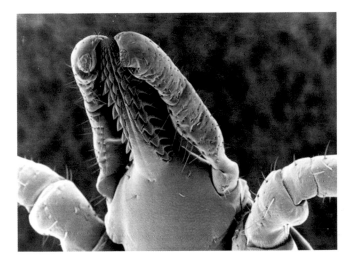

**FIGURE 10.5**

Mouth parts of *Ixodes Scapularis*. Scanning electron microscopy.

*Courtesy of NIAID/David Dorward.*

They prefer temperatures and humidity levels that are moderate; this partly accounts for the greater density of Lyme disease cases along the Atlantic and Pacific coast in the northeast and western regions of the United States. Perhaps to protect themselves from excessive heat and to find higher humidity, ticks seek refuge under leaf litter, in tall grasses, and in low-lying vegetation. Ticks also do not do well under extremely cold weather conditions, although they can find warmth and insulation under a bed of snow.

## PREVENTION RECOMMENDATIONS

### Avoid Tick-Prevalent Areas

In the United States, certain regions are known to be heavily laden with black-legged ticks (*Ixodes scapularis* and *Ixodes pacificus*)—particularly the northeast, mid-Atlantic, upper Midwest, and Pacific coastal states. People engaged in outdoor activity in these regions in particular should be vigilant to the risk of tick bites. It should be noted, however, that while disease-carrying ticks are found throughout the United States, only the *Ixodes* black-legged ticks have been shown to transmit *B. burgdorferi*. The ticks that carry Lyme disease are gradually spreading farther south and west. Birds that carry *Ixodes* ticks to new locations play a key role in the geographic spread of Lyme disease.

### Use Personal Protection Measures

- **Timing.** Because *Ixodes* ticks in the northeastern United States are most active from April to September, local residents and visitors should be particularly alert to the possibility of tick bites during these months. In many climates, however, especially as the winters become warmer, ticks can be active and bite humans through the fall and winter as well. In northwestern California, for example, *Ixodes pacificus* nymphs can be found from January through October and adult ticks can be found from late fall through the spring.

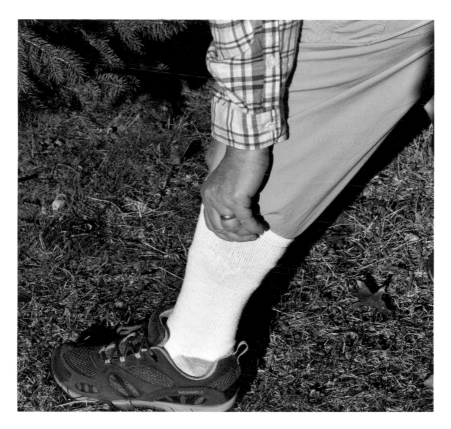

FIGURE 10.6

Light colored clothing will make spotting ticks easier. Tucking pants into socks and
shirt into pants will help prevent ticks from becoming attached to the skin.

*Courtesy of Barbara Strobino.*

- **Clothing.** If working or hiking in tick-infested areas, it is advisable
  to minimize skin exposure by adopting protective measures such as
  wearing long pants and long-sleeved shirts as well as tucking one's
  pants into one's socks. Unlike mosquitoes, ticks cannot penetrate
  clothing. Wearing light-colored clothing enables ticks to be more
  readily seen.

# Use Tick Repellent

## HUMANS

**On the body:**

- An insect repellent that contains 20 to 35 percent DEET applied to exposed areas of skin can be effective in repelling ticks. This lower concentration of DEET is as effective as formulations that contain 100 percent DEET. DEET can be toxic, so it is important to avoid the eyes, mouth, or any open wounds during the application process. To reduce the risk of adverse effects, it is wise to use the lowest effective concentration of DEET (20 to 35 percent) and to wash off the application after being outdoors, including washing both the skin and clothes. Parents should carefully apply this to children, avoiding their hands, eyes, mouth, or open wounds.
- Picaridin is effective in repelling mosquitoes and flies and at higher concentrations (20 percent or greater) does repel ticks as well. Picaridin has been used in Europe since 1998.
- IR3535 is a formulation that may be safer than DEET and is derived from a common amino acid (beta-alanine). Formulations containing IR3535 are widely used in Europe and can be found in the United States as well.
- Oil of Lemon Eucalyptus is a tick and insect repellant that is a chemically synthesized version of a plant oil. In a concentration of 30% it may be effective for up to 6 hours.
- DEET and IR3535 have the longest duration of action when applied to the skin, lasting 8–10 hours.
- For children and infants, parents should consult their pediatrician regarding the safest tick repellants for the skin.

**On the clothes:**

- Individuals living in tick-prevalent areas may choose to apply the insecticide (and acaracide) permethrin to clothing to repel and kill ticks. Permethrin can be sprayed onto shoes, socks, pants, shirts, and hats; this should be done before the clothing is worn in a well-ventilated outdoor environment without wind. Various companies that make outdoor products sell clothing that has been pretreated with permethrin. Such clothing can continue to repel and kills ticks for twenty to forty washes. Care should be taken with permethrin, however, as it should not be applied directly to skin.

## PETS

Tick collars can be an effective strategy in repelling ticks from pets; however, they are more effective in small pets rather than larger ones. Another approach for dogs in particular is a spot-on insecticide applied at monthly intervals to the skin of the neck, enabling the distribution of a tick repellant through the bloodstream to the skin of the dog.

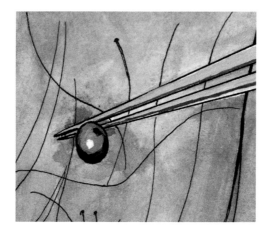

**FIGURE 10.7**

Tick removal: Use fine-tipped tweezers to remove an attached tick. Get as close as possible to the skin surface and pull up.

*Courtesy of the Connecticut Agricultural Experiment Station/Dr. Kirby Strafford.*

## Perform Tick Checks

### HUMANS

After being outside, individuals living in Lyme endemic areas should check their clothes and bodies for ticks as soon as possible. This should include a visual inspection as well as a manual inspection feeling around the body (through the hair, for example) for ticks. During peak tick-biting season, tick checks should be done at least once daily. Areas to check in particular include under the arms, in and around the ears, inside the belly button, behind the knees, between the legs, around the waist, and in the hair using a fine-tooth comb.

Bathing or showering as soon as possible after coming indoors is an ideal way to wash off any unattached ticks. Early detection and removal of ticks is important because research studies suggest that the sooner the removal, the less likely the transmission of *B. burgdorferi* (des Vignes et al. 2001). Washing one's clothes does not kill ticks, even after an hour in the washing machine. However, one hour in a dryer on high heat will kill ticks.

### PETS

Pets should be checked for ticks given that they often run through the woods or brush, serving as "tick drags." Pets can either get bitten themselves or bring the ticks into the house, exposing pet owners.

## Perform Landscape Management

Landscape management tactics can markedly reduce the risk of being bitten by a tick. The Connecticut Agricultural Experiment Station has an invaluable free guide for tick control and landscape management that can be found online. The general principles of management for individual homeowner are as follows:

- Clear tall grasses and brush around your home and remove leaf litter. Removing leaf litter on the edge of the yard has itself been shown to reduce the number of ticks by up to 70 percent (Stafford 1993).

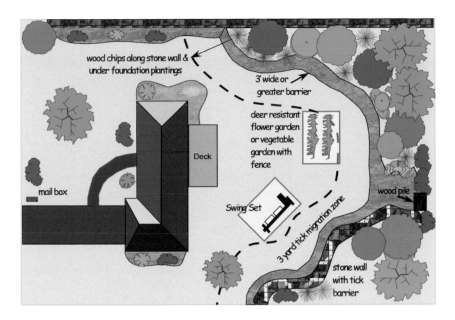

**FIGURE 10.8**

Landscaping techniques can help reduce tick habitat and isolate parts of the yard from tick hot spots.

*Courtesy of the Connecticut Agricultural Experiment Station/Dr. Kirby Strafford.*

- Put wood chips under foundation plantings.
- Create a mulch or wood chip barrier at least three feet wide around the property perimeter.
- Keep children's play areas such as swing sets away from the areas where ticks are most densely found—the woods, stone walls, and the perimeter of one's property where the grass meets the woods.
- Eliminate Japanese Barberry bushes from the property because their presence has been associated with higher tick abundance; in one study, their removal resulted in a reduction in the density of spirochete-infected adult ticks to nearly 60 percent that of unmanaged infestation (Williams et al. 2009.)
- Consider hiring a licensed landscape care company to apply an acaracide, a tick pesticide, in the yard. This approach is often used in the northeastern United States in the spring to reduce the nymphal

tick population and in the fall to reduce the adult tick population. Children and household pets should stay off the treated areas for at least twenty-four hours. Landscape companies can provide more specific guidelines.

## Target the Carriers or Hosts of Ticks

White-tailed deer are the primary host for the adult black-legged tick. Deer fencing and deer culling (by large amounts—90 percent) have been shown to decrease risk (Stafford 1993; Daniels, Fish, and Schwartz 1993). A study over thirteen years of permanent residents from one Connecticut community demonstrated that deer culling greatly reduced the number of resident-reported cases of Lyme disease (by 80 percent) and also greatly reduced the tick abundance in that community (by 76 percent) (Kilpatrick, LaBonte, and Stafford 2014). This study concluded that densities of thirteen deer per square mile significantly reduced the risk of contracting Lyme disease.

**FIGURE 10.9**

White-tailed deer are the primary host for the adult black-legged tick.

*Courtesy of Barbara Strobino. Image from Westchester County, New York.*

**FIGURES 10.10A, 10.10B, 10.10C**

The most common reservoir for *Borrelia burgdorferi* is the white-footed mouse. Other hosts include common rodents like chipmunks and squirrels, as well as veery, a thrush that forages on the ground in wooded areas.

*Figure 10.10A courtesy of the Connecticut Agricultural Experiment Station/Dr. Kirby Stafford.*
*Figures 10.10B and 10.10C courtesy of Barbara Strobino.*

While the impact of dramatic reduction or elimination of deer on the reproduction of black-legged ticks can be substantial, this approach to prevention of Lyme disease really only works well on small islands or geographically isolated areas in which it is possible to keep the deer population extremely low. Deer culling is thus not recommended as an

**FIGURE 10.11**

Purple finch with multiple attached ticks.

*Courtesy of Bill Hilton Jr., www.hiltonpond.org.*

effective approach to Lyme disease prevention in most Lyme endemic regions (Kugeler et al. 2016). Methods that kill ticks on small animals have been examined. Bait boxes work when small animal tick carriers enter them (such as the white-footed mouse, chipmunk, vole, or shrew); in the bait box, these animals are brushed with an acaracide, killing ticks.

The key to these approaches is to have most residences in a geographic area using them. Spotty use by one household but not by others would be unlikely to yield a large benefit.

## Test Ticks for Microbes

If a tick has been retained after removal (e.g., in a baggy), it can be tested to see if it contains *B. burgdorferi* or other microbes. Two labs that do accept samples from throughout the United States include the University of Massachusetts at Amherst Tick Lab (www.tickreport.com) and the University of Rhode Island Tick Lab (www.tickencounter.org). These labs will identify the type of tick, estimate the duration of attachment based on size, and test the tick contents for microbes. If a tick does contain *B. burgdorferi*, for example, the patient should have a cost-benefit discussion with his or her physician about whether a prophylactic course of treatment is warranted. If the tick is estimated to have been attached longer than thirty-six hours, treatment would be indicated because *B. burgdorferi* transmission is more likely.

## TRANSMISSION

The only known way to contract Lyme disease is to be bitten by an *Ixodes* tick. Studies indicate that when a tick feeds for thirty-six hours or more, the likelihood of transmission is greatly increased. A tick that has had a prior partial blood meal when biting a new individual will rarely be able to transmit *B. burgdorferi* infection in less than twenty-four hours, possibly because the *Borrelia* spirochetes had already migrated from the midgut to the salivary gland during the prior partial blood meal. One study (Piesman et al. 2001) demonstrated that spirochetes in tick salivary glands increased more than seventeenfold during tick attachment, from 1.2 per salivary gland pair before tick feeding to 20.8 at seventy-two hours after attachment. The period of greatest increase in the number of spirochetes

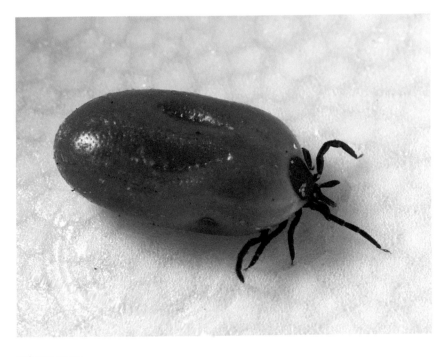

**FIGURE 10.12**

Engorged female black-legged Ixodes tick.

*Courtesy of the CDC/Dr. Gary Alpert, Urban Pests—Integrated Pest Management (IPM).*

in the salivary glands was forty-eight to sixty hours after tick attachment, coinciding with the time period of greatest risk of transmission during nymphal tick feeding.

The spirochetes that cause Lyme disease disseminate through the skin after a tick bite and may then briefly enter and get disseminated by the bloodstream to various tissues of the body, such as the brain, joints, collagen, and heart. For this reason, the American Red Cross does not accept blood donations from patients with active infection of *B. burgdorferi.*

## Antibiotic Treatment After Tick Bites for Prevention of Lyme Disease

One study evaluated the potential benefit of one dose of doxycycline, the primary antibiotic used to treat early Lyme disease, after a tick bite to determine if it reduced the risk of *B. burgdorferi* infection. The conclusion was that one 200-mg dose of doxycycline did confer a greater benefit than placebo; however, it did not prevent the emergence of Lyme disease in all patients (Nadelman et al. 2001). One patient in the single-dose doxycycline group did develop an *erythema migrans* rash. However, because significantly more individuals in the placebo group developed EM compared to the antibiotic-treated group, the study reported "effectiveness" for the single-dose prophylaxis approach.

Based on this study, it is not uncommon for doctors working in Lyme endemic areas to prescribe a dose of doxycycline or amoxicillin after a tick bite, particularly if the tick has been attached for a longer duration. The value of antibiotic prophylaxis increases when ticks have been attached for more than thirty-six hours because the longer the attachment, the greater the likelihood of transmission of microbes from the tick to the human.

Critics of this one-dose prophylaxis study pointed out that the follow-up period may have been too short—only six weeks—and that a longer follow-up interval is needed to confirm that the single 200-mg dose of doxycycline is more effective than placebo. This is a reasonable concern given that some manifestations of Lyme disease, such as Lyme arthritis, may not emerge until six months or more after initial infection. Critics also raised the point that insufficient early antibiotic treatment may not serve to reduce the spirochetal load enough such that an effective antibody response is not mounted, leading to the possibility of disease emergence without the individual testing positive on the antibody tests for Lyme disease. Finally, critics have expressed concern that this prophylactic approach may give patients a false sense of safety (and reduce personal tick bite reduction prevention measures) because antibiotic prophylaxis with doxycycline will not prevent the transmission of other microbes from ticks, such as viruses or *Babesia microti*.

On this topic, there are quite different guidelines recommended by the IDSA versus the ILADS. The IDSA guidelines from 2006 recommend a single dose of doxycycline after an *Ixodes* tick bite if the tick attachment was thirty-six hours or more, if the local rate of tick infection with *B. burgdorferi* is 20 percent or greater, and if treatment can begin within seventy-two hours of tick removal. The ILADS guidelines from 2014 recommend doxycycline treatment for a minimum of twenty days for all *Ixodes* tick bites in which there is evidence of tick feeding, regardless of the degree of tick engorgement or the infection rate in the local tick population. Both organizations encourage education about reducing the risk of tick bites. These quite different treatment recommendations highlight the need for a longer-duration study to assess the relative benefit of these different approaches to prevention.

A meta-analysis (an analysis of studies pooled together) tried to address some of these questions (Warshafsky et al. 2010). Among the four randomized trials included in this meta-analysis, follow up after tick bite ranged from 1.5 to 36 months. The conclusion was that antibiotic prophylaxis significantly reduced the odds of developing Lyme disease compared to placebo in endemic areas after an *Ixodes* tick bite. Other than the Nadelman and colleagues study (2001), which gave antibiotics (doxycycline) for only one day, the other studies provided a longer course of antibiotic treatment for prevention of Lyme disease after tick bite: penicillin (1,000 mg/day for ten days), amoxicillin (750 mg/day for ten days), and tetracycline (1,000 mg/day for ten days).

A more recent study (Schwameis et al. 2017) evaluated the effectiveness of azithromycin cream versus placebo applied to the skin for three days within seventy-two hours of a tick bite. The primary outcome was the number of treatment failures among 995 study participants, defined as seroconversion (from negative to positive on the antibody blood tests) or development of EM. The results demonstrated that topical azithromycin was well tolerated but the percentage of treatment failures was comparable in the azithromycin and placebo groups. Topical azithromycin did not lead to enhanced prevention compared to topical placebo.

## Sexual Transmission of Lyme Disease

This topic is of considerable concern for patients. This is a reasonable issue to address, particularly because it is well known that another spirochetal infection, syphilis, can be sexually transmitted. At present, however, the preponderance of evidence does not support sexual transmission of Lyme disease. We describe a study (Middelveen et al. 2014) that explored this topic.

- To address the question of whether *B. burgdorferi* spirochetes are even present in human sexual encounters, these investigators conducted a controlled study that searched for *B. burgdorferi* spirochetes in the semen and vaginal secretions of individuals with and without a history of Lyme disease. Varied detection techniques were conducted, such as silver staining, immunohistochemistry, polymerase chain reaction (PCR), and culture. The authors reported having found *Borrelia* spirochetes in nearly all of the patients' specimens with a history of Lyme disease and none of the controls. The authors of the study note that this article does not claim to report sexual transmission, but rather demonstrates that *Borrelia* spirochetes are present in genital fluids and so sexual transmission is a possibility. The authors also note that this study requires replication with a much larger sample.
  - The findings from this study sent shudders through the patient community, frightening many couples into considering not having unprotected sexual intercourse. Since publication, the study has been heavily scrutinized. Researchers have expressed concerns about the methodology and reporting: not having provided sufficient clinical history of the patient sample to confirm that they had had prior Lyme disease, not having provided sufficient data regarding the results of the assays on the control samples, and using laboratories with unclear validation methods for the assays. Two of the post-publication reviewers of this article had substantial reservations about the study's methodology, leading them to be highly skeptical of the findings and the study's implications. A future study should be conducted by different investigators with

samples from healthy controls and patients with well-documented Lyme disease sent in a blinded fashion to independent academic research laboratories with recognized excellence in Lyme research; these measures would enhance credibility and serve as a critical next step to assess the validity of the findings from this study.

- Although syphilis is a sexually transmitted disease caused by the spirochete *Treponema pallidum*, there are important differences between syphilis and Lyme disease that make sexual transmission of *B. burgdorferi* highly unlikely. *Treponema pallidum* produces open skin lesions in the genital or oral mucosa, called chancres, that enable transmission of the spirochete into the bloodstream. In contrast, *B. burgdorferi* cannot survive on the skin and does not cause open skin lesions in the genital or oral mucosa. In addition, *B. burgdorferi* cannot penetrate the skin on contact; *B. burgdorferi* instead requires transmission into the deeper skin layers by an external method, such as by a tick bite or a blood transfusion.

- To address the question about sexual transmission, the CDC published their review of the evidence online:

There is no credible scientific evidence that Lyme disease is spread through sexual contact. Published studies in animals do not support sexual transmission (Moody [and Barthold] 1991; Woodrum [and Oliver] 1999), and the biology of the Lyme disease spirochete is not compatible [with] this route of exposure (Porcella [and Schwan] 2001). The ticks that transmit Lyme disease are very small and easily overlooked. Consequently, it is possible for sexual partners living in the same household to both become infected through tick bites, even if one or both partners doesn't remember being bitten.

(CDC 2017)

## LYME DISEASE AND PREGNANCY

Because certain infections during pregnancy have been associated with serious congenital abnormalities, there has been concern about how Lyme disease during pregnancy would affect the fetus. Some early case reports and small studies suggested a link between maternal Lyme disease and miscarriage or birth defects. However, more recent, larger studies have not shown any definable congenital Lyme disease syndrome. While these data are partially reassuring, many believe that we simply do not yet have enough information to definitively say whether Lyme disease acquired during pregnancy confers any short- or long-term risk to the fetus. Therefore, for the health of the mother and of the fetus, it is important to promptly and effectively treat Lyme disease or any other tick-borne coinfection acquired during pregnancy.

Furthermore, pregnant women in Lyme endemic areas should be particularly vigilant about avoiding areas with high tick exposure. Women who contract Lyme disease during pregnancy might also consider having the placenta examined histologically and by PCR after childbirth. Some specialty laboratories do offer PCR assays of *B. burgdorferi* on human tissue. Pregnant patients with newly acquired Lyme disease are usually treated with amoxicillin or penicillin rather than doxycycline, because of concerns about risks of doxycycline to the fetus. More recent reviews of research suggest that short courses of doxycycline may be safe for young children but concerns about use in pregnancy remain; guidelines on the use of doxycycline are currently being re-evaluated (Cross et al. 2016). Patients should discuss these issues with their physician in consultation with an infectious disease specialist.

The good news is that research suggests that women who contracted Lyme disease prior to pregnancy and who have been treated adequately with antibiotics appear to be at no increased risk of adverse fetal outcomes compared to women who did not have a history of Lyme disease. Furthermore, there is also no evidence suggesting that a history of treated *B. burgdorferi* infection affects a woman's ability to become pregnant in the future.

Specific research reports indicate the following:

- *Borrelia* spirochetes were cultured from the fetal liver of four aborted fetuses. In one of these cases, there was evidence of positive fluorescence after a monoclonal mouse antibody specific for *B. burgdorferi* was applied to the tissue (MacDonald 1986).
- A case series reported on nineteen women who acquired Lyme disease during pregnancy; of these, thirteen received antibiotic therapy. Adverse outcomes occurred in five of the nineteen pregnancies, but

the varied outcomes could not be definitely linked to Lyme disease (Markowitz et al. 1986).

- In a study of 143 pregnant women who had been serum tested for Lyme disease, only one of the twelve women who miscarried had tested positive for Lyme disease antibodies. This led the investigators to conclude that a positive serum Lyme test does not increase risk of miscarriage over the general population (Dlesk et al. 1989).

- In a review of data from ninety-five women from Hungary who were diagnosed with Lyme disease during pregnancy, loss of pregnancy (n=7) and cavernous hemangioma (n=4) were the most common adverse outcomes. Adverse pregnancy outcome was significantly more common in those who did not receive antibiotics than in those who did. Because the investigators were not able to identify spirochetes in the fetal tissue, they were unable to prove causation. They concluded that untreated infection during pregnancy confers risk but a specific syndrome representing congenital Lyme disease was unlikely.

- There were three large epidemiologic studies that shed valuable light on the risk of Lyme disease to the fetus.

  ○ One study looked at prenatal exposure to Lyme disease in which a history of Lyme disease and blood tests for Lyme disease antibodies were conducted at the time of the first visit to delivery. Of 1,290 women tested twice, only one woman had a test that went from negative to positive (i.e., seroconverted), and this woman who had an untreated flu-like illness had a healthy child. This study found that neither the diagnosis of Lyme disease in the past nor living in a highly endemic area were associated with fetal death, low birth weight, or congenital malformations (Strobino et al. 1993).

  ○ Another study reported on an umbilical cord serologic survey of five thousand babies: one cohort from an endemic area and one from a nonendemic area. Infants were followed up to six months of age. Mothers of infants in the endemic area were five to twenty times more likely to have been exposed to B. burgdorferi in the past compared to mothers of infants in the nonendemic area (based on history and/or cord blood serology). Within the endemic cohort, there were no differences in the rate of major or minor malformations or birth weight by maternal Lyme disease history or cord blood serology (Williams et al. 1995).

o A case control study was conducted in a Lyme endemic area designed to specifically address the risks of congenital heart disease and maternal Lyme disease. Cases comprised 796 children with congenital heart defects. Seven hundred and four controls were selected from among children with no abnormalities seen at the same pediatric cardiology service. There was no association between congenital heart disease and maternal tick bite or maternal Lyme disease within three months of conception or during pregnancy (Strobino, Abid, and Gewitz 1999).

## Lyme Disease and Pregnancy Summary

Case reports and small series raise concern that infection with *B. burgdorferi* during pregnancy may lead to adverse outcomes. The large epidemiologic studies are limited by the rare occurrence of untreated infection acquired during pregnancy. These epidemiologic studies suggest that prior Lyme disease that has been treated, or antibody positivity alone, does not confer increased risk for adverse outcomes. However, given the plausibility that *B. burgdorferi* acquired during pregnancy could be transmitted to the fetus as a result of intravascular dissemination, physicians recommend prompt antibiotic treatment—for the health of both the mother and the fetus. It is also important to diagnose and promptly treat any coinfections.

## Coinfections and Pregnancy

There are only a few reports of the impact of other tick-borne diseases, such as Babesiosis and human granulocytic anaplasmosis, during pregnancy.

- In 2007, a small study of six women diagnosed with anaplasmosis during pregnancy showed that all six had excellent responses to rifampin or doxycycline therapy (Dhand et al. 2007). Perinatal transmission was found in one woman's baby; the baby also responded well to treatment. Overall there did not appear to be any long-term sequelae in these mothers or their children twenty-one months later.

- A study in 2012 reviewed five cases in which the agent of Babesiois had been demonstrated to cross the placenta either during pregnancy or during delivery and cause congenital infection. In all of these cases, although the mothers were asymptomatic, the infants fell ill between nineteen and forty-one days after birth. All infants responded well to antimicrobial therapy (Joseph et al. 2012).

## THE LYME DISEASE VACCINES

The first Lyme disease vaccine in the United States, LYMErix, was approved for use in 1998 and was taken off the market in 2002. This Lyme vaccine had limitations. It had an efficacy of approximately 80 percent, meaning that 20 percent of fully vaccinated individuals were still at risk of getting Lyme disease. Full vaccination also required three vaccine administrations: the initial dose, then one month and twelve months later. Among patients who received these three vaccine doses, there was uncertainty regarding whether the LYMErix vaccine would confer long-term immunity. When the vaccine was first considered for approval by the FDA, there was also concern about the safety of the vaccine among patients who carry the HLA-DR4 gene. Past research had indicated that patients who carry this marker are at increased risk for developing a chronic treatment-refractory arthritis after infection with *B. burgdorferi* (Steere, Dwyer, and Winchester 1990). This fact then raised fear among patients that the vaccine itself could cause symptoms in a genetically vulnerable population who might carry this HLA-DR4 gene. After the approval in 1998, the FDA received case reports of patients who developed arthritis after receiving the vaccine. According to the FDA, the frequency of this occurrence had not been greater than one would expect for the development of arthritis in the community at large. Nevertheless, because of the increasing concern generated by these cases, the FDA convened a special committee hearing in 2001. The conclusion of this committee reportedly was that the data did not yet indicate that the vaccine caused an increased risk of arthritis; however, the concern was great enough to warrant recommendation of a change in the package insert and the aggressive pursuit of more safety data from a larger sample of patients. It was not clear at that time what the long-term safety of the vaccine would be, given that patients would need to be revaccinated on an ongoing basis in order to keep the protective antibody levels elevated. The vaccine was discontinued in 2002 due to unclear reasons that may include low consumer demand, less than 100 percent effectiveness, and safety concerns that received substantial media attention (Nigrovic and Thompson 2007).

## New Developments in Vaccines

- **OspC Vaccine**. This vaccine—by focusing on outer surface protein C, which is expressed by *B. burgdorferi* during early infection in the human—has the advantage of providing sustained prevention without the need for frequent boosters as in the OspA-based vaccines. One version of an OspC vaccine, recently shown effective and now available for use in dogs, is being modified for human studies (Rhodes et al. 2013).

  In a departure from traditional approaches in vaccine development, which typically utilize a recombinant form of a protein that is normally produced by the infecting organism, this vaccine was developed using an approach that created totally new proteins comprised of only the most immunologically relevant portion of their natural *B. burgdorferi* counterparts (Earnhart and Marconi 2007). These novel recombinant proteins are referred to as chimeritopes. Chimeritopes offer several advantages over traditional subunit vaccines.
  - Regions of a vaccine candidate protein that do not elicit productive immunological responses (i.e., non-productive epitopes), or regions that are associated with adverse events, can be eliminated allowing for the amplification of protective immune responses.
  - Due to the modular design of chimeritopes and the ability to include numerous diverse epitopes, this vaccine would convey broad protection. In the context of a Lyme disease vaccine, these chimeritopes can be designed in such a way as to protect against all Lyme disease spirochete species associated with human infection; this would include, for example, both the United States and European genospecies.

○ Theoretically, a chimeritope-styled vaccine could be developed that protects not only against *B. burgdorferi* but also against multiple tick borne pathogens such as *Anaplasma, Ehrlichia,* and *Babesia.*

- **OspA vaccines.** Although the prior OspA vaccine was not a success in the United States for reasons noted earlier, two companies have developed variants of the OspA vaccine that offer promise in providing protection against Lyme disease in both the United States and Europe (Plotkin 2016). One company developed a vaccine candidate in which parts of two OspA molecules were fused to make three separate antigens; to enhance public acceptance and possibly for safety, developers of this vaccine removed the OspA epitope that some experts thought might put patients at risk of autoimmune disease. For unclear reasons, further development of this vaccine has been stopped. Another company has developed an OspA-based multivalent vaccine (VLA15) that is now being tested in both the United States and Europe and is similarly designed to provide a broad range of protection against the majority of Borrelia species pathogenic to humans.

- **OspA-treated mice.** If the number of ticks infected with *B. burgdorferi* could be reduced, then the risk to humans from ticks would be reduced. One approach is to vaccinate the white-footed mouse; this approach has been shown to be helpful in reducing the tick infection rates in field studies. The approach is similar to the one that was used for the original human Lyme vaccine in which the human was vaccinated to develop protective antibodies. These antibodies worked not by killing spirochetes in the human but during the tick's blood meal when the antibodies were sucked into the tick's abdomen. How does one vaccinate wildlife such as mice? The vaccine is administered as part of a food product distributed as bait. A recent study demonstrated that after two years of feeding mice the vaccine-laced oatmeal, 23 percent fewer tick nymphs were infected with *B. burgdorferi* (Gomes-Solecki 2014). After five years of treatment, 76 percent fewer tick nymphs were infected. In other words, the greater the number of years of bait treatment with the reservoir-targeted vaccine, the lower the infectivity rate of the ticks. This would be expected to translate into a decreased risk of Lyme disease for people living in the geographic areas where the mice were vaccinated. The limitation of course is that large geographic areas would have to employ these bait vaccine treatments to have a meaningful impact on lowering human Lyme disease rates.

## NEW DEVELOPMENTS IN PREVENTION

### Genetic Modification of the Mouse to Prevent Tick-Borne Disease

One of the most significant breakthroughs in science over the past decade occurred when CRISPR-Cas9 technology was first described (Jinek et al. 2012). CRISPR (clustered regularly interspaced short palindromic repeats) is a revolutionary new genome engineering tool—an enzymatic scalpel—that enables one to cut DNA at any desired sequence. This new gene-editing technology was recognized by scientists around the world as a transformative tool to assist in research on human disease, agriculture, and the environment. Why was this such a big breakthrough? Before CRISPR, scientists wanting to learn the impact of changing gene expression (turning it "on" or "off") needed to do mouse studies, which would take months to achieve. Now, using CRISPR, it is possible to see the impact of a "gene knockout" study in days. The speed of research on human cancer cells and genetically inherited disease has now dramatically accelerated as a result of CRISPR technology.

How can CRISPR be applied to Lyme disease prevention? A research group in Massachusetts (Esvelt et al. 2014) is now guiding a project to disrupt the transmission cycle in the wild by permanently immunizing wild white-footed mice, which are the primary reservoir of tick-borne diseases in the northeastern United States. The primary concept is that if every mouse from birth produced antibodies conferring protective immunity against *B. burgdorferi* infection, the primary transmission cycle of Lyme disease will be broken. If mice are not infected, the ticks cannot get infected by feeding on the mice, and thus humans would not become infected if bitten by these ticks. Although there are other animals that serve as reservoir carriers of *B. burgdoreri* and so a smaller percentage of ticks would still acquire infection after feeding on these other carriers (e.g, moles), the vast majority of tick-acquired *B. burgdorferi* infection occurs by feeding on the mouse. This method—if it works—would dramatically reduce the environmental risk to humans and reduce Lyme disease rates. If there are fewer infected ticks, there will be less Lyme disease.

How would this project proceed? This research group is currently identifying gene sequences in vaccinated mice that produce protective antibodies conferring resistance to Lyme disease. The research team will then encode these "protective" sequences into the mouse genome to create mice that are immune from birth. Releasing these engineered mice on small islands in reasonable numbers over multiple generations would stably introduce the trait (i.e., ongoing production of protective antibodies) to a large fraction of the native mouse population, thus dramatically reducing the percentage of ticks that get infected after feeding on a mouse. Similarly, if the team is able to identify a way to modify the mouse genome such that it produced antibodies that prevented sustained tick attachment to the mouse (possibly by interfering with the anti-inflammatory effects of tick salivary proteins), this method would provide protection not only against Lyme disease but also against other tick-borne diseases, such as Babesiosis and Anaplasmosis.

Unusually, the project is not controlled by the researchers but by local communities and health officials from two Lyme endemic island communities in Massachusetts: Nantucket and Martha's Vineyard. These communities will select an uninhabited island for initial tests of safety and efficacy, then decide whether to release mice onto their own islands. If successful, the approach could eventually be spread to interested mainland communities using local gene drive systems and perhaps one day extended to all of eastern North America using an evolutionarily stable global drive system (Esvelt et al. 2014; Noble et al. 2016).

Could this approach permanently prevent many tick-borne diseases? That is the hope. While this research endeavor is only just beginning, we report it here partly because it is so novel and intriguing. We also present it to alert the reader that scientific research on prevention with potentially profound public health impact is underway.

# 11

## SUGGESTIONS TO THE PATIENT SEEKING EVALUATION OR TREATMENT

Patients who have a very complex history associated with Lyme disease can be overwhelming to a doctor at the time of a new evaluation. Given physicians' limited time and sometimes narrow range of expertise, many prefer to focus on one or two problems. The patient with a history of Lyme disease, however, may present with numerous problems—arthralgias, myalgias, headaches, cognitive problems, mood issues, severe fatigue, impaired sleep, and/or neuropathic pain. A thorough medical history and physical exam for a patient with multisystemic symptoms and a long history may take two to three hours; however, most physicians only have forty-five minutes or less for a new evaluation. Given the time limitations of physicians for an initial office visit, patients should be advised to organize their medical history prior to the evaluation and to focus on the key symptoms causing current distress when meeting with the doctor. This kind of preparation will assist the physician in staying focused on the most pressing problems in the context of the broader clinical history in order to be most helpful to the patient. This chapter discusses tips for a patient seeking a more satisfying doctor-patient encounter.

### HOW TO APPROACH THE VISIT

Keep an open mind about causation. You may feel strongly that your symptoms are due to one cause, but the doctor may find evidence suggesting other etiologies. If you arrive with a pre-set conviction regarding the cause of your symptoms and discount the doctor's judgment and recommendations without even trying them, you may well be doing yourself a disservice.

Recognize that clinical medicine does not always yield definitive diagnoses and that both the patient and the physician may need to accept a level of uncertainty in the diagnostic and treatment planning process. If your symptoms started after exposure to a Lyme endemic area and you were walking in tick-infested areas and you developed prominent flu-like symptoms but you never developed the well-recognized "CDC surveillance clinical signs" of Lyme disease, then a doctor's differential diagnosis will be broad. The physician should consider that you may have acquired a tick-borne infection and order blood tests. If your antibody test results for Lyme disease are highly suggestive but not fully positive, this could indicate that you never had Lyme disease or it could reflect markers of past infection or of one so new that the full panel of antibodies haven't yet developed. Alternatively the indeterminate result could reflect false positive bands due to cross-reactive antibodies. A thoughtful clinician would view your clinical presentation as a puzzle that needs to be figured out with a careful differential diagnosis. Your symptoms could be due to a tick-borne infection and/or due to multiple other causes unrelated to infection or tick-borne diseases.

However, if other reasonable possible causes have been ruled out and your symptoms are disabling or distressing, your health care provider might start to discuss a trial course of antibiotic treatment for "probable" or "possible" Lyme disease. The risks and benefits of this approach would be discussed with you. If your symptoms resolve after antibiotic treatment, that still does not prove you had Lyme disease; it does, however, suggest that you had an "antibiotic-responsive illness." You should know that antibiotics have multiple modes of action—for example, doxycycline is effective in both fighting infection and in reducing inflammation. Therefore you should not be surprised if a doctor states that although he or she is happy that you have gotten better, the etiology of your symptoms still is unclear.

If your doctor suggests another course of treatment that is not related to Lyme disease and your symptoms do not strongly point to Lyme disease, you could agree to try the recommended course of treatment for a defined period of time for the alternate diagnosis he or she has made. The health care provider might also agree to reevaluate the alternate diagnosis and treatment plan after an agreed-upon period of time if you are not feeling substantially better. With this strategy, the doctor-patient relationship remains collaborative, respectful, and is more likely to lead to a solution.

If you feel that the doctor has not listened carefully or conducted a sufficiently thorough evaluation, you should discuss this with the doctor. It could be that the doctor had a bad day for whatever reason. Give your doctor a chance to listen more carefully. If this approach does not work, you might decide to seek a second opinion from another doctor.

If you have been exposed to a Lyme endemic area and if you go to your physician with an expanding red rash (without other reasonable explanations), you should not be told to wait until the blood tests are back to start treatment. In the presence of a characteristic rash suggestive of Lyme disease from an individual exposed to a Lyme endemic area, antibiotic treatment should be started right away because the rash is most likely a Lyme disease rash. In early Lyme disease, as noted earlier in this book, the Lyme disease tests are negative as often as 50 percent of the time. Onset of treatment should not be delayed for many reasons, one of which is that the diagnostic tests for early Lyme disease are insensitive.

## WHAT TO BRING TO THE APPOINTMENT

Be prepared. Having the information below with you will provide your doctor with a more complete picture of your illness.

### Typed Summary of Medical History

- A clear timeline of your history is very helpful to doctors. If you can, write a short (one to three pages *maximum*) summary of your symptom history indicating when each symptom began. Include answers to questions such as:
  - When did your illness start? Did it come on suddenly over days or gradually over weeks?
  - When did you last feel fully well for a sustained period of time such as 3 months or more?
  - What was the progression of symptoms?

- ○ Have your symptoms been steadily getting worse?
- ○ Has your illness had more of a waxing and waning course, meaning sometimes you are well but sometimes you are sick?
- ○ Has any treatment or behavior led to an improvement or worsening of your symptoms?
- ○ When (if ever) were you admitted to the hospital?
- ○ What were your treatments—what dose, how long, and were they helpful?
- ○ Are you immune suppressed or have you been treated with immune suppressive mediations, such as steroids?
- ○ Have you had any tick bites in the past, severe flu-like illnesses, atypical rashes, or prior diagnoses of Lyme disease or other tick-borne diseases?
- ○ Have you traveled to tick-infested areas?
- ○ Have you had a blood transfusion?
- Include a paragraph about any past medical illnesses, surgeries, brain injury (e.g., concussion), or allergies.
- Note any significant illnesses experienced by your first-degree relatives (parents, siblings, children).
- Note any major recent stressors in your life (e.g., divorce, death, loss of job).
- If you do not remember this information or are having memory problems in general, it can be helpful to ask a spouse or relative to help you recreate your history or go with you to your appointment.

## Medications

- Bring a list of current and past medications to your appointment, including the names of the medications, the doses, the dates you took them, and a note as to whether they helped. You might want to bring the bottles containing your current medications.
- Include all medications prescribed for other medical problems, sleep issues, or mood problems as well as herbal or homeopathic pills. For example, some patients with neuropathic symptoms (e.g., numbness or stabbing pains) may be taking extra vitamin B6 without realizing that vitamin B6 in excess (i.e., leading to higher blood levels than the

normal range) can actually cause neurologic symptoms. If the patient does not tell the health care provider about taking vitamin B6, this possible explanation for neuropathic symptoms might not be considered.

- Be sure to tell your physician about any previous treatments you have had for Lyme disease. All of this information is important for the physician's assessment.

## Previous Test Results

- Bring a copy of all test results from the past two years (including routine tests and endocrine, inflammatory, and other diagnostic tests) to leave with your doctor.
- For the period prior to the past two years, narrow what you bring to include:
  ○ test results that were abnormal,
  ○ all previous Lyme disease test results (including all Lyme enzyme-linked immunosorbent assay, IgG Western blot, IgM Western blot, polymerase chain reaction assays, and spinal or joint fluid results),
  ○ prior test results, if available, for other tick-borne and infectious illnesses (e.g., Babesia, Ehrlichia, Anaplasma, Mycoplasma, *Bartonella*, viruses, etc.),
  ○ dates and results of any neurologic tests (including brain imaging, nerve conduction studies, electroencephalograms, and biopsy results from small nerve fiber studies), and
  ○ copies of evaluation reports by any specialists (e.g., in neurology, infectious disease, rheumatology, neuropsychology, psychiatry).

## SEEKING A SECOND OPINION

It is smart to seek a second opinion if your symptoms persist despite current treatments. This is not a sign of disrespect toward your doctor. In fact, you should discuss this with your doctor, who may be able to guide you to physicians with additional expertise. Physicians are often well-intentioned and expert in certain areas, but they cannot be experts in all areas of medicine. Just as the diagnosis of Lyme disease or another tick-borne disease can be missed by a doctor not familiar with its many manifestations, the diagnosis of another treatable illness can be missed by a doctor who has incorrectly attributed a variety of symptoms to Lyme disease or another tick-borne disease.

It is not surprising that there is misdiagnosis because we are dealing with a disease for which diagnostic tests are not always definitive. Because Lyme disease can affect so many different organ systems, it can be helpful to have the input of several medical specialists in order to be confident of the diagnosis and to identify any new treatments that may have emerged for symptoms. Some patients may have Lyme disease and other concurrent illnesses that are unrelated to one another. Or Lyme disease may have triggered another disorder that requires nonantibiotic therapies for cure or symptom reduction. Or another disorder completely unrelated to Lyme disease or another tick-borne disease may have arisen de novo. Seeking a fresh medical opinion is therefore a good idea and may lead to a breakthrough in your health.

Some patients seek "Lyme-literate doctors." From one perspective, this makes sense because Lyme disease is a complex disease with a rapidly expanding knowledge base. If Lyme disease and other tick-borne diseases are a possible explanation for one's symptoms, a doctor who has evaluated and treated many such patients might use a wider set of tools for diagnosis or have experience using different approaches to help patients with persistent symptoms. This scenario would be comparable to a patient with persistent headaches who has not found help from the local primary care doctor and so is referred to a neurologist specializing in headaches for consultation. However, it is unclear what "Lyme literacy" means because it often has a highly politicized connation that identifies the health care provider as being on one side of the many debates associated with Lyme disease diagnosis and treatment. On a practical level, there is no specific specialty training requirement or nationally recognized credentialing process for "Lyme literacy." In other words, the self-advertised "Lyme literate" doctor may or may not be well-informed; he or she may or may not have studied and critically appraised the literature on Lyme disease.

Any doctor, regardless of whether he/she is considered "Lyme literate," who concludes on the first visit, "I know what you have, and this is what you should do" may well make the patient feel much relieved as finally a clear diagnosis and treatment plan are provided; the diagnostic impression by this doctor may be correct, but it is also possible that the overly enthusiastic and confident conclusion represents the views of a doctor who has lost the objective and critical mindset necessary for the fresh evaluation and care of the complex patient. When patients present with a cluster of symptoms that are common to many disorders, then a broad differential diagnosis needs to be kept in mind so as not to miss the correct diagnosis. A thoughtful and reasonable doctor spends time with the patient clarifying the uncertainties associated with test results (both false positives and false negatives), explains the factors taken into account when narrowing down the differential diagnosis, and discusses the risks, benefits, and evidence associated with different treatment options.

## TIPS FOR NAVIGATING ONLINE HEALTH INFORMATION

Today many patients seek information about their health online. There is a lot of helpful information on the Internet and it is important for patients to be proactive and knowledgeable about their health. However, in some cases online research can provoke unnecessary anxiety, particularly when the information is inaccurate, out of date, or does not apply to that particular patient. In other cases, patients may be misled and fall victim to a fraudulent scheme.

For individuals who already have a tendency toward illness anxiety, surfing the Internet for health information can become a black hole from which the individuals emerge hours later with even more anxiety. Our research at Columbia has shown that individuals without preexisting health anxiety are often better able to make productive use of Internet-related health information searches than those who are more preoccupied and fearful about illness concerns (Doherty-Torstrick 2016). Indeed, our research shows that those with preexisting illness anxiety who turn to the Internet for "answers and reassurance" end up feeling far worse after checking than prior to surfing the web. Therefore our recommendation is that individuals with preexisting illness anxiety *avoid* use of the Internet for health-related information and reassurance and instead rely on a health care provider.

Some tips for navigating the Internet include:

- Ask a trusted physician or health professional to recommend reliable sites.
- Show a healthy skepticism. Not everything that is posted online is true. Consider:
  - Who are the authors?
  - What is their motivation or bias?
  - Do they have a financial interest at stake?
  - What sources are they citing?
  - Do the authors convey a paranoid, disdainful view of health care providers that suggests that most health care providers can't be trusted?
  - What is the purpose of the site?
  - Is anyone checking or approving the site to make sure the information is true?
  - When was the site last updated?
- Be suspicious if the site promises rapid dramatic results or "cures," especially if the authors do not cite sources of information or if the site is supposed to be for patients but uses a lot of technical medical language. Reliable websites will not promise anything unrealistic or attempt to persuade readers by using jargon.
- Know that some information online might be totally inaccurate and other information might be partially accurate but does not apply to every patient.
- Check more than one site to have more complete information.
- Chat rooms and message boards can be risky. Most often, these sites are visited not by those who are well and recovered but by those who are still suffering. Hence, the information is often biased toward more severe, chronic, or rare manifestations of an illness. While some information may be helpful and accurate, misinformation can often be inadvertently perpetuated. Individuals can sound "smart and well-informed" because of the studies cited, but these individuals may not have the training or qualifications needed to properly critique or understand ongoing research and medical debates. Further compounding the risk associated with relying on these resources is that

some individuals may be using these sites to promote products without revealing their true financial motivations.

- Note that the last part of the URL may provide helpful clues on trustworthiness:
  - .com sites are often but not always commercial sites selling products.
  - .org can be any organization.
  - .gov sites are government run.
  - .edu sites are associated with a school or university.

For additional tips, the U.S. FDA has an extensive guide on how to effectively navigate information online at http://www.fda.gov/Drugs/Resources ForYou/Consumers/BuyingUsingMedicineSafely/BuyingMedicines OvertheInternet/ucm202863.htm.

# 12

## THE EXPERIENCE OF THE PATIENT
## WITH CHRONIC SYMPTOMS

When Lyme disease is treated early with antibiotics, many patients recover fully following a short-duration mild or moderately severe illness. Some patients, however, experience a more protracted course of illness. These may be individuals for whom the infection was detected long after the tick bite. Or these may be individuals who had a family history of a rheumatologic illness and a genetic predisposition for autoimmune sequelae. Or they may be individuals with a history of chronic illness, such that the immune system is primed to overreact. For those patients who remain symptomatic following supposedly adequate treatment, not only are the symptoms themselves hard to bear but so too are the responses of the medical community and even of friends and loved ones who do not understand their suffering.

In many ways, these patients' experiences are similar to that of the figure of Job in the Bible (see figure 12.1). Job was a just man who had a big family and a large farm. Afflicted with the death of his children, the loss of his livelihood, and a body covered with boils, Job was accused by his neighbors of having done something to offend God. His friends and neighbors seemed to say, "It's your fault—you brought this on yourself." Job felt desperate, confused, and abandoned.

Some patients with Lyme disease feel that others are accusing them of exaggerating their symptoms or using their illness for secondary gain. They may have lost their jobs, depleted the family savings on health care bills, and become socially and functionally disabled. Marriages may start to falter and parents may feel inadequate and guilty for not being more available to their children. Like Job, they have been assailed with manifold

**FIGURE 12.1**

William Blake, *Job Rebuked by His Friends*, 1826.

losses. The emotional, physical, interpersonal, and financial consequences of this illness are at times overwhelming and feel unbearable.

This chapter will address the experience of post-treatment Lyme disease itself and the interpersonal context in which it occurs. Our focus here is on the patient. What is it like to have chronic symptoms after Lyme disease? What are the characteristic challenges that such patients face? The psychological aspects of Lyme disease, especially when the symptoms have become persistent, are manifold and multidetermined.

Certain characteristics of this disease render it particularly challenging to the affected patient. The features we delineate below have been culled from our work with thousands of patients over the past twenty-five years. Among them are:

- The politically charged climate and its impact on the physician-patient relationship
- The protean nature of the presentations of Lyme disease
- The variability of course: waxing and waning symptoms
- The psychological ramifications of an "invisible" chronic illness
- The fact that Lyme disease can affect the brain and sensorium
- Uncertainty surrounding diagnosis, treatment, and prognosis

We shall take up these issues one by one, hoping to give an overview of some of the distinctive determinants of the patient experience of Lyme disease.

We will begin with a section on the effects of the politically charged climate surrounding Lyme disease on the patient and on the physician-patient relationship. Then, in a series of shorter sections, we will take up some of the more direct effects of the illness. We return to the broader social context in a penultimate section on the effects of uncertainty. Finally, we will offer some perspectives on the role of mental health care for those suffering from chronic symptoms and the importance of resiliency in recovery from illness. We hope to convey the very real suffering that many patients experience while at the same time offering a sense of hope.

## THE POLITICALLY CHARGED CLIMATE AND ITS IMPACT ON THE PHYSICIAN-PATIENT RELATIONSHIP

The politically charged climate surrounding Lyme disease—as delineated in chapter 5—renders the patient experience complex from the very beginning. Most patients will have read about Lyme disease in the popular press, and those in endemic areas may have friends, neighbors, and relatives who have been affected. Many will have recovered, having received antibiotics promptly. Others may have suffered for years before diagnosis and sustained significant personal and financial losses. Some patients may be unduly frightened by rumors of difficulties in treatment and chronicity. Others may wonder what is wrong with them when their own disease fails to respond to standard courses of antibiotics, as their neighbors and doctor indicate that it should.

## Destruction of Patient-Physician Relationships

Faced with persistent symptoms after standard treatment for Lyme disease, most patients return to their primary care physician seeking help. Some of these encounters may leave the patient feeling confused, angry, and hurt. Why?

When going into the physician's office, there is an expectation of care. Instead some patients feel as if they are treated as the enemy without knowing why. Patients who have had a good relationship with their physician, upon developing Lyme disease that does not respond fully to a standard course of treatment, may find that there is suddenly a rift between physician and patient. It is as if the prior positive, caring relationship has been replaced by one of mistrust or accusation. Patients may start to feel disbelieved, marginalized, or abandoned by the medical community.

## How Might a Doctor Respond to a Patient with Relapsing Symptoms?

If one is confident in the wisdom of academic experts that one course of antibiotic treatment is curative for most patients, a reasonable approach by a health care provider when faced with a patient whose symptoms have not improved would include searching for another possible illness that has not yet been considered.

- The patient may be depressed or overly anxious because there is a combination of low energy, irritability, and changes in sleep patterns.
- The patient may have fibromyalgia because there is widespread pain.
- The patient may have chronic fatigue syndrome because daily sleep intervals extend to twelve to fourteen hours and the patient's physical functioning has dramatically declined.

Consideration of these alternative explanations is reasonable and part of good medical practice, especially given that we now know that certain environmental triggers (such as infection) can lead to residual mood disorders, persistent fatigue, and musculoskeletal pain. The problem is not that the physician is considering these other possibilities to enhance care of the patient; indeed, these other diagnostic considerations may provide new directions for treatment. The problem is that the physician may be completely opposed to the possibility that the patient may still have residual infection and/or that another course of antibiotic therapy might confer benefit. The physician may take umbrage when patients bring in articles or relate anecdotes suggesting that repeated antibiotic treatment for some cases of Lyme disease may be necessary. The patient comes to feel shut out, unheard, and uncertain whom to trust. Even in instances in which the doctor's recommendations might in fact have validity, the patient who feels unheard will remain doubtful about the doctor's judgment and unlikely to follow through.

When the patient's symptoms not only persist but become more numerous, the patient becomes alarmed and somatically preoccupied. Whereas

"The bad news is...you have Lyme disease. The good news is, I don't believe in that disease so you are fine!"

FIGURE 12.2

when there is an explanation and plan of action, or even the sense that the doctor has absorbed the information and is giving it thought and attention, patients are better able to relax their vigilance. When the doctor responds by blaming or brushing the patient off, the patient will feel doubly traumatized. As a result of this physician-patient interaction, the subjective experience of pain and confusion imposed by the illness becomes compounded by a kind of physician-induced post-traumatic stress disorder.

Doctors are trained to be able to give answers and find solutions. When a patient presents with a litany of symptoms that do not fit into the doctor's known paradigms or that are unsupported by laboratory evidence, that doctor may be tempted to discount those aspects of the patient story that do not fit. The doctor may not want to treat that patient, knowing that he or she does not know how to help or fearing that engagement with this patient might take him into controversial medical waters.

The current climate in health care delivery poses particular challenges for the patient with a complex or atypical disease presentation, such as those manifest in many of our patients with late-stage post-treatment Lyme disease symptoms. The traditional functions of the physician—listening carefully to the patient's history in order to create a differential diagnosis and sitting by the patient's side to offer human comfort in the face of physical and mental suffering—have been marginalized to the periphery in favor of a checklist of questions and laboratory tests. Instead of looking at the patient and listening, the physician of today is often found staring at a computer screen, typing in answers to questions that look good for the medical record but are not necessarily focused on unraveling the individual patient's complex presentation.

This means that doctors are deprived of an invaluable source of information: the patient him- or herself. Patients and their family members have important insights to provide the physician regarding their former functioning and how the current presentation differs from their habitual selves. Lyme disease is one of those illnesses that remind us of the value of old-school medicine: knowing the patient as a person, knowing how the current presentation fits into his or her life as a whole, and listening very carefully to the details of the clinical history.

Guidelines that were developed to convey and clarify the typical presentation and course of an illness fail to address the outliers whose lab values or clinical trajectory fall outside of the norm. Could this patient be an outlier? Could this patient have Lyme disease even if the presentation and course are atypical? Even if the lab tests are equivocal? Some physicians ask themselves such questions. Others do not. Some doctors love the complicated patient, experiencing such encounters as a challenge, an opportunity for a "Dr. House" moment—finding the thread that unravels the disease and revealing the elusive diagnosis. Other doctors may feel quite uncomfortable evaluating patients who do not fit known patterns and whose symptoms seem to defy the doctor's expertise. Such encounters take time—a commodity that few doctors now have.

## Why Would a Patient, Previously Well Regarded by the Physician, Be So Readily Dismissed?

Aspects of Lyme disease itself may contribute to the perplexing response of physicians. Patients generally appear healthier than they feel, and symptoms are not only subjective but also quite variable, so that the patient presents differently from visit to visit. One day the symptoms appear more neurologic—ranging from sharp stabbing pains or shooting pains to dizziness, migraines, and problems with short-term memory. On another day, the symptoms appear more rheumatologic, with migrating joint and muscle pains. On yet another day, the patient appears to be much better symptomatically. In addition, the patient may be cognitively impaired, making it hard for him or her to retrieve details of symptom history and present them in an organized way. The lack of consistency in the patient's presentation may make the patient appear flaky and unreliable. The multiplicity of presentations may suggest to the physician that the underlying diagnosis is more likely a somatic symptom disorder, a stress disorder, or even a fabrication for secondary gain.

## How Does the Patient Feel?

Patients may come to feel like a pariah within the medical community, part of a marginalized group. Once "chronic Lyme disease" is in the medical chart, doctors and other health care providers may have an immediate negative bias: this patient is "bad news," won't respond well to interventions, and will have all kinds of preconceived and benighted notions of what is going on with them.

The experience of being disbelieved or even disliked by physicians can be not only demoralizing but also destructive to good patient care. Sensing the doctor's disbelief or distrust, the patient learns to screen his or her statements so as not to agitate the doctor and be further discredited. The net result is that the doctor ends up not hearing the full clinical picture and the patient ends up increasingly isolated.

Adding insult to injury, the same patient who has been told that "there is no such thing as chronic Lyme disease" may be dismayed and enraged to discover that past Lyme disease is an exclusion factor for life insurance. The patient then asks, "If chronic symptoms after Lyme disease don't exist or aren't serious, then why is a past history of Lyme disease a reason for exclusion from life insurance?" Others may find that even when treatments (such as intravenous antibiotics) are prescribed by their doctors, insurance companies refuse to pay, citing articles or calling upon "experts" who diagnose and treat Lyme disease according to very narrow criteria. The medical controversy has the effect of adding substantially to the financial burden of the illness on patients.

The experience of being disbelieved and misrepresented over and over is inherently traumatizing. Some patients, following eventual recovery from hard to diagnose and/or complex cases of Lyme disease, have identified this atmosphere of disbelief (and the resulting social isolation and self-doubt) as the single most stressful aspect of their illness experience.

## PROTEAN NATURE OF THE PRESENTATIONS OF LYME DISEASE

As indicated in earlier sections of this book, Lyme disease can affect nearly every organ and system in the human body: the skin, the joints, the nervous system, the eyes, the heart, and the brain. These protean presentations may occur simultaneously or serially, and symptoms may come and go. Lyme disease, "the new great imitator," is arguably an even better medical mime than its predecessor, syphilis. And although there have been tremendous advances in medical science since the pre-antibiotic era when syphilis was rampant, there are also disadvantages to being a patient with a potentially multisystemic illness in the current medical climate.

For example, in this era of medical specialization, illnesses that cut across different organ systems are particularly difficult to diagnose. Patients may see an ophthalmologist for diminished visual clarity, conjunctivitis, or scotomas, a rheumatologist or orthopedist for a swollen knee, a neurologist for burning or stabbing pain, a psychiatrist for depression, and a dermatologist for a recurrent rash. Especially when doctors are hurried—a common occurrence in the context of managed care in which each office visit is limited to one complaint only—the connection between these various presentations may be missed.

The patient him- or herself is left with a mystifying experience of multiple seemingly unrelated ailments among which only afterward can he or she discern the common thread. For example: A summer "flu." Months later, episodes of vertigo, skipped heartbeats, diffuse muscle twitches. A year later, one knee becomes achy and swollen but resolves in a week. Next come backaches, stiff neck, and lancinating pains that wake the patient from sleep. Numbness and tingling on the left side of the face and down the left leg crop up, along with a tendency to bump into door frames on the left side, "brain fog," and crushing fatigue. A seemingly nonsensical parade of symptoms.

One patient remarked, "This illness is like a Halloween party. First one thing pops out at me, and then another. I don't know whether I'm coming or going." One's familiar body—suddenly unreliable, mercurial—becomes like a foreign country.

Patients often make connections themselves that doctors have not yet made. Or it may be a psychotherapist or alternative health care provider who is able to put the puzzle pieces together and guide the patient toward a more comprehensive understanding.

## THE VARIABILITY OF COURSE: WAXING AND WANING SYMPTOMS

Symptoms tend to wax and wane dramatically during the course of later-stage or post-treatment Lyme disease. The patient's level of pain, sensory sensitivities, cognition, functional status, and outlook can vary greatly from day to day. This renders it nearly impossible to plan ahead. Patients may take on a work project during the course of a day or week when their symptoms are relatively mild only to find that the project becomes impossible to complete when the diffuse muscle pain or "brain fog" returns. Or they may turn down desired activities based on how ill they are feeling only to find that when the day comes, they are chipper enough to have been able to participate. Usually feeling better is reward enough in itself, but it is easy to feel down on oneself for having disappointed others and frustrated at having needlessly missed out.

Schoolchildren may vary considerably in their performance from day to day. Parents and teachers may suspect a psychological basis for the child's ability to function one day and not the next. Tutors working with children suffering from late-stage effects from Lyme disease have remarked on such variability. It is very important for the professionals involved in the child's care to educate tutors and school systems about this odd characteristic of the disease. Adults referred for neuropsychological testing may similarly manifest variable capacities in working memory and verbal fluency, performing better on one day of testing than on the next.

The variability in symptoms characterizing the illness itself is compounded by the fact of a paradoxical worsening of symptoms during antibiotic treatment (see prior sections regarding this Jarisch-Herxheimer–like reaction, a worsening of symptoms during antibiotic treatment of spirochetal diseases thought to be due to increased inflammation in reaction to release of spirochetal fragments).

Symptom variability is often augmented by the patient's own reactions to it. On "good days," it is tempting to "seize the day," especially because one never knows when the next "good day" will arrive. But this can backfire. We have seen this pattern repeatedly: a young person, suddenly freed from the daily drag of fatigue and malaise, goes for a twenty-mile bike ride, finishes up a long-overdue school project, and then goes out partying with friends late into the night. The next day symptoms and fatigue return "with a vengeance," intensified by virtue of the person's having overdone it during the "good spell." It can be very helpful for the mental health professional or primary care physician to work with the patient on finding a "middle ground" to maximize functioning month by month rather than day by day. For example, some level of physical activity is important for mood, flexibility, strength, and circulation. Patients do best by finding what level of physical activity is sustainable without leading to greater levels of fatigue and debilitation on the subsequent day. For example, the patient would be well advised to perform some level of exercise on a daily basis where feasible—even if it is very mild, such as easy stretching and breathing exercises or gentle walking—for thirty to sixty minutes, tailoring the level of activity to what is tolerable on a given day. The level (and/or duration) can then be very gradually increased.

Patients with fluctuating persistent symptoms after Lyme disease not uncommonly find that their family, friends, and doctors start to doubt them. "You've received the curative treatment—so why are you still sick?" Some may suggest psychological causes for these persistent symptoms. A spouse may ask: "Why are you sick one day, but better the next? How can it be that often when we make plans, your sickness acts up and we need to cancel?" Although these questions can be recognized as a response to frustrated longings for a return to a normal life, patients nevertheless feel hurt and disbelieved. Friends, family, and doctors alike may falsely assume that variable symptoms signify a psychogenic cause.

## PSYCHOLOGICAL RAMIFICATIONS OF AN "INVISIBLE" CHRONIC ILLNESS

### Features of Chronic Illness

Acute illness is characterized by sudden onset and, most often, the expectation of a return to prior functioning in the near future. In the event of mild illness, the patient may have the luxury of just "calling in sick" and be excused from responsibilities for the expected short duration of the illness. If the illness is severe, social supports often gather quickly, seeing the situation as temporary and novel.

The experience of chronic illness is not one of imminent danger so much as an insidious, corrosive "slow drip" that gradually and imperceptibly wears one down. Friends and loved ones return to "business as usual," leaving the patient alone with the arduous task of adapting to a new, long-term reality. Symptoms become familiar. The patient may experience periods of grief over the loss of prior functioning, but, over time, a range of new coping skills may emerge.

Support groups may be of help in the instance of some chronic illnesses. Lyme disease support groups (usually attended by those with late-stage or chronic disease) may be very helpful sources of information for some patients, but for others may be frightening or depressing, populated (as they tend to be) by those who fail to get better. Conversely, it can be very hard for patients to see others in the group respond to treatments to which they themselves fail to respond.

Young people with chronic illness may feel a particularly intense sense of isolation. The "invulnerability" characteristic of the mindset of late adolescence and early adulthood does not keep good company with those who have become suddenly quite vulnerable. By middle age, more individuals will have had direct or close experience with morbidity and mortality. Chronic illness is more likely to be experienced by middle-aged individuals as part of the human condition. For young people, such vulnerability may seem like a foreign country. On the other hand, among the young people whom we have seen dealing with this illness over the years, a silver lining may take the form of maturity and compassion gained at a young age. Some have changed career paths, taking a greater interest in the poor or in those from developing nations who do not have the assumed advantages that we have. Many have become interested in psychology, legal advocacy, or medicine as a result of their experience with Lyme disease. The luxury and tyranny of being "one of the pack" in their adolescent/young adult peer groups is not open to them.

Chronic illness raises questions of identity and eventually forces changes in one's self-concept and modus operandi. Those with "type A" personalities—who have perceived themselves as indomitable, the one who goes the extra mile—may face particular challenges. They will need to reconfigure their sense of self—for better or for worse.

## The Experience of "Invisible" Illness

Patients whom we have seen with Lyme disease who later had cancer or quadruple bypass surgery have noted the markedly different social responses to their different illnesses. Whereas during Lyme disease patients felt they were struggling in isolation, assailed with doubts from all sides, during treatment for cancer or heart disease they found a plethora of social and institutional supports: rehab programs, rides to and from chemo appointments, volunteers at the hospital offering counsel and support. They have expressed immense emotional relief to find that society gathers around them, views them as "courageous," "battling with cancer," "survivors," even though their physical and emotional distress may much of the time have been less with these diseases than from the effects of Lyme disease. Ironically, the fact that for the most part Lyme disease is not life-threatening (notable exceptions exist) mitigates the active research and social supports that exist for many other diseases. The "sick role" that is socially sanctioned when dealing with cancer or heart disease is often not sanctioned when it comes to Lyme disease. The fact that biomarkers of active disease are not yet reliably available to document ongoing physiologic disease makes the patient's report of illness symptoms more subjective and open to question (Rebman et al. 2015).

Furthermore, often the level of subjective distress does not correlate well with external manifestations, leaving the patient feeling more alone. Anyone can relate to a broken leg or the visible evidence of a cast, a bruise, or swelling; it is harder to grasp how utterly transformed a person can feel—with crushing fatigue, "brain fog," spatial disorientation, odd jabbing pains, and extreme sensitivity to light or sound—while looking more or less the same as they had before. It can be hard for the patient him- or herself to sort out what may be direct effects of the disease from his or her own reaction to them. Patients have reported feeling they were "just going crazy" based on the pervasiveness and apparent inexplicability of their fluctuating and invisible symptoms. Others have said, "If I were to make something up, I would choose something a heck of a lot more believable than this!"

Similar to post-treatment Lyme disease, certain rheumatologic diseases may also be characterized by an absence of external objective signs of disease that would otherwise serve to "legitimize" the pain, fatigue, and cognitive lapses in the eyes of others and of the patients themselves. Recent research indicates that individuals with these "invisible" diseases are at risk of negative social interactions characterized by lack of understanding and discounting. These negative experiences are collectively labeled as "invalidation" (Kool et al. 2009). Discounting includes disbelief, nonacceptance of symptom fluctuations, rejection, and suspicion that the symptoms have a purely psychological characteristic or are being exaggerated. Positive social responses are associated with better health in various studies, while negative social responses—particularly the experience of being discounted—are associated with poor mental and physical health (Kool et al. 2012). Recent research suggests that invalidation contributes to pain amplification, social isolation, and the overall burden of disease (Santiago et al. 2017). These findings imply that family members and health professionals may be able to help the patient struggling with the "invisible" illness of post-treatment Lyme disease by educating themselves about the disease, providing emotional support, and avoiding the potentially harmful impact of invalidating and rejecting interpersonal interactions.

## Different Challenges for Different Age Groups

As the foregoing examples suggest, the experience of chronic disease differs profoundly depending on the age when it strikes. Young children have the advantage of having caretakers and social services in place, but the potential deleterious effects on manifold aspects of development are more profound for them. On the other hand, so too are the resilience and capacity to rebound of young children, provided treatment is effective. Latency-aged children have the challenge of school where they are expected to achieve certain milestones at particular grades levels and to track in parallel with their age group. Controversies over receipt of special services affect this group to the greatest extent. Adolescents are caught in their conflicting need to be independent—to differentiate themselves from their parents—versus their need to rely on parents and caretakers because of their illness. This group is often most affected by loss of and alienation from friends their own age. Among adolescents for whom FOMO (fear of missing out) is rampant, there may be little room to consider hanging out with a sick friend. Adolescent patients may push themselves to the point of exhaustion in an effort to keep up with social activities with peers in defiance of parents and teachers, thus inspiring doubt as to the validity of their subsequent complaints.

Adult patients, on the other hand, have greater burdens of responsibility: wage earning, child rearing, and elder care among them. These responsibilities do not take a "time-out" for chronic illness. Because of the controversies surrounding Lyme disease, workman's compensation and disability benefits may be particularly difficult to obtain, thus placing a greater financial burden on the patient and/or other family members. Children of chronically ill parents may suffer varying kinds of neglect. Conversely, they may develop resilience and a (for better or for worse) precocious capacity to fend for themselves. Symptoms of Lyme disease developing or recurring in old age may be more easily disregarded as effects of aging, thus delaying diagnosis and/or depriving such patients of potentially useful treatment modalities.

## Effects on Families

There can be tremendous strain on a family from any chronic illness, but once again, Lyme disease brings particular challenges, largely due to the controversies surrounding it. Parents may be split in their views of a sick child, for example. One parent may be in the medical field, swayed by the advice of doctors in tertiary care facilities who diagnose strictly according to CDC criteria and follow IDSA guidelines exclusively. The other may be closer to the child's everyday experience and be more cognizant of changes in the child's behavior, personality, and cognitive performance. The parent may have heard from other parents with similar experiences whose child has been helped by a doctor in the community who diagnoses using broader criteria and treats more aggressively. One parent may be acutely aware of the financial burdens imposed by multiple medical consultations with only marginal results. This may be the parent with primary financial responsibility, who sees genuine hardship ahead as savings and college funds are depleted. The other parent may be acutely attuned to the child's suffering and want to leave no stone unturned in the quest for answers and relief. Where there are preexisting strains within a marriage, the decisions about the management of the child's illness may be particularly fraught. The child may feel not only sick but also responsible for the tensions in the household.

## THE FACT THAT LYME DISEASE CAN AFFECT THE BRAIN AND SENSORIUM

It is hard to feel sound and strong of mind when the very organ generating mind and coping skills is itself compromised by the disease.

Lyme disease can directly affect the brain and sensorium in multiple ways: via direct infection, systemic immune effects, changes in neurotransmitter balance, and altered neural pathways (as in central sensitization). It can affect cognition, emotional experience, and sensory processing.

### Cognitive Effects

As mentioned in chapter 2, the symptoms and sequelae from Lyme disease can include cognitive effects, most typically short-term memory problems (especially working memory), word-finding problems, dyslexic changes, executive problems (difficulties with planning and organization, difficulties with multitasking), and mental slowing. The latter is often described by patients as "brain fog" or "like my thoughts are wading through molasses."

Patients may have difficulty reading and find that when they move on to the next paragraph, they have forgotten what they read before. One patient who eventually got better with additional antibiotic treatment said, "It was like I'd had intellectual tunnel vision: I could hold only one thought in mind. Now I can see the whole landscape. I can remember the pages I've just read and relate them to what I'm reading now."

Patients may have spatial disorientation such that familiar routes become suddenly difficult to navigate or appear unfamiliar. Patients may have new-onset dyslexic changes, reversing numbers or letters when writing or words and phrases when speaking. They may confuse left and right and may find themselves making verbal errors that are uncharacteristic of them. The patient who remarked, "I'm not feeling well today. Oh well, maybe I'll feel better yesterday," was manifesting a kind of temporal dyslexic error. This tendency abated following antibiotic treatment. Other examples of cognitive errors might include placing the cereal box in the refrigerator or asking one's spouse to please put the milk back in the radiator. Such errors are readily recognized soon after the fact, but may be sources of alarm or perplexity to the patient and to his or her family.

Difficulties in executive functioning and slowed thinking may make it more difficult to retain perspective or to seek needed medical care. It may seem overwhelming and exhausting to track down doctors who might be able to help or to organize a coherent history in preparation for a new doctor visit. A patient struggling to keep up appearances at work may speak up in a meeting only to lose track midsentence of the point he or she wished to convey. Ordinary quotidian tasks, such as planning a menu or cooking a meal, may seem overwhelming; the patient may find that he or she has left out significant steps or ingredients. Such difficulties can be very frightening to patients, sources of mild embarrassment or of intense shame, and a far greater obstacle to functioning in the world than are the physical symptoms—and more difficult for other people to comprehend.

One patient described her cognitive difficulties in this way: "Most days, it's like there's an egg beater in my head: my thoughts get scrambled. Other days, it's like the egg beater isn't plugged in." She compared this to how she feels when her cognition is better: "Even if I'm stuck in bed all day, it's okay, because at least I can think. Read. Daydream. I can follow and make sense of my own thoughts, and I don't feel so utterly lost."

## Effects on the Sensorium

Lyme disease can affect the sensorium early and severely, and such effects, in some cases, persist beyond recovery from other symptoms. These effects also cut to the core of one's identity and to one's sense of reality, one's sense of "being in the world." Most of us take for granted that our senses provide us with a more or less accurate representation of the external world. But when colors appear suddenly too intensely bright, or normal ambient sounds, rather than being soothing, grate against us like a rasp on metal or fingernails on a blackboard, then there is a brutal awakening to the fact that we are, in our very essential being, at the mercy of our sensory apparatus.

Most common is sensitivity to light—particularly bright or flickering lights, such as fluorescent lighting in supermarkets or strobe lighting during electroencephalogram testing. Exposure to light may lead to head-aches, eye pain, or even panic attacks. It can be very helpful to recognize that the feeling of extreme anxiety in certain settings is related to sensory issues rather than coming out of the blue or in reaction to interpersonal tension. One patient noted that each time she did the food shopping in a certain aisle of the supermarket, she became acutely anxious to the point of panic. Later she realized that the light in that section was flickering erratically. Waiting rooms of doctors who care for those with persistent symptoms from Lyme disease are populated with patients wearing sun-glasses, even on cloudy days!

Also common is hypersensitivity to sound (hyperacusis). One patient reported that the sound of a hard candy bumping against her husband's teeth would cause her to jump and scream. Another reported constantly needing to turn down the volume on the television, not recognizing that he was listening to it at a far lower volume than normal.

Indeed, hyperacuities can occur across sensory modalities. A patient with hyperacute vibration sensitivity took her car to a mechanic because she thought it had lost its ball bearings and was vibrating dangerously, only to find that the problem was not in her car, but in her own altered sensorium. Associated hyperacuities to taste, touch, and smell may occur as well. In addition to hypersensitivities, Lyme disease can cause loss of vision or hearing (Steere et al. 1985; Peeters et al. 2013; Bertholon et al. 2012), although this is far less common.

Perhaps related to subtle sensory changes or perhaps to cognitive and emotional factors, many patients report experiences of depersonaliza-tion and derealization: feeling "there and not there," "going through the motions," "not myself," or "like I'm watching a movie—not real life." For some, this sense of dislocation and unreality is profound—and devas-tating. One patient said, "I feel like the walking dead. I can be out with friends talking, and they're laughing and responding to me like nothing's wrong, but for me the whole world has changed."

We include these many examples not because every patient with per-sistent symptoms manifests them, but to give a flavor for how bizarre and perplexing the illness experience can be for the individual patient. And there are many more examples that we could give; this list is by no means an exhaustive summary.

## UNCERTAINTY SURROUNDING DIAGNOSIS, TREATMENT, AND PROGNOSIS

The uncertainty surrounding diagnosis, treatment, and prognosis may be the single most salient feature of the patient experience. The fact that doctors—good doctors and "experts" in the field —disagree regarding so many aspects of this disease, from diagnosis to treatment to prognosis, leads patients to feel they must become de facto experts in their own care. They must choose among rival camps or find a physician who can translate the reasons for these rivalries for them and help guide them in their choices. They must trust their physician while taking in stride the many dissenting voices in the lay press, among their physician friends, or among their family, friends, and neighbors. They must choose a path knowing that science or experience may bear them out in the long run or else prove them wrong. Or they must educate themselves sufficiently to feel comfortable going against their physician and seeking a second, third, or fourth opinion. Patients who seek such multiple opinions are often accused of "doctor shopping" and viewed as "suspect" by subsequent physicians. Nonetheless, many patients in our practices have seen ten or more physicians before coming up with a diagnosis and course of treatment that brought about remission or cure. Some seek professional help from a variety of health care providers, engaging in expensive treatments with substantial side effects without ever achieving significant therapeutic gains.

### How Doctors Deal with Uncertainty

Doctors vary in their capacity to acknowledge and/or tolerate uncertainty. In the face of uncertainty about diagnostic tests or treatment, some doctors adhere strictly to the CDC surveillance criteria for diagnosis in deciding when and whether to treat, while others place greater emphasis on clinical history and prior responses to treatment. Some end up underdiagnosing, while others err more in the direction of overdiagnosis. Some are very open about the uncertainty, giving the patient many treatment options from which to make an "informed" choice (which may risk leaving the patient frightened and confused), while others peddle what we might consider false certainty (which carries its own risks of doing harm).

Often it is the doctor who can state that he or she believes that the patient has an illness but cannot specify the cause who is—paradoxically—the most reassuring. Facing uncertainty honestly is calming and validating for the patient. In other words, the clinician who is willing to accompany the patient in trying to understand the illness, even though the diagnosis is not clear, is often a source of considerable comfort.

Uncertainty requires doctors to draw upon many different sources of information in order to make decisions. These include the patient's history, the physical exam, the results of diagnostic tests, articles about the disease in medical journals, diagnostic or treatment guidelines published by experts, and the doctors' wealth of clinical experience. At times the physician may make a diagnosis and recommend treatment with 90 percent certainty, while at other times he or she may be quite uncertain—perhaps only 60 percent confident—leading the physician to have to balance the potential benefits of treatment against the potential risks of serious adverse side effects.

Parents advocating for a sick child would be wise to pose the following question to their doctors: What would you do if it were your child? The physician may hesitate when faced with this question, realizing that guidance about treatment that might be appropriate for the majority of patients with the disease and presented from a podium at a lecture may not be the same as recommendations optimized for a particular individual. This question forces the doctor to address the difference between public health concerns relating to the population in general (e.g., overuse of antibiotics) and the potential benefit for a given child of empirical treatment for otherwise debilitating symptoms.

Patients seeking care for persistent symptoms may seek help from doctors whom they normally might not approach. Patients will be referred by friends to new practitioners—"the only one who really understands Lyme disease." Some of these doctors provide sound medical care and monitor their patients carefully. Others venture into more experimental treatments, some of which may help, and others not. Patients may be vulnerable to persuasion by the doctor whose caring manner, magnetic personality, and/or reassuring certainty provide hope for the recovery they have long sought. Some health care providers, perhaps with good intentions, may use diagnostic methods that have no proven value but are presented with absolute confidence. These health care providers may also recommend treatments that have little justification given what is known about the spirochetal cause of Lyme disease. By providing a new approach to diagnosis and treatment, they may attract patients who have become disenfranchised from traditional Western medicine; these patients may then expend considerable resources of time and money on a marginal and potentially quite expensive treatment path.

Some have equated this scenario to health care in the nineteenth and early twentieth century, when scientific testing of treatments was not yet routinely conducted. In those years, bloodletting was standard practice only because clinicians believed it to work—and this practice was advocated by highly respected academic clinicians!

Medicine of the twenty-first century requires evidence in order for a diagnostic test and treatment approach to be deemed proven helpful. Much of what patients consume and alternative health care providers recommend has not been adequately tested. This is not to say that it cannot be helpful, only that, until further research has been done, we are limited in our capacity to predict which of these alternative treatments and diagnostic protocols will be beneficial to whom.

Patients with chronic symptoms face a dilemma: To what lengths should they go to seek help for ongoing symptoms? Some may experience significant improvements in their quality of life in response to one or more of these "unproven" treatments. But for those who are not so fortunate, trying these alternative approaches can become a more than full-time job. Patients with ongoing symptoms wonder: When does this stop? When will the symptoms go away? When will I find an effective treatment? Should I keep trying these different treatments that my doctors tell me to try or should I focus on acceptance and find a way to live with my symptoms? Each patient struggles to find a balance between the search for solutions and acceptance of uncertainty and of one's current symptom complex.

To complicate matters further, often "cure" of the disease does not automatically or immediately result in relief from the illness. What do we mean by this? What we mean is that there are secondary effects of the infection that may persist after the organism is eradicated. Some of the details as to how this happens have been elucidated in prior chapters.

Alternative treatment approaches (such as mindfulness, anti-inflammatory diets, acupuncture, and neurofeedback) may aid in the recuperation process, if not in the "cure" per se.

## THE ROLE OF MENTAL HEALTH CARE AND RESILIENCY

Recuperation from the potentially life-changing effects of Lyme disease can be greatly aided by having someone to talk to. This observation may seem commonplace, but it cannot be overemphasized. There are far-reaching psychological benefits to just putting one's experience into words. To do so can lend form and coherence to what is otherwise an overwhelming and demoralizing ordeal. Part of what leads many patients to abandon Western medicine and conventional treatments is not only the fact of not getting better but also the lack of confidence that there is anyone out there who understands. The experience of being listened to—deeply listened to, not as a case study or example of a disease process, but as a whole person—is particularly important for the patient with chronic symptoms who has had the experience of (repeatedly) being discounted and misunderstood. The presence of a listening ear can help the patient draw from his or her experience of illness whatever life lessons and potentialities might be available from it: perhaps greater mental flexibility, maturity, and/or compassion for others in distress. Some patients have been obliged to learn new skills—mindfulness, yoga, therapeutic movement—as a matter of survival, but have then come to embrace these skills as ongoing sources of enrichment in their lives.

Many patients choose to avoid seeking mental health care even if there is marked emotional distress due to fear that others will say: "See I told you . . . it was all in your head!" This avoidance is an unfortunate corollary of both the misunderstandings about Lyme disease and the still pervasive stigma associated with issues related to mental health—as if seeing a mental health professional were evidence of moral weakness or suggestive that one's symptoms are imaginary. That depression and anxiety are a common part of the experience of patients with chronic symptoms after treated Lyme disease has been well-described in the published literature (Hassett et al. 2008; Fallon and Nields 1994). That the spirochete itself has been shown to cross the blood–brain barrier within weeks of initial skin infection is well documented (Garcia-Monoc et al. 1990). That the blood flow and metabolism of the brain is altered in subgroups of patients with chronic neuropsychiatric symptoms associated with Lyme disease is also well documented (Fallon et al. 2009). Thus both because Lyme disease affects the brain and sensorium and because of the complex climate surrounding chronic Lyme-related symptoms, many patients might benefit from—and indeed many do end up—seeking mental health care. Perhaps ironically, it is often the therapist or psychiatrist who says to the patient "there are atypical features to your depression. I suspect there is something more going on." Or they may say, "You have tolerated this particular antidepressant without difficulty in the past, why should it suddenly be giving you panic attacks? And perhaps it is significant that when you have dizziness and numbness and tingling, you are also running a low-grade temperature and having joint pains."

The mental health professional can play a key role: by listening to the patient and validating the patient's experience, by understanding that the experience of medical symptoms is shaped by personality, genetic profile, and life history, by helping the patient navigate a confusing health care system in which there may appear to be no captain to steer the patient in the right direction, no general to organize the troops, and by providing psychological and pharmacologic interventions to improve quality of life and emotional stability.

In our work with patients who have Lyme disease, we have seen a great deal of suffering. We have also been privileged to witness the quiet courage of patients of all ages in dealing with their illness. We have seen the many creative ways in which some of our patients have found meaning in their lives, despite and sometimes as a result of their illness experience. Some have contributed to knowledge of the disease, participating in research studies or writing articles or books. Some have founded support groups that have become springboards for fundraising and political activism. Some have gone on to become health care providers, armed with invaluable firsthand knowledge of the patient's perspective. Some have become lawyers, devoted to helping others who have been oppressed by society or denied insurance coverage. Some have found expression through creative writing, art, and photography, finding in the particulars of their illness windows onto universals of human suffering and the search for meaning. Once an illness has become chronic, it requires a reworking of identity: it becomes an aspect of the self that must be integrated into one's self-concept and functioning. "Resilience" is the capacity to take what comes and find some way to make meaning through it, to "bounce back," perhaps forever changed, perhaps with significant losses in certain areas of functioning and opportunity, yet with some new understanding and source of motivation. We have seen some remarkable examples of such resiliency among the many patients who have come through our clinic and practices.

## CONCLUSION

The experience of the patient with chronic or relapsing and remitting symptoms after antibiotic treatment for Lyme disease is often one of confusion and profound disorientation. Invisible symptoms mean that others cannot tell how it feels inside. Waxing and waning symptoms make it impossible to plan. Medical controversy means that individuals may find themselves at odds with a previously trusted physician. The lack of a clear social consensus regarding the illness means that even friends may view them with skepticism and doubt. Families may be pulled apart and suffer severe financial setbacks, either due to lost earning power or to extensive medical expenses. Uncertainty and doubt may exist in the patient him- or herself, at a loss as to whether to "push through it," see yet another health care provider, or resign him- or herself to more or less permanent lifestyle changes. Like Job, these patients are assailed from within and without, feeling that the powers that be have left them in the lurch, friends doubt them, and all their good efforts have come to naught.

The story of Job ends—in a somewhat tacked-on ending—with the return of Job's health, family, and property. It is unclear how or why this happens, except that Job has witnessed and acknowledged the enormity and complexity of what he is up against—of God and of creation, the workings of which he had thought he understood, but which in fact were more vast, inscrutable, and powerful than he could possibly fathom. He thought he knew the rules, and realizing that he did not was the first step in his restoration.

Medical professionals are gradually waking up to the complexity of Lyme disease and to the real suffering of patients with chronic symptoms and, instead of blaming patients for their misfortune, are working hard and across disciplines to try to restore them, like Job, to their former well-being and good grace. The issues surrounding the treatment of patients with chronic symptoms, and the ways of the spirochete itself, are far more challenging than previously imagined. This awareness by the medical and scientific community represents the first step toward elucidating the biological underpinnings of these chronic symptoms and providing solace and hope to those who suffer with this illness.

# 13

## FREQUENTLY ASKED QUESTIONS

### SIGNS, SYMPTOMS, AND DIAGNOSIS

**Can you get a new case of Lyme disease if you have been treated successfully once before? How do you tell if the Lyme is a new case or just a second bout of a previous infection?**

You can still get a new case of Lyme disease even if you have had it previously and have been treated successfully with antibiotics. If you are exposed to the bacteria again through another tick bite, you can become reinfected and require treatment. If you develop symptoms after initial treatment and recovery, you should see your doctor to determine if it is a new infection or a recurrence of symptoms from an earlier infection. It can be difficult to distinguish whether your symptoms are the result of a new infection or a previous infection. If you have not been exposed again to tick bites, a symptom recurrence may be due to either another unrelated illness, a tick-borne coinfection that was not previously identified, or a *Borrelia*-triggered immune-mediated symptom complex that now has its own timeline for resolution. Additionally, the return of symptoms may be due to the reemergence of the initial infection that had been only partially treated. In most cases, a solo *erythema migrans* (EM) rash and fever would be a sign of a new acute infection. Serologic testing carried out by your physician may help in the interpretation of your current symptoms. For example, if the quantity of antibodies in the serum as determined by a specific test such as the C6 enzyme-linked immunosorbent assay (ELISA) shows a marked increase compared to what had been seen in a prior test conducted months after treatment, that would most likely reflect a reinfection because the quantity of *B. burgdorferi* spirochetes present to stimulate the immune system after a new tick bite is going to be vastly higher than what might occur from a prior infection.

**What percent of cases of reasonably proven Lyme disease present without the EM rash?**

According to the annual reporting by the Centers for Disease Control (CDC), based on cases reported to them for national surveillance, EM rash occurs in 70 percent of confirmed cases. Based on these estimates, 30 percent of confirmed cases do not present with an EM rash, but rather present with other classic features of disseminated Lyme disease included in their surveillance case definition (e.g., meningitis, arthritis, facial palsy). The CDC's surveillance data, however, tells only part of the story because patients may also present with flu-like symptoms such as fatigue, muscle pain, low-grade fever, and headaches that commonly occur in early localized Lyme disease.

Another way to answer this question is to go back to the early days of Lyme disease before the signs and symptoms were widely known and recognized. In the early studies in Connecticut, among those patients who presented with new-onset migrating arthritis, the recollection of a rash was—not surprisingly—much lower; only 25 percent recalled having had an EM rash. This means that in geographic areas where Lyme disease is less well known, the rash would be recalled far less frequently.

In the Lyme vaccine studies, patients were very carefully monitored for the emergence of new symptoms during the first several months after injection with either the vaccine or placebo (Steere and Sikan 2003). The investigators in that study were surprised to learn that 18 percent did not present with any of the classic signs of Lyme disease, but rather presented only with flu-like symptoms; they were confident the patients had been newly infected with *B. burgdorferi* because the patients' blood tests had converted from negative to positive. In other words, based on this carefully conducted study, it is reasonable to estimate that nearly one in five patients who contract Lyme disease would not be detected if the physician relies solely on the CDC's surveillance criteria for diagnosis.

For epidemiologic surveillance purposes, to be considered a "confirmed" case by the CDC in the absence of a rash, a person has to have

laboratory evidence of infection and at least one late manifestation of
Lyme disease. Late manifestations of Lyme disease considered
in the surveillance criteria are joint swelling, facial nerve palsy, other
signs of nervous system involvement, or specific cardiac problems.
Notably, for the purposes of epidemiologic surveillance, encephalopathy is not recognized as a late manifestation of Lyme disease, and
diffuse flu-like symptoms are not recognized as an early manifestation.
The CDC also has criteria for a "probable" case, defined as a physician-
diagnosed Lyme disease that has laboratory evidence of infection. In these
cases, the typical "objective signs" are not present, but a physician has
been impressed enough by the clinical presentation and the laboratory
tests to make a diagnosis of Lyme disease.

**At what point do I stop antibiotics for the psychological symptoms
of Lyme disease and conclude that these symptoms will not go away
through antibiotics?**

This is a complex question because the answer depends on what is
causing the psychological symptoms. While psychological symptoms can
be triggered by a systemic or central nervous system infection, psychological symptoms in the context of Lyme disease may also arise for other
reasons. In some patients with Lyme disease, the mood symptoms may be
a direct result of active infection itself, causing local inflammation in the
brain or in the periphery—each of which can contribute to psychological
symptoms. In other patients, these symptoms may represent a psychological reaction to having a challenging illness associated with severe stressors. In yet others, the mood symptoms may reflect the residual effects of
prior infection, such that the brain's neural networks or neurotransmitters
have been changed.

Each of these causes has a different treatment approach.

- A psychological reaction to illness is common to all people afflicted
  with an illness that impacts functional status or causes marked
  distress; therefore we often recommend that patients with chronic
  illness consider psychotherapy to help the individual reorient to this
  changed view of his or her physical and mental self and to maximize
  coping skills.

- For the patient with acute infection with Lyme disease who develops new-onset depressive symptoms, irritability, or cognitive disturbances, a course of antibiotic therapy can often lead to remarkable improvement in physical, cognitive, and emotional symptoms.
- If the psychological symptoms persist or if the initial mood symptoms are severe, it is very important that the patient consult with a psychiatrist to determine how best to treat these symptoms apart from—or in addition to—the antibiotic therapy.

When symptoms continue even after a repeated course of antibiotic therapy, this could be due to an ongoing hyperactivated immune response leading to the production of cytokines that themselves lead to altered mood. Or it could be that the neural networks were altered by the prior infection. In the case of active inflammation that persists after the infection has been treated, an immune-modulating therapy may be helpful. In the case of altered neural networks or altered neurotransmitter balance, a more pharmacologically focused therapy or a brain stimulation therapy (e.g., transcranial magnetic stimulation) may be necessary.

It is worth noting that some studies indicate that as many as 40 percent of patients with post-treatment Lyme disease syndrome (PTLDS) may have a major mood disorder (Hassett et al. 2008). In many patients with symptoms that persist after antibiotic therapy, more antibiotic treatment does not help resolve the depression. This may have something to do with how the infection with Lyme disease altered the brain's neural networks or neurotransmitter functioning. We suspect this is the case because patients with a history of Lyme disease and persistent cognitive symptoms may have changes in brain metabolism evident on functional brain imaging (Fallon et al. 2009) and because patients who do not have clear histories of prior Lyme disease but who believe they have Lyme disease do not have such high rates of depressive symptoms (Hassett et al. 2008). The good news here is that antidepressant treatment and psychotherapy can often be extremely helpful in resolving the Lyme-triggered depression. With treatment, patients may gradually or even suddenly find they have more energy, improved memory, less irritability, less pain, and a greater motivation to reengage with life.

When in the course of Lyme disease should the patient seek psychiatric or psychological help? It is our opinion that all patients dealing with persistent or relapsing-remitting multisystemic symptoms that impair functioning or cause marked distress can benefit from the expertise of a mental health provider; this is true whether the cause is Lyme disease, cancer, lupus, multiple sclerosis, or another serious disease. Therefore we recommend mental health consultation when the patient finds him- or herself struggling with significant emotional or cognitive changes. The clinician may serve several roles. As an expert in the health care system, the clinician may help the patient navigate among providers and make decisions about whose recommendations to follow. As an expert in psychotherapy, the clinician can help the patient cope with the numerous stressors and not get buried by the burden of illness. As an expert in treating mood disorders and pain, the clinician may provide behavioral or pharmacologic help to improve sleep, decrease neuropathic pain, stabilize mood, and improve daily functioning.

## OVERLAP OF LYME DISEASE WITH OTHER DISEASES

**Is there a link between Lyme disease and chronic fatigue?**

Chronic fatigue is a common problem after any infection. In many cases, the fatigue dissipates after the infection has resolved. In a subgroup of patients, the fatigue may persist for many months and sometimes longer. It is unknown why some patients go on to develop post-infectious fatigue and others do not. There is evidence that some patients carry genetic markers that may increase their risk for post-infectious fatigue (Gow et al. 2009). It is estimated that more than two million people in the United States have chronic fatigue syndrome (CFS) (also called myalgic encephalitis). Reasearch suggests that the problem of persistent fatigue is mediated by immune dysregulation (with pro-inflammatory cytokine activiation tracking with fatigue severity) (Montoya et al. 2017), the autonomic nervous system, hormonal mechanisms (hypothalamic-pituitary-adrenal axis abnormalities), and genetic predisposition.

A recent metabolomics study (Naviaux et al. 2016) of forty-five patients with CFS and thirty-nine normal controls found that 80 percent of the diagnostic metabolites were decreased in the CFS patients, consistent with a hypometabolic syndrome. The authors suggest that CFS is a "highly concerted hypometabolic response to environmental stress that traces to mitochondria." This study not only identified a common metabolomic signature among people whose CFS was triggered by many different stressors but also suggested a new direction for studies of pathophysiology and treatment. This study requires validation in a much larger patient and control sample size before the conclusions can be accepted, but the finding is provocative and gives new hope to patients with CFS. A similar metabolomic study should be conducted comparing patients with chronic fatigue with a history of Lyme disease to those who have recovered fully from Lyme disease.

Fatigue is a common problem in many disorders; therefore before attributing fatigue to infection or a post-infectious state, a thorough evaluation should be done to rule out other causes of fatigue, such as thyroid abnormalities, anemia, or cancer. With regard to Lyme disease, we assume that after an initial course of antibiotic treatment some patients have persistent fatigue as a result of post-infectious processes, whereas others may still harbor a small amount of persistent infection that may require retreatment. Indeed, in people with PTLDS struggling with fatigue, research by Dr. Alaedini and others at Columbia University Medical Center has shown that there is elevated activity of cytokine interferon-alpha; this is important because interferon-alpha can itself cause fatigue and cognitive problems (Jacek et al. 2013). Fatigue is in fact one of the most debilitating problems in PTLDS.

PTLDS and CFS, however, are not the same entities. While the symptom profiles overlap, the cerebrospinal fluid biomarkers differ. Research by Dr. Schutzer and the Pacific Northwest National Laboratory using the cerebrospinal fluid from patients with Lyme encephalopathy study demonstrated that the spinal fluid contains over 690 unique proteins not found in the spinal fluid of those with CFS (Schutzer et al. 2011). The serum biomarkers have also been shown to differ. Unlike the earlier studies that demonstrated an increased level and frequency of IgG antineural antibodies in the serum of patients with PTLDS (49.4 percent) compared to patients who recovered from Lyme disease (18.5 percent) and healthy controls (15 percent) (Chandra et al. 2010), no elevation of antineural antibodies was found in patients with CFS/myalgic encephalomyelitis (7.8 percent) compared to healthy controls (13.2 percent) (Ajamian et al. 2015).

Both PTLDS and CFS are debilitating conditions characterized by prominent fatigue, but they are clearly distinct entities.

**Is it possible for Lyme disease to be misdiagnosed as amyotrophic lateral sclerosis (ALS)? Are there similarities in symptoms between these two diseases?**

The question of a relationship between Lyme disease and amyotrophic lateral sclerosis (ALS) first received significant academic attention when a neurologist at Stony Brook conducted a study that compared the frequency of blood test positivity to *B. burgdorferi* among patients with ALS to community controls. The results indicated a higher percentage of the ALS patients were seropositive for Lyme disease (Halperin, Kaplan, et al. 1990). Since then, there have been isolated case reports in the media and rarely in the academic literature indicating that a patient had been misdiagnosed with an ALS-like illness only later to be rediagnosed and treated for Lyme disease with good clinical response. As a result of these rare reports, there have also been many desperate patients with ALS who have sought treatment for possible Lyme disease with intravenous (IV) ceftriaxone. Most have shown no benefit. We suspect that there are individuals who develop some of the features of an ALS-like illness who are misdiagnosed as having ALS and who instead are suffering with neurologic symptoms triggered by Lyme disease. However, the overwhelmingly vast majority of patients with ALS are not misdiagnosed patients with undiagnosed Lyme disease. It can be expected that in a Lyme endemic area, Lyme disease may occur as a comorbid but causally unrelated condition in ALS. A clinical trial was recently completed that demonstrated that two grams of ceftriaxone administered twice daily did not result in a significant benefit among patients with ALS (Cudkowicz et al. 2014). Because ceftriaxone up-regulates the glutamate transporter and thereby reduces the nervous system excitotoxicity caused by glutamate, researchers hoped that IV ceftriaxone would be beneficial; unfortunately, ceftriaxone was not helpful.

**Can Lyme disease be misdiagnosed as autism? What research is there to prove this? Can a child with autism be successfully treated for Lyme disease?**

It would be extremely unusual to misdiagnose a child with Lyme disease as having autism because the symptom profiles are so different. In both conditions, however, sensory hyperacuities may occur. Lyme disease typically gets diagnosed when a child has joint and muscle pains along with fatigue, positive blood tests, and central or peripheral nervous system involvement. Certainly, a child with autism may also get Lyme disease and thus have two disorders at the same time. In that situation, treatment of Lyme disease should result in a resolution of the Lyme disease, but it would not likely result in a change in the autism symptoms. The question of interest to us is whether there are cases of "regressive autism" that have been induced by a central nervous system infection, such as with *B. burgdorferi*. In this scenario, a child with a mild preexisting autistic spectrum disorder who gets a central nervous system infection causing encephalitis may experience a sudden worsening of the underlying mild autistic syndrome. This child who previously had barely detectable autism spectrum symptoms may now appear to have new-onset autism. If this occurs due to *B. burgdorferi* infection, antibiotic treatment should lead to a resolution of the encephalitis and the clinical picture of "regressive autism" such that the child returns to the prior baseline state of neuropsychiatric health. This, however, does not mean that Lyme disease causes autism. Instead it means that the infection with *B. burgdorferi* and inflammation has exacerbated an underlying vulnerability in the central nervous system, as would occur in other cases of encephalitis. In this case, because the child would be expected to have an abnormal spinal fluid suggestive of central nervous system invasion by *B. burgdorferi*, spinal fluid studies are strongly recommended.

**My child had Lyme disease, got treated, and is now depressed. Could this be a sign of a relapse?**

Part of the answer to this question depends on the temporal relationship of the depressive symptoms to the Lyme disease, the child's personal and family history of mood disorders, and whether the Lyme disease was treated early or later in the course of infection. In most cases, if depression is present after antibiotic treatment and if other systemic symptoms of Lyme disease are not present (e.g., muscle and joint pain, neuropathies), a mental health provider would be the best person to evaluate your child because it is likely he or she could feel a lot better with standard approaches to the treatment of depression.

"Depression" is a word that encompasses physical, cognitive, and emotional components. The physical symptoms include poor sleep, fatigue, and low energy. The cognitive symptoms include poor concentration, impaired memory, and trouble making decisions. The emotional component includes feeling guilty, hopeless, even suicidal, and being unable to enjoy life in most aspects. PTLDS is most often associated with physical symptoms such as insomnia, fatigue, headaches, pain, and sometimes with cognitive symptoms such as poor memory and problems with word retrieval. In other words, PTLDS is most often associated with the physical and cognitive parts of the depressive picture and less often with the emotionally despairing part. While mild levels of depressive symptoms are common among patients with PTLDS, most studies indicate that only a much smaller percentage develop severe depression. When psychiatric symptoms do become more severe, however, it is particularly important for that individual to seek mental health care.

The emotional aspects of depression might occur secondarily to being sick with a physical illness or directly from an infection affecting the brain or from immune products (e.g., cytokines) affecting the brain that were released by infection outside of the brain. If a patient does not have other features of Lyme disease present, such as marked fatigue, headaches, joint pain, and muscle pain, it seems less likely that the depression is a sign of a relapse.

Signs of a medical illness underlying depression include atypical physical symptoms accompanying the depression (e.g., shooting pains, paresthesias, joint pain), a poor response to good psychiatric treatments, or physical symptoms that are more prominent than the emotional ones. It should be noted that the elderly often present with primarily physical complaints—not emotional ones—as their leading manifestation of primary depression.

While these guidelines are generally true, it should also be recognized that when a person has a central nervous system infection (e.g., encephalitis), the emotional part of depression can be very dramatic. The person might be suddenly tearful for no apparent reason, have very poor frustration tolerance, become angered at the least provocation, and appear to have a personality change. These would be considered neuropsychiatric manifestations of a central nervous system infection.

Because Lyme disease is most often a multisystemic illness with multisystemic symptoms, individuals who present with only psychiatric symptoms are much less likely to have Lyme disease as the cause. In order to assess these issues further, it is helpful to consult both a psychiatrist and a medical practitioner to receive psychiatric and medical workups. The medical workup might include repeat blood tests, neuropsychological tests, magnetic resonance imaging (MRI) a lumbar puncture to examine the spinal fluid, and--when neuropathic symptoms are present—nerve conduction studies to assess peripheral nerve function.

**Is there any relationship between sleep apnea and Lyme disease?**

No evidence exists that links Lyme disease to sleep apnea, although sleep apnea has been associated with other encephalitic disorders. This is an area that has not been well studied among patients with Lyme disease. Sleep apnea symptoms can be similar to Lyme disease symptoms. For example, patients with sleep apnea may be difficult to arouse when asleep, will have excessive daytime sleepiness, and may complain of insomnia. They may have morning headaches, inattentiveness, and a decline in school or work performance. Hypertension, or high blood pressure, may also occur. Although the risk for sleep apnea increases with obesity, one can have sleep apnea without being obese. The problem can occur in children as well as adults. The diagnosis is confirmed at a sleep lab after special tests of respiratory function and all-night polygraphic sleep monitoring. Patients with central sleep apnea may have lesions in the brain that cause difficulty with speech or swallowing. Patients with obstructive sleep apnea tend to be overweight and to have large tonsils. At night, these patients may snore. Apneic spells are characterized by ten- to thirty-second periods when breathing appears to stop, following by a slight awakening with a deep breath, and then return to sleep with no awareness of the sleep events. Treatment is guided by both the severity and type of symptoms. In central apnea, certain medications can be helpful. Treatments for the obstructive type include weight loss, breathing devices (continuous positive airway pressure [CPAP] devices are most common), and surgery.

**How does one distinguish between multiple sclerosis and neurologic Lyme disease?**

It is sometimes challenging to distinguish neurologic manifestations of multiple sclerosis (MS) from those due to Lyme disease. Clinical features may overlap. In addition, Lyme disease may initiate a first attack of MS or complicate a preexisting condition. The susceptibility of MS to infectious triggers is well known and not unique to *B. burgdorferi* infection. When a patient has markers of both MS and Lyme disease, antibiotic treatment for Lyme disease should be given. Immune modulatory therapy such as steroids can be started once antibiotics are on board.

Clinically isolated syndromes such as optic neuritis or myelitis may occur in Lyme disease and as an initial manifestation of MS. Evaluation for these syndromes includes MRI imaging of brain and spine and examination of spinal fluid that includes Lyme antibody titers, oligoclonal bands, and IgG index. These syndromes may occur prior to seroconversion so that serologic tests for Lyme disease may be misleadingly negative. Serology should be repeated in four to eight weeks. Treatment decisions should assess risk for exposure and the presence of extraneural symptoms such as fatigue and joint pain. Immune modulatory therapy is indicated because both optic neuritis and myelitis results are immunologically mediated. Intravenous steroids or immunoglobulin may be given, along with antibiotics for suspected Lyme.

Similar to MS, infection with *B. burgdorferi* can cause a progressive illness affecting both the brain and spinal cord. Referred to as Lyme encephalomyelitis, this is a very rare presentation of Lyme disease. In these cases, Lyme disease may be characterized by partial or full paralysis (para- or tetraspastic pareses), walking difficulties, poor coordination, bladder and bowel dysfunction, and visual disorders. Hyperintense lesions on MRI scans are seen in MS and Lyme disease, but the distribution differs. In both MS and Lyme encephalomyelitis, the cerebrospinal fluid typically shows signs of inflammation and oligoclonal bands (Hansen et al. 1990). In Lyme disease, however, the presence of an elevated Lyme index (higher level of antibodies against *B. burgdorferi* in the cerebrospinal fluid compared to the serum) confirms current or past central nervous system infection.

Cerebrospinal fluid culture or polymerase chain reaction (PCR) studies for *B. burgdorferi* DNA are not particularly helpful tests in neurologic

Lyme disease, with detection occurring in only 10 to 30 percent of cases (Strle and Stanek 2009). CXCLXIII is a chemokine biomarker often found in the cerebrospinal fluid of patients with acute neurologic Lyme disease; though not diagnostic of Lyme disease, it is a sensitive surrogate marker of active infection according to European studies (Borde et al. 2012).

MRI scans can also be informative in differentiating Lyme disease from MS. The MRI of individuals with MS often shows at least one well-demarcated oval/round lesion and the periventricular lesions tend to align perpendicular to the ventricles (Dawson's fingers). The MRI and clinical criteria for MS diagnosis are outlined in the McDonald criteria (Polman et al. 2011).

In MS, the most diagnostic abnormal cerebrospinal fluid laboratory studies are the presence of oligoclonal bands (in 90 to 95 percent of patients with MS), along with intrathecal antibody production that is not specific to Lyme disease (in 70 to 90 percent) and myelin basic protein. Except for fatigue, MS patients do not have symptoms and findings outside of the nervous system, as is often the case in patients with neurologic manifestations of Lyme (arthralgias, arthritis, myalgias, *erythema migrans*, carditis). In contrast to Lyme disease, about 50 percent of patients with MS have abnormal evoked potentials. The cerebrospinal fluid of patients with MS, but not Lyme disease, often demonstrates antibodies against measles and mumps (Heller et al. 1990; Mygland et al. 2010).

If cerebrospinal fluid studies show intrathecal production of antibodies against *B. burgdorferi* with inflammatory markers and an appropriate clinical syndrome, the diagnosis of Lyme encephalomyelitis is confirmed. If studies show elevated myelin basic protein and oligoclonal bands and no signs of intrathecal Lyme antibody production, the diagnosis of MS is more likely. Oligoclonal bands may arise in response to central nervous system infections such as with *B. burgdorferi*, but they are not as prominent as in MS, nor are they sustained.

### What is the relationship between obsessive compulsive disorder and Lyme disease?

Obsessive compulsive disorder (OCD) is a neuropsychiatric illness that is quite common, occurring in one in forty individuals. Typically it starts in either childhood or young adulthood. The cause is undoubtedly multifactorial, but there is a strong genetic contribution. The neural circuitry underlying OCD is complex and involves several parts of the brain, including the orbitofrontal cortex, the basal ganglia, and the thalamus. If there is injury to this circuitry in a healthy person, OCD may result.

Some infections are associated with immune-mediated injury to the basal ganglia. Antibodies produced to fight the infection cross the blood–brain barrier and affect neuronal structures involved in thinking, movement, and emotions, sometimes resulting in obsessive and compulsive thinking or behavior. Sudden-onset OCD was reported after a viral epidemic in the 1920s described by Von Economo and again more recently among children after strep infection (Swedo 2010). Similarly, although uncommon, we have seen children and young adults develop new-onset OCD shortly after getting Lyme disease.

In one well-known published case, described earlier in chapter 3, a twelve-year-old boy was admitted to a psychiatric facility for anorexia because his weight had dropped far too low due to compulsive bicycling (Pachner 1988). He did not have body image or food issues; rather, his weight was low because he had a compulsion to continue bicycling. When the consulting neurology fellow, Dr. Andrew Pachner, took his history and learned that he had previously had Lyme arthritis followed shortly thereafter by depression, interpersonal isolation, uncommunicativeness, and compulsive behaviors, the possibility that *B. burgdorferi* infection might be related to the OCD with depressive symptoms was raised. Although the neurology exam was normal, a spinal tap was conducted and revealed findings consistent with central nervous system Lyme disease. The child was treated with IV penicillin for two weeks and the compulsive bicycling stopped. He regained weight and interpersonal skills. The child remained well at long-term follow-up. We have seen other similar cases, sometimes also responding to oral antibiotics. Given that some of the individuals who developed OCD did not have a family history of OCD or other predisposing features (such as trauma or other obsessive compulsive spectrum disorders), it seems reasonable to suspect that *B. burgdorferi* infection may trigger the onset of OCD in some individuals. This intriguing relationship requires further study.

## Do epileptic or nonepileptic seizures occur in Lyme disease?

Brain infections, including Lyme disease, may cause cellular damage and lead to the development of epileptic seizures. Seizures are a rare complication of Lyme disease. If they do occur in a patient with an active bacterial central nervous system infection (as in Lyme disease), antibiotic treatment should lead to resolution of the seizure disorder. Seizures in the context of Lyme neuroborreliosis that do not remit after antibiotic treatment raise the possibility of an unrelated concomitant seizure trigger or residual tissue damage from the prior infection that is now serving as a seizure focus. Other noninfectious causes of seizures include abnormal levels of medications, toxic exposures, structural abnormalities or brain scars, or blood sugar levels that are too low or too high, among many other causes.

Any disease or stressful life experience can result in the development of nonepileptic seizures (also known as "functional seizures") that are not due to abnormal electrical discharges in the brain. People with nonepileptic seizures do not have conscious, voluntary control over them. These episodes can appear quite frightening, similar to grand mal epileptic seizures. They are believed to be physical reactions to psychological stress. The risk of developing nonepileptic seizures is increased among patients with a prior history of emotional trauma or a current experience of severe emotional stress. We speculate that months or years of unexplained arthritic and neurologic symptoms prior to being diagnosed correctly with Lyme disease can itself be a severe stressor that triggers nonepileptic seizures. Patients with nonepileptic seizures are not helped by antiseizure medication. Some patients may have both—actual seizures (confirmed by an electroencephalogram [EEG] that detects electrical activity) and nonepileptic functional seizures (that do not have an abnormal electrical discharge). Long-term video EEG recording in a neurology inpatient unit is the best way to make a diagnosis and then plan for appropriate treatment. While it may be surprising to the patient to learn that the seizure-like behaviors have a psychological origin, this is actually excellent news as most patients with functional seizures can make dramatic progress through a combination of physical therapy and psychotherapy.

In some cases, patients mistakenly characterize nonepileptiform involuntary movements such as paroxysmal dystonia or myoclonus as seizures. It is important to seek evaluation by a movement disorder specialist if the

EEG is normal in a patient with repetitive involuntary movements before the designation of pseudoseizures.

**I have heard that strep infection can cause sudden-onset OCD in children through an autoimmune process. Are there any other autoimmune diseases that can cause sudden psychiatric problems in adults?**

Anti-NMDA receptor encephalitis is an autoimmune disorder characterized by the sudden onset of memory problems, personality changes, paranoia, hallucinations, abnormal movements, and seizures. This phenomenon was originally discovered in young women with ovarian tumors, but it has now been found in people of all ages with diverse triggers. It occurs when a disease, such as cancer or an autoimmune condition, results in the formation of antibodies that attack the NMDA receptors in the central nervous system, affecting memory, behavior, and cognition. When the causative disease is cancer, this condition is considered a "paraneoplastic syndrome" and tends to have a poorer prognosis. When the causative disease is an autoimmune condition, patients usually make a full recovery (Wandinger et al. 2011).

Anti-NMDA receptor encephalitis can be diagnosed by looking for anti-NMDA antibodies in the blood or cerebrospinal fluid. Treatments for anti-NMDA receptor encephalitis include intravenous immunoglobulin (IVIG), plasma exchange, cyclophosphamide, and rituximab. This condition may be relevant to the field of Lyme disease because some patients with post-treatment Lyme symptoms have elevated levels of antineuronal antibodies (Chandra et al. 2010). In the laboratory setting, these antineuronal antibodies among patients with PTLDS have been shown to attach to neural cells of the brain's cerebral cortex and the spinal cord's dorsal root ganglia. In the human host, however, it has not yet been demonstrated that these antineuronal antibodies are causing chronic Lyme disease-related symptoms.

## TESTING AND TREATMENT FOR LYME DISEASE

**What is the significance of band 41 on the IgM and IgG Western blot? There is much controversy over this band. I know it is a band included in list of important bands by the CDC, but I also know that the CDC**

requires more bands to be present before making a diagnosis. What else could cause that to be positive if not Lyme Disease?

The 41 kDa band is often positive on the Western blot, even among those who have never had Lyme disease. At Columbia University we did a study in which we looked at the banding patterns of patients with a prior history of Lyme disease and compared these findings to the banding patterns of healthy controls from the inner city of New York who have never had Lyme disease. We found that a large percentage of the healthy controls tested positive on the 41 kDa band. For that reason, we conclude that the 41 kDa band does not have much value in guiding us as to whether a person has been exposed to *B. burgdorferi*. One reason a positive 41 kDa band might emerge is that our mouths contain nonpathogenic spirochetes that contain a protein similar to that found at the 41 kDa band site; it is known that some of these oral spirochetes may harmlessly seed the bloodstream from time to time, with our immune system producing antibodies against the protein segments on these non-Lyme spirochetes. These cross-reactive antibodies may be responsible for the positive results on the 41 kDa band on the Western blot (a false positive band) that may be found even among those who have never been to a Lyme endemic area.

**I have already been treated for Lyme disease. Is it dangerous to have Lyme antibodies in my blood?**

No, it is not dangerous. In fact, it is a good thing because antibodies are needed to help fight infection. The presence of antibodies in the IgG class against *B. burgdorferi* indicates that your immune system has mounted a specific attack against the Lyme disease microbe. The antibodies can be found in your blood for many years after the initial infection—like an army serving to protect against previously encountered invaders. This is similar to what happens in your blood after getting a vaccine. However, if you are sick and think you may have Lyme disease now, you should be evaluated by a physician.

**Is it correct to conclude that if a lab is CLIA certified by the federal government that I can trust their tests are valid? What is the difference between "FDA test clearance" and certification of a lab by "Clinical Laboratory Improvement Amendments"?**

FDA clearance of a test means that the test developers have conducted careful study of the test and provided this data to the federal government, specifically the FDA, for their review, and that the FDA review has confirmed that the test meets standards for a clinically valid test.

CLIA certification of a lab primarily means that the lab facility meets a set of basic quality standards for the testing of specimens from humans. CLIA certification tells us much less about whether a specific test is accurate or valid in identifying disease in humans. FDA clearance requires demonstration of clinical validity in humans; in other words, samples from patients with the disease will generally test positive and those without will test negative. This is a fundamentally different and higher standard of proof than demonstrating the test's ability to detect a particular analyte in a test tube that has been "spiked" with the microbe of interest.

Many tests that are available from individual laboratories are not FDA cleared. For example, not one of the PCR tests that are commercially available to detect *B. burgdoferi* DNA has been FDA cleared. Certainly there are reliable labs that provide clinically valid PCR assays that have not been FDA cleared. That is partly because there is substantial financial cost to conducting the validation studies necessary to support a submission to the FDA for "clearance" of an assay.

**Can you have Lyme disease without any symptoms? I had blood work that showed I have Lyme but I don't have any symptoms.**

If a person has no signs or symptoms of Lyme disease, the person does not have Lyme disease, as the definition of disease requires the presence of symptoms. When a positive test for Lyme disease is found in otherwise healthy people or people with fatigue or pain from other causes, the results should not be viewed as indicative of an active infection with the bacteria causing Lyme disease. Those who believe otherwise are misinformed.

There are several reasons why a healthy person might have a positive test for Lyme disease. Among them are the following:

- *Infection that was cleared by the person's immune system without antibiotic treatment.* In other words, the person was previously infected by *B. burgorferi*, but did not develop significant symptoms; the immune system eradicated the bacteria, but the memory of the prior infection is still there and that is why the antibodies are still positive. These anti-bodies may persist for many months or even years, when active infec-tion is no longer present. Over time, however, the ELISA titer should decrease in magnitude because infection is no longer present.

- *Infection that was cleared by the person's immune system with the help of antibiotics.* In this case, the patient may have been on antibiotics for other reasons when the tick bite and infection occurred or shortly after the initial skin infection; in this case, the person may not recall having had Lyme disease because the rash may not have been seen or may not have developed. *Borrelia* spirochetes were killed through the combined action of the antibiotics and the immune response. The antibodies may remain for months or years.

- *A positive test may indicate that there is a small amount of persis-tent Lyme bacteria continuing to stimulate the immune system.* These residual persister organisms may be metabolically less active than the initial invasive spirochetes at the time of acute infection; that is, the bacteria might be in a quiescent or dormant state and thus not cause any evident disease symptoms. In this case, the antibody tests may stay elevated for long periods without a gradual decline.

- *The positive result may be a false positive.* This is more likely to occur if the positive test is only an ELISA or an IgM Western blot, as opposed to the more specific IgG Western blot. It is well known, for example, that concurrent viral infections, such as Epstein-Barr virus that causes mononucleosis, may result in a false positive Lyme ELISA. However, if the positive test is an IgG Western blot or a C6 Lyme ELISA, it is very unlikely that either of these tests would be falsely positive. A positive result on these latter tests would be excellent evidence to indicate past or recent infection.

## If a second Western blot is still positive for IgM or IgG antibodies months after treatment, does that mean the Lyme disease is still active and further treatment is necessary?

No, it does not necessarily mean that the *B. burgdorferi* infection that causes Lyme disease is still present. The positive IgM or IgG Western blot indicates that your immune system is generating antibodies against some of the surface proteins of the *B. burgdorferi* spirochete. Your immune system, however, may continue to generate these antibodies long after the infection has left your body. It is not clear at this point how long the "immunologic memory" of prior infection stays active. The problem is that the Western blot does not tell you about the presence of the spirochete itself—it only tells you indirect information about the immune system's response to the spirochete (either present or past).

Some doctors argue that the IgM Western blot, if positive, is indicative of current infection. This is understandable because in medical training we were taught that for most infections the IgM antibody response is a marker of recent infection and that it goes away when the infection is gone. However, many academic scientists have concluded that this traditional teaching is not applicable to Lyme disease. In other words, the presence of IgM antibodies does not necessarily mean that one has a new or recent infection. Why? Several research groups have shown that the IgM Western blot can remain positive for many months after receiving antibiotics and after all clinical symptoms of Lyme disease have resolved.

Others argue that the presence of the IgM Western blot for Lyme disease later in the course of illness may be falsely positive due to the well-known cross-reactivity that can occur due to infection with other bacteria or viruses; the Lyme IgM Western blot in this scenario would be positive not because of an infection with *B.burgdorferi* but because of infection with one of these other microbes.

The CDC conveys that the IgM Western blot is only reliably informative in the early stages of infection; after that, the IgG Western blot is the test of choice. The IgM Western blot also has poorer specificity, meaning that false positives are more likely to occur with the IgM Western blot than with the more specific IgG Western blot. In a study (Schriefer 2015) that compared Lyme disease Western blots among patients with other diseases and no known exposure or history of Lyme disease, false positive results were noted on the IgM Western blot from samples from patients with other diseases (9.1 percent in multiple sclerosis, 14.7 percent in mononucleosis, and 20 percent in syphilis) but no false positives were noted when the IgG Western blot was used.

Most importantly, clinicians who order these tests need to take into account the clinical symptoms and the risk of exposure to a Lyme endemic area. For example, a positive ELISA and IgM Western blot is much more likely to be a true positive if the patient comes from a Lyme disease endemic area than if the patient comes from a country where Lyme disease has never been reported and where *Ixodes* ticks do not even exist.

The gold standard of diagnosis of current active infection is culture, but culture is rarely achievable in later phases of Lyme disease. Second best is the presence of the *B. burgorferi* DNA detectable by PCR, but this is also not often found because the *B.burgdorferi* spirochete spends only a very short period of time in the blood vasculature, most often in the earliest stage of infection. Unfortunately, we do not yet have definitive, fully reliable, and sensitive laboratory indicators of when the infection has been eradicated. Such a test would be of enormous clinical value in helping guide treatment decisions. As we described in the laboratory test chapter of this book, there are many new developments in laboratory testing that may give us the test we need in the near future.

**Is it possible to have a negative Western blot test and have Lyme disease?**
Yes, it is possible to have a negative IgM and IgG Western blot and have Lyme disease; this is most likely to occur early in the course of infection. The Western blot is a test that tells us what antibodies exist in the blood serum against proteins of a certain molecular weight. A Western blot report reveals which bands or antibodies were identified. In many ways, the IgG Western blot test is a more informative test than the standard whole-cell sonicate ELISA because it is more specific. For example, at most labs, a positive IgG Western blot is 100 percent specific for exposure to *B. burgdorferi*. A positive ELISA, however, is much less specific because it does not separate out the antibodies that are more highly specific for Lyme disease from the antibodies that arise from cross-reactivity against proteins that are shared in common by many microbes, as one might see among patients with other diseases such as lupus or mononucleosis. This general statement about ELISA vs Western blot is accurate; however it is now also clear that cross-reactive antibodies can also lead to false positive bands on the Western blot. More accurate immunoblots are available that use recombinant or synthetic proteins that reduce the likelihood of false positive results.

However, low sensitivity and false negative results remain a concern as well. The IgM and IgG Western blots are well known to have insufficient sensitivity in very early Lyme disease, meaning they may show a false negative result when a patient truly does have Lyme disease. The IgM Western blot is more sensitive and reliable two to three weeks after the initial infection, as that is the time it takes for the antibodies to appear. The IgG Western blot becomes positive later than the IgM Western blot; this may not occur until six or more weeks after the initial infection. Another factor that may contribute to false negative results is the impact of early antibiotic therapy. If a person has been given antibiotics early in the course of infection, the immune response may be partially blunted as the spirochetal load is less, resulting in a false negative ELISA or Western blot test.

While the IgG Western blot is nearly always positive among patients with Lyme arthritis in the United States, the IgG Western blot among patients with neurologic Lyme disease in the United States has been less sensitive, with an early study showing rates ranging from 64 to 72 percent (Dressler et al. 1993). Later studies using the two-tiered strategy revealed a higher detection rate of 87 percent, but even this indicates that 13 percent of true cases would be missed (Bacon et al. 2003).

It is important to remember that when the requirement for five bands to be positive on the IgG Western blot was agreed upon by a group of U.S. researchers in the mid-1990s and then recommended by the CDC for laboratory confirmation of a case of Lyme disease, this was based on a mathematical probability that optimized sensitivity and specificity. More simply stated, five bands led to a near 100 percent likelihood that if a sample was identified as positive, that that patient did indeed have prior *B. burgdorferi* infection. However, it should be noted that four bands also led to a very high specificity—not as perfect as the 100 percent obtained by requiring five bands, but still extremely high. The clinician should therefore make sure to look at the number of bands on the IgG Western blot; if the clinical picture is highly consistent with Lyme disease and the person has been exposed to a Lyme endemic area, it would be reasonable to consider it highly probable that an IgG Western blot with four bands positive in this patient reflects prior infection with *B. burgdorferi*.

**How reliable are the labs that conduct the Lyme test? If I get a negative result from one lab, should I ask that my blood be sent to another lab? Do some labs have their own "in-house" criteria for interpreting the Western blot? Are these better than the CDC criteria?**

Because doctors often rely on blood tests to make important clinical decisions, we have also been very interested in these questions. We conducted a study that enrolled thirty-seven patients with post-treatment Lyme symptoms and forty individuals who were healthy and had no known history of prior Lyme disease (Fallon et al. 2014). We drew their blood and divided each person's serum into four tubes. We then sent serum from each of these study participants to four different labs—a university lab, a national commercial lab, and two private Lyme specialty labs. The results were surprising.

First, we learned that on the ELISA and the IgG Western blot nearly all labs detected similar percentages of cases as positive. In other words, the positivity rate within each of the labs was comparable—no difference was detected between the commercial lab, the Lyme specialty labs, and the university lab. However, we also learned that there was discordance between labs; they were not always reporting the same cases as positive or negative. This happened as often as 30 percent of the time.

Second, we learned that the IgM Western blot was positive about 20 percent of the time among healthy controls at one of the Lyme specialty labs when the CDC criteria were used, even though these people felt healthy and had no recollection of prior tick bite or prior infection with *B. burgdorferi*. When the "in-house" criteria rather than the CDC surveillance criteria were used for interpretation, the lab results became even more confusing—more than 35 percent of the samples among the healthy controls were IgM Western blot positive. If one combined both the IgM Western blot and the IgG Western blot and applied the "in-house" criteria, more than half of the time the healthy controls would have had a positive result on at least one of these two assays. These results demonstrated that the IgM Western blot can be quite misleading, especially if non-CDC criteria are used for interpretation, as otherwise healthy people without symptoms of disease might be offered antibiotic treatment if these tests were used as the sole basis of clinical decision making. This is not good clinical practice of course; most physicians would not treat an asymptomatic person with antibiotics even if the blood test is positive.

However, consider the following extreme case. Imagine a person has never traveled outside of his or her home town and comes from an area where there are no confirmed Lyme disease cases and no *Ixodes* ticks.

In other words, to our knowledge, he or she could not have been exposed to ticks that carry *B. burgdorferi*. Now imagine that this person has muscle and joint pain and gets a positive result on a single Lyme test. Now consider that this single positive test is an IgM Western blot using only "in-house" criteria. How likely is it that this person has Lyme disease? This is a question often asked by patients. Most physicians would say that the likelihood of this test result being a true positive test is extremely low. They would educate the patient that both the ELISA and the IgM Western blot should be examined together in sequence (i.e., not as isolated tests) and that the IgM Western blot is really most useful only in the early stages of testing for Lyme disease. Given that this hypothetical patient has never been to a Lyme endemic area and given that the IgM Western blot is known to have false positives due to cross-reactivity or when "in-house" criteria are used for interpretation, the physician would reasonably conclude that this test result is a false positive.

**For chronic symptoms of Lyme disease, does treatment with intravenous immunoglobulin help?**

To our knowledge, intravenous immunoglobulin (IVIG) has never been studied in a controlled fashion as a treatment for PTLDS. However, some physicians are using this treatment for patients whose symptoms and neurologic studies suggest that they have autoimmune-mediated neurologic sequelae from Lyme disease that persist after antibiotic treatment; uncontrolled data suggest potential benefit among these patients both for symptoms and for improving small nerve fiber density (Katz and Berkley 2009). This is an area of research that is worth pursuing. Certainly, given that there is evidence that IVIG may be beneficial for a variety of inflammatory and autoimmune diseases, such as relapsing and remitting multiple sclerosis (MS), myasthenia gravis, pemphigus, polymyositis, dermatomyositis, Wegener's granulomatosis, and chronic inflammatory demyelinating polyneuropathy (CIDP), it is reasonable to investigate whether it may also be beneficial for patients with PTLDS particularly if there is evidence indicative of an autoimmune-mediated process that may be leading to neuropathic pain. The lack of controlled data, however, precludes conclusions about whether or not IVIG treatment has acute or sustained benefit for patients with persistent symptoms after being treated with antibiotics for Lyme disease. IVIG is an expensive treatment. Although studies in other diseases indicate that IVIG is generally well tolerated with only mild side effects, serious adverse events such as renal failure, aseptic meningitis, and thromboembolic events have been reported. Given the absence of controlled studies to determine whether or not IVIG is beneficial in the treatment of autoimmune neuropathies after Lyme disease, at present, IVIG for PLTDS remains an investigative treatment.

**What can patients with chronic pain or neuropsychiatric symptoms from Lyme disease do to get proper treatment if our doctors aren't that familiar with Lyme disease?**

The central question associated with the chronic neuropsychiatric symptoms triggered by Lyme disease is whether the Lyme disease has been adequately treated. If there is evidence to support central nervous system involvement and if the patient has only been treated previously with oral antibiotic therapy, a course of intravenous antibiotics may have a valuable role in improving outcome. If a comprehensive evaluation indicates that the Lyme disease has been adequately treated with antibiotics, the focus should turn to nonantibiotic approaches to address the persistent pain and neuropsychiatric symptoms. There are a variety of nonantibiotic approaches that appear promising for the remediation of these symptoms that may have been triggered by Lyme disease, but are no longer due to active infection.

Consultation with someone who has had considerable experience evaluating patients with PTLDS can be helpful. For example, rheumatologists, neurologists, and psychiatrists often treat patients with chronic symptoms, such as pain, fatigue, and neuropsychiatric symptoms. These specialists may then be able to guide you and your doctor regarding the next phase of treatment. Most doctors would appreciate the recommendation of a colleague with more extensive expertise. It helps both the treating doctor and the patient.

We wish to add, however, that we have seen many patients who have avoided going to their local medical doctors or mental health providers out of fear of being misunderstood. This can be risky because it leads to delays in recognizing and treating disabling symptoms. Lyme disease related–depression and chronic pain can lead to suicidal thoughts. Because of the life-threatening risks associated with untreated or inadequately treated depression, it is critical that patients with depression seek help from a mental health professional. One does not necessarily need to be an expert on post-treatment Lyme disease to treat depression, irritability, pain, cognitive problems, or fatigue related to PTLDS. Often the standard treatments used by psychiatrists work well among patients with ongoing neuropsychiatric symptoms after antibiotic treatment for Lyme disease.

**What criteria do doctors use to choose different antibiotics?**

Most often doctors rely on what has been shown in published studies to be effective for Lyme disease. For neurologic Lyme disease, the best-tested antibiotic is IV ceftriaxone. For early Lyme disease, the best-tested antibiotics include oral doxycycline, cefuroxime, and amoxicillin. As with most infectious diseases, if one antimicrobial agent does not prove to be effective, a different antibiotic might be chosen for the second round of treatment.

In some cases, after poor response to standard antibiotics, physicians may use other antibiotics have not yet been subjected to large placebo-controlled studies. For example, because several in vitro studies indicate that *B. burgdorferi* can penetrate and lodge inside cells (Klempner et al. 1993; Livengood and Gilmore, Jr. 2006), some doctors might select medications that have good intracellular penetration such as clarithromycin for the second course of treatment. Further, some doctors add hydroxychloroquine to clarithromycin based on the hypothesis that this leads to enhanced intracellular killing of spirochetes by clarithromycin; one report from a large uncontrolled clinical series using this combination regimen indicated a good response among patients with chronic symptoms (Donta 2003). Other doctors recommend against this approach as they are concerned about the rare irreversible risks to the retina associated with long-term use of hydroxychloroquine and the absence of placebo-controlled trials to assess efficacy. Could this treatment combination of clarithromycin and hydroxychloroquine confer additional benefit if given after intravenous ceftriaxone to patients with persistent symptoms despite prior treatment? A recent large placebo-controlled study concluded that the addition of three months of this combined therapy did not add any additional benefit to improvement in outcome (Berende et al. 2016).

More recently there has been interest in the in vitro studies that have shown that the standard antibiotics for Lyme disease are not very effective against the "persister *Borrelia*." These in vitro studies (Feng, Auwaerter, and Zhang 2015; Sharma et al. 2015) have suggested different approaches for eradicating persisters in the lab setting. One group has found that combinations of different antibiotics are most effective against both active and persister *B. burgdorferi* in the lab setting. Another group has recommended pulse dosing; this means giving a dose of antibiotics followed by an antibiotic-free interval and repeating this cycle a certain number of times. Both approaches have been found helpful in reducing or eliminating persisters in vitro. These research findings are now being tested in animal models and may also be tested in the future in controlled human trials to see if the promising findings of efficacy in the lab setting can be transferred to the setting of real disease in the animal or human. Unfortunately, many antibiotics that look promising in the in vitro setting fail to show benefit in the animal or human studies.

Other factors that go into the decision include whether the patient is allergic to a particular family of antibiotics or whether the patient can tolerate oral medications. Oral medication intolerance might suggest the use of intramuscular penicillin, whereas if a person is allergic to penicillins or cephalosporins, intramuscular penicillin is not an option.

### How do I know whether I have received a sufficiently long course of antibiotic therapy?

Resolution of the patient's symptoms suggests that the duration of treatment was adequate. However, the resolution or marked improvement of symptoms may not occur until several weeks or months after the antibiotic treatment has ended. This has been well demonstrated in both European and U.S. studies of Lyme disease (Krupp et al. 2003; Oksi et al. 2007). Therefore the scientific studies suggest that physicians should not base duration of antibiotic treatment on symptom resolution.

Approximately 5 to 20 percent of patients continue to have symptoms after a course of antibiotic therapy for Lyme disease, particularly in the later stages of Lyme disease. Some doctors argue that the antibiotics themselves should not be stopped until all of the signs and symptoms of disease are gone, given the possibility of persistent infection. The latter rationale, however, is too simplistic because improvement can take time and because there are many possible causes for persistent symptoms that are not related to persistent infection (e.g., residual damage from the prior infection, a hyperactivated immune response, central sensitization, unrecognized coinfection, tissue damage, or neural network changes). It is also clear that while antibiotics can be helpful in treating infectious disease, they can also lead to unintended negative consequences, such as the development of clostridium difficile colitis, gall bladder sludge and abdominal pain, or alterations of the gut microbiome with yet to be determined long-term consequences.

A middle of the road approach used by many physicians is to consider a repeated course of antibiotic therapy if the symptoms have not cleared up several months or more after the initial antibiotic course. Most valuable would be for the physician to use objective methods to measure change in response to treatment, such as neuropsychological testing or validated clinical assessment instruments—such as the PROMIS self-report clinical measures (freely available online). The use of these objectively validated tests before, during, and after treatment allows the clinician to assess the magnitude of change in a consistent and reliable manner.

In an initial study using objective measures to assess whether repeated antibiotic therapy is helpful, our Columbia team in collaboration with private physicians conducted a pilot study using neuropsychological testing before and after retreatment (Fallon et al. 1999); the results of this open-label study indicated that patients given a repeated course of IV antibiotic therapy showed considerable cognitive improvement. A limitation of this study, however, was that there was no control group. When subjected to the more rigorous scrutiny of a placebo-controlled trial, ten weeks of repeated IV antibiotic therapy did not show sustained improvement in cognition; both the antibiotic-treated and placebo-treated groups showed the same improvement at the six-month end-point (Fallon et al. 2008).

One important question is whether repeated antibiotic therapy has ever been shown to be helpful in a well-designed placebo-controlled study for any of the major symptoms of PTLDS. The answer is yes—with qualifications. There have now been four NIH-funded placebo-controlled U.S. studies of treatment for persistent symptoms after Lyme disease. Two studies (Klempner et al. 2001) using one month of IV ceftriaxone and two months of oral doxycycline showed no benefit in functional status with continued antibiotic treatment compared to placebo. One study (Krupp et al. 2003) using one month of IV ceftriaxone showed sustained improvement in fatigue at six months to a significantly greater extent in the drug-treated group than in the placebo-treated group; a similar finding of sustained improvement in fatigue after a course of IV ceftriaxone compared to IV placebo was reported as a secondary finding in our later study (Fallon et al. 2008). A fourth study (Fallon et al. 2008) found a marginal benefit in overall cognition after ten weeks of IV ceftriaxone, but this improvement was lost when patients were off antibiotics for the following fourteen weeks. However, in a planned secondary analysis, this study also reported that patients who had more pain or physical dysfunction at the start of the study were more likely to show improvement in these domains if given IV ceftriaxone compared to IV placebo, and that this improvement was sustained even after being off antibiotics for the following fourteen weeks.

Taken together, these study results suggest that repeated antibiotic therapy may be beneficial for a certain subgroup of patients. These studies also indicate that a substantial proportion of patients with chronic persistent symptoms did not improve with these courses of repeated antibiotic therapy. It is important to note that all four studies reported that some patients experienced troubling adverse effects associated with the IV antibiotic therapy. These adverse effects included systemic infection (sepsis), formation of thrombi from the intravenous line leading to pulmonary embolus in one case, and biliary stones leading to cholecystectomy in another. Given these significant risks, it is clear that other safer and more durable treatments are needed for patients with persistent symptoms. It is also clear in this age of personalized medicine that we need to have biomarkers or tests that can tell us prior to initiating treatment whether or not a patient is likely to respond to repeated antibiotic therapy or another treatment approach.

Finally, a recent trial from The Netherlands (Berende et al. 2016) of 280 patients with persistent symptoms attributed to Lyme disease asked whether adding a twelve-week course of antibiotic therapy after a two week course of IV ceftriaxone leads to greater clinical benefit than adding twelve weeks of placebo. The study failed to show a benefit to *extended* antibiotic therapy because there was no difference among patient groups on improvement in physical functioning; those who got placebo performed just as well as those who got randomly assigned to receive either doxycycline or the clarithromycin/hydroxychloroquine combination. This trial was novel in that it assessed the benefit of longer term compared to shorter term therapy among patients— most of whom had been previously treated for Lyme disease. While there are limitations and problems with this study as noted in chapter 7, the study findings do not support the use of longer courses of antibiotic therapy for patients with PTLDS as given in this trial. Although this one study alone does not settle the question of whether extended therapy is helpful, this large clinical trial does represent an important first study to address this issue.

Another finding from The Netherlands study, however, was that all groups improved over time; this is notable because all of the patients received two weeks of intravenous ceftriaxone prior to being randomized to extended antibiotic therapy or placebo. What does this mean? While this suggests that *repeated* antibiotic therapy may be useful, it does not prove it. Why? Because there was no placebo control group when the IV ceftriaxone was first given. It is possible that patients may have improved with the passage of time alone and that the administration of IV ceftriaxone was not the instrument of change. There are other design limitations to this study that limit our ability to draw useful clinical conclusions (e.g., the heterogeneous nature of the study sample that included some patients for enrollment whose documentation consisted of only an IgM Western blot—as previously discussed in the lab test section, these patients may or may not have had prior Lyme disease).

**I've been on antibiotics now for many months and I'm not getting better. I've read on the Internet that if I get worse, that's a good sign—it indicates I still have spirochetes in my system and that the antibiotics are killing the spirochetes. Is that true?**

If one is not getting better, the most logical conclusion is that the antibiotics that you are taking are not helping and that you may have another problem causing your symptoms. While some patients may experience a short-duration worsening of symptoms when antibiotics are initiated, antibiotic treatment in Lyme disease—if active infection is present—should lead to a reduction of symptoms. An ongoing worsening of symptoms is not a Herxheimer reaction; rather, a worsening of symptoms raises the question of drug toxicity, incorrect diagnosis, or incorrect treatment.

## TICKS

**What is the best way to remove a tick and what if I did not get the entire tick out?**

The tick should be removed as soon as it is noticed. With fine-tipped tweezers, firmly grasp the tick as close to the skin as possible and, with a steady motion, pull the tick's body away from the skin. It is important to avoid crushing the tick's body because that might cause the bodily contents to be squeezed into the skin, promoting infection. If the tick is accidentally squeezed or crushed, remove it and then clean the skin with soap and warm water or alcohol. Do not use petroleum jelly, a hot match, nail polish, or other products to remove a tick.

To see a diagram of how to remove a tick, see figure 10.7 or go to http://www.cdc.gov/lyme/removal/index.html.

**How long does it typically take after the tick bite for Lyme symptoms to appear? Is it possible to test the tick to see if it is infected?**

In most cases, it takes from three to thirty days after being bitten by a tick to develop the initial symptoms of Lyme disease. In order for the spirochete to be transmitted, the tick usually has to be attached for at least twenty-four to thirty-six hours. However, transmission of *B. burgdorferi* after shorter-duration attachments has been recorded. The key is that the shorter the duration of attachment, the lesser the risk of acquiring infection. Because the risk of transmission also depends on the infection rate in ticks in the area where the bite occurred, not all tick bites place a person at risk of getting Lyme or other tick-borne diseases. Testing ticks to see if they are infected is not routinely done, but if you live in a Lyme endemic area, you could check with your local or state health departments to see if they do PCR testing on submitted ticks. Some Lyme specialty labs do test ticks. Two universities offer tick testing services on a national basis (the University of Massachusetts at Amherst and the University of Rhode Island). Just as everyone who is bitten does not come down with Lyme disease, not everyone who has Lyme disease recalls being bitten by a tick. This is because the tick is small and can fall off without the person's awareness of having been bitten or because the tick bite occurred in an area of the body that is not readily visible.

**How can I tell if a red rash is an insect bite or a tick bite?**

The best-known description of the EM rash from Lyme disease is a red rash that is usually at least two inches across or larger, with pink to red edges, gradually developing a paler central clearing, classically described as a "bull's eye." Rashes that are smaller than two inches in diameter that occur within the first day or two after the tick bite most likely represent an inflammatory response to the tick bite itself rather than to the microbial contents from the tick's abdomen (which can take twenty-four to forty-eight hours to reach the mouthparts of the tick). However, while the bull's eye appearance is widely considered by the public to be the most common appearance of the EM rash, up to 80 percent of the time the EM rash does not have a central clearing but rather is uniformly red. Other EM rashes can have a bluish-red color or a raised central region. The rash can also appear as multiple red patches spread across the skin. Patients usually get the EM rash three to thirty days after the tick bite. How then does one distinguish this rash from other rashes? It is not always possible given the diverse presentations of Lyme EM rashes. The main helpful feature of the Lyme rash, however, is that in most patients this rash expands in size over time to two inches or greater; drawing a line around the rash on the skin will enable the patient to easily assess whether the rash is expanding. While it can be warm to the touch and slightly itchy, most often it is not very itchy. While there may be no pain or only mild pain at the site of the EM rash, more extreme pain would be atypical. Patients should be treated with antibiotics even if the rash has spontaneously resolved because we know that without antibiotic treatment the infection may persist and the patient would be at increased risk of developing more serious late manifestations of Lyme disease.

## MISCELLANEOUS

**Where can I get geographical statistics on areas with high rates of Lyme disease?**

The CDC publishes national statistics and identifies those counties with the highest rates of Lyme disease in the United States. The websites of state health departments may provide data on Lyme disease by town of residence.

**Is Lyme disease a new disease?**

While the EM rash and Lyme arthritis were first described in the United States in the 1970s, clinical reports of patients with histories quite typical of Lyme disease exist in Europe from the late nineteenth century. In the early part of the twentieth century, this disease was often referred to as Garin-Bujadoux syndrome or Bannwarth syndrome. Only later when the spirochetal cause of Lyme disease was discovered and tests existed to assess the antibody response did it become possible to clarify that these European syndromes, which also had an EM rash followed by neurologic or arthritic symptoms, were indeed also examples of Lyme disease. However, the agent of Lyme disease has been around far longer. Confirmation that the microbe that causes Lyme disease has likely caused human disease for millenia came when the genetic material of *B. burgdorferi* was identified from Otzi—the Ice Man Mummy—who is estimated to have lived 5,300 years ago (Keller et al. 2012). His corpse was first found in 1991 on the mountainous border between Austria and Italy.

**Does it make a difference whether you get bitten by a tick carrying one type of *Borrelia* spirochete or another? I've heard there are many different species and strains.**

This is true. There are at least ten to twenty genospecies. In the United States, *B. burgdorferi sensu strictu* causes most cases of human Lyme disease. The prominent European genospecies, however, are *Borrelia garinii*, *Borrelia afzelii*, and *B. burgdorferi sensu strictu*. *Borrelia garinii* causes a primarily neurologic illness with meningitis and radicular pains. *Borrelia afzelii* causes a primarily dermatologic illness with a late manifestation known as *acrodermatitis chronica atrophicans*. However, even within these different genospecies, you will find additional manifestations of

Lyme disease as well. For example, *Borrelia afzelii*, which primarily affects the skin, has been found in the cerebrospinal fluid of patients with multiple EM rashes. Instead of reporting the typical neurologic symptoms of radicular pains and/or meningitis that are common among patients with *B. garnii*, these patients with *B. afzelii* in their cerebrospinal fluid more often reported dizziness. The investigators who conducted this retrospective chart review reported that the clinical diagnosis of neuroborreliosis was readily made in nineteen of twenty-three *B. garinii* cases but missed in nine of ten *B. afzelii* cases because the symptomatic presentation was less specific (Strle et al. 2006). Other recently discovered genospecies that cause disease in humans include *B. valaisiana* in East Asia and Europe; *B. lusitaniae* in Asia, North Africa, and Europe; *B. bissettii* in the United States and Europe *B. mayonii* in the United States; and *B. spielmanii* in Europe. There is emerging evidence that the different genospecies might have slightly different sensitivities to the standard antibiotics against Lyme disease; however, the differences are small and unlikely to be of clinical significance.

There is also evidence that *Borrelia* spirochetes from the United States cause a greater inflammatory response in the human than *Borrelia* spirochetes from Europe. This could have important implications when comparing U.S. versus European Lyme disease, as greater inflammation would lead to a broader set of symptoms and possibly lead to a larger percentage of patients who have chronic post-treatment symptoms.

What is less clear is whether the many different "strains" of *B. burgdorferi* spirochetes that differ only slightly in their genetic profile have different clinical manifestations. This is harder to study because there are so many strains. It does appear, however, that certain *B. burgdorferi* strains stay localized in the skin, while other strains are more invasive, spreading rapidly through the skin and into the bloodstream and leading to disseminated disease.

**I would like to find a support group (online or other) specifically for people diagnosed with chronic symptoms from Lyme disease. Can you make some recommendations?**

Support groups can be found by calling the Lyme clinics or Lyme disease organizations in your state. You might also call a national organization such as the Lyme Disease Association for the names of support groups in your area.

**What is the Rife machine? And is there evidence to support its use in Lyme disease?**

A 2013 *New Yorker* article titled "The Lyme Wars" discusses a patient with Lyme disease who reported that the Rife machine helped her symptoms improve (Specter 2013). Some have stated that this machine generates radio frequencies that can destroy bacteria, including *B. burgdorferi* spirochetes; we could not find published evidence to support this claim. The Rife machine was invented in the 1930s and over the recent years its popularity has increased, despite the fact that there are no published studies in peer-reviewed journals to show that it works. In 2007, the *Seattle Times* reported on a fraud case in which a couple who had no medical training was operating an underground clinic in which they used the Rife machine to treat serious diseases. A thirty-two-year-old man with testicular cancer died after refusing his physician's recommendation for an immediate surgery and instead undergoing Rife therapy for a year. Many physicians are therefore concerned that an unsubstantiated belief in the benefit of the Rife machine may result in a patient delaying acceptance of therapy with a proven effective treatment. However, anecdotal reports from patients with Lyme disease have said that the Rife machine has helped them. In 2016, we conducted a PubMed Search using the key words "Rife and Lyme" and "Rife and *Borrelia*," but no medical articles appeared. To our knowledge, there have been no peer-reviewed published studies demonstrating the effectiveness of the Rife machine in treating Lyme disease or other tick-borne infections.

**What are biofilms? Are they involved in Lyme disease?**

Biofilms form when bacteria stick to surfaces in moist environments, forming a slimy, glue-like substance. Examples of biofilms include the plaque that forms on your gums and teeth as well as the slippery coating on rocks in a river. They are held together by sugary molecular strands called extracellular polymeric substances (EPS). These slimy colonies of bacteria are better able to resist host immune defenses than regular bacteria. Biofilms can allow bacterial diseases that are usually easily treatable to become more chronic. It has been suggested by some scientists that biofilms may play a role in Lyme disease that does not easily respond to antibiotic treatment (Sapi et al. 2012). While biofilms have been demonstrated in the laboratory setting, the possible role of biofilms in human Lyme disease is an area of controversy. It is still not completely understood and remains under active investigation.

**How do stress and depression affect the brain? Can these effects be reversed with treatment?**

The hippocampus, which is involved in learning, memory, and stress response, is the part of the human brain that has been proven to continue producing new cells throughout adulthood. This is known as "neurogenesis" and "neuroplasticity." Recent animal studies as well as observation of the human response to antidepressant treatments demonstrate that stress and depression can impair hippocampal neurogenesis or the development of new neurons. These studies suggest that psychosocial stress, adverse life events, and depression can lead to decreased formation of new neural connections between nerve cells. In humans, it has been shown that the volume of the hippocampus is decreased in adults with major depressive disorder. The good news is that studies now show that antidepressant pharmacotherapy can reverse stress-induced decrease in hippocampus volume and result in the restoration of new nerve cell growth (Dranovsky and Hen 2006). Some clinicians have referred to the effect of these therapies as "Miracle Grow" for the brain. After several weeks of treatment, antidepressants medications decrease depression and anxiety, possibly by increasing neurogenesis. We suspect that the increased neurogenesis in the hippocampus seen after antidepressant pharmacotherapy would also be seen after other effective therapies for anxiety and depression, such as psychotherapy, stress management, transcranial magnetic stimulation, and electroconvulsive therapy. The effect of stress on the brain is an ongoing area of research. When patients avoid medications because they worry about the impact of medication on the brain, they should also be aware that their decision not to treat the anxiety/depression may allow pervasive anxiety or depression to continue unabated and this can itself be harmful to the brain, reducing the growth of new nerve cells and thus decreasing brain volume in certain areas. Both patients and physicians need to be aware of these new research findings so that optimal care can be provided.

# 14

## THE GOOD NEWS EMERGING FROM LYME DISEASE RESEARCH

In this closing chapter, we wish to reemphasize the good news about research, its place in the history of Lyme disease, and the hope it provides for patients. For decades there has been a tension between the patient community and the academic community. This tension arose because patients in Lyme endemic areas were sick, not able to get definitive diagnoses, and not sure what treatment options to pursue.

The times are changing. In recent years, there has been a seismic shift in our understanding of Lyme disease. The good news is that the great divide that previously separated the patient community with chronic symptoms from the academic ivory tower is now being bridged as a result of careful research—some of it funded by the NIH in the United States or by governmental agencies in other countries and some funded by generous private donors and foundations. What is remarkable is that the current research is shaking up the encrusted views that have long polarized the medical and patient community. These are indeed exciting times in the world of Lyme disease. The following are a few examples of advances in our understanding of Lyme disease.

### RECOGNITION THAT *BORRELIA* PERSIST

Researchers from UC Davis (Hodzic et al. 2008), Tulane (Embers et al. 2012), Cornell (Straubinger 2000), Yale (Bockenstedt et al. 2002; Bockenstedt et al. 2012), and Finland (Yrjanainen et al. 2007) have documented that *Borrelia* spirochetes or pieces of spirochetes can persist in the animal host despite antibiotic therapy; this has been demonstrated either by immunohistochemistry, which allows visualization of the spirochete, or by PCR assays, which identify the genetic material of the spirochete. Some of the dormant organisms become active again months after treatment. These persister spirochetes differ from the initial infecting spirochetes because they do not grow in the standard culture medium. In mice, persistent infection was associated with altered cytokine expression in the mouse tissue consistent with recognition of the spirochetal infection (Hodzic et al. 2014). In the rhesus macaque study (Embers et al. 2012), three of the treated monkeys had signs of cardiac muscle inflammation. Why would these findings be considered good news? Because recognition of persistent infection despite antibiotic treatment in the animal model has led to a new openness to exploring why this occurs and to consider the possibility that persistent symptoms in the human may, at least in some cases, be due to persistent infection. That this question is finally being taken seriously by the academic research community is a remarkable advancement. Some of the pressing questions that need to be funded and researched are these:

> Can the findings of *Borrelia* persistence in the animal models also be demonstrated in humans?
> What are these persistent organisms doing? Are they causing disease?
> Are the cytokines that are expressed leading to systemic fatigue, cognitive impairment, and muscle pain?
> Are the persistent *Borrelia* triggering antibodies that then attack human tissue through the process of molecular mimicry?

## *Borrelia* Detection Requires Special Techniques

Researchers have demonstrated that one of the mistakes we have made all along is assuming that a negative blood culture or a negative PCR test for DNA in tissue or blood means that the organism is not present. These gold standard tests in medicine have now been shown to lead to false conclusions when dealing with Lyme disease.

In this circumstance, the tick itself has helped us. A very old diagnostic approach known as "xenodiagnosis" has been enormously helpful. When this method is applied to Lyme disease studies, an uninfected laboratory raised tick is allowed to feed on a previously *B. burgdorferi*–infected animal (e.g., mouse or rhesus macaque) that months earlier received antibiotic treatment. After feeding, the body of the tick is then examined by PCR, microscopy, or culture to see if the *Borrelia* spirochete can be detected. What we learned from these studies is that the tick can often suck up spirochetes from the previously treated animal that a mere blood test would never have been able to find (Hodzic et al. 2008; Embers et al. 2012). In other words, this xenodiagnostic approach has been able to confirm that the *Borrelia* organism can persist despite antibiotics.

Based on these novel findings in the animal models of Lyme disease, an intriguing similar study among humans was then conducted (Marques et al. 2014). In this study, to determine if persistent infection in humans could be documented, uninfected ticks were allowed to feed on humans with chronic symptoms to see if these ticks could similarly suck up *B. burgdorferi* spirochetes from the blood. Clever? Absolutely—and essential. This NIH-funded study revealed that while intact spirochetes could not be found in the feeding ticks after antibiotic treatment of the human Lyme disease, the ticks did show DNA evidence of the *Borrelia* spirochete in one of the individuals with chronic symptoms who was serologically positive by C6 peptide enzyme-linked immunosorbent assay; this supports the hypothesis that *B. burgdorferi* spirochetes or *B. burgdorferi* fragments can persist in the human host.

## REPEATED ANTIBIOTICS CAN HELP

Researchers (Krupp et al. 2003) have demonstrated that repeated treatment with antibiotics among patients who had already received standard courses of treatment is three times more likely to lead to sustained improvement in fatigue than treatment with placebo; this finding was supported by nearly identical results in a retreatment study that we conducted at Columbia. In our study, although repeated antibiotics did not lead to sustained improvement in the primary outcome of cognition, repeated antibiotic therapy did lead to sustained improvement in the secondary outcome of fatigue among those who had moderate to high levels of fatigue at study entry

(Fallon et al. 2008; Fallon et al. 2012). While other larger clinical trials of repeated antibiotic therapy failed to show a beneficial effect in improving physical functioning (Klempner et al. 2001), the fact that two trials found significant improvement in fatigue does support the clinical observation that at least one of the cardinal symptoms of post-treatment Lyme disease syndrome (i.e., fatigue) can be meaningfully reduced with repeated antibiotic therapy. These studies also demonstrated that intravenous antibiotic therapy is associated with significant risks. Although repeated antibiotic therapy for post-treatment Lyme fatigue was shown to be effective, the study authors did not recommend repeated antibiotic therapy due to the overall risks associated with intravenous therapy (Krupp et al. 2003). Oral antibiotic therapies with good tissue and central nervous system penetration need to be evaluated to determine whether they can be similarly effective and safer for persistent fatigue among patients with post-treatment Lyme disease syndrome. It is also essential that studies be conducted to test other disease-modifying nonantibiotic approaches because persistent infection is only one of several possible explanations for persistent symptoms.

## PERSISTER *BORRELIA BURGDORFERI* SPIROCHETES MAY NECESSITATE DIFFERENT TREATMENT APPROACHES

While the standard antibiotics against Lyme disease, such as doxycycline and amoxicillin, are known to be quite effective against actively replicating *B. burgdorferi*, recent studies in the laboratory setting indicate that these gold standard antibiotics are not very effective against those *B. burgdorferi* that are more quiescent; these are called "persisters." Numerous research groups have now identified different compounds that in the laboratory setting have efficacy not only against the actively replicating *B. burgdorferi* but also against the more quiescent forms (Feng et al. 2014; Sharma et al. 2015; Feng et al. 2017). This laboratory based research is still in its early stages, and what has been learned from the lab setting now needs to be tested in the animal setting—and then later in the human setting. It should be noted that these studies conducted in the laboratory demonstrating persister *B. burgdorferi* differ markedly from the in vivo setting in which microbes such as the *Borrelia* spirochetes are killed not only by antibiotics but also by the immune response. Whether these "persister" *Borrelia* are the cause of persistent symptoms in humans remains to be demonstrated. However, should persister *B. burgdorferi* spirochetes be present and causing symptoms (i.e., not just acting as innocuous non-disease causing bacteria), then these new antimicrobial agents may offer a new way to tackle post-treatment Lyme disease symptoms.

## RECOGNITION THAT PERSISTENT SYMPTOMS AFTER TREATMENT FOR LYME DISEASE HAVE BEEN ASSOCIATED WITH OBJECTIVE BIOLOGIC FINDINGS

Some of these patients have been shown to have elevated levels of antineuronal antibodies in blood comparable to what is seen in lupus (Chandra et al. 2010), elevated inflammatory cytokine activity in the serum (Jacek et al. 2013; Strle et al. 2014), higher likelihood of expression of antibody to endothelial cell growth factor (Strle et al. 2014), and expression of immune proteins in the spinal fluid surrounding the brain (Schutzer et al. 2011). In other words, these patients have biologic evidence of an overactive immune response. The critical research question now is this: Could it be that some patients with chronic symptoms after antibiotic treatment for Lyme disease suffer from a persistently activated immune response that now requires immunologic therapies rather than or in addition to antimicrobial therapies to achieve symptom improvement or remission? Furthermore, what exactly is triggering this persistent immune activation? Is it persistent infection, persistent remnants of infection, or is it now an autonomous autoimmune response?

## RECOGNITION THAT LYME DISEASE INFECTION MAY LEAD TO ABNORMALLY ACTIVE NEURAL PATHWAYS

Research using functional brain imaging scans (e.g, positron emission tomography and SPECT) has demonstrated altered brain function and blood flow among individuals with chronic symptoms after Lyme disease (Fallon et al. 2009; Logigian et al. 1997). Could it be that the prior infection with *B. burgdorferi* altered the brain neurochemistry and altered the neural activation patterns such that clinical improvement requires brain-focused treatments? In other words, while persistent infection and immune hyperactivation may indeed be important pieces of the puzzle, it appears that so too is altered brain function. If altered brain function is contributing to chronic symptoms, then treatment approaches that target the brain rather than infection may play an important role in the treatment of post-treatment Lyme disease symptoms.

## "OMICS RESEARCH" CAN HELP IMPROVE DIAGNOSTICS AND CLARIFY PATHOPHYSIOLOGY

"Omics research" starts from the most basic level and proceeds up the information chain, generating "big data" from blood samples—genomics (DNA) to transcriptomics (mRNA) to proteomics (proteins) to metabolomics (metabolites of cellular processes)—as well as big data from neural connectomics (in vivo studies of brain function). Discovery-based approaches search in an unbiased way for what is present as opposed to the more traditional and reductionist approaches that start with a hypothesis about what is present and then search for a particular gene or protein. This research requires careful collection of biological samples from patients at all stages of disease. When these patients are followed prospectively over time with good clinical assessments and sample collection, one can then probe the samples to clarify disease pathogenesis and to identify biomarkers associated with treatment response or relapse. The last decade has seen a particular focus on building new large repositories with prospective long-term patient follow up (Aucott et al. 2013). Several examples of how omics research has yielded valuable discoveries in Lyme disease are as follows:

- Applying proteomic approaches to cerebrospinal fluid, a collaborative investigation (Schutzer et al. 2011) demonstrated that the cerebrospinal fluid of individuals with post-treatment Lyme disease syndrome from our Columbia Lyme encephalopathy study contained over six hundred unique proteins not present in the cerebrospinal fluid of individuals with chronic fatigue syndrome, demonstrating for the first time that these similar syndromes have different pathophysiologic profiles.

- Applying metabolomic approaches to the blood of patients with early Lyme disease, a collaborative investigation led to the development of a new diagnostic assay that was shown to be twice as sensitive as the CDC's two-tiered assay (88 percent versus 42 percent) for the detection of early Lyme disease (Molins et al. 2015).

- Applying omics approaches to the study of inflammatory markers ("inflammatomics"), investigators discovered that patients with early Lyme disease had elevated levels of inflammatory markers and acute phase inflammatory reactants (C-reactive protein and serum amyloid A), collectively creating a biosignature that distinguishes patients with acute Lyme disease from normal controls (Soloski et al. 2014).

These important findings—made possible through advances in biotechnology, systems biology, and bioinformatics—demonstrate the power of these new approaches to help improve our understanding and diagnosis of Lyme disease.

This research also demonstrates that progress requires collaboration. Given the extensive expertise in multiple fields required for probing samples, the expense of the biotechnology, and the need for sophisticated bioinformatics to integrate information from very large data sets, collaborations across multiple research centers as well as academic and governmental institutions are needed. The good news is that such collaborations are now increasingly common in the field of Lyme disease.

## IDENTIFICATION OF A NEW TICK-BORNE INFECTION CAUSING SYMPTOMS SIMILAR TO LYME DISEASE

The clinical community has known for a long time that other tick-borne organisms, such as Babesia, Anaplasma, and Erhlichia, cause dangerous diseases. Researchers have reported that 30 percent of ticks in the northeastern United States contain more than one microbe that causes human disease (Tokarz et al. 2010). Powassan virus, for example, has been found in 2 percent of the ticks in certain areas of New York and Connecticut;

this can cause encephalitis with permanent neurologic sequelae and in some cases death. *B. miyamotoi* was identified in ticks over a decade ago, but more recently researchers from Russia and the United States have proven that it can actually cause human disease that looks a lot like Lyme disease (Krause et al. 2013; Gugliotta et al. 2013). After a tick bite, these patients develop fever, headaches, fatigue, and muscle aches. They usually test negative for Lyme disease but respond well to antibiotic therapy. This might help explain why some patients have told us for years that after a tick bite they got a Lyme-like illness, that they tested negative for Lyme disease, but that this tick-related illness responded well to antibiotics. In other words, the patients were right in saying that antibiotics helped and the doctors were right in saying it was not Lyme disease. In this example, science has vindicated both parties and clinical care has been enhanced.

## NEW PREVENTION STRATEGIES

New prevention strategies offer promise of a massive reduction in the incidence of Lyme disease. As described in chapter 10, a new vaccine based on OspC proteins has been shown to be effective against Lyme disease in dogs and is now being modified for testing in humans (Rhodes et al. 2013). A new multivalent OspA vaccine is now being tested in human trials that has the potential to protect against *Borrelia burgdorferi* infection both in the United States and Europe (Plotkin 2016). A bait vaccine has been developed that vaccinates mice such that over time the percentage of ticks infected with *Borrelia* spirochetes is markedly reduced (Gomes-Solecki 2014). And a public health strategy is being explored that genetically modifies mice in the community setting such that they are no longer effective carriers of the *Borrelia* spirochete, thus markedly reducing the likelihood that ticks will acquire *Borrelia* spirochetes when they attach to mice (Esvelt et al. 2014). Fewer infected ticks means fewer people will get Lyme disease after a tick bite.

While it is distressing that tick-borne diseases are spreading throughout the United States, that tick control measures are still inadequate, and that we do not yet have a definitive diagnostic test for Lyme disease that can tell us whether or not infection is still present, these examples demonstrate that there are many reasons to be optimistic.

Research scientists pursue questions that intrigue them, designing studies to test hypotheses based on their pre-set assumptions. It is hard to change rigidly held beliefs, even in the face of mounting evidence that disproves those beliefs. Researchers who for decades had argued that *B. burgdorferi* could not possibly persist are now reconsidering their views. Such a radical paradigm shift—one that is indisputably evidence based—occurs through the convergence of scientific research from a multitude of international investigators.

It is essential that government agencies in the United States and other countries continue to build on the momentum of the past decade and pursue the questions that these new provocative, paradigm-shifting, and exciting research findings have raised. These agencies should set a priority on funding new research studies on persistent organisms, diagnostics, biomarkers, treatment, vaccines, and tick reduction. With the remarkable biotechnology now available to address these areas, the funding needs to be provided so the research can get done.

Physicians need to have better tools to determine why patients have persistent symptoms, they need to have diagnostic tests that identify those patients who still have active infection, and they need to have a broader array of effective treatment strategies from which to choose to help those patients whose lives have been devastated by this illness. These are issues that the patient community has long asked us to address. The medical and scientific communities are finally listening to them.

# GENERIC (BRAND) DRUG NAMES

## ANTIBIOTICS

amoxicillin (Amoxil, Augmentin)
atovaquone (Mepron)
azithromycin (Zithromax)
carbomycin (Geocillin)
cefoperazone (Cefobid)
cefotaxime (Claforan)
cefotiam (Pansporin)
ceftriaxone (Rocephin)
cefuroxime (Zinacef, Ceftin)
ciprofloxacin (Cipro, Ciloxam, Neofloxin)
clarithromycin (Biaxin)
clindamycin (Cleocin, Dalacin, Clinacin)
clofazimine (Lamprene)
daptomycin (Cubicin)
doxycycline (Monodox, Vibramycin, Doryx, Oracea)
erythromycin (Eryc, Erythrocin, Benzamycin)
gentamicin (Gentak, Garamycin)
ketoconazole (Nizoral)
levofloxacin (Levaquin, Tavanic, Iquix)
minocycline (Solodyn Minocin, Minomycin, Akamin)
penicillin
streptomycin
sulfamethoxazole (Gantanol)

tetracycline (Sumycin)
tigecycline (Tygacil)

## OTHER DRUGS

alprazolam (Xanax, Niravam)
amantadine (Symmetrel)
amitriptyline (Elavil, Amitrip, Levate)
atomoxetine (Strattera)
bupropion (Wellbutrin, Zyban)
carbamazepine (Tegretol, Carbatrol, Epitol)
citalopram (Celexa, Cipramil)
clonazepam (Klonopin, Antelepsin, Rivotril)
clonidine (Catapres, Kapvay, Nexiclon)
cyclobenzaprine (Amrix, Fexmid, Flexeril)
cyclophosphamide (Endoxan, Cytoxan, Neosar)
desvenlafaxine (Pristiq, Desfax, Ellefore)
dextroamphetamine (Dexedrine, Metamina, Attentin)
diphenhydramine (Benadryl, Unisom, Sominex)
doxepin (Sinequan, Prudoxin, Zonalon)
duloxetine (Cymbalta)
escitalopram (Lexapro, Cipralex)
eszopiclone (Lunesta)
fludrocortisone (Florinef)
fluoxetine (Prozac, Sarafem, Adofen)
fluvoxamine (Faverin, Fevarin, Floxyfral, Dumyrox, Luvox)
gabapentin (Neurontin)
gamma globulin (Gammagard,Gamunex, gamaSTAN, Gammaplex)
guanfacine (Afken, Estulic, Intuniv, Tenex)
hydrocortisone (Cortef, Solu-Cortef)
hydroxychloroquine (Plaquenil)
isotretinoin (Accutane)
levomilnacipran (Fetzima)
lisdexamfetamine (Tyvense, Elvanse, Venvanse, Vyvanse)

lorazepam (Ativan, Tavor, Temestra)

meptazinol (Meptid)

methotrexate (Trexall, Xatmep, Rheumatrex)

methylphenidate (Ritalin, Concerta, Aptensio, Biphentin)

midodrine (Amatine, ProAmatine, Gutron)

milnacipran (Savella, Ixel, Joncia, Dalcipran)

mirtazapine (Remeron)

modafinil (Provigil, Alertec, Modavigil)

naltrexone (Revia, Vivitrol)

oxycodone (OxyContin, Roxicodone)

paroxetine (Paxil, Seroxat)

prednisone (Deltasone, Rayos, Prednicot, Sterapred)

pregabalin (Lyrica)

quetiapine (Seroquel, Temprolide)

quinine (Qualaquin, Quinate, Quinbisul)

ramelteon (Rozerem)

rituximab (Rituxan, MabThera)

sertraline (Zoloft)

suvorexant (Belsomra)

temazepam (Restoril, Normison, Nortem)

trazodone (Oleptro)

valproate (Convulex, Depakote, Epilim, Stavzor)

venlafaxine (Effexor)

zaleplon (Sonata, Starnoc, Andante)

zolpidem (Ambien)

# GLOSSARY OF TERMS

**Antibody:** Also known as immunoglobulin, the antibody is a protein produced by the immune system to defend against microbes such as spirochetes, other bacteria, and viruses. The antibody binds to a protein (called an "antigen") on the microbe (e.g., on the outer surface of the spirochete) to facilitate killing of the microbe.

**Antigen:** An antigen is a molecule that induces an immune response. The smaller piece of this antigen that is the precise site for antibody binding is called an epitope.

**B. burgdorferi:** The spirochetal bacterium that causes Lyme disease, transmitted by ticks of the *Ixodes* species.

**Centers for Disease Control (CDC):** A U.S. government agency mandated to improve public health through health promotion, disease surveillance, and prevention.

**Cerebrospinal fluid:** The continuously produced watery fluid that flows in the ventricles and around the surface of the brain and spinal cord. A lumbar puncture ("spinal tap") is used to collect cerebrospinal fluid to detect signs of disease or infection.

**Chemokine:** A type of cytokine that guides white blood cells to sites of infection.

**Cross-reactivity:** This occurs when an antibody produced in response to a region on one microbe also binds to similar regions on other microbes. This can cause false positive reactions in antibody-based tests.

**Cytokines:** Hormone-like cell signaling molecules that aid cell-to-cell communication and stimulate the other cells to move toward sites of inflammation, infection, and trauma. Examples include interferon, interleukin, and tumor necrosis factor.

**DNA sequencing:** The method used to determine the precise order of nucleotides within a DNA molecule. DNA sequencing is used in many areas of biology and medicine to identify sequences of individual genes or entire genomes of an organism. It is also used to search for genetic variations and/or mutations that may play a role in the development or progression of a disease. Advances in sequencing technologies (high-throughput or next-generation sequencing) have led to greater speed and lower cost and facilitate not only genome sequencing but also transcriptome profiling (RNA) and epigenomic studies.

**Enzyme-linked immunosorbent assay (ELISA):** A method of detecting and quantifying substances, such as antibodies, in the blood or cerebrospinal fluid. Also referred to as enzyme immunoassay (EIA), this is often the first test for Lyme disease.

**Encephalitis:** Inflammation of the brain. Patients may experience confusion, irritability, hallucinations, spontaneous tearfulness, headaches, fever, weakness, sleep disturbance, and impaired cognition (such as problems with memory, attention, and/or verbal fluency).

**Encephalomyelitis:** Inflammation of the brain and spinal cord. Patients may experience symptoms affecting the brain common to encephalitis as well as signs of spinal cord involvement such as weakness, sensory loss in the legs, and urinary problems. The cerebrospinal fluid typically shows abnormalities such as increased white blood cells. Encephalomyelitis may be triggered or perpetuated by viral or other infections such as spirochetal infection with *B. burgdorferi*.

**Encephalopathy:** A disturbance or disease of the brain. In Lyme disease, this term usually refers to the patient who has developed prominent cognitive problems later in the course of Lyme disease.

***Erythema migrans* (EM):** An expanding rash that is characteristic of Lyme disease, occurring shortly after the tick bite in many but not all patients. Satellite rashes may occur at later points in the illness. Most commonly, the rash is a solid red to pink color and oval or round in shape. While the "bull's eye"—a red rash with central clearing that gradually enlarges—is the most readily recognized EM rash, only 20 percent of EM rashes have this appearance.

**Genomics:** The study of an organism's entire genome. Typically the entire DNA sequence of an organism is mapped, with a particular interest in observing interactions between loci and alleles within the genome. This method is different from standard techniques in molecular biology that focus on identifying the functions of specific genes. More broadly speaking, some researchers consider genomics to refer to the study of all of the genes of a cell or tissue at the level of the genotype (DNA), transcriptome (mRNA), or proteome (protein).

**Herxheimer reaction:** This typically refers to an exacerbation of symptoms or new onset of symptoms shortly after starting antibiotic therapy. This is thought to be due to a flare of the immune system in response to the killing of microbes. This inflammatory reaction usually manifests as an intensification of the patient's existing symptoms. This has been reported in a variety of spirochetal diseases, including syphilis, relapsing fever, and Lyme disease.

**In vitro/in vivo:** "In vitro" studies of microbes refer to the study of microbes outside of their natural biological context. These studies might be conducted in petri dishes or test tubes, for example. This is distinct from "in vivo" studies that take place in the natural context, such as in an animal model of disease or in the human. The distinction between these two approaches to studying disease is important because what occurs in vitro may not be the same as what occurs in vivo. For example, certain outer surface proteins (OSP) are expressed in the lab setting that aren't expressed in the in vivo setting; certain OSP proteins of the *Borrelia* spirochete that are expressed in the human are not expressed when grown in culture in the petri dish. Similarly, certain antibiotics that work in the lab setting against *Borrelia* spirochetes do not work when tested in the animal model or in humans. While helpful and a critical first step in experimental research, in vitro studies have limitations.

***Ixodes* ticks:** "Hard-bodied" ticks that carry microbes (e.g., viruses, bacteria, and protozoan parasites), some of which can be transmitted by the bite of a tick to humans to cause disease. Ticks are considered "vectors" because they transmit infection.

**Lyme borreliosis:** Another term for Lyme disease, commonly used outside of the United States.

**Meningitis:** Inflammation of the meninges surrounding the brain. Patients may experience headaches, light sensitivity, pain when moving the head, nausea, and vomiting. Patients with Lyme disease typically develop this as an early neurologic reaction to infection with *B. burgdorferi*.

**Neuroborreliosis:** This is an alternate term for neurologic Lyme disease. Neuroborreliosis is caused by *B. burgdorferi*. In the United States, neurologic Lyme disease is caused by *B. burgdorferi sensu stricto*, while in Europe the most common cause is *Borrelia garinii*.

**Neuropathy:** Damage to or malfunction of the nerves of the body. One common type affects the peripheral nervous system causing symptoms such as tingling, intense pain, or weakness.

**Neuropsychological testing:** This is not the same as a neuropsychiatric evaluation. A neuropsychiatric evaluation usually refers to an interview conducted by a psychiatrist who asks about mood, medical status, and cognition (sometimes performing a small set of tests of memory and attention in the office). Neuropsychological testing refers to a formal battery of tests of brain functions, such as auditory and visual memory, auditory and visual attention, visual motor performance, intelligence, speed of mental processing, verbal fluency, planning and executive abilities, and mental flexibility. A comprehensive battery, usually performed by a neuropsychologist, may take three to eight hours or more.

**Polymerase chain reaction (PCR):** A test used to detect genetic material (DNA or RNA), such as that of the microbe *B. burgdorferi*. Unlike the ELISA and Western blot tests, which only tell you that the immune system has generated antibodies to the spirochete, the PCR actually identifies pieces of the genetic material of the organism. This test is considered to be a strong indication that *B. burgdorferi* is actually present in the tissue or fluid being examined.

**Post-treatment Lyme Disease Syndrome (PTLDS):** This term describes patients with a history of well-documented Lyme disease who have persistent symptoms despite having been treated with standard duration IDSA-recommended antibiotics for Lyme disease. These symptoms commonly include fatigue, pain, and cognitive problems, start within six months of Lyme disease diagnosis and treatment, and are associated with functional impairment.

**Proteomics:** The use of biotechnology to study the entire array of proteins produced by an organism or system. Protein expression varies depending on both the genes and environmental stressors. In the past, protein expression was studied by mRNA analysis, but because mRNA is not always translated into protein, proteomics has stepped in to confirm the presence and quantity of protein.

**Radiculoneuropathy:** A disturbance in the nerve that may cause shooting pain, numbness, or tingling in the distribution of a nerve root. It emanates from the spinal cord. "Sciatica" is a good example of radicular pain in that it starts from the spinal cord and shoots down the leg.

**Serologic test:** A blood test that detects antibodies against microbes.

**Seronegativity:** This refers to the situation in which an individual is infected with a microbe but the blood tests are negative; they fail to indicate current infection. Some patients may in fact test negative because they are being tested too soon after the tick bite or because they have been treated with antibiotics that diminish the immune response.

**Spirochete:** A helical-shaped bacteria; for example, *B. burgdorferi*, the bacterium that causes Lyme disease.

**Systems biology:** Because the human body is complex and because certain illnesses (like Lyme disease) affect the body diffusely, studies that focus on just one aspect of the organism or disease process may not yield sufficient information to change the course of disease. Systems biology views the body as a system composed of an interacting network of genes, proteins, and biochemical reactions. The immune response to fight infections, for example, does not arise from a single protein or gene, but rather is the finely tuned interaction between the external environment and the individual's genes, proteins, and biochemical mechanisms. Systems biologists therefore focus on the individual components and the interactions among them to help understand health and disease.

**Vasculitis:** Inflammation of the blood vessels. Many diseases can cause a vasculitis, such as lupus, syphilis, cocaine abuse, Lyme disease, and primary angiitis of the central nervous system.

**Vectors:** A vector is an organism (such as a mosquito or tick) that does not cause disease itself but which spreads infection by conveying pathogens from one host to another.

**Western blot (immunoblot):** A method of detecting which antibodies are present in a serum sample; it is often ordered as the second test after the ELISA for Lyme disease.

**Xenodiagnosis:** A diagnostic method that is used to enhance the detection of microbes. In Lyme disease research this refers to allowing an uninfected laboratory-raised tick to feed on an infected animal and then examining the previously uninfected tick (e.g., by PCR or culture) for the presence of *B. burgdorferi* that it may have ingested during its blood meal.

# REFERENCES

Ackermann, R., E. Gollmer, and B. Rehse-Küpper. 1985. "Progressive *Borrelia* Encephalomyelitis: Chronic Manifestation of Erythema Chronicum Migrans Disease of the Nervous System." *Dtsch Med Wochenschr.* 110, no. 26: 1039–42.

Adelson, M. E., R. V. Rao, R. C. Tilton, K. Cabets, E. Eskow, L. Fein, J. L. Occi, and E. Mordechai. 2004. "Prevalence of *B. burgdorferi, Bartonella* spp., *Babesia Microti,* and *Anaplasma Phagocytophila* in Ixodes Scapularis Ticks Collected in Northern New Jersey." *J Clin Microbiol.* 42, no. 6: 2799–801.

Afari Maxwell, E., F. Marmoush, M. U. Rehman, U. Gorsi, and F. J. Yammine. 2016. "Lyme Carditis: An Interesting Trip to Third-Degree Heart Block and Back." *Case Reports in Cardiology.* 5: 1–3.

Afzelius, A. 1921. "Erythema Chronicum Migrans." *Acta Dermato-Venereol.* 2: 120–25.

Aguero-Rosenfeld, M. E., G. Wang, I. Schwartz, and G. P. Wormser. 2005. "Diagnosis of Lyme Borreliosis." *Clin Microbiol Rev.* 18, no. 3: 484–509.

Ajamian, M., M. Cooperstock, G. P. Wormser, S. D. Vernon, and A. Alaedini. 2015. "Anti-Neural Antibody Response in Patients with Post-Treatment Lyme Disease Symptoms versus Those with Myalgic Encephalomyelitis/Chronic Fatigue Syndrome." *Brain Behav Immun.* 48: 354–55.

Alaedini, A. and N. Latov. (2005). "Antibodies against OspA epitopes of Borrelia burgdorferi cross-react with neural tissue." *Journal of Neuroimmunology,* 159, no. 1: 192–195.

Ali, A. "Lyme Disease". In: Integrative Medicine, Fourth Edition. David Rakel, Editor. Philadelphia, Elsevie4, 2018. 218–228.

American Board of Internal Medicine, Consumer Reports. "Dental Fillings that Contain Mercury." Choosing Wisely. Last updated March 2014. http://www.choosingwisely.org/patient-resources/dental-fillings-that-contain-mercury/.

American Psychiatric Association. *Somatic Symptom Disorder. DSM-5.* Last updated in 2013. Available at http://www.dsm5.org/Documents/Somatic Symptom Disorder Fact Sheet. Accessed May 6, 2016.

Anderson, A., H. Bijlmer, P. E. Fournier, S. Graves, J. Hartzell, G. J. Kersh, G. Limonard, T. J. Marrie, and R. F. Massung. "Management of Q Fever—United States, 2013."

*MMWR. Recommendations and Reports: Morbidity and Mortality Weekly Report. Recommendations and Reports/Centers for Disease Control.* 62, no. RR-03: 1–30.

Arnaboldi, P. M. and R. J. Dattwyler. 2015. "Cross-Reactive Epitopes in *Borrelia burgdorferi* p66." *Clin Vaccine Immunol.* 22, no. 7: 840–43.

Arnold, L. M., J. I. Hudson, E. V. Hess, A. E. Ware, D. A. Fritz, M. B. Auchenbach, L. O. Starck, and P. E. Keck Jr. 2004. "Family Study of Fibromyalgia." *Arthritis Rheum.* 50, no. 3: 944–52.

Arvikar, S. L., J. T. Crowley, K. B. Sulka, and A. C. Steere. 2017. "Autoimmune Arthritides, Rheumatoid Arthritis, Psoriatic Arthritis, or Peripheral Spondyloarthritis Following Lyme Disease." *Arthritis Rheumatol.* 69, no. 1: 194–202.

Arvikar, S. L. and Steere, A. C. 2015. "Diagnosis and Treatment of Lyme Arthritis." *Infec Dis Clin North Am.* 29, no. 2: 269–80.

Aucott, J. N., L. A. Crowder, and K. B. Kortte. 2013. "Development of a Foundation for a Case Definition of Post-Treatment Lyme Disease Syndrome." *Int J Infect Dis.* 17: 443–49.

Aucott, J. N., A. W. Rebman, L. A. Crowder, and K. B. Kortte. 2013. "Post-Treatment Lyme Disease Syndrome Symptomatology and the Impact on Life Functioning: Is There Something Here?" *Quality of Life Research.* 22: 75–84.

Auwaerter, P. G., J. S. Bakken, R. J. Dattwyler, J. S. Dumler, J. J. Halperin, E. McSweegan, R. B. Nadelman, S. O'Connell, E. D. Shapiro, S. K. Sood, A. C. Steere, A. Weinstein, and G. P. Wormser. 2011, September. "Antiscience and Ethical Concerns Associated with Advocacy of Lyme Disease." *Lancet Infect Dis.* 11, no. 9: 713–19.

Bacon, R. M., B. J. Biggerstaff, M. E. Schriefer, R. D. Gilmore Jr., M.T. Philipp, A. C. Steere, G. P. Wormser, A. R. Marques, and B. J. Johnson. 2003. "Serodiagnosis of Lyme Disease by Kinetic Enzyme-Linked Immunosorbent Assay Using Recombinant VlsE1 or Peptide Antigens of *B. burgdorferi* Compared with 2-Tiered Testing Using Whole-Cell Lysates." *J Infect Dis.* 187, no. 8: 1187–99.

Bakken, J. S., and S. Dumler. 2008. "Human Granulocytic Anaplasmosis." *Infect Dis Clin North Am.* 22, no. 3: 433–48, viii.

Balakrishnan, N., M. Ericson, R. Maggi, and E. B. Breitschwerdt. 2016, May. "Vasculitis, Cerebral Infarction and Persistent *Bartonella henselae* Infection in a Child." *Parasit Vectors.* 9, no. 1: 254. http://doi.org/10.1186/s13071-016-1547-9.

Bamunuarachchi, G. S., W. D. Ratnasooriya, S. Premakumara, and P. V. Udagama. 2013. "Antimalarial Properties of Artemisia Vulgaris L. Ethanolic Leaf Extract in a Plasmodium Berghei Murine Malaria Model." *J Vector Borne Dis.* 50, no. 4: 278–84.

Banerjee, R., J. J. Liu, H. M. Minhas. 2013. "Lyme Neuroborreliosis Presenting with Alexithymia and Suicide Attempts." *J Clin Psychiatry.* 74, no. 10: 981.

Bannwarth, A. 1941. "Chronische Lymphocytäre Meningitis, Entzündliche Polyneuritis und Rheumatismus." *Archive für psychiatrie und Nervenkrankheiten.* 113: 284–376.

Barbour AG. Lyme Disease. 1st edition, 1996. 2nd edition, 2015. Johns Hopkins University Press.

Barr, W. B., R. Rastogi, L. Ravdin, and E. Hilton. 1999. "Relations among Indexes of Memory Disturbance and Depression in Patients with Lyme Borreliosis." *Applied Neuropsychology* 6: 12–18.

Barthold, S. 2012. "Persistence of Non-Cultivable *Borrelia burgdorferi* Following Antibiotic Treatment." In *Global Challenges in Diagnosing and Managing Lyme Disease—Closing Knowledge Gaps: Hearing before the Subcommittee on Africa, Global Health, and Human Rights of the Committee on Foreign Affairs House of Representatives,* 112 Cong., 2nd sess., July 17, Serial No. 112-169: 10–23.

Barthold, S. W., E. Hodzic, D. M. Imai, S. Feng, X. Yang, and B. J. Luft. 2010, February. "Ineffectiveness of Tigecycline against Persistent Borrelia burgdorferi." *Antimicrob Agents Chemother.* 54, no. 2: 643–51.

Batheja, S., J. Nields, A. Landa, and B. A. Fallon. 2013. "Post-Treatment Lyme Syndrome and Central Sensitization." *J Neuropsychiatry Clin Neuroscience.* 25: 176–86.

Bechtold, K. T., A. W. Rebman, L. A. Crowder, D. Johnson-Greene, and J. N. Aucott. 2017. "Standardized Symptom Measurement of Individuals with Early Lyme Disease Over Time." *Arch Clin Neuropsychol.* 32, no. 2: 129–141.

Belongia, E. A., K. D. Reed, P. D. Mitchell, P. H. Chyou, N. Mueller-Rizner, M. F. Finkel, and M. E. Schriefer. 1999. "Clinical and Epidemiological Features of Early Lyme Disease and Human Granulocytic Ehrlichiosis in Wisconsin." *Clin Infec Dis* 29: 1472–77.

Benach, J. L., F. M. Bosler, J. P. Hanrahan,, J. L. Coleman, G. S. Habicht, T. F. Bast, D. J. Cameron, J. L. Ziegler, A. G. Barbour, W. Burgdorfer, R. Edelman, and R. A. Kaslow. 1983. "Spirochetes Isolated from the Blood of Two Patients with Lyme Disease." *N Engl J Med.* 308, no. 13: 740–42.

Berende, A., H. J. ter Hofstede, F. J. Vos, H. van Middendorp, M. L. Vogelaar, M. Tromp, F. H. van den Hoogen, A. R. Donders, A. W. Evers, and B. J. Kullberg. 2016, March. "Randomized Trial of Longer-Term Therapy for Symptoms Attributed to Lyme Disease." *N Engl J Med.* 374, no. 13: 1209–20.

Berghoff, W. 2012. "Chronic Lyme Disease and Co-Infections: Differential Diagnosis." *Open Neurol J.* 6: 158–78.

Bertholon, P., C. Cazoria, A. Carricajo, A. Oletski, and B. Laurent. 2012. "Bilateral Sensorineural Hearing Loss and Cerebellar Ataxia in the Case of Late Stage Lyme Disease." *Braz J Otorhinolaryngol.* 78, no. 6: 124.

Biesiekierski, J. R., E. D. Newnham, P. M. Irving, J. S. Barrett, M. Haines, J. D. Doecke, S. J. Shepherd, J. G. Muir, and P. R. Gibson. 2011. "Gluten Causes Gastrointestinal Symptoms in Subjects without Celiac Disease: A Double-Blind Randomized Placebo-Controlled Trial." *Am J Gastroenterol.* 106, no. 3: 508–14.

Biggs, H. M., C. B. Behravesh, K. K. Bradley, F. S. Dahlgren, N. A. Drexler, J. S. Dumler, S. M. Folk, C. Y. Kato, R. R. Lash, M. L. Levin, R. F. Massung, R. B. Nadelman, W. L. Nicholson, C. D. Paddock, B. S. Pritt, and M. S. Traeger. 2016, May 13. "Diagnosis and Management of Tickborne Rickettsial Diseases: Rocky Mountain Spotted Fever and Other Spotted Fever Group Rickettsioses, Ehrlichioses, and Anaplasmosis—United States. A Practical Guide for Health Care and Public Health Professionals. Recommendations and Reports." *MMWR.* 65, no. 2: 1–44.

Blanc, F., N. Philippi, B. Cretin, C. Kleitz, L. Berly, B. Jung, S. Kremer, I. J. Namer, F. Sellal, B. Jaulhac, and J. de Seze. 2014. "Lyme Neuroborreliosis and Dementia." *J Alzheimers Dis.* 41, no. 4: 1087–93.

Block, K. E., Z. Zheng, A. L. Dent, B. L. Kee, and H. Huang. 2016. "Gut Microbiota Regulates K/BxN Autoimmune Arthritis through Follicular Helper T but Not Th17 Cells." *J Immunol.* 196, no. 4: 1550–57.

Bloom, B. J., P. M. Wyckoff, H. C. Meissner, and A. C. Steere. 1998. "Neurocognitive Abnormalities in Children After Classic Manifestations of Lyme Disease." *Pediatr Infect Dis J.* 17, no. 3: 189–96.

Bockenstedt, L. K., D. G. Gonzalez, A. M. Haberman, and A. A. Belperron. 2012. "Spirochete Antigens Persist Near Cartilage After Murine Lyme Borreliosis Therapy." *J Clin Invest.* 122, no. 7: 2652–60.

Bockenstedt, L. K., J. Mao, E. Hodzic, S. W. Barthold, and D. Fish. 2002. "Detection of Attenuated, Noninfectious Spirochetes in *B. burgdorferi*-Infected Mice After Antibiotic Treatment." *J Infect Dis.* 186, no. 10: 1430–47.

Borde, J. P., S. Meier, V. Fingerle, C. Klier, J. Hübner, and V. K. Winfried. 2012. "CXCL 13 May Improve Diagnosis In Early Neuroborreliosis with Atypical Laboratory Findings." *BMC Infect Dis.* 2012; 12: 344.

Borovikova, L. V., S. Ivanova, M. Zhang, H. Yang, G. I. Botchkina, L. R. Watkins, H. Wang, N. Abumrad, J. W. Eaton, K. J. Tracey. 2000. "Vagus Nerve Stimulation Attenuates the Systemic Inflammatory Response to Endotoxin." *Nature.* 405, no. 6785: 458–62.

Branda, J. A., M. E. Aguero-Rosenfeld, M. J. Ferraro, B. J. Johnson, G. P. Wormser, and A. C. Steere. 2010. "2-Tiered Antibody Testing for Early and Late Lyme Disease Using only an Immunoglobulin G Blot with the Addition of a VlsE Band as the Second-Tier Test." *Clin Infect Dis.* 50, no. 1: 20–26.

Branda, J. A. and E. S. Rosenberg. 2013. "*Borrelia* Miyamotoi: A Lesson in Disease Discovery." *Ann Intern Med.* 159, no. 1: 61–62.

Bransfield, R. C. 2012. "The Psychoimmunology of Lyme/Tick-Borne Diseases and Its Association with Neuropsychiatric Symptoms." *Open Neurol J.* 6: 88–93.

Bravo, J. A., P. Forsythe, M. V. Chew, E. Escaravage, H. M. Savignac, T. G. Dinan, J. Bienenstock, and J.F. Cryan. 2011. "Ingestion of Lactobacillus Strain Regulates Emotional Behavior and Central GABA Receptor Expression in a Mouse via the Vagus Nerve." *Proc Natl Acad Sci USA.* 108, no. 38: 16050–55.

Breitschwerdt, E. B. 2014. "Bartonellosis: One Health Perspectives for an Emerging Infectious Disease." *ILAR Journal.* 55, no. 1: 46–58.

Brorson, Ø, S.H. Brorson, J. Scythes, J, MacAllister, A. Wier, and L. Margulis L. 2009. "Destruction of Spirochete *Borrelia burgdorferi* Round-Body Propagules (RBs) by the Antibiotic Tigecycline." *Proc Natl Acad Sci USA.* 106, no. 44: 18656–661.

Brunoni, A. R., A. Chaimani, A. H. Moffa, L. B. Razza, W. F. Gattaz, Z. J. Daskalakis, and A. F. Carvalho. 2016, December 28. "Repetitive Transcranial Magnetic Stimulation for the Acute Treatment of Major Depressive Episodes: A Systematic Review with Network Meta-Analysis." *JAMA Psychiatry.* (Epub ahead of print).

Burgdorfer, W., A. G. Barbour, S. F. Hayes, J. L. Benach, E. Grunwaldt, and J. P. Davis. 1982. "Lyme Disease-a Tick-Borne Spirochetosis?" *Science.* Jun 18; 216: 1317–19.

Burkitt, T. R., M. E. Schriefer, and S. A. Larsen. 1997. "Cross-Reactivity to *B. burgdorferi* Proteins in Serum Samples from Residents of a Tropical Country Nonendemic for Lyme Disease." *J Infect Dis.* 175, no. 2: 466–69.

Burton, E., C. Campbell, M. Robinson, S. Bounds, L. Buenaver, and M. Smith. 2016. "Sleep Mediates the Relationship between Central Sensitization and Clinical Pain." *The Journal of Pain.* 17, no. 4: S56.

Busch, A. J., K. A. Barber, T. J. Overend, P. M. Peloso, and C. L. Schachter. 2007. "Exercise for Treating Fibromyalgia Syndrome." *Cochrane Database Syst Rev.* Oct 17, no. 4: CD003786.

Cadavid, D., P. G. Auwaerter, J. Rumbaugh, and H. Gelderblom. 2016. "Antibiotics for the Neurological Complications of Lyme Disease." *Cochrane Database Syst Rev.* 12: CD006978. doi: 10.1002/14651858.CD006978.pub2.

Callaway, E. 2012. "Iceman's DNA Reveals Health Risks and Relations." *Nature.* doi:10.1038/nature.2012/10130.

Callister, S. M., D. A. Jobe, A. Stuparic-Stancic, M. Miyamasu, J. Boyle, R. J. Dattwyler, and P. M. Arnaboli. 2016. "Detection of IFN-γ Secretion by T Cells Collected Before and After Successful Treatment of Early Lyme Disease." *Clin Infect Dis* 62, no. 10: 1235–41.

Cameron, D. J., L. B. Johnson, and E. L. Maloney. 2014. "Evidence Assessments and Guideline Recommendations in Lyme Disease: The Clinical Management of Known Tick Bites, Erythema Migrans Rashes and Persistent Disease." *Expert Review of Anti-Infective Therapy.* 12: 1103–35.

"Case 29-1984 — A 21-Year-Old Man with Headache, Fever, and Facial Diplegia." 1984. *N Engl J Med.* 11: 172–181.

Charlton, N. and K. L. Wallace. 2010. "American College of Medical Toxicology Position Statement on Post-Chelator Challenge Urinary Metal Testing. *J Med Toxicol.* 6, no.1: 74-5.

Centers for Disease Control and Prevention (CDC). 1995. "Recommendations for Test Performance and Interpretation from the Second National Conference on Serologic Diagnosis of Lyme Disease." *Morb Mortal Wkly Rep.* 44, no. 31: 590–91.

——. "Chronic Fatigue Syndrome (CFS)." http://www.cdc.gov/cfs/general/index.html.

——. "Lyme Disease." http://www.cdc.gov/lyme.

——. "Q Fever." http://www.cdc.gov/qfever/.

——. "Rocky Mountain Spotted Fever (RMSF)." http://www.cdc.gov/rmsf/.

——. "Southern Tick-Associated Rash Illness." http://www.cdc.gov/stari/.

——. "Tick-Borne Relapsing Fever." http://www.cdc.gov/relapsing-fever/.

——. "Can Lyme Disease Be Transmitted Sexually?" https://www.cdc.gov/lyme/faq/.

Celik, T., U. Celik, M. Komur, O. Tolunay, C. Donmezer, and D. Yildizdas. 2016. "Treatment of Lyme Neuroborreliosis with Plasmapheresis." *J Clin Apher.* 31: 476–78.

Chandra, A., N. Latov, G. P. Wormser, A. R. Marques, and A. Alaedini. 2011. "Epitope Mapping of Antibodies to VlsE Protein of *Borrelia burgdorferi* in Post-Lyme Disease Syndrome." *Clin Immunol.* 141, no. 1: 103–10.

Chandra, A., G. P. Wormser, M. S. Klempner, R. P. Trevino, M. K. Crow, N. Latov, and A. Alaedini. 2010. "Anti-Neural Antibody Reactivity in Patients with a History of Lyme Borreliosis and Persistent Symptoms." *Brain Behav Immun.* 24, no. 6: 1018–24.

Chapin, H., E. Bagarinao, and S. Mackey. 2012. "Real-Time fMRI Applied to Pain Management." *Neurosci Lett.* 520, no. 2: 174–81.

Chen, L. F. and D. J. Sexton. 2008. "What's New in Rocky Mountain Spotted Fever?" *Infect Dis North Am.* 22, no. 3: 415–32.

Cheung, C. S. F., K. W. Anderson, K. Y. V. Benitez, M. J. Soloski, J. N. Aucott, K. W. Phinney, and I. V. Turko. 2015. "Quantification of *Borrelia burgdorferi* Membrane Proteins in Human Serum Is a New Concept for Detection of Bacterial Infection." *Anal Chem.* 87, no. 22: 11383–88.

Clauw, D. J. 2014. "Fibromyalgia: A Clinical Review." *JAMA.* 311, no. 15: 1547–55.

Commins, S. P., and T. A. E. Platts-Mills. 2013. "Delayed Anaphylaxis to Red Meat in Patients with IgE Specific for Galactose Alpha-1,3-Galactose." *Curr Allerg Asthma Rep.* 13: 72–77.

Cotté, V., S. Bonnet, D. Le Rhun, E. Le Naour, A. Chauvin, H. J. Boulouis, B. Lecuelle, T. Lilin, and M. Vayssier-Taussat. 2008, July. "Transmission of *Bartonella henselae* by Ixodes Ricinus." *Emerg Infect Dis.* 14, no. 7: 1074–80.

Coyle, P. K., S. E. Schutzer, Z. Deng, L. B. Krupp, A. L. Belman, J. L. Benach, and B. J. Luft. 1995. "Detection of *B. burgdorferi*-Specific Antigen in Antibody-Negative Cerebrospinal Fluid in Neurologic Lyme Disease." *Neurology.* 45: 2010–15.

Cross, R., C. Ling, N. P. J. Day, R. McGready, and D. H. Paris. 2016. "Revisiting Doxycycline in Pregnancy and Early Childhood—Time to Rebuild Its Reputation?" *Expert Opinion on Drug Safety.* 15: 367–82.

Crumeyrolle-Arias, M., M. Jaglin, A. Bruneau, S. Vancassel, A. Cardona, V. Daugé, L. Naudon, and S. Rabot. 2014. "Absence of the Gut Microbiota Enhances Anxiety-Like Behavior and Neuroendocrine Response to Acute Stress in Rats." *Psychoneuroendocrinology.* 42: 207–17.

Cryan, J. F. and T. G. Dinan. 2012. "Mind-Altering Microorganisms: The Impact of the Gut Microbiota on Brain and Behaviour." *Nat Rev Neurosci.* 13, no. 10: 701–12.

Cudkowicz, M. E., S. Titus, M. Kearney, H. Yu, A. Sherman, D. Schoenfeld, D. Hayden, A. Shui, B. Brooks, R. Conwit, D. Felsenstein, D. J. Greenblatt, M. Keroack, J. T. Kissel, R. Miller, J. Rosenfeld, J. D. Rothstein, E. Simpson, N. Tolkoff-Rubin, L. Zinman, and J. M. Shefner. 2014. "Safety and Efficacy of Ceftriaxone for Amyotrophic Lateral Sclerosis: A Multi-Stage, Randomised, Double-Blind, Placebo-Controlled Trial." *Lancet Neurol.* 13, no. 11: 1083–91.

Cunha, B. A. 2013, January 31. "Rocky Mountain Spotted Fever." Retrieved August 13, 2013. emedicine.com.

Cunha, B. A., Mickail, N., and Laguerre, M. 2012. "Babesiosis Mimicking Epstein Barr Virus (EBV) Infectious Mononucleosis: Another Cause of False Positive Monospot Tests." *J Infect.* 64, no. 5: 531–32.

Daniels, T. J., D. Fish, and I. Schwartz. 1993. "Reduced Abundance of Ixodes Scapularis (Acari: Ixodidae) and Lyme Disease Risk by Deer Exclusion." *J Med Entomol.* 30, no. 6: 1043–49.

Dantzer, R. 2009. "Cytokine, Sickness Behavior, and Depression." *Immunol Allergy Clin North Am.* 29, no. 2: 247–64.

Dantzer, R., J. C. O'Connor, G. G. Freund, R. W. Johnson, and K. W. Kelley. 2008, January. "From Inflammation to Sickness and Depression: When the Immune System Subjugates the Brain." *Nat Rev Neurosci.* 9, no. 1: 46–56.

Darbinyan, V., A. Kteyan, A. Panossian, E. Gabrielian, G. Wikman, and H. Wagner. 2000. "Rhodiola Rosea in Stress Induced Fatigue–a Double Blind Cross-over Study of a Standardized Extract SHR-5 with a Repeated Low-Dose Regimen on the Mental Performance of Healthy Physicians During Night Duty." *Phytomedicine.* 7, no. 5: 365–71.

Dattwyler, R. J., and J. J. Halperin. 1987. "Failure of Tetracycline Therapy in Early Lyme Disease." *Arth and Rheum.* 30: 448–51.

Dattwyler, R. J., J. J. Halperin, H. Pass, and B. J. Luft. 1987. "Ceftriaxone as Effective Therapy in Refractory Lyme Disease." *J Infect. Dis.* 155: 1322–25.

Dattwyler, R. J., J. J. Halperin, D. J. Volkman, and B. J. Luft. 1988. "Treatment of Late Lyme Borreliosis—Randomized Comparison of Ceftriaxone and Penicillin." *Lancet* 1, no. 8596: 1191–94.

Dattwyler, R. J., D. J. Volkman, S. M. Conaty, S. P. Platkin, and B. J. Luft. 1990. "Amoxicillin Plus Probenecid versus Doxycycline for Treatment of Erythema Migrans Borreliosis." *Lancet* 336: 1404–6.

Dattwyler, R. J., D. J. Volkman, B. J. Luft, J. J. Halperin, J. Thomas, and M. G. Golightly. 1988. "Seronegative Lyme Disease. Dissociation of Specific T- and B-Lymphocyte Response to *B. burgdorferi*." *N Engl J Med.* 319: 1441–46.

De la Fuente-Fernandez, R., T.J. Ruth, V. Sossi, M. Schulzer, D. B. Calne, and A. J. Stoessl. 2001. "Expectation and Dopamine Release: Mechanism of the Placebo Effect in Parkinson's Disease." *Science.* 293, no. 5532: 1164–66.

Delong, A. K., B. Blossom, E. L. Maloney, and S. E. Phillips. 2012. "Antibiotic Retreatment of Lyme Disease in Patients with Persistent Symptoms: A Biostatistical Review of Randomized, Placebo-Controlled, Clinical Trials." *Contemp Clin Trials.* 33, no. 6: 1132–42.

Dennis, D. T., T. S. Nekomoto, J. C. Victor, W. S. Paul, and J. Piesman. 1998. "Reported Distribution of Ixodes Scapularis and Ixodes Pacificus (Acari: Ixodidae) in the United States." *J Med Entomol.* 35: 629–38.

Dersch, R., H. Sommer, S. Rauer, and J. J. Meerpohl. 2016. "Prevalence and Spectrum of Residual Symptoms in Lyme Neuroborreliosis after Pharmacological Treatment: A Systematic Review." *J Neurol.* 263, no. 1: 17–24.

Des Vignes, F., J. Piesman, R. Heffernan, T. L. Schulze, K. C. Stafford III, and D. Fish. 2001. "Effect of Tick Removal on Transmission of Borrelia Burgdorferi and Ehrlichia Phagocytophila By Ixodes Scapularis Nymphs." *J Infectious Disease.* 183: 773–78.

Dhand, A., R. B. Nadelman, M. Aguero-Rosenfeld, F. A. Haddad, D. P. Stokes, and H. W. Horowitz. 2007. "Human Granulocytic Anaplasmosis During Pregnancy: Case Series and Literature Review." *Clin Infect Dis.* 45, no. 5: 589–93.

Dlesk, A., S. K. Broste, P. G. Harkins, P. A. McCarty, and P. D. Mitchell. 1989. "Lyme Seropositivity and Pregnancy Outcome in the Absence of Symptoms of Lyme Disease." *Arthritis Rheum.* 32 (Suppl): S46.

Doherty-Torstrick, E. R., K. E. Walton, and B. A. Fallon. 2016. "Cyberchondria: Parsing Health Anxiety from Online Behavior." *Psychosomatics.* 57, no. 4: 390–400.

Donta, S.T. 2003. "Macrolide Therapy of Chronic Lyme Disease." *Med Sci Monit.* 9, no. 11: Pl136–42.

Doron, S and D. R. Snydman. 2015. "Risk and Safety of Probiotics." *Clin Infec Dis.* 60, Suppl. 2: S129–34.

Dranovsky, A. and R. Hen. 2006. "Hippocampal Neurogenesis: Regulation by Stress and Antidepressants." *Biol Psychiatry.* no. 59: 1135–43.

Dressler, F., J. A. Whalen, B. N. Reinhardt, and A. C. Steere. 1993. "Western Blotting in the Serodiagnosis of Lyme Disease." *J Infect Dis.* 167: 392–400.

Dumler, J. S., A. F. Barbet, C. P. Bekker, G. A. Dasch, G. H. Palmer, S. C. Ray, Y. Rikihisa, and F. R. Rurangirwa. 2001. "Reorganization of Genera in the Families Rickettsiaceae and Anaplasmataceae in the Order Rickettsiales: Unification of Some Species of Ehrlichia with Anaplasma, Cowdria with Ehrlichia and Ehrlichia with Neorickettsia, Descriptions of Six New Species Combinations and Designation of Ehrlichia Equi and 'HGE Agent' as Subjective Synonyms of Ehrlichia Phagocytophila." *Int J Syst Evol Microbiol.* 51, pt. 6: 2145–65.

Dumler, J. S., J. E. Madigan, N. Pusterla, and J. S. Bakken. 2007. "Ehrlichioses in Humans: Epidemiology, Clinical Presentation, Diagnosis, and Treatment." *Clin Infect Dis.* 45, Suppl 1: S45–51.

Dworkin, M. S., T. G. Schwan, D. E. Anderson Jr., and S. M. Borchardt. 2008. "Tick-Borne Relapsing Fever." *Infect Dis Clin North Am.* 22, no. 3: 449–68.

Dworkin, M. S., P. C. Shoemaker, C. L. Fritz, M. E. Dowell, and D. E. Anderson Jr. 2002. "The Epidemiology of Tick-Borne Relapsing Fever in the United States." *Am J Trop Med Hyg.* 66, no. 6: 753–58.

Earnhart, C. G. and R. T. Marconi. 2007. "An Octavalent Lyme Disease Vaccine Induces Antibodies that Recognize All Incorporated OspC Type-Specific Sequences." *Hum Vaccin.* 3, no. 6: 281–89.

Ebel, G. D. 2010. "Update on Pawassan Virus: Emergency of a North American Tick-Borne Flavivirus." *Annu Rev Entomol.* 55: 95–110.

Ebel, G. D., I. Foppa, A. Spielman, and S. R. Telford. 1999. "A Focus of Deer Tick Virus Transmission in the Northcentral United States." *Emerging Infectious Diseases.* 5, no. 4: 570–74.

Edlow, J. A. and D. C. Mcgillicuddy. 2008. "Tick Paralysis." *Infect Dis Clin North Am.* 22, no. 3: 397–413.

Edlow, J. A. 2004. *Bull's Eye: Unraveling the Medical Mystery of Lyme Disease.* New Haven: Yale University Press. 2nd edition.

Eikeland, R., U. Liøstad, A. Mygland, K. Herlofson, G. C. Løhaugen. 2012. "European Neuroborreliosis: Neuropsychological Findings 30 Months Post-Treatment." *Eur J Neurol.* 19, no. 3: 480–7.

Eikeland, R., A. Mygland, K. Herlofson, and U. Liøstad. 2011. "European Neuroborreliosis: Quality of Life 30 Months after Treatment." *Acta Neurol Scand.* 124, no. 5: 349–54.

Eikeland, R., A. Mygland, K. Herlofson, and U. Liøstad. 2013. "Risk Factors for a Non-Favorable Outcome after Treated European Neuroborreliosis. *Acta Neurol Scand.* 127, no. 3: 154–60.

Eisen, R. J., L. Eisen, and C. B. Beard. 2016. "County-Scale Distribution of *Ixodes Scapularis* and *Ixodes Pacificus* (Acari: Ixodidae) in the Continental United States." *J Medical Entomology.* 53, no. 2: 349–86.

Elkins, L. E., D. A. Pollina, S. R. Scheffer, and L. B. Krupp. 1999. "Psychological States and Neuropsychological Performances in Chronic Lyme Disease." *Appl Neuropsychol.* 6, no. 1: 19–26.

Elsner, R. A., C. J. Hastey, K. J. Olsen, and N. Baumgarth. 2015. "Suppression of Long-Lived Immunity Following *Borrelia burgdorferi* Induced Lyme Disease." *PLoS Pathog.* 11, no. 7: e1004976.

Embers, M. E., S. W. Barthold, J. T. Borda, L. Bowers, L. Doyle, E. Hodzic, M. B. Jacobs, N. R. Hasenkampf, D. S. Martin, S. Narasimhan, K. M. Phillippi-Falkenstein, J. E. Purcell, M. S. Ratterree, M. T. Philipp. 2012. "Persistence of *B. burgdorferi* in Rhesus Macaques following Antibiotic Treatment of Disseminated Infection." *PLoS ONE.* 2012; 7, no. 1: e29914.

Eshoo, M. W., C. C. Crowder, A. W. Rebman, M. A. Rounds, H. E. Matthews, J. M. Picuri, M. J. Soloski, D. J. Ecker, S. E. Schutzer, and J. N. Aucott. 2012. "Direct Molecular Detection and Genotyping of *B. burgdorferi* from Whole Blood of Patients with Early Lyme Disease." *PLoS ONE.* 7, no. 5: e36825.

Eskow, E. and R. S. Rao. 2001. "Concurrent Infection of the Central Nervous System by *B. burgdorferi* and *Bartonella henselae*: Evidence for a Novel Tick-Borne Disease Complex." *Arch Neurol.* 58, no. 9: 1357–63.

Estruch, R., E. Ros, J. Salas-Salvadó, M. I. Covas, D. Corella, F. Arós, E. Gómez-Gracia, V. Ruiz-Gutiérrez, M. Fiol, J. Lapetra, R. M. Lamuela-Raventos, L. Serra-Majem, X. Pintó, J. Basora, M. A. Muñoz, J. V. Sorlí, J. A. Martínez, and M. A. Martínez-González; PREDIMED Study Investigators. 2013. "Primary Prevention of Cardiovascular Disease with a Mediterranean Diet." *N Engl J Med.* 368, no. 14: 1279–90.

Esvelt, K. M., A. L. Smidler, F. Catteruccia, and G. M. Church. 2014. "Concerning RNA-Guided Gene Drives for the Alteration of Wild Populations." *eLife* e03401. doi:10.7554/eLife.03401.

Fallon, B. A., H. Bird, C. Hoven, D. Cameron, M. R. Liebowitz, and D. Shaffer. 1994. "Psychiatric Aspects of Lyme Disease in Children and Adolescents: A Community Epidemiologic Study in Westchester, New York." *J Spirochetal & Tick-Borne Diseases.* 1: 98–100.

Fallon, B. A., S. Das, J. J. Plutchok, F. Tager, K. Liegner, and R. Van Heertum. 1997. "Functional Brain Imaging and Neuropsychological Testing in Lyme Disease." *Clinical Infectious Disease.* 25; Suppl 1: S57–63.

Fallon, B. A., J. G. Keilp, K. M. Corbera, E. Petkova, C. B. Britton, E. Dwyer, I. Slavov, J. Cheng, J. Dobkin, D. R. Nelson, and H. A. Sackeim. 2008. "A Randomized, Placebo-Controlled Trial of Repeated IV Antibiotic Therapy for Lyme Encephalopathy." *Neurology.* 70, no. 13: 992–1003.

Fallon, B. A., E. S. Levin, P. J. Schweitzer, and D. Hardesty. 2010, March. "Inflammation and Central Nervous System Lyme Disease." *Neurobiol Dis.* 37, no. 3: 534–41.

Fallon, B. A., R. B. Lipkin, K. M. Corbera, S. Yu, M. S. Nobler, J. G. Keilp, E. Petkova, S. H. Lisanby, J. R. Moeller, I. Slavov, R. Van Heertum, B. D. Mensh, and H. A. Sackeim. 2009. "Regional Cerebral Blood Flow and Metabolic Rate in Persistent Lyme Encephalopathy." *Arch Gen Psychiatry.* 66, no. 5: 554–63.

Fallon, B. A. and J. A. Nields. 1994. "Lyme Disease: A Neuropsychiatric Illness." *American Journal of Psychiatry* 151, no. 11: 1571–83.

Fallon, B. A., J. A. Nields, J. J. Burrascano, K. Liegner, D. DelBene, and M. R. Liebowitz. 1992, Spring. "The Neuropsychiatric Manifestations of Lyme Borreliosis." *Psychiatr Q.* 63, no. 1: 95–117.

Fallon, B. A., J. M. Kochevar, A. Gaito, and J. A. Nields. 1998. "The Underdiagnosis of Neuropsychiatric Lyme Disease in Children and Adults." *Psychiatr Clin North Am.* 21, no. 3: 693–703, viii.

Fallon, B. A., M. Pavlicova, S. W. Coffino, and C. Brenner. 2014. "A Comparison of Lyme Disease Serologic Test Results from 4 Laboratories in Patients with Persistent Symptoms after Antibiotic Treatment." *Clin Infect Dis.* 59, no. 12: 1705–10.

Fallon, B. A., E. Petkova, J. G. Keilp, and C. B. Britton. 2012. "A Reappraisal of the U.S. Clinical Trials of Post-Treatment Lyme Disease Syndrome." *Open Neurol J.* 6: 79–87.

Fallon, B. A., F. Tager, J. Keilp, N. Weiss, M. R. Liebowitz, L. Fein, and K. Liegner. 1999. "Repeated Antibiotic Treatment in Chronic Lyme Disease." *Journal of Spirochetal Diseases.* 6, no. 4: 94–102.

Feng, J., P. G. Auwaerter, and Y. Zhang. 2015 "Drug Combinations against *B. burgdorferi* Persisters in Vitro: Eradication Achieved by Using Daptomycin, Cefoperazone and Doxycycline." *PLoS ONE* 10, no. 3: e0117207.

Feng, J., W. Shi, S. Zhang, D. Sullivan, P. G. Auwaerter, and Y. Zhang. 2016a. "A Drug Combination Screen Identifies Drugs Active against Amoxicillin-Induced Round Bodies of In Vitro *Borrelia burgdorferi* Persisters from an FDA Drug Library." *Front Microbiol.* 7: 743.

Feng J., T. Wang, W. Shi, S. Zhang, Sullivan, P. G. Auwaerter, and Y. Zhang. 2014. "Identification of Novel Activity against *Borrelia burgdorferi* Persisters using an FDA Approved Drug Library." *Emerg Microbes Infect.* 3, no. 7: e49.

Feng, J., S. Zhang, W. Shi, N. Zubcevik, J. Miklossy, and Y. Zhang. 2017. "High Activity of Selective Essential Oils against Stationary Phase *Borrelia burgdorferi* as a Persister Model." *BioRxiv*. (preprint) doi: https://doi.org/10.1101/130898.

Feng, J., S. Zhang, W. Shi, and Y. Zhang. 2016b. "Ceftriaxone Pulse Dosing Fails to Eradicate Biofilm-Like Microcolony *B. burgdorferi* Persisters which are Sterilized by Daptomycin/Doxycycline/Cefuroxime without Pulse Dosing." *Front Microbiol*. 7: 1744.

Ferrucci, R., M. Vergari, F. Cogiamanian, T. Bocci, M. Ciocca, E. Tomasini E, M. De Riz, E. Scarpini, and A. Priori. 2014. "Transcranial Direct Current Stimulation (tDCS) for Fatigue in Multiple Sclerosis." *NeuroRehabilitation*. 34, no. 1: 121–27.

Fonseca, D. M., T. W. Hand, S. J. Han, M. Y. Gerner, A. Glatman Zaretsky, A. L. Byrd, O. J. Harrison, A. M. Ortiz, M. Quinones, G. Trinchieri, J. M. Brenchley, J. F. Brodsky, R. N. Germain, G. J. Randolph, and Y. Belkaid. 2015. "Microbiota-Dependent Sequelae of Acute Infection Compromise Tissue-Specific Immunity." *Cell*. 163, no. 2: 354–66.

Fowler, A., L. Forsman, M. Eriksson, and R. Wickström. 2013. "Tick-Borne Encephalitis Carries a High Risk of Incomplete Recovery in Children." *The Journal of Pediatrics* 163, no. 2: 555–60.

Fraser, C. 1997. "Genomic Sequence of a Lyme Disease Spirochaete, *B. burgdorferi*." *Nature*. 390: 580–86.

Garcia-Monco, J. C., B. F. Villar, J. C. Alen, and J. L. Benach. 1990. "*Borrelia* in the Central Nervous System: Experimental and Clinical Evidence for Early Invasion." *J Infect Dis*. 161: 1187–93.

Garin, C., and C. Bujaudoux. 1922. "Paralysie par les Tiques." *Journal dé Medecine, Lyon*. 7: 765–67.

Garkowski, A., J. Zajkowska, A. Zajkowska, A. Kułakowska, O. Zajkowska, B. Kubas, D. Jurgilewicz, M. Hładuński, U. Łebkowska. 2017. "Cerebrovascular Manifestations of Lyme Neuroborreliosis: A Systematic Review of Published Cases." *Front Neurol*. Apr 20, no. 8: 146. doi: 10.3389/fneur.2017.00146. eCollection 2017.

Goldenberg, J. Z., S. S. Ma, J. D. Saxton, M. R. Martzen, P. O. Vandvik, K. Thorlund, G. H. Guyatt, and B. C. Johnston. 2013. "Probiotics for the Prevention of *Clostridium difficile*-Associated Diarrhea in Adults and Children." *Cochrane Database Syst Rev*. May 31, no. 5: CD006095.

Gomes-Solecki, M. 2014. "Blocking Pathogen Transmission at the Source: Reservoir Targeted OspA-Based Vaccines against *B. burgdorferi*." *Front Cell Infect Microbiol*. 4: 136.

Gorthi, S. P. 2012. "Chronic Inflammatory Demyelinating Polyradiculoneuropathy (CIDP): Current Perspectives." *Medicine Update*. 22: 580–85.

Gow, J. W., S. Hagan, P. Herzyk, C. Cannon, P. O. Behan, and A. Chaudhuri. 2009. "A Gene Signature for Post-Infectious Chronic Fatigue Syndrome." *BMC Med Genomics*. 2: 38.

Gugliotta, J. L., H. K. Goethert, V. P. Berardi, and S. R. Telford III. 2013. "Meningoencephalitis from *Borrelia miyamotoi* in an Immunocompromised Patient." *N Engl J Med*. 368, no. 3: 240–45.

Halperin, J. J., G. P. Kaplan, S. Brazinsky, T. F. Tsai, T. Cheng, A. Ironside, P. Wu, J. Delfiner, M, Golightly, R. H. Brown, R. J. Dattwyler, and B.J. Luft. 1990. "Immuno-logic Reactivity against *B. burgdorferi* in Patients with Motor Neuron Disease." *Arch Neurol.* 47, no. 5: 586–94.

Halperin, J. J., L. B. Krupp, M. G. Golightly, and D. J. Volkman. 1990, September. "Lyme Borreliosis-Associated Encephalopathy." *Neurology.* 40, no. 9: 1340–43.

Hammoud, K. A. 2012, October 17. "Bartonellosis." Retrieved August 13, 2013. emedicine.com.

Hansen, K., J. M. Bangsborg, H. Fjordvang, N. S. Pedersen, and P. Hindersson. 1988. "Immunochemical Characterization of and Isolation of the Gene for a *Borrelia burgdorferi* Immunodominant 60-Kilodalton Antigen Common to a Wide Range of Bacteria." *Infect Immun.* 56, no. 8: 2047–53.

Hansen, K, M. Cruz, and H. Link. 1990. "Oligoclonal *Borrelia burgdorferi*–Specific IgG Antibodies in Cerebrospinal Fluid in Lyme Neuroborreliosis." *J Infec Dis.* 161, no. 6: 1194–202.

Hassett, A. L., D. C. Radvanski, S. Buyske, S. V. Savage, M. Gara, J. I. Escobar, and L. H. Sigal. 2008. "Role of Psychiatric Comorbidity in Chronic Lyme Disease." *Arthritis Care & Research.* 59, no. 12: 1742–49.

Heimlich, H. J. 1990. "Should We Try Malariotherapy for Lyme Disease?" *N Engl J Med.* 322: 1234–35.

Heller, J., G. Holzer, and K. Schimrigk. 1990."Immunological Differentiation between Neuroborreliosis and Multiple Sclerosis." *J Neurol.* 237, no. 8, 465–70.

Hellerstrom, S. 1930. "Erythema Chronicum Migrans Afzelii." *Acta Derm Venereol (Stockh.).* 1: 315–21.

Hellerstrom, S. 1951. "Erythema Chronicum Migrans, Afzelius, with Meningitis." *Acta Derm Venereol.* 31: 227–34.

Hess, A., J. Buchmann, U. K. Zettl, S. Henschel, D. Schlaefke, G. Grau, and R. Benecke. 1999. "*Borrelia burgdorferi* Central Nervous System Infection Presenting as an Organic Schizophrenia-Like Disorder." *Biol Psychiatry.* 45, no. 6: 795.

Hildenbrand, P., D. E. Craven, R. Jones, and P. Nemeskal. 2009. "Lyme Neuroborreliosis: Manifestations of a Rapidly Emerging Zoonosis." *Am J Neuroradiol.* 30, no. 6: 1079–87.

Hodzic, E., S. Feng, and S.W. Barthold. 2013. "Assessment of Transcriptional Activity of *Borrelia burgdorferi* and Host Cytokine Genes During Early and Late Infection in a Mouse Model." *Vector Borne Zoonotic Dis.* 13, no.10: 694–711.

Hodzic, E., S. Feng, K. Holden, K. J. Freet, and S. W. Barthold. 2008. "Persistence of *B. burgdorferi* following Antibiotic Treatment in Mice." *Antimicrob Agents Chemother.* 52, no. 5: 1728–36.

Hodzic, E., D. Imai, S. Feng, and S. W. Barthold. 2014. "Resurgence of Persisting Non-Cultivable *B. burgdorferi* following Antibiotic Treatment in Mice." *PLoS ONE.* 9, no. 1: e86907.

Hollstrom, E. 1951. "Successful Treatment of Erythema Migrans Afzelius." *Acta Derm Venereol (Stockh.).* 31: 235–43.

Hollstrom, E. 1958. "Penicillin Treatment of Erythema Chronicum Migrans Afzelius." *Acta Derm Venereol (Stockh.)*. 38: 285–89.

Holl-Wieden, A., S. Suerbaum, and H. J. Girschick. 2007. "Seronegative Lyme Arthritis." *Rheumatol Int*. 27, no. 11: 1091–93.

Horowitz, H. W., M. E. Aguero-Rosenfeld, D. Holmgren, D. McKenna, I. Schwartz, M. E. Cox, and G. P. Wormser. 2013. "Lyme Disease and Human Granulocytic Anaplasmosis Coinfection: Impact of Case Definition on Coinfection Rates and Illness Severity." *Clin Infect Dis*. 56, no. 1: 93–99.

Hoyo-Becerra, C., J. F. Schlaak, and D.M. Hermann. 2014. "Insights from Interferon-α-Related Depression for the Pathogenesis of Depression Associated with Inflammation." *Brain Behav Immun*. 42: 222–231.

Hughes, R. A. C., P. Bouche, D. R. Cornblath, E. Evers, R. D. M. Hadden, A. Hahn, I. Illa, C. L. Koski, J. M. Leger, E. Nobile-Orazio, J. Pollard, C. Sommer, P. Van den Bergh, P. A. van Doom, and I. N. van Schaik. 2006. "European Federation of Neurological Societies/Peripheral Nerve Society Guideline on Management of Chronic Inflammatory Demyelinating Polyradiculoneuropathy: Report of a Joint Task Force of the European Federation of Neurological Societies and the Peripheral Nerve Society." *European J Neurology*. 13: 326–32.

Hunfeld, K. P., E. Ruzic-Sabljic, D. E. Norris, P. Kraiczy and F. Strle. 2005. "In Vitro Susceptibility Testing of *Borrelia burgdorferi Sensu Lato* Isolates Cultured from Patients with Erythema Migrans Before and After Antimicrobial Chemotherapy. *Antimicrob Agents Chemother*. 49, no. 4: 1294–301.

Ismail, N., K. C. Bloch, and J. W. Mcbride. 2010. "Human Ehrlichiosis and Anaplasmosis." *Clin Lab Med*. 30, no. 1: 261–92.

Jacek, E., B. A. Fallon, A. Chandra, M. K. Crow, G. P. Wormser, and A. Alaedini. 2013. "Increased IFNα Activity and Differential Antibody Response in Patients with a History of Lyme Disease and Persistent Cognitive Deficits." *J Neuroimmunol*. 255, no. 1–2: 85–91.

Jarvis, W. T. "Rife Devices." The National Council Against Health Fraud. http://www.ncahf.org/articles/o-r/rife.html.

Jensen, M. P., S. Hakimian, L. H. Sherlin, and F. Fregni. 2008. "New Insights into Neuromodulatory Approaches for the Treatment of Pain." *J Pain*. 9, no. 3: 193–99.

Jinek, M., K. Chylinski, I. Fonfara, M. Hauer, J. A. Doudna, and E. Charpentier. 2012. "A Programmable Dual-RNA-Guided DNA Endonuclease in Adaptive Bacterial Immunity." *Science*. 337, no. 6096: 816–21.

Joseph, J. T., K. Purtill, S. J. Wong, J. Munoz, A. Teal, S. Madison-Antenucci, H. W. Horowitz, M. E. Aguero-Rosenfeld, J. M. Moore, C. Abramowsky, and G. P. Wormser. 2012. "Vertical Transmission of Babesia microti, United States." *Emerging Infect Dis*. 18, no. 8: 1318–21.

Johnson, B. J., M. A. Pilgard, and T. M. Russell. 2014, March. "Assessment of New Culture Method for Detection of *Borrelia* Species from Serum of Lyme Disease Patients." *J Clin Microbiol*. 52, no. 3: 721–24.

Johnson, L., and R. B. Stricker. 2010, June. "The Infectious Diseases Society of America Lyme Guidelines: A Cautionary Tale about the Development of Clinical Practice Guidelines." *Philos Ethics Humanit Med.* 9, no. 5: 1–17.

——. 2004, August. "Treatment of Lyme Disease: A Medicolegal Assessment." *Expert Rev Anti Infect Ther.* 2, no. 4: 533–57.

Jowett, N., R. A. Gaudin, C. A. Banks, and T. A. Hadlock. 2017. "Steroid Use in Lyme Disease-Associated Facial Palsy Is Associated with Worse Long-Term Outcomes." *Laryngoscope.* 127, no. 6: 1451–1458.

Kalina, P., A. Decker, E. Kornel, and J. J. Halperin. 2005. "Lyme Disease of the Brainstem." *Neuroradiology.* 47, no. 12: 903–7.

Kanjwal, K., B. Karabin, Y. Kanjwal, and B. P. Grubb. 2011. "Postural Orthostatic Tachycardia Syndrome following Lyme Disease." *Cardiol J.* 18, no. 1: 63–66.

Kaplan, R. F. and L. Jones-Woodward. 1997, March. "Lyme Encephalopathy: A Neuropsychological Perspective." *Semin Neurol.* 17, no. 1: 31–37.

Kappelmann, N., G. Lewis, R. Dantzer, P. B. Jones, and G. M. Khandaker. 2016. "Antidepressant Activity of Anti-Cytokine Treatment: A Systematic Review and Meta-Analysis of Clinical Trials of Chronic Inflammatory Conditions." *Mol Psychiatry.* doi: 10.1038/mp.2016.167. (Epub ahead of print).

Karouia, F., K. Peyvan, and A. Pohorille. 2017. "Toward Biotechnology in Space: High-Throughput Instruments for In Situ Biological Research Beyond Earth." *Biotechnol Adv.* S0734–9750, no. 17: 30042–3.

Katon, W. and P. Ciechanowski. 2012, July 3. "Panic Disorder: Epidemiology, Clinical Manifestations, and Diagnosis." Retrieved August 13, 2013. uptodate.com.

Katz, A., and J. M. Berkley. 2009. "Diminished Epidermal Nerve Fiber Density in Patients with Antibodies to Outer Surface Protein A (OspA) of *B. burgdorferi* Improves with Intravenous Immunoglobulin Therapy." *Neurology.* 72, S3: A55.

Keilp, J. G., K. Corbera, I. Slavov, M. J. Taylor, H. A. Sackeim, and B. A. Fallon. 2006, January. "WAIS-III and WMS-III Performance in Chronic Lyme Disease." *J Int Neuropsychol Soc.* 12, no. 1: 119–29.

Keller, A., M. Graefen, M. Ball, M. Matzas, V. Boisguerin, F. Maixner, P. Leidinger, C. Backes, R. Khairat, M. Forster, B. Stade, A. Franke, J. Mayer, J. Spangler, S. McLaughlin, M. Shah, C. Lee, T. T. Harkins, A. Sartori, A. Moreno-Estrada, B. Henn, M. Sikora, O. Semino, J. Chiaroni, S. Rootsi, N. M. Myres, V. M. Cabrera, P. A. Underhill, C. D. Bustamante, E. E. Vigl, M. Samadelli, G. Cipollini, J. Haas, H. Katus, B. D. O'Connor, M. R. Carlson, B. Meder, N. Blin, E. Meese, C. M. Pusch, and A. Zink. 2012. "New Insights into the Tyrolean Iceman's Origin and Phenotype as Inferred by Whole-Genome Sequencing." *Nat Commun.* 3: 698.

Killmaster, L. F. and M. L. Levin. 2016, July. "Isolation and Short-Term Persistence of *Ehrlichia ewingii* in Cell Culture." *Vector Borne Zoonotic Dis.* 16, no. 7: 445–48.

Kilpatrick, H. J., A. M. LaBonte, and K. C. Stafford. 2014. "The Relationship between Deer Density, Tick Abundance, and Human Cases of Lyme Disease in a Residential Community." *J Med Entomol.* 51, no. 4: 777–84.

King, C. and N. Sarvetnick. 2011. "The Incidence of Type-1 Diabetes in NOD Mice is Modulated by Restricted Flora Not Germ Free Conditions." *PLoS ONE.* 6, no 2: e17049.

Klempner, M. S., L.T. Hu, J. Evans, C. H. Schmid, G. M. Johnson, R. P. Trevino, D. Norton, L. Levy, D. Wall, J. McCall, M. Kosinski, and Weinstein A. 2001a. "Two Controlled Trials of Antibiotic Treatment in Patients with Persistent Symptoms and a History of Lyme Disease." *N Engl J Med.* 345, no. 2: 85–92.

Klempner, M. S., P. J. Baker, E. D. Shapiro, A. Marques, R. J. Dattwyler, J. J. Halperin, and G. P. Wormser. 2013. "Treatment Trials for Post-Lyme Disease Symptoms Revisited." *Am J Med.* 126, no. 8: 665–69.

Klempner, M. S., R. Noring, and R. A. Rogers. 1993. "Invasion of Human Skin Fibroblasts by the Lyme Disease Spirochete, *Borrelia burgdorferi.*" *J Infect Dis.* 167, no. 5: 1074–81.

Klempner, M. S., C. H. Schmid, L. Hu, A. C. Steere, G. Johnson, B. McCloud, R. Noring, and A. Weinstein. 2001b. "Intralaboratory Reliability of Serologic and Urine Testing for Lyme Disease." *Am J Med.* 110, no. 3: 217–19.

Kool, M. B., H. van Middendorp, H. R. Boeije, and R. Geenen. 2009. "Understanding the Lack of Understanding: Invalidation from the Perspective of the Patient with Fibromyalgia." *Arthritis Rheum.* 61: 1650–56.

Kool, M. B., H. van Middendorp, M. A. Lumley, J. W. J. Bijlsma, and R. Geenen. 2012. "Social Support and Invalidation by Others Contribute Uniquely to the Understanding of Physical and Mental Health of Patients with Rheumatic Diseases." *J Health Psychology.* 18, no. 1: 86–95.

Koopman, F. A., S. S. Chavan, S. Miliko, S. Grazio, S. Sokolovic, P. R. Schuurman, A. D. Mehta, Y. A. Levine, M. Faltys, R. Zitnik, K. J. Tracey, and P. P. Tak. 2016. "Vagal Nerve Stimulation Inhibits Cytokine Production and Attenuates Disease Severity in Rheumatoid Arthritis." *PNAS* 113, no. 20: 8284–89.

Kowalski, T. J., S. Tata, W. Berth, M. A. Mathiason, and W. A. Agger. 2010. "Antibiotic Treatment Duration and Long-Term Outcomes of Patients with Early Lyme Disease from a Lyme Disease-Hyperendemic Area." *Clin Infect Dis.* 50, no. 4: 512–20.

Kraiczy, P., C. Skerka, M. Kirschfink, P. F. Zipfel, and V. Brade. 2002. "Immune Evasion of *B. burgdorferi*: Insufficient Killing of the Pathogens by Complement and Antibody." *Int J Med Microbiol.* 291, Suppl 33: 141–46.

Krause, P. J., S. Narasimhan, G. P. Wormser, L. Rollend, E. Fikrig, T. Lepore, A. Barbour, and D. Fish. 2013. "Human *Borrelia miyamotoi* Infection in the United States. *N Engl J Med.* 368, no. 3: 291–93.

Krause, P. J., D. Fish, S. Narasimhan, and A. G. Barbour. 2015. "*Borrelia* Miyamotoi Infection in Nature and in Humans." *Clin Microbiol Infect.* 21, no. 7: 631–39.

Krause, P. J., K. McKay, C. A. Thompson, V. K. Sikand, R. Lentz, T. Lepore, L. Closter, D. Christianson, S. R. Telford, D. Persing, J. D. Radolf, and A. Spielman; Deer-Associated Infection Study Group. 2002. "Disease-Specific Diagnosis of Coinfecting Tickborne Zoonoses: Babesiosis, Human Granulocytic Ehrlichiosis, and Lyme Disease." *Clin Infect Dis.* 34, no. 9: 1184–81.

Krause, P. J., S. R. Telford III, A. Spielman, V. Sikand, R. Ryan, D. Christianson, G. Burke, P. Brassard, R. Pollack, J. Peck, and D. H. Persing. 1996. "Concurrent Lyme Disease and Babesiosis: Evidence for Increased Severity and Duration of Illness." *JAMA*. 275: 1657–60.

Krupp, L. B., L. G. Hyman, R. Grimson, P. K. Coyle, P. Melville, S. Ahnn, R. Dattwyler, and B. Chandler. 2003. "Study and Treatment of Post Lyme Disease (STOP-LD): A Randomized Double Masked Clinical Trial." *Neurology*. 60, no. 12: 1923–30.

Kugeler, K. J., R. A. Jordan, T. L. Schulze, K. S. Griffith, and P. S. Mead. 2016. "Will Culling White-Tailed Deer Prevent Lyme Disease?" *Zoonoses Public Health*. 63, no. 5: 337–45.

Kullberg, B. J., A. Berende, and A. W. Evers. 2016. "Longer-Term Therapy for Symptoms Attributed to Lyme Disease." *N Engl J Med* 375, no. 10: 998.

Kumar, M., R. Singh, and M. Rashid. 2016. "Lyme Polyradiculitis Masquerading Guillain-Barre Syndrome." *J Pediatr Neurosci*. 11: 384–85.

Lahey, L. J., M. V. V. Panas, R. Mao, M. Delanoy, J. J. Flanagan, S. R. Binder, A. W. Rebman, J. G. Montoya, M. J. Soloski, A. C. Steere, R. J. Dattwyler, P. M. Arnaboldi, J. N. Aucott, and W. H. and Robinson. 2015. "Development of a Multiantigen Panel for Improved Detection of *B. burgdorferi* Infection in Early Lyme Disease." *J Clin Microbiol*. 53: 3834–41.

Lakos, A., and N. Solymosi. 2010. "Maternal Lyme Borreliosis and Pregnancy Outcome." *Int J Infect Dis*. 14, no. 6: e494–8.

Lam, R. W., A. J. Levitt, R. D. Levitan, M. W. Enns, R. Morehouse, E. E. Michalak, and E. M. Tam. 2006. "The Can-SAD Study: A Randomized Controlled Trial of the Effectiveness of Light Therapy and Fluoxetine in Patients with Winter Seasonal Affective Disorder." *Am J Psychiatry*. 163, no. 5: 805–12.

Landa, A., B. S. Peterson, and B. A. Fallon. 2012, September. "Somatoform Pain: A Developmental Theory and Translational Research Review." *Psychosom Med*. 74, no. 7: 717–27.

Lange, G., M. N. Janal, A. Maniker, J. Fitzgibbons, M. Fobler, D. Cook, and B. H. Natelson. 2011, September. "Safety and Efficacy of Vagus Nerve Stimulation in Fibromyalgia: A Phase I/II Proof of Concept Trial." *Pain Med*. 12, no. 9: 1406–13.

Lantos, P. M., W. A. Charini, G. Medoff, M. H. Moro, D. M. Mushatt, J. Parsonnet, J. W. Sanders, and C. J. Baker. 2010. "Final Report of the Lyme Disease Review Panel of the Infectious Diseases Society of America." *Clin Infect Dis*. 51: 1–5.

Larun, L., K. G. Brurberg, J. Odgaard-Jensen, and J. R. Price. 2016, February 7. "Exercise Therapy for Chronic Fatigue Syndrome." *Cochrane Database Syst Rev*. 2: CD003200. doi: 10.1002/14651858.CD003200.pub4.

Lawrence, C., R. B. Lipton, F. D. Lowy, and P. K. Coyle. 1995. "Seronegative Chronic Relapsing Neuroborreliosis." *Eur Neurol*. 35, no. 2: 113–17.

Lee, M., S. Silverman, H. Hansen, V. B. Patel, and L. Manchikanti. 2011. "A Comprehensive Review of Opioid-Induced Hyperalgesia." *Pain Physician*. 14: 145–61.

Lee, Y. K., J. S. Menezes, Y. Umesaki, and S. K. Mazmanian. 2011. "Proinflammatory T-cell Responses to Gut Microbiota Promote Experimental Autoimmune Encephalomyelitis." *PNAS*. 108, suppl.1: 4615–22.

Li, X., G. A. McHugh, N. Damie, V. K. Sikand, L. Glickstein, and A. C. Steere. 2011. "Burden and Viability of *Borrelia burgdorferi* in Skin and Joints of Patients with Erythema Migrans or Lyme Arthritis." *Arthritis Rheum.* 63, no. 8: 2238–47.

Liang, F. T., A. C. Steere, A. R. Marques, B. J. Johnson, J. N. Miller, and M. T. Philipp. 1999. "Sensitive and Specific Serodiagnosis of Lyme Disease by Enzyme-Linked Immunosorbent Assay with a Peptide Based on an Immunodominant Conserved Region of *B. burgdorferi* vlsE." *J Clin Microbiol.* 37, no. 12: 3990–96.

Liegner, K. 1993. "Lyme Disease: The Sensible Pursuit of Answers." *J Clinical Microbiology.* 31: 1961–63.

Liegner, K. B., P. Duray, M. Agricola, C. Rosenkilde, L. A. Yannuzzi, M. Ziska, R. Tilton, D. Hulinska, J. Hubbard, and B. A. Fallon. 1997. "Lyme Disease and the Clinical Spectrum of Antibiotic Responsive Chronic Meningoencephalitis." *J Spirochetal and Tick-Borne Diseases.* 4: 61–73.

Lindenbaum, J., E. B. Healton, D. G. Savage, J. C. Brust, T. J. Garrett, E. R. Podell, P. D. Marcell, S. P. Stabler, and R. H. Allen. 1988. "Neuropsychiatric Disorders Caused by Cobalamin Deficiency in the Absence of Anemia or Macrocytosis." *N Engl J Med.* 318: 1720–28.

Lindquist, L. and O. Vapalahti. 2008. "Tick-Borne Encephalitis." *Lancet.* 371, no. 9627: 1861–71.

Livengood, J. A. and R. D. Gilmore, Jr. 2006. "Invasion of Human Neuronal and Glial Cells by an Infectious Strain of *Borrelia burgdorferi*." *Microbes Infect.* 8, nos. 14–15: 2832–840.

Logigian, E. L., K. A. Johnson, M. F. Kijewski, R. F. Kaplan, J. A. Becker, K. J. Jones, B. M. Garada, B. L. Holman, and A. C. Steere. 1997. "Reversible Cerebral Hypoperfusion in Lyme Encephalopathy." *Neurology.* 49, no. 6: 1661–70.

Logigian, E. L., R. F. Kaplan, and A. C. Steere. 1990. "Chronic Neurologic Manifestations of Lyme Disease." *N Engl J Med.* 323, no. 2:1438–44.

Logigian, E. L., R. F. Kaplan, and A. C. Steere. 1999. "Successful Treatment of Lyme Encephalopathy with Intravenous Ceftriaxone." *J Infect Dis.* 180: 377–83.

Londoño, D., D. Cadavid, E. E. Drouin, K. Strle, G. McHugh, J. M. Aversa, and A. C. Steere. 2014. "Antibodies to Endothelial Cell Growth Factor and Obliterative Microvascular Lesions in the Synovium of Patients with Antibiotic-Refractory Lyme Arthritis." *Arthritis Rheumatol.* 66, no. 8: 2124–33.

Luft, B. J., P. D. Gorevic, W. Jiang, P. R. Munoz, and R. J. Dattwyler. 1991. "Immunologic and Structural Characterization of the Dominant 66-to 73-kDa Antigens of *Borrelia burgdorferi*." *J Immunol.* 146, no. 8: 2776–82.

Luft, B. J., D. J. Volkman, J. J. Halperin, and R. J. Dattwyler. 1988. "New Chemotherapeutic Approaches in the Treatment of Lyme Borreliosis." *Ann NY Acad Sci.* 539: 252–561.

Macdonald, A. B. 1986. "Human Fetal Borreliosis, Toxemia of Pregnancy, and Fetal Death." *Zentralbl Bakteriol Mikrobiol Hyg A.* 263, nos. 1–2: 189–200.

Magnarelli, L. A., J. N. Miller, J. F. Anderson, and G. R. Riviere. 1990. "Cross-Reactivity of Nonspecific Treponemal Antibody in Serologic Tests for Lyme Disease." *J Clin Microbiol.* 28, no. 6: 1276–79.

Magni, R., B. H. Espina, K. Shah, B. Lepene, C. Mayuga, T. A. Douglas, V. Espina, S. Rucker, R. Dunlap, E. F. Petricoin, M. F. Kilavos, D. M. Poretz, G. R. Irwin, S. M. Shor, L. A. Liotta, and A. Luchini. 2015, November 4. "Application of Nanotrap Technology for High Sensitivity Measurement of Urinary Outer Surface Protein A Carboxyl-Terminus Domain in Early Stage Lyme borreliosis." *J Transl Med.* 13: 346.

Marchand, W. R. 2014. "Neural Mechanisms of Mindfulness and Meditation: Evidence from Neuroimaging Studies. *World J Radiol.* 6, no.7: 471–79.

Markowitz, L. E., A. C. Steere, J. L. Benach, J. D. Slade, and C. V. Broome. 1986. "Lyme Disease During Pregnancy." *JAMA.* 255, no. 24: 3394–96.

Marques, A. 2008. "Chronic Lyme Disease: An Appraisal." *Infec Dis Clin North Am.* 22: 341–60.

Marques, A. R. 2015. "Laboratory Diagnosis of Lyme Disease – Advances and Challenges." *Infect Dis Clin North Am.* 29, no. 2: 295–307.

Marques, A., S. R. Telford III, S. P. Turk, E. Chung, C. Williams, K. Dardick, P. J. Krause, C. Brandeburg, C. D. Crowder, H. E. Carolan, M. W. Eshoo, P. A. Shaw, and L. T. Hu. 2014. "Xenodiagnosis to Detect *B. burgdorferi* Infection: A First-in-Human Study." *Clin Infect Dis.* 58, no. 7: 937–45.

Mast, W. E., and W. M. Burrows. 1976a. "Erythema Chronicum Migrans and 'Lyme Arthritis.'" *Letter* 236: 2392.

——. 1976b. "Erythema chronicum migrans in the United States." *JAMA* 236: 859–60.

Masters, E. J., C. N. Grigery, and R. W. Masters. 2008. "STARI, or Masters Disease: Lone Star Tick-Vectored Lyme-Like Illness." *Infect Dis Clin North Am.* 22, no. 2: 361–76.

Mathey, E. K., S. B. Park, R. A. C. Hughes, J. D. Pollard, P. J. Armati, M. H. Barnett, B. V. Taylor, P. J. B. Dyck, M. C. Kiernan, and C. S-Y Lin. 2015. "Chronic Inflammatory Demyelinating Polyradiculoneuropathy: From Pathology to Phenotype." *J Neurol Neurosurg Psychiatry.* 86: 973–85.

Maurelus, K. 2011, April 19. "Tularemia in Emergency Medicine." Retrieved August 13, 2013. emedicine.com.

May, A. 2008. "Chronic Pain May Change the Structure of the Brain." *Pain.* 137, no. 1: 7–15.

Mayberg, H. S., P. Riva-Posse, and A. L. Crowell. 2016, May 1. "Deep Brain Stimulation for Depression: Keeping an Eye on a Moving Target." *JAMA Psychiatry.* 73, no. 5: 439–40.

Mayo Clinic. 2012, August 20. "Tularemia." Retrieved August 13, 2013. mayoclinic.com /health/tularemia/ds00714.

McGuigan, M. A. 2012. "Chronic Poisoning: Trace Metals and Others." In *Goldman's Cecil Medicine*, 24th edition, edited by R. Cecil, L. Goldman, and A. Schafer. pp. 88–97. Philadelphia, PA: WB Saunders.

Mead, P. 2004. Public Hearing on Lyme disease, State of Connecticut, Department of Public Health, January 29. http://www.ct.gov/ag/lib/ag/health/0129lyme.pdf.

Mead, P.S. 2015. "Epidemiology of Lyme Disease." *Infect Dis Clin North Am.* 29, no. 2: 187–210.

Meldrum, S. C., G. S. Birkhead, D. J. White, J. L. Benach, D, L. Morse. 1992. "Human Babesiosis in New York State: An Epidemiological Description of 136 Cases." *Clin Infect Dis* 15, no. 6: 1019-1023. https://doi.org/10.1093/clind/15.6.1019.

Middelveen, M. J., J. Burke, E. Sapi, C. Bandoski, K. R. Filush, Y. Wang, A. Franco, A. Timmaraju, H. A. Schlinger, P. J. Mayne, and R. B. Stricker. 2014. "Culture and Identification of *Borrelia* Spirochetes in Human Vaginal and Seminal Secretions." *F1000Research* 3:309.

Miller, A. H. and C. L. Raison. 2016, January. "The Role of Inflammation in Depression: From Evolutionary Imperative to Modern Treatment Target." *Nat Rev Immunol.* 16, no. 1: 22–34.

Miller, A. H. Andrew H., V. Maletic, and C. L. Raison. 2009. "Inflammation and its Discontents: The Role of Cytokines in the Pathophysiology of Major Depression." *Biol Psychiatry.* 65, no. 9: 732–741.

MMWR. 2012, July 13. "Babesiosis Surveillance—18 States, 2011." *Morb Mortal Wkly Rep* 61, no. 27: 505–9.

Molins, C. R., L. V. Ashton, G. P. Wormser, A. M. Hess, M. J. Delorey, S. Mahapatra, M. E. Schriefer, and J. T. Belisle. 2015. "Development of a Metabolic Biosignature for Detection of Early Lyme Disease." *Clin Infect Dis.* 60, no. 12: 1767–75.

Molins, C. R., M. J. Delorey, C. Sexton, and M. E. Schriefer. 2016. "Lyme Borreliosis Serology: Performance of Several Commonly Used Laboratory Diagnostic Tests and a Large Resource Panel of Well-Characterized Patient Samples." *J Clin Micro.* 54: 2726–34.

Montoya, J. G., T. H. Holmes, J. N. Anderson, H. T. Maecker, Y Rosenberg-Hasson, I. J. Valencia, L.Chu, J. W. Younger, C. M. Tato, M. M. Davis. 2017. "Cytokine signature associated with disease severity in chronic fatigue syndrome patients" *PNAS.* epub doi: 10.1073/pnas.1710519114

Moody, K. D. and S. W. Barthold. 1991. "Relative Infectivity of *Borrelia Burgdorferi* in Lewis Rats by Various Routes of Inoculation." *Am J Trop Med Hyg.* 44:135–39.

Mozaffarian, D., M. B. Katan, A. Ascherio, M. J. Stampfer, and W. C. Willett. 2006. "Trans Fatty Acids and Cardiovascular Disease." *N Engl J Med.* 354, no. 15: 1601–13.

Murray, P. 1996. *The Widening Circle: A Lyme Disease Pioneer Tells Her Story.* New York: St. Martin's Press.

Mygland, A., U. Liøstad, V. Fingerle, T. Rupprecht, E. Schmutzhard, and I. Steiner; European Federation of Neurological Societies. 2010. "EFNS Guidelines on the Diagnosis and Management of European Lyme Neuroborreliosis." *Eur J Neurol.* 17, no. 1: 8–16.

Nadelman, R. B., J. Nowakowski, D. Fish, R. C. Falco, K. Freeman, D. McKenna, P. Welch, R. Marcus, M. E. Agüero-Rosenfeld, D. T. Dennis, and G. P. Wormser; Tick Bite Study Group. 2001. "Prophylaxis with Single-Dose Doxycycline for the Prevention of Lyme Disease After an *Ixodes scapularis* Tick Bite." *N Engl J Med.* 345, no. 2: 79–84.

Nagy-Szakal, D., B.L. Williams, N. Mishra, X. Che, B. Lee, L. Bateman, N. G. Klimas, A. L. Komaroff, S. Levine, J. G. Montoya, D. L. Peterson, D. Ramanan, K. Jain, M. L.

Eddy, M. Hornig, and W. I. Lipkin. 2017. "Fecal Metagenomic Profiles in Subgroups of Patients with Myalgic Encephalomyelitis/Chronic Fatigue Syndrome." *Microbiome*. 5, no. 1, 44.

Naro, A., D. Milardi, M. Russo, C. Terranova, V. Rizzo, A. Cacciola, S. Marino, R. S. Calabro, and A. Quartarone. 2016, July 27. "Non-Invasive Brain Stimulation, a Tool to Revert Maladaptive Plasticity in Neuropathic Pain." *Front Hum Neurosci*. https://doi.org/10.3389/fnhum.2016.00376.

Natelson, B. H., D. Vu, X. Mao, N. Weiduschat, F. Togo, G. Lange, M. Blate, G. Kang, J. D. Coplan, and D. C. Shungu. 2015, November. "Effect of Milnacipran Treatment on Ventricular Lactate in Fibromyalgia: A Randomized, Double-Blind, Placebo-Controlled Trial." *J Pain*. 16, no. 11: 1211–19.

National Digestive Diseases Information Clearinghouse (NDDIC). 2012, January 27. "Celiac Disease." Retrieved August 13, 2013. http://digestive.niddk.nih.gov/diseases/pubs/celiac/.

National Institute of Neurological Disorders and Stroke, NIH. 2011, October 4. "NINDS Postural Tachycardia Syndrome Information Page." Retrieved August 13, 2013. http://www.ninds.nih.gov/disorders/postural_tachycardia_syndrome/postural_tachycardia_syndrome.htm.

Naviaux, R. K., J. C. Naviaux, K. Li, A. T. Bright, W. A. Alaynick, L. Wang, A. Baxter, N. Nathan, W. Anderson, and E. Gordon. 2016, September 13. "Metabolic Features of Chronic Fatigue Syndrome." *Proc Natl Acad Sci USA*. 113, no. 37: E5472–80.

Nelson, C., S. Elmendorf, and P. Mead. 2015. "Neoplasms Misdiagnosed as 'Chronic Lyme Disease.'" *JAMA Intern Med*. 175, no. 1: 132–33.

Nelson, C., S. Hojvat, B. Johnson, J. Petersen, M. Schriefer, C. B. Beard, L. Petersen, and P. Mead. 2014, April 18. "Concerns Regarding a New Culture Method for *B. burgdorferi* Not Approved for the Diagnosis of Lyme Disease." *Morb Mortal Wkly Rep*. 63, no. (15): 333.

Nelson, C.A., S. Saha, K. J. Kugele, M. J. Delorey, M. B. Shankar, A. F. Hinckley, and P. S. Mead. 2015. "Incidence of Clinician-Diagnosed Lyme Disease, United States, 2005–2010." *Emerg Infect Dis*. 21, no. 9: 1625–31.

Nields, J. A., B. A. Fallon, and P. J. Jastreboff. 1999. "Carbamazepine in the Treatment of Lyme Disease-Induced Hyperacusis." *J Neuropsychiatry Clin Neurosci*. 11, no. 1: 97–99.

Nigrovic, L. E. and K. M. Thompson. 2007. "The Lyme Vaccine: A Cautionary Tale." *Epidemiology and Infection*. 135, no. 1: 1–8.

Nigrovic, L. E. and S. L. Wingerter. 2008. "Tularemia." *Infect Dis Clin North Am*. 22, no. 3: 489–504.

NIMH. "PANDAS: Frequently Asked Questions about Autoimmune Neuropsychiatric Disorders Associated with Streptococcal Infections." Retrieved August 13, 2013. http://www.nimh.nih.gov/health/publications/pandas/index.shtml.

——. "Panic Disorder." Retrieved August 13, 2013. http://www.nimh.nih.gov/health/topics/panic-disorder/index.shtml.

——. "Psychotherapies." Retrieved August 8, 2013. http://www.nimh.nih.gov/health/topics/psychotherapies/index.shtml.

Noble, C., J. Olejarz, K. Esvelt, G. Church, and M. Nowak. 2016. "Evolutionary Dynamics of CRISPR Gene Drives." *bioRxiv*: 057281.

Nocton, J. J., F. Dressler, B. J. Rutledge, P. N. Rys, D. H. Persing, and A. C. Steere. 1994. "Detection of *Borrelia* burgdorferi DNA by Polymerase Chain Reaction in Synovial Fluid from Patients with Lyme Arthritis." *N Engl J Med*. 330: 229–34.

Norris, S. J. 2006. "Antigenic Variation with a Twist –the *Borrelia* Story." *Mol Microbiol*. 60, no. 6: 1319–22.

Nowalk, A. J., R. D. Gilmore, Jr., and J. A. Carroll. 2006. "Serologic proteome analysis of Borrelia burgdorferi membrane-associated proteins." *Infect Immun*. 74: 3864–3873.

Oczko-Grzesik, B., and L. Kępa, Puszcz-Matlińska, M., Pudło, R., Żurek, A., & Badura-Głąbik, T. (2017). Estimation of cognitive and affective disorders occurrence in patients with Lyme borreliosis. *Ann Agric Environ Med*. 24, no. 1: 33–38.

Oksi, J., H. Kalimo, R. J. Marttila, M. Marjamaki, P. Sonnimen, J. Nikoskelainen, and M. K. Viljanen. 1996. "Inflammatory Brain Changes in Lyme Neuroborreliosis: A Report on Three Patients and Review of the Literature." *Brain*. 119: 2143–54.

Oksi, J., M. Marjamaki, J. Nikoskelainen, and M. K. Viljanen. 1999. "*B. burgdorferi* Detected by Culture and PCR in Clinical Relapse of Disseminated Lyme Borreliosis." *Ann Med*. 31: 225–32.

Oksi, J., J. Nikoskelainen, H. Hiekkanen, A. Lauhio, M. Peltomaa, A. Pitkäranta, D. Nyman, H. Granlund, S. A. Carlsson, I. Seppälä, V. Valtonen, and M. Viljanen. 2007. "Duration of Antibiotic Treatment in Disseminated Lyme Borreliosis: A Double-Blind, Randomized, Placebo-Controlled, Multicenter Clinical Study." *Eur J Clin Microbiol Infect Dis*. 26, no. 8: 571–81.

Pachner, A. R. 1988. "*Borrelia burgdorferi* in the Nervous System: The New 'Great Imitator.'" *Ann N Y Acad Sci*. 539: 56–64.

Pasareanu, A. R., A. Mygland, and O. Kristensen. 2012, March 6. "A Woman in Her 50s with Manic Psychosis." *Tidsskr Nor Laegeforen*. 132, no. 5: 537–59.

Pavia, C. S. 2003. "Current and Novel Therapies for Lyme Disease." *Expert Opin Investig Drugs*. 12, no. 6: 1003–16.

Peeters, N., B. Y. van der Kolk, S. F. Thijsen, and D. R. Colnot. 2013. "Lyme Disease Associated with Sudden Sensorineural Hearing Loss: Case Report and Literature Review." *Otol Neurotol*. 34, no. 5: 832–37.

Pfingsten, M., E. Leibing, W. Harter, B. Kröner-Herwig, D. Hempel, U. Kronshage, and J. Hildebrandt. 2001. "Fear Avoidance Behavior and Anticipation of Pain in Patients with Chronic Low Back Pain: a Randomized Controlled Study." *Pain Med*. 2, no. 4: 259–66.

Philipp, M. T., G. P. Wormser, A. Marques, S. Bittker, D. S. Martin, J. Nowakowski, and L. G. Dally. 2005. "A Decline in C6 Antibody Titer Occurs in Successfully Treated Patients with Culture-Confirmed Early Localized or Early Disseminated Lyme Borreliosis." *Clin Diag Lab Immunolog*. 12: 1069–74.

Piesman, J., B. S. Schneider, and N. S. Zeidner. 2001. "Use of Quantitative PCR to Measure Density of *B. burgdorferi* in the Midgut and Salivary Glands of Feeding Tick Vectors." *J Clin Microbiology*. 39: 4145–48.

Pinto-Sanchez, M. I., G. B. Hall, K. Ghajar, A. Nardelli, C. Bolino, J. T. Lau, F. P. Martin, O. Cominetti, C. Welsh, A. Rieder, J. Traynor, C. Gregory, G. De Palma, M. Pigrau, A. C. Ford, J. Macri, B. Berner, G. Bergonzelli, M. G. Surette, S. M. Collins, P. Moayyedi, and P. Bercik. 2017. "Probiotic Bifidobacterium Longum NCC3001 Reduces Depression Scores and Alters Brain Activity: A Pilot Study in Patients with Irritable Bowel Syndrome." *Gastroenterology* (May 5, 2017). doi: 10.1053/j.gastro.2017.05.003. (Epub ahead of print).

Plotkin, S. A. 2016. "Need for a New Lyme Disease Vaccine." *N Engl J Med*. 375, no. 10: 911–13.

Pollina, D. A., M. Sliwinski, N. K. Squires, and L. B. Krupp. 1999. "Cognitive Processing Speed in Lyme Disease." *Neuropsychiatry Neuropsychol Behav Neurol* 12, no. 1: 72–78.

Polman, C. H., S. C. Reingold, B. Banwell, M. Clanet, J. A. Cohen, M. Filippi, K. Fujihara, E. Havrdova, M. Hutchinson, L. Kappos, F. D. Lublin, X. Montalban, P. O'Connor, M. Sandberg-Wollheim, A. J. Thompson, E. Waubant, B. Weinshenker, and J. S. Wolinsky. 2011. "Diagnostic Criteria for Multiple Sclerosis: 2010 Revisions to the McDonald Criteria." *Ann Neurol*. 69: 292–302.

Porcella, S. F. and T. G. Schwan. 2001. "*Borrelia Burgdorferi* and *Treponema Pallidum*: A Comparison of Functional Genomics, Environmental Adaptations, and Pathogenic Mechanisms." *J Clin Invest*. 107: 651–56.

Preac-Mursic, V., K. Weber, H. W. Pfister, B. Wilske, B. Gross, A. Baumann, and J. Prokop. 1989. "Survival of *B. burgdorferi* in Antibiotically Treated Patients with Lyme Borreliosis." *Infection*. 17: 355–59.

Priem, S., G. R. Burmester, T. Kamradt, K. Wolbart, M. G. Rittig, and A. Krause. 1998. "Detection of *Borrelia burgdorferi* by Polymerase Chain Reaction in Synovial Membrane, but Not in Synovial Fluid from Patients with Persisting Lyme Arthritis After Antibiotic Therapy." *Ann Rheum Dis*. 57, no. 2: 118–21.

Pritt, B. S., P. S. Mead, D. K. Johnson, D. F. Neitzel, L.B. Respicio-Kingry, J. P. Davis, E. Schiffman, L. M. Sloan, M. E. Schriefer, A. J. Replogle, S. M. Paskewitz, J. A. Ray, J. Bjork, C. R. Steward, A. Deedon, X. Lee, L. C. Kingry, T. K. Miller, M. A. Feist, E. S. Theel, R. Patel, C. L. Irish, and J. M. Petersen. 2016. "Identification of a Novel Pathogenic *Borrelia* Species Causing Lyme Borreliosis with Unusually High Spirochaetaemia: A Descriptive Study." *Lancet Infect Dis*. 16: 556–64.

Puledda, F., and P. J. Goadsby. 2016. "Current Approaches to Neuromodulation in Primary Headaches: Focus on Vagal Nerve and Sphenopalatine Ganglion Stimulation." *Curr Pain Headache Rep*. 20: 47.

Purdy, J. 2013. "Chronic Physical Illness: A Psychophysiological Approach for Chronic Physical Illness." *The Yale Journal of Biology and Medicine*. 86, no. 1: 15–28.

Raveche, E. S., S. E. Schutzer, H. Fernandes, H. Bateman, B. A. McCarthy, S. P. Nickell, and M. W. Cunningham. 2005. "Evidence of Borrelia Autoimmunity-Induced Component of Lyme Carditis and Arthritis." *J Clin Microbiol.* 43, no. 2: 850–56.

Rebman, A. W., J. N. Aucott, E. R. Weinstein, K. T. Bechtold, K. C. Smith, and L. Leonard. 2015. "Living in Limbo: Contested Narratives of Patients with Chronic Symptoms following Lyme Disease." *Qual Health Research.* 27, no. 4: 543–46.

Reis, C., M. Cote, D. Le Rhun, B. Lecuelle, M. L. Levin, M. Vayssier-Taussat, and S. I. Bonnet. 2011. "Vector Competence of the Tick *Ixodes ricinus* for Transmission of *Bartonella birtlesii.*" *PLoS Negl Trop Dis.* 5, no. 5: e1186.

Rhodes, D. V., C. G. Earnhart, T. N. Mather, P. F. Meeus, and R. T. Marconi. 2013. "Identification of *B. burgdorferi* ospC Genotypes in Canine Tissue following Tick Infestation: Implications for Lyme Disease Vaccine and Diagnostic Assay Design." *Vet J.* 198, no. 2: 412–18.

Rolain, J. M., P. Brouqui, J. E. Koehler, C. Maguina, M. J. Dolan, and D. Raoult. 2004. "Recommendations for Treatment of Human Infections Caused by *Bartonella* Species." *Antimicrob Agents Chemother.* 48, no. 6: 1921–33.

Romero, J. R., and K. A. Simonsen. 2008. "Powassan Encephalitis and Colorado Tick Fever." *Infect Dis Clin North Am.* 22, no. 3: 545–59.

Rothermel, H., T. R. Hedges, and A. C. Steere. 2001. "Optic Neuropathy in Children with Lyme Disease." *Pediatrics.* 108, no. 2: 477–81.

Rupprecht, T. A., M. Elstner, S. Weil, and H. W. Pfister. 2008. "Autoimmune-Mediated Polyneuropathy Triggered by *Borrelial* Infection?" *Muscle Nerve.* 37, no. 6: 781–85.

Saeed, S., J. Quintin, H. H. Kerstens, N. A. Rao, A. Aghajanirefah, F. Matarese, S. C. Cheng, J. Ratter, K. Berentsen, M. A. van der Ent, N. Sharifi, E. M. Janssen-Megens, M. Ter Huurne, A. Mandoli, T. van Schaik, A. Ng, F. Burden, K. Downes, M. Frontini, V. Kumar, E. J. Giamarellos-Bourboulis, W. H. Ouwehand, J. W. van der Meer, L. A. Joosten, C. Wijmenga, J. H. Martens, R. J. Xavier, C. Logie, M. G. Netea, and H. G. Stunnenberg. 2014. "Epigenetic Programming of Monocyte-to-Macrophage Differentiation and Trained Innate Immunity." *Science.* 345, no. 6204: 1251086.

Saez-Lara, M. J., C. Gomez-Llorente, J. Plaza-Diaz J., and A. Gil. 2015. "The Role of Probiotic Lactic Acid Bacteria and Bifidobacteria in the Prevention and Treatment of Inflammatory Bowel Disease and Other Related Diseases: A Systematic Review of Randomized Human Clinical Trials." *BioMed Research International.* 505878. http://doi.org/10.1155/2015/505878

Sakkas, H., P. Gousia, V. Economou, V. Sakkas, S. Petsios, and C. Papadopoulou. 2016. "In Vitro Antimicrobial Activity of Five Essential Oils on Multidrug Resistant Gram-negative Clinical Isolates." *J Intercult Ethnopharmacol.* 5, no. 3: 212–18.

Santiago, M. G., A. Marques, M. Kool, and R. Geenen. 2017. "Invalidation in Patients with Rheumatic Diseases: Clinical and Psychological Framework." *J Rheumatology.* 44, no. 4: 512–518.

Sapi, E., S. L. Bastian, C. M. Mpoy, S. Scott, A. Rattelle, N. Pabbati, A. Poruri, D. Burugu, P. A. Theophilus, T. V. Pham, A. Datar, N. K. Dhaliwal, A. MacDonald, M. J. Rossi, S. K. Sinha, and D. F. Luecke. 2012. "Characterization of Biofilm Formation by *B. burgdorferi* in Vitro." *PLoS ONE*. 7, no. 10: e48277.

Sapi, E., N. Pabbati, H. Datar, E. M. Davies, A. Rattelle, and B. A. Kuo. 2013. "Improved Culture Conditions for the Growth and Detection of *Borrelia* from Human Serum." *International Journal of Medical Sciences*. 10, no. 4: 362–76.

Schlesinger, P. A., P. H. Duray, P. A. Burke, A. C. Steere, and M. T. Stillman. 1985. "Maternal–Fetal Transmission of the Lyme Disease Spirochete, *B. burgdorferi*." *Ann Intern Med*. 103: 67–68.

Schmidt, C., A. Plate, B. Angele, H. W. Pfister, M. Wick, U. Koedel, and T. A. Rupprecht. 2011. "A Prospective Study on the Role of CXCL13 in Lyme Neuroborreliosis." *Neurology*. 76, no. (12): 1051–58.

Schriefer, M. E. 2015. "Lyme Disease Diagnosis: Serology." *Clin Lab Med*. 35, no. 4: 797–814.

Schur, P. H. 2012a, May 29. "Patient Information: The Antiphospholipid Syndrome (Beyond the Basics)." Retrieved August 13, 2013. uptodate.com.

Schur, P. H. 2012b, June 6. "Patient Information: Systemic lupus erythematosus (SLE) (Beyond the Basics)." Retrieved August 13, 2013. uptodate.com.

Schutzer, S. E., T. E. Angel, T. Liu, A. A. Schepmoes, T. R. Clauss, J. N. Adkins, D. G. Camp, B. K. Holland, J. Bergquist, P. K. Coyle, R. D. Smith, B. A. Fallon, and B. H. Natelson. 2011. "Distinct Cerebrospinal Fluid Proteomes Differentiate Post-Treatment Lyme Disease from Chronic Fatigue Syndrome." *PLoS ONE*. 6, no. 2: e17287.

Schutzer, S. E., P. K. Coyle, P. Reid, and B. Holland. 1999. "*B. burgdorferi*-Specific Immune Complexes in Acute Lyme disease." *JAMA*. 282: 1942–46.

Schwameis, M., T. Kündig, G. Huber, L. von Bidder, L. Meinel, R. Weisser, E. Aberer, G. Härter, T. Weinke, T. Jelinek, G. Fätkenheuer, U. Wollina, G. D. Burchard, R. Aschoff, R. Nischik, G. Sattler, G. Popp, W. Lotte, D. Wiechert, G. Eder, O. Maus, P. Staubach-Renz, A. Gräfe, V. Geigenberger, I. Naudts, M. Sebastian, N. Reider, R. Weber, M. Heckmann, E. C. Reisinger, G. Klein, J. Wantzen, and B. Jilma. 2017. "Topical Azithromycin for the Prevention of Lyme Borreliosis: A Randomised, Placebo-Controlled, Phase 3 Efficacy Trial." *Lancet Infect Dis*. 17, no. 3: 322–329.

Scrimenti, R. J. 1970. "Erythema Chronicum Migrans." *Arch Dermatol*. 102: 104–5.

Skogman, B. H., K. Glimaker, M. Nordwall, M. Vrethem, L. Odkvist, & P. Forsberg. 2012. "Long-Term Clinical Outcome After Lyme Neuroborreliosis in Childhood." *Pediatrics*. 120, no. 2: 262–269.

Sharma, B., A. V. Brown, N. E. Matluck, L. T. Hu, and K. Lewis. 2015. "*B. burgdorferi*, the Causative Agent of Lyme Disease, Forms Drug-Tolerant Persister Cells." *Antimicrob Agents Chemother*. 59, no. 8: 4616–24.

Singh, S. K. and H. J. Girschick. 2004. "Molecular Survival Strategies of the Lyme Disease Spirochete *B. burgdorferi*." *Lancet Infect Dis*. 4, no. 9: 575–83.

Smith, H. S., D. Bracken, and J. M. Smith. 2011 "Pharmacotherapy for Fibromyalgia." *Frontiers in Pharmacology*. no. 2: 17.

Soloski, M. J., L. A. Crowder, L. J. Lahey, C. A. Wagner, W. H. Robinson, and J. N. Aucott. 2014. "Serum Inflammatory Mediators as Markers of Human Lyme Disease Activity." *PLoS ONE*. 9, no. 4: e93243.

Specter, M. 2013, July 1. "The Lyme Wars." *The New Yorker*.

Stabler, S. P. 2013. "Vitamin B12 Deficiency." *N Engl J Med*. 368: 149–60.

Stafford, K. C. and L. A. Magnarelli. 1993. "Spatial and Temporal Patterns of *Ixodes scapularis* (Acari: Ixodidae) in Southeastern Connecticut." *J Med Entomol*. 30, no. 4: 762–71.

Stafford, K. C. 1993. "Reduced Abundance of *Ixodes scapularis* (Acari: Ixodidae) with Exclusion of Deer by Electric Fencing." *J Med Entomol*. 30, no. 6: 986–96.

Stanek G., J. Klein, R. Bittner, and D. Glogar. 1990. "Isolation of *Borrelia Burgdorferi* from the Myocardium of a Patient with Long-Standing Cardiomyopathy." *N Engl J Med*. 322, no. 4: 249–252.

Steere, A. C. and S. M. Angelis. 2006. "Therapy for Lyme Arthritis: Strategies for the Treatment of Antibiotic-Refractory Arthritis." *Arthritis & Rheumatism*. 54, no. 10: 3079–86.

Steere, A. C., J. Coburn, and L. Glickstein. 2004. "The Emergence of Lyme Disease." *J Clin Invest*. 113, no. 8: 1093–1101.

Steere, A. C., P. H. Duray D. J. Kauffmann, and G.P. Wormser. 1985. "Unilateral Blindness Caused by Infection with the Lyme Disease Spirochete, *Borrelia burgdorferi*." *Ann Inter Med*. 103, no. 3: 382–84.

Steere, A. C., E. Dwyer, and R. Winchester. 1990. "Association of Chronic Lyme Arthritis with HLA-DR4 and HLA-DR2 Alleles." *N Engl J Med*. 323, no. 4: 219–23.

Steere, A. C., R. L. Grodzicki, A. N. Kornblatt, J. E. Craft, A. G. Barbour, W. Burgdorfer, G. P. Schmid, E. Johnson, and S. E. Malawista. 1983. "The Spirochetal Etiology of Lyme Disease." *N Engl J Med*. 308, no.13: 733–40.

Steere, A. C., S. E. Malawista, J. H. Newman, P. N. Spieler, and N. H. Bartenhagen. 1980, July. "Antibiotic Therapy in Lyme Disease." *Ann Intern Med*. 93, no. 1: 1–8.

Steere, A. C., S. E. Malawista, D. R. Snydman, R. E. Shope, W. A. Andiman, M. R. Ross, and F. M. Steele. 1977. "Lyme Arthritis: An Epidemic of Oligoarticular Arthritis in Children and Adults in Three Connecticut Communities." *Arthritis Rheum*. 20: 7–17.

Steere, A. C., R. T. Schoen, and E. Taylor. 1987. "The Clinical Evolution of Lyme Arthritis." *Ann Intern Med*. 107. no. 5: 725–31.

Steere, A. C. and V. K. Sikand. 2003. "The Presenting Manifestations of Lyme Disease and the Outcomes of Treatment." *New Engl J Med*. 348: 2472–74.

Steere, A. C., F. Strle, G. P. Wormser, L. T. Hu, J. A. Branda, J. W. R. Hovius, X. Li, and P. S. Mead. 2016. "Lyme Borreliosis." *Nature Reviews: Disease Primers*. 2: 1–18.

Straubinger, R. K. 2000. "PCR-Based Quantification of *B. burgdorferi* Organisms in Canine Tissues over a 500-Day Postinfection Period." *J Clin Microbiol*. 38, no. 6: 2191–99.

Straubinger, R. K., B. A. Summers, Y. F. Chang, and M. J. G. Appel. 1997. "Persistence of *B. burgdorferi* in Experimentally Infected Dogs After Antibiotic Treatment." *J Clin Microbiol*. 35: 111–16.

Stricker, R. 2007. "Counterpoint: Long-Term Antibiotic Therapy Improves Persistent Symptoms Associated with Lyme Disease." *Clin Infect Dis.* 45: 149–57.

Strle, F., V. I. Maraspin, S. Lotric-Furian, E. Ruzić-Sabljić, and J. Cimperman. 1996. "Azithromycin and Doxycycline for Treatment of *Borrelia* Culture-Positive Erythema Migrans." *Infection.* 24: 64–68.

Strle, F., V. Preac-Mursic, J. Cimperman, V. Ruzic E, Maraspin, M. Jereb. 1993. "Azithromycin versus Doxyxycline for Treatment of Erythema Migrans: Clinical and Microbiological Findings." *Infection.* 21, no. 2: 83–88.

Strle, F., E. Ruzić-Sabljić, J. Cimperman, S. Lotric-Furlan, and V. Maraspin. 2006. "Comparison of Findings for Patients with *Borrelia garinii* and *Borrelia afzelii* Isolated from Cerebrospinal Fluid." *Clin Infect Dis.* 43, no. 6: 704–10.

Strle F and G. Stanek. 2009. "Clinical Manifestations and Diagnosis of Lyme Borreliosis." *Curr Probl Dermatol.* 37: 51–110.

Strle, K., D. Stupica, E. E. Drouin, A. C. Steere, and F. Strle. 2014. "Elevated Levels of IL-23 in a Subset of Patients with Post-Lyme Disease Symptoms following Erythema Migrans." *Clin Infect Dis.* 58, no. 3: 372–80.

Strobino, B., S. Abid, and M. Gewitz 1999. "Maternal Lyme Disease and Congenital Heart Disease: A Case-Control Study in an Endemic Area." *Am J Obstet Gynecol.* 180: 711–16.

Strobino, B. A., C. L. Williams, S. Abid, R. Chalson, and P. Spierling. 1993. "Lyme Disease and Pregnancy Outcome: A Prospective Study of Two Thousand Prenatal Patients." *Am J Obstet Gynecol.* 169, no. 2, pt. 1: 367–74.

Struble, K. 2013, April 15. "Q Fever." Retrieved August 13, 2013. emedicine.com.

Swedo, S. E. 2010. "Streptococcal Infection, Tourette Syndrome, and OCD: Is There a Connection? PANDAS: Horse or Zebra?" *Neurology.* 74, no. 17: 1397–99.

Telford, S. R., H. K. Goethert, P. J. Molloy, V. P. Berardi, H. R. Chowdri, J. L. Gugliotta, and T. J. Lepore. 2015. "*Borrelia* Miyamotoi Disease (BMD): Neither Lyme Disease Nor Relapsing Fever." *Clin Lab Med.* 35, no. 4: 867–82.

Thomas, S., J. Izard, E. Walsh, K. Batich K, P. Chongsathidkiet, G. Clarke, D. A. Sela, A. J. Muller, J. M. Mullin, K. Albert, J. P. Gilligan, K. DiGuilio, R. Dilbarova, W. Alexander, and G. C. Prendergast. 2017. "The Host Microbiome Regulates and Maintains Human Health: A Primer and Perspective for Non-Microbiologists." *Cancer Res.* 77, no. 8: 1783–1812.

Tissot-Dupont, H. and D. Raoult. 2008. "Q Fever." *Infect Dis Clin North Am.* 22, no. 3: 505–14.

Tokarz, R., K. Jain, A. Bennett, T. Briese, and W. I. Lipkin. 2010. "Assessment of Polymicrobial Infections in Ticks in New York State." *Vector Borne Zoonotic Dis.* 10, no. 3: 217–21.

Topakian, R., K. Stieglbauer, K. Nussbaumer, and F. T. Aichner. 2008. "Cerebral Vasculitis and Stroke in Lyme Neuroborreliosis." *Cerebrovascular Dis.* 26: 455–61.

Tutolo, J. W., J. E. Staples, L. Sosa, and N. Bennett. 2017. "Notes from the Field: Powassan Virus Disease in an Infant—Connecticut, 2016." *MMWR Morb Mortal Wkly Rep.* 66, no. 15: 408–409.

Uhde, M., M. Ajamian, G. Caio, R. De Giorgio, A. Indart, P. H. Green, E. C. Verna, U. Volta, and A. Alaedini. 2016. "Intestinal Cell Damage and Systemic Immune

Activation in Individuals Reporting Sensitivity to Wheat in the Absence of Coeliac Disease." *Gut.* 65, no. 12: 1930–37.

Uher, R., K. E. Tansey, T. Dew, W. Maier, O. Mors, J. Hauser, M. Z. Dernovsek, N. Henigsberg, D. Souery, A. Farmer, and P. McGuffin. 2014. "An Inflammatory Biomarker as a Differential Predictor of Outcome of Depression Treatment with Escitalopram and Nortriptyline." *Am J Psychiatry.* 171, no. 12: 1278–86.

University of Montana Center for Biofilms Engineering. "Biofilm Basics." Retrieved August 13, 2013. http://www.biofilm.montana.edu/node/2390.

van Burgel, N. D., F. Bakels, A. C. Kroes, and A. P. van Dam. 2011. "Discriminating Lyme Neuroborreliosis from Other Neuroinflammatory Diseases by Levels of CXCL13 in Cerebrospinal Fluid." *J Clin Microbiol.* 49: 2027–30.

van Middendorp, H., M. A. Lumley, J. W. Jacobs, J. W. Bijlsma, and R. Geenen. 2010, October. "The Effects of Anger and Sadness on Clinical Pain Reports and Experimentally-Induced Pain Thresholds in Women with and without Fibromyalgia." *Arthritis Care Res (Hoboken).* 62, no. 10: 1370–76.

Vannier, E., B. E. Gewurz, and P. J. Krause. 2008. "Human Babesiosis." *Infect Dis Clin North Am.* 22, no. 3: 469–88.

Vannier, E. and P. J. Krause. 2012. "Human Babesiosis." *N Engl J Med.* 366: 2397–407.

Van den Bergh, P. Y. K., R. D. M. Hadden, P. Bouche, D. R. Cornblath, A. Hahn, I. Illa, C. L. Koski, J.-M. Leger, E. Nobile-Orazio, J. Pollard, C. Sommer, P. A. van Doorn, and I. N. van Schaik. 2010. "European Federation of Neurological Societies/Peripheral Nerve Society Guideline on Management of Chronic Inflammatory Demyelinating Polyradiculoneuropathy: Report of a Joint Task Force of the European Federation of Neurological Societies and the Peripheral Nerve Society—First Revision." *European J Neurology.* 17: 356–63.

Vedanarayanan, V., W. H. Sorey, and S. H. Subramony. 2004. "Tick Paralysis." *Semin Neurol.* 24, no. 2: 181–14.

Vrethem, M, L. Hellblom, M. Widlund, M. Ahl, O. Danielsson, J. Ernerudh, and P. Forsberg. 2002. "Chronic Symptoms Are Common in Patients with Neuroborreliosis-A Questionnaire Follow-Up Study." *Acta Neurol Scand.* 106, no. 4: 205–208.

Wandinger, K. P., S. Saschenbrecker, W. Stoecker, and J. Dalmau. 2011. "Anti-NMDA Receptor Encephalitis: A Severe, Multistage, Treatable Disorder Presenting with Psychosis." *J Neuroimmunol.* 231, nos. 1–2: 86–91.

Wang, T. J., M. H. Liang, O. Sangha, C. B. Phillips, R. A. Lew, E. A. Wright, V. Berardi, A. H. Fossel, and N. A. Shadick. 2000. "Coexposure to *Borrelia burgdorferi* and *Babesia microti* Does Not Worsen the Long-Term Outcome of Lyme Disease." *Clin Infect Dis.* 31, no. 5: 1149–54.

Warshafsky, S., D. H. Lee, L. K. Francois, J. Nowakowski, R. B. Nadelman, and G. P. Wormser. 2010. "Efficacy of Antibiotic Prophylaxis for the Prevention of Lyme disease: An Updated Systematic Review and Meta-Analysis." *J Antimicrob Chemother.* 65, no. 6: 1137–44.

Watkins, L. R., L. E. Goehler, J. K. Relton, N. Tartaglia, L. Silbert, D. Martin, and S. F. Maier. 1995. "Blockade of Interleukin-1 Induced Hyperthermia by Subdiaphragmatic

Vagotomy: Evidence for Vagal Mediation of Immune-Brain Communication." *Neurosci Lett.* 183, nos. 1–2: 27–31.

Weintraub, P. 2013. *Cure Unknown: Inside the Lyme Epidemic.* New York: St. Martin's Press.

Weissenbacher, S., J. Ring, and H. Hoffman. 2005. "Gabapentin for the Symptomatic Treatment of Chronic Neuropathic Pain in Patients with Late-Stage Lymeborreliosis: A Pilot Study." *Dermatology.* 211, no. 2: 123–27.

Weitzner, E., D. McKenna, J. Nowakowski, C. Scavarda, R. Dornbush, S. Bittker, D. Cooper, R. B. Nadelman, P. Visintainer, I. Schwartz, and G. P. Wormser. 2015. "Long-Term Assessment of Post-Treatment Symptoms in Patients with Culture-Confirmed Early Lyme Disease." *Clin Infect Dis.* 61, no. 12: 1800–6.

Williams, C. L., B. Strobino, A. Weinstein, P. Spierling, and F. Medici. 1995. "Maternal Lyme Disease and Congenital Malformations: A Cord Blood Serosurvey in Endemic and Control Areas." *Paediatr Perinat Epidemiol.* 9: 320–30.

Williams, S. C., J. S. Ward, T. E. Worthley, and K. C. Stafford III. 2009, August. "Managing Japanese Barberry (Ranunculales: Berberidaceae) Infestations Reduces Blacklegged Tick (Acari: Ixodidae) Abundance and Infection Prevalence with *B. burgdorferi* (Spirochaetales: Spirochaetaceae)." *Environ Entomol.* 38, no. 4: 977–84.

Wolver, S. E., D. R. Sun, S. P. Commins, and L. B. Schwartz LB. 2013, February. "A Peculiar Cause of Anaphylaxis: No More Steak? The Journey to Discovery of a Newly Recognized Allergy to Galactose-Alpha-1,3-Galactose Found in Mammalian Meat." *J Gen Intern Med.* 28, no. 2: 322–25.

Woodrum, J.E. and J.H. Oliver Jr. 1999. "Investigation of Venereal, Transplacental, and Contact Transmission of the Lyme Disease Spirochete, *Borrelia Burgdorferi*, in Syrian hamsters." *J Parasitol.* 85: 426–30.

Wormser, G. P., S. Bittker, D. Cooper, J. Nowakowski, R. B. Nadelman, and C. Pavia. 2001. "Yield of Large-Volume Blood Cultures in Patients with Early Lyme Disease." *J Infect Dis.* 184: 1070–72.

Wormser, G. P., E. Masters, D. Liveris, J. Nowakowski, R. B. Nadelman, D. Holmgren, S. Bittker, D. Cooper, G. Wang, and I. Schwartz. 2005. "Microbiologic Evaluation of Patients from Missouri with Erythema Migrans." *Clin Infect Dis.* 40, no. 3: 423–28. doi: 10.1086/427289.

Wormser, G. P., R. J. Dattwyler, E. D. Shapiro, J. J. Halperin, A. C. Steere, M. S. Klempner, P. J. Krause, J. S. Bakken, F. Strle, G. Stanek, L. Bockenstedt, D. Fish, J. S. Dumler, and R. B. Nadelman. 2006. "The Clinical Assessment, Treatment, and Prevention of Lyme Disease, Human Granulocytic Anaplasmosis, and Babesiosis: Clinical Practice Guidelines by the Infectious Diseases Society of America." *Clin Infect Dis.* 43, no. 9: 1089–134.

Wormser, G.P., A. Levin, S. Soman, O. Adenikinju, M. V. Longo, and J. A. Branda. 2013. "Comparative Cost-Effectiveness of Two-Tiered Testing Strategies for Serodiagnosis of Lyme Disease with Noncutaneous Manifestations." *J Clin Microbiol.* 51, no. 12: 4045–49.

Wormser, G. P., R. B. Nadelman, R. J. Dattwyler, D. T. Dennis, E. D. Shapiro, A. C. Steere, T. J. Rush, D. W. Rahn, P. K. Coyle, D. H. Persing, D. Fish, and B. J. Luft. 2000. "Practice Guidelines for the Treatment of Lyme Disease." *Clin Infect Dis.* 31, Suppl 1: 1–14.

Wormser, G.P., M. Schriefer, M.E. Aguero-Rosenfeld, A. Levin, A. C. Steere, R. B. Nadelman, J. Nowakowski, A. Marques, B. J. Johnson, and J. S. Dumler. 2013. "Single-Tier Testing with the C6 Peptide ELISA Kit Compared with Two-Tier Testing for Lyme Disease." *Diagn Microbiol Infect Dis.* 75, no. 1: 9–15.

Wormser, G. P. and I. Schwartz. 2009. "Antibiotic Treatment of Animals Infected with *B. burgdorferi.*" *Clin Microbiol Rev.* 22, no. 3: 387–95.

Wutte, N., J. Archelos, B. A. Crowe, W. Zenz, E. Daghofer, F. Fazekas, and E. Aberer. 2014. "Laboratory Diagnosis of Lyme Neuroborreliosis Is Influenced by the Test Used: Comparison of Two ELISAs, Immunoblot and CXCL13 Testing." *J Neurol Sci.* 347, nos. 1–2: 96–103.

Yang, Q., Z. Zhang, E. W. Gregg, W. D. Flanders, R. Merritt, and F. B. Hu. 2014. "Added Sugar Intake and Cardiovascular Diseases Mortality among US Adults." *JAMA Intern Med.* 174, no. 4: 516–24.

Younger, J., L. Parkitny, and D. McLain. 2014. "The Use of Low-Dose Naltrexone (LDN) as a Novel Anti-Inflammatory Treatment for Chronic Pain." *Clin Rheumatol.* 33, no. 4: 451–9.

Yrjanainen, H., J. Hytonen, X. Y. Song, J. Oksi, K. Hartiala, and M. K. Viljanen. 2007. "Anti-Tumor Necrosis Factor-Alpha Treatment Activates *B. burgdorferi* Spirochetes 4 Weeks After Ceftriaxone Treatment in C3H/He mice." *J Infect Dis.* 195, no. 10: 1489–96.

# INDEX

# DATE DUE

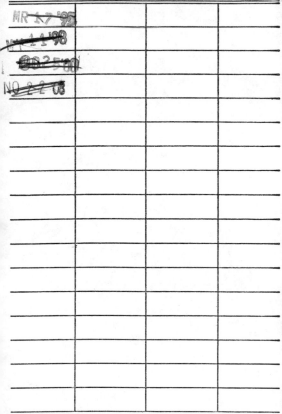